SPEED KING

MEN OF ACTION SERIES

AHREN SANDERS

Ahren Sanders

Editing: Kendra Gaither at Kendra's Editing and Book Services
Cover Photo: Rafa Garcia
Cover Model: Alex Badia
Cover Design: Melissa @MG BookCovers and Designs

MEN OF ACTION SERIES

SPEED KING

AHREN SANDERS

CONTENTS

PROLOGUE

ALMOST 11 YEARS AGO

ACHILLES

"I CAN'T BELIEVE today's the day." Harley's voice quivers.

My fingers lace with hers and squeeze lightly. "We've talked about this. You promised you wouldn't cry."

"Doesn't change the fact that I hate it. It feels like punishment."

"Joining the Marines isn't punishment. It's an honor."

Her blue eyes are loaded with misery. "I know. It's selfish of me. But you are my best friend. I don't have many of those. Girls are so complicated. With you, it's always been easy."

"That's because high school girls are bitches. Plain and simple. They're jealous of you."

Her eyes bulge in disbelief, and she makes a waving gesture up and down her body. "Jealous? Please. Look at me. There is nothing special here. My hair's a mess most days, my style isn't cool, and people think I'm a nerd."

I grind my teeth at her perception of herself. My gaze roams down her body, appreciating the way her sundress highlights her curves. She's wearing her favorite faded pink Chucks. "Your hair is pretty, your style is cool, and being smart isn't nerdy. It's commendable. You've already been awarded scholarships to two of your top colleges."

"If there is any jealousy, it's none of that. They're envious of you. After prom, the rumors started you took me as your pity date. Tons of girls wanted you to ask them. That makes me think I may have coerced you into going with me."

Fury boils in my gut. I'd heard that rumor, too, and now regret not shutting that shit down. I bring our joined hands to her cheek, running my thumb along her jaw. "Fucking bitches, Harley. Every girl in that school knows they had no chance. If it wasn't for you, I'd have ditched the whole thing. It wasn't coercion; it was a privilege."

Her lips curl, and she gives me a small smile. "I'll miss you."

"Boot camp is no joke. But I'll message if I can."

"You better. Dad, Mom, and I will be at your graduation."

"Don't break too many hearts your senior year."

This time, she rolls her eyes high to the sky. "Forget about that. Dad won't let me date. You're the only guy he ever let me go out with alone. He's so protective."

"Rich is wise and knows how precious you are. I understand exactly where he's coming from."

"Recruits! Board up!" A man in uniform barks out the order sharply.

"Do you need to say goodbye to Sandy again?"

I follow her line of sight to my mom, who is standing with Harley's parents, Amanda and Rich. Notably absent is my father. Harley didn't mention it, but her expression when Mom arrived alone gave away her curiosity.

She knows my home life was messed up, but she doesn't know the extent of it. Rich and Amanda are salt of the earth, good-to-the-soul people. They may have some faults, but I doubt it. Whereas my parents, Pete and Sandy Kingston, have a lifetime of fuck-ups behind them. Dysfunction is putting it mildly.

My dad's currently sobering up in a detox facility. Rich has promised to monitor his progress and push to keep him on track.

"Nah, Mom will start crying again and it will be awkward."

I've barely turned my head when Harley lunges into me, wrapping her arms tight. She lightly pecks over my cheek, neck, and ear before whispering, "I'm so proud of you. Please be safe."

I clear my throat, her sweet floral scent washing over me, and the skin she kissed tingling.

God, she feels good against me. The teenage boy comes alive. My cock stirs, and I bite my tongue to tame it down. "I'll be good."

She steps away, reaches inside her pocket, and shoves a folded piece of paper into my hand. "Don't read this 'til you're gone."

I nod.

Slowly, she backs away, not breaking eye contact until she gets to her parents. I give them all a chin jerk and shift the bag in my hand, then get on the bus.

The mood is solemn and quiet, nothing like the chatter and bustling outside. I nab a window seat and look out in time to see Harley crumble into her dad, her body rocking violently. Tears streak down Mom and Amanda's cheeks. Rich stares back at me with a look that blows straight through me, piercing somewhere deep.

Pride, admiration, respect.

The bus drives away, and I open the note.

Achilles,

~~*Thank you for being my friend.*~~

Thank you for being the best, most wonderful, most loyal friend in my life.

Thank you for letting me know the incredible person you are hiding from the rest of the world.

Thank you for not embarrassing me that first day when I declared we were friends and you weren't getting rid of me.

There are a thousand little things to thank you for, but last, I'll say thank you for being such a good man.

All my love,

Harley

A knot coils tight in my stomach, and my heart thunders in my chest.

I type a quick text to Rich—*Take care of her.*

His reply comes back within the minute—*Always. Do good, son. Go become the man you want to be.*

I power the phone off, knowing that was the last communication with my life as I know it. In a few hours, all personal belongings will be stripped and bagged.

Go become the man you want to be, replays in my head, fueling my determination.

This is the beginning, the first step of finding the man inside me that is good enough for Harley Christine Jacobs.

No matter how long it takes. Because when I find that man, I'm coming back for her.

1

ACHILLES

"We're applying for SWAT." I lay it out, not wanting to prolong this more than necessary.

Major and Talon stand to my right and Ford to my left. Without looking, I know we stand in solidarity—legs planted, arms crossed, and serious expressions. This is not up for discussion. Our decision is firm.

The statement hangs in the air as Chief Boyd's face hardens and his eyes move over us. He has no idea who the four of us are outside of our applications and any documentation of records in the academy. I'm surprised he even accepted my request for a meeting today

"Pardon me?"

"We're applying for SWAT," I repeat.

"I'm not deaf. I'm wondering where you four rookies got the balls to come into my office and make that announcement. You haven't completed your first round of field training, and you're already looking to move up the ranks."

"It's not balls, it's respect."

"Respect? You men may be ex-Marines, but you're on my force now and I call the shots."

"Marines," I correct him. The temperature in the room chills, all giving off the same disapproval of his assessment.

"What?"

"Marines. We're not ex-Marines. We're Marines."

"Being in the Reserves doesn't make you active."

Major lets out a low, bitter sound, pulling Captain's attention to him.

"I've already had to jump through hoops and fast track your asses through the academy. There are some pissed-off people in this department who think you received special treatment because of who you know."

This is another trigger point and I close my eyes, mentally getting a hold of my temper. It pisses me off when anyone insinuates we've gotten here because of special treatment. The four of us have worked our asses to the bone, risking our lives countless times for this country, and we are exactly where we deserve to be.

"SWAT division has a waiting list that takes years to get through. Men and women with much more experience are already chomping for the call to interview," he goes on. "Hell, you four are so green, there're barely any scuffs on your shoes."

"We know what we need to do."

"Yeah? You think? What makes you think you're SWAT material?"

"We know," I reiterate.

"The probability of the four of you moving so quickly is improbable."

"We're a team," Talon speaks up. "We go together."

"Cocky big shots who have no regard for how things work. Funny how that was missing in your personnel files."

"We're not cocky; we're good at what we do," I correct him.

"How could we know that with less than a month on the streets?"

I raise an eyebrow, remaining quiet while the guys chuckle. Captain Boyd leans back in his chair, not amused. "You think one arrest makes you a novice?" There's a little less anger in his tone.

"Nope, just getting started."

"Cocky," he says, shaking his head.

"You don't even qualify for —"

"Eleven months," I cut him off, finishing his sentence.

"It takes the best of the best for consideration. Not to mention a recommendation."

"Best of the best is not a problem. And we're counting on you for the recommendation."

"Why are you here telling me this? To fire me up? Piss me off that you've barely started and already have a foot out the door? Not sure it's a good way to start a relationship."

Once again, I remain quiet. He scans my face, his eyes piercing into mine, and it's obvious the instant it dawns on him. It's like watching the proverbial light bulb switch. He's figuring me out.

"What's your full name, rookie?"

"Ace Kingston." I don't disclose my birth name. Almost everyone knows me as Ace.

"Holy shit, you're the one." His expression takes on a new form of understanding. "Achilles Kingston. How in the hell did I miss this? You're Rich's boy."

A knot curls in my gut, and I force myself to stand still. A new round of tension fills the air as he puts the pieces of my screwed-up puzzle together. And from the look on his face, he knows a hell of a lot more than I'd hoped. I'd come this far with only a few people knowing my story. Rich Jacobs is the pinnacle that helped get me on track. And that is why I came clean with the captain about my future plans—Rich suggested it.

"Rich thinks highly of you," is all I say.

Boyd rises, coming to stand in front of us, and keeps his eyes locked with mine. "We have rules, regulations, and protocols in this department. You understand?"

"I know all about living a strict code."

"That's why I'm not kicking your asses to parking patrol for the next year."

"Appreciate it."

His lips twitch, and he breaks our stare, shaking his head in amusement. "Fucking ex-special forces, badass fighters, awards of excellence. Right here on my team."

The guys shift uncomfortably as he summarizes us.

"Your files are locked tight. I didn't understand why there was so much pressure to push you through the academy at rapid speed. I have gone rounds with my team about who would work with y'all because of the rumors swirling of special treatment."

"We didn't think it was necessary to tell our life history."

"Not my place to do so, but I see things in a whole new light. You men want SWAT, I won't stop you. But I'm also not softening the expectations."

"No need."

"A word of advice. Keep your intentions under wraps. It won't make you popular amongst your peers if they think you aren't committed to the department."

"Advice appreciated, but we're not here to be popular."

He moves his gaze toward us again. "I didn't think so, but remember who's in charge."

"Of course." I jerk my chin and turn to leave, the others doing the same.

"One more thing," he calls out, and my heart sinks at the sound of his tone. I can guess what's coming.

I glance over my shoulder, waiting.

"Rich and I have worked together for a long time. Even though I didn't know you, I was around years ago when all that went down with your dad. He took it personally that they involved you in the mess. Glad to know it's worked out for the best."

I dip my head and walk out. It goes without explanation I owe Rich more than I can ever repay. What no one knows, except the three men at my side, is that Rich shaped my life.

But it was his daughter who was the driving force. Harley Jacobs… my Harley.

Everything I've done, everything I've accomplished… everything that has gone well in my life up to this point… it has all been for her.

And hopefully soon… for us.

"We've got company," Talon announces, strolling into the room with another round. "Security cameras show a grey SUV."

We all know who the vehicle belongs to. He's laying it out to gauge my reaction. I've been in a shit-fucking mood since we came home and, besides the occasional comment on the game, no one has spoken directly to me.

"Guess I shouldn't be surprised." I pop the cap off a cold beer and straighten from my lounging position.

"Want privacy?" Talon asks.

"No need. My guess is he isn't alone."

There's a quick rap at the door before Ford answers. My guess was right. Amanda is standing next to Rich with her motherly smile bright.

I stand and wait my turn to greet them. There are a lot of muffled voices as Amanda doles out congratulatory hugs and Rich gives strong-armed handshakes.

When they get to me, Amanda's eyes pool with tears. "God, Ace! I am proud of you!" she gushes, throwing herself in my arms. She's said this many times over the years, but today is different.

"Thanks, Amanda." This is the first time I've seen her in months. A twinge of guilt creeps in, knowing I should have attempted to visit, but my focus was on other things. "It's good to see you, but you could have called instead of driving all the way out here."

"I wasn't giving you a chance to come up with an excuse. It was time I saw you face to face." I'm aware they were at the graduation a few weeks ago, but we ducked out immediately after the commissioner finished speaking. It was a dick thing to do, but there was a good reason.

Rich has been a member of the Nashville Police Department for over thirty years. The last fifteen as a detective. He exchanges a look with Amanda that tells me all I need to know. This is more than a social drop-in.

"We came to talk," Rich confirms my suspicions.

"We sure as hell did!" Amanda raises her face, eyes now on fire. "I should strangle all of you!"

She twists her head to the other guys, who shrink back like scolded boys.

"It's my fault." I take the blame, knowing it's useless. She's gearing up for lecture mode.

"It's all your faults. Graduation was an important day—why weren't any of your parents there?"

"It was a formality, and we made it low-key," I explain. "We're having a celebratory weekend soon."

This is the truth. Talon, Ford, and Major's families are visiting in a few weeks.

"Well, that's fine, but what about Pete and Sandy?" Amanda pushes.

My spine goes straight at the mention of my parents.

"Not going there."

"Son, Pete's been sober for over ten years. It's time to get over the grudge. When will you cut him some slack?" Rich poses the same question he's been asking for a while.

"There is no grudge. Let that shit go a long time ago."

"What about your poor mother? She loves you so much. This rift is putting her through hell." Amanda's also repeating the same thing she's said for years.

"There is no rift. It wasn't a big deal. I'll invite her to lunch soon."

The unspoken question hangs in the air, and Major shuffles his feet uncomfortably.

"Go ahead and ask, Amanda."

"What about Harley?"

"What about her?"

"I've almost given up on mending the fences with your parents, but poor Harley? You used to be so close. She's been waiting to hear from you."

"She's busy, didn't want to bother her." It's a sorry-ass excuse. Actually, it's a bald-faced lie and sounds exactly like it.

"Bother her? You've been in town for over six months. She had tears in her eyes the whole ceremony. She has always been incredibly proud of you. Then you ran like a coward!"

I try to beat the guilt clawing at my insides. I knew she was there, felt her before we even entered the floor. It was easy to spot her, sitting with her parents in the section for personnel. She looked incredible in the navy-blue dress. Her silky auburn hair was hanging straight, the usual curls blown out. I fucking loved her curls, but she was gorgeous any way she came.

It had been three years since I'd seen Harley in person. Her grandfather's funeral. I didn't know the man well, but the heartbreak in her voice on the phone had me boarding the first flight available. My intentions were to slip away unnoticed, but my three overly interfering friends ended up by my side, claiming their support. I knew it was bullshit. They wanted to meet the woman who had me so far wrapped up that I never showed interest in anyone else.

Major, Ford, Talon, and I met in boot camp and became quick friends. Our goals and drive were identical, knowing we were all on the same path with our military careers. They were the closest things to brothers I would ever have. Hell, our brotherhood was stronger than most sibling relationships I'd witnessed.

Marines, brothers, and now partners. They were family, and outside of Harley, the most important people in my life. Over the years, and many nights, they learned about Harley. She came to know them, too, through stories.

In those early years, they understood my position. She was too young and too much was at stake. But after she went to college, they took a different stance. A standpoint that encouraged me to tell her the truth.

A suggestion I refused to follow through.

The years away, I allowed myself the communication. It was safe, and even with my feelings, I could compartmentalize, making myself think of Harley as a girl.

That weekend home changed everything. I lost the fight and was forced to face the truth. My beautiful, sweet girl was now all woman. Three days was all it took for me to fall even deeper under her spell. I was fucked.

Totally fucked.

And then I made the mistake… breaking every promise I vowed as an eighteen-year-old when I left her to join the Marines. *Just one kiss*, I told myself. One kiss wouldn't change anything between us.

The instant my lips touched hers and I finally had her in my arms, I was toppling over the edge of insanity. It took every bit of strength to walk away, claiming it was wrong.

I thought I lost her for good that time. The look of raw devastation on her face is etched in my brain, and I swore if I ever had the chance, it would never be there again. She may have thought I didn't love her, but she was wrong.

It took a while, but I finally heard from her again.

Please let me know you are safe.

The email came through while I was overseas, and it took days to see it. For the first time in my life, I was at a crossroads about how to react. Ignoring her was not an option, but this was a chance to make a clean break. Then that damn angelic face filled my head. I couldn't let her worry.

I remembered my end game.

Her… everything I was doing was for her.

So I typed out a generic response and opened myself up again. It wasn't my choice to be an elusive asshole; it was a necessity. Our position and role in the Marines was active combat. Until we decided to get out, I needed her to live her life free of worry and be happy.

"Amanda, we should mind our own business," Rich says, bringing me back to the present with all eyes on me.

She shoots Rich a daring glare that now has me shifting uncomfortably.

"I wish I could go back in time all those years ago and tape your overbearing, opinionated, stupid mouth shut! You should be ashamed! You took something beautiful and innocent and made a colossal mess of things."

Rich hangs his head, running his hands through his salt and pepper hair, and then focuses back on me. "I am ashamed. I made a mistake."

"You did what any father would do. Harley was too good for me. If it wasn't for you, I'd probably have a few stints in jail under my belt. I'm the man I am because of your push. Never let that fact go unnoticed."

"What I did was chastise an eighteen-year-old young man that had a shitty home life and got caught up in his father's mess. You were doing what you had to do to survive. I was too hard on you."

"We knew I was enlisting and leaving. Stringing Harley along would have been the wrong thing to do. She deserved better."

"But you wouldn't string her along. You were a better man at eighteen than most men I know. And you only got better from there. I never should have intervened."

"You did the right thing, and it was over a decade ago. Time to let it go."

"I'll let it go when you tell me you're stepping up."

"I've got it handled."

"Really?" He arches his eyebrows, rolling his eyes in a way that tells me he knows I'm full of shit. "Four grown men hauling ass out of their own graduation ceremony to hide from a woman that wanted nothing more than to congratulate you? Bunch of chickens. That's not stepping up."

The guys all shuffle their feet. I press my lips tight, unable to argue. He's right; it was cowardly.

"Don't wait too long." His words are simple, but there's a meaning behind them that sets me on edge.

"What's that supposed to mean?"

"There's a new guy coming around. He's been persistent."

Major blows out a breath, prying the beer bottle from my hand. At the mention of this guy, my body goes rigid.

"If you care about her in any way, she needs to know," Amanda suggests.

"Can't stop her from dating." The words come out grave and clipped, ripping a hole in my gut.

"Ugh! You are extraordinarily bull-headed." She actually stomps, her face flaming red. Her actions remind me so much of Harley's that some of my irritation slips away.

"Another reason we came by is to let you know Boyd called me after your little meeting today," Rich breaks in. "Can't predict the future, but if you boys don't screw up, you have the recommendation."

"That's good to know."

"It's a long road, Ace, and I'll support your career. But like Amanda said, don't wait too long to really start your life. Especially if you want that life to include Harley. A lot has changed in the three years since you were here."

Rich is digging deep. He knows how I feel about his daughter.

Always has. We go into a stare-down, the boiling in my gut spreading through my veins. His lips twitch, one side curling up.

"See I may have finally made my point. Word of warning, the woman has a temper like her mama."

Amanda nods in agreement "Us Jacobs women know how to hold our own."

"I'll keep that in mind."

2

HARLEY

It's only seven o'clock and my feet are already throbbing in agony. The next three hours will be hell.

"Please don't tell me Tom changed the dress code." My best friend, Jewls, joins me behind the bar, ready to start her shift.

"I forgot my clothes at home this morning so I'm stuck wearing these." I wave to my business attire from my day job.

"You look nice."

"You're lying."

"Maybe you look a tad out of place. Why don't you change your shirt?"

"I tried, but Tom doesn't have any more in my size."

Her eyes light up as she reaches to the underside of the bar, digging in her bag, and a blur of blue zips across the space. "Found one," she chirps.

"Jewls, you're a size smaller than me."

"Half a size, technically, and this shirt has been worn. It's stretched out."

"Gross." I wrinkle my nose.

"It's clean, you freak, just perfectly worn."

"Fine."

I roll my eyes on the way to the restroom to change. It's a little snug in the chest, but the rest is loose and it's a much better choice. When I look in the mirror, my eyes bug out. Snug isn't the right word.

My chest is bursting at the hem of the V-neck, barely covering the lace of my bra. I glance at the cream ruffled blouse in my hand and contemplate putting it back on when there's a banging on the bathroom door.

"Jewls needs you! The rush has started," Tom barks gruffly.

"Too late to change my mind now," I mutter, hurrying to the bar.

An hour later, we have a chance to breathe and I catch the sly grin on Jewls' face as she whispers something to Tom. He looks at me, then back to her, walking away, shaking his head.

"What was that about?"

"He's acting like an old man," she replies, wiping the bar top.

"How so?"

"Something about you showing skin in his bar."

"What the hell? He loves skin." The girls who work the floor and man the bar on the weekends wear much more provocative outfits, and he encourages it.

"That's what I told him. This is much sexier than the stiff, stuck-up wardrobe they force you to wear daily."

I ignore her comments about my clothes, mainly because I agree. Being a junior marketing executive at my firm requires a certain level of conservatism. While I'm not one to show a lot of skin, I wish the dress code was looser.

"Don't worry about him. This should cheer you up." She waves a wad of cash in front of me before dropping it in the tip jar below the bar. "We are getting closer to our vacation."

Our vacation. Two weeks in Europe. Jewls and I bouncing around from city to city, visiting my cousin, and closing the trip with a Mediterranean Cruise.

That's why we are working here. Every bit of this money goes to our trip. Tom is an old colleague of my dad's who retired and opened the bar years ago. He traded his uniform-wearing structured life to laid-back, t-shirt-casual bar-owner. He secured a perfect location that brings in heavy clientele, especially from the force. Everyone supports him.

He agreed to hire us with little experience and trained us in what he labeled 'his way'. We aren't typically scheduled weekend shifts, but the nights we work provide a good amount to pad our European Fund.

"You ready to talk to me?" Jewls' question brings me from my thoughts.

"About what?"

"It's been days. I've been patient enough."

I shrug, glancing around the bar, hoping someone needs a drink so I can avoid her inquisition. Unfortunately, everyone is glued to the baseball playoffs on the overhead screens.

"Nothing to say. His responses to my texts have been short and distant. He doesn't have time to get together right now, even for coffee. Doesn't take a genius to see he's not interested."

"I'm sorry."

"No big deal," I lie.

It is a big deal. My head has been in a complete daze since seeing Achilles at his graduation.

It did not surprise my parents when I asked them to get me a ticket with them. Dad's position on the force gives him floor seats, and I knew it would work to my advantage. Luck was on my side, and all four of the men were directly in my line of sight during the whole ceremony. I knew he was planning an escape. The tension in his body rolled off in waves.

Once, only once, did he glance my way. When his dark eyes connected with mine, I forgot how to breathe.

Dazzling... That's the only way to describe them.

He let his guard down, and I felt the heat between us. There was a dash of hope in that split second before he broke the connection.

When he fisted his thigh and flicked two fingers, that was my cue. He made the mistake of looking to his left. I followed his eyes to the exit, and I was on my feet, inching that way before the commissioner was through speaking. I had no clue what to expect, but enough was enough. He'd been evading me for too long. I tried to stop him, make him talk to me, but I was too late.

"Earth to Harley." A palm waves in my face.

"I'm pretty sure he's cut me off again," I whisper softly, hating to admit it. "He's been back in town for over six months. Things are definitely different between us. Even communication with the guys is turning weird."

She slides her hand in mine and squeezes sympathetically. There's no use in telling me to get over Achilles and move on.

"I'm not going out with John again." I change the subject.

"Not surprised. You can't have chemistry with anyone when your whole mind is consumed with Ace," she pauses, her gaze moving over my shoulder and her eyes lighting up. "Although, I think the tides may turn soon," she giggles.

I twist to see what she's referring to and suck in a deep breath. Major, Talon, and my dad are all sitting at the end of the bar. Major and Talon are staring at me with wide eyes while my dad is wearing his signature grin. As I walk closer, I peer past them to see if Achilles is following, but Dad gives me a quick shake, indicating he's not here.

"What a pleasant surprise." I lean across and give my dad a half-hug.

"These rookies needed to be introduced to Tom's," he answers, swiping a handful of bar nuts.

"Hi, guys." I try to reach across and hug them both, but they remain stiff.

"I thought you worked in a swanky marketing firm?" Major asks flatly.

"I do, but I work here a few nights a week."

"This is a bar."

"I'm aware of that."

"It's a blue bar."

It's true, ninety-percent of the clientele are active or retired police, but that shouldn't matter. "So?"

"If you're working in any bar, it should be the kind that has crystal chandeliers and serves drinks for twenty dollars a pop. Not this."

"What's wrong with this?" I prop my hand on my hip, narrowing my eyes. "Are you implying I'm a snob?"

"Hell no, but Ace will flip his fucking shit when he finds out," Talon spits out.

"Why?"

"Look at you," he waves his hand. "What are you wearing?"

Humiliation heats my skin, and I know splotches are crawling up my neck. "I'm wearing a shirt, Talon. And these are called boobs. A lot of women have them. What is that Marine slang? SITFU?"

The acronym scrolls through my head, making sure the letters are correct. *Suck it the fuck up.*

The slap of my dad's hand on the hard wood draws my attention his way, and he's dropped his chin to his chest, roaring in laughter, and clearly enjoying this.

"Dad, what's wrong with you?"

"I couldn't have set this up better if I tried. Damn."

"Set what up?"

"Hey, guys, I hear congratulations are in order." Jewls slides three bottles of beer to them, thankfully interrupting the ridiculous conversation.

"Jewls?" It's slight, but there's a flicker of surprise in Major's eyes.

"Hey, Major, Talon." She smiles.

Talon jerks his chin, but Major's expression has gone blank.

"Cat got your tongue?" she teases him.

"I just… You…" he stumbles over his words.

"I've grown up? Three years in a long time." She helps him out.

"Obviously," he mutters.

Jewls and I met in college and, after graduation, she decided to stay in Nashville. She's known about Achilles and his friends since the beginning of our friendship. At my grandfather's funeral, she met them for the first time. During the weekend, I was too wrapped up with Achilles, but watching this exchange, I have to wonder if something happened between her and Major.

"Lookin' good, Jewls." Talon shoots her a grin.

"Thanks, Talon. Welcome to Nashville."

"You're working here, too?" Talon questions.

"Part-time, like Harley. We cover the bar three nights a week."

Right as she answers, a regular from the other end calls my name, and I give a wave, leaving them to serve him. As I turn, I catch the glint in my dad's eye, and suspicion settles in the pit of my stomach.

What is that all about?

3

ACE

"You have an admirer," Ford smirks as I place the weight bar back in the cradle.

"Not interested."

"You may think differently once you see her."

"It's never mattered, let's roll."

"Too late. Five… four… three… two…"

"Hello there," a sultry voice sounds, and I spin to find a woman standing two feet away. She's dressed in skin-tight clothes with a perfectly styled ponytail and a face full of make-up. At barely seven-thirty in the morning, she looks out of place in a gym full of men and women trying to get in a workout before their day begins. It's even more obvious when her eyes fill with unmistakable intent as she steps closer.

"Hey."

"I've seen you in here before."

Not shocking since I'm here six days a week. I've noticed her, too, and avoided all contact. She's attractive if you're into the assertive cat-and-mouse chase. Most men would jump at the opportunity to play her game.

I'm not most men… and she's not Harley.

"My name is Mia."

"Ace."

"Ace." My name rolls off her tongue, and her gaze roams over my arms appreciatively. "I really like your ink. I have a tattoo as well, but it's in a more intimate area."

Ford's chuckle turns into a cough when I spear him with a look of irritation.

She takes my silence as an invitation to keep talking. "Are you new to the force?" Her perfectly manicured finger points to my sweaty and ripped MNPD shirt.

"I am." My instincts tell me she already knows the answer since men and women on the force frequent this gym. The proximity to the station makes it convenient.

My suspicions are confirmed when her gaze grows hungrier and she licks her lips. "I have great respect for those who protect our city. Maybe you and I could grab—"

"Ace!" She's cut off by a thunderous shout across the floor.

I whip around to find Talon and Major striding my way, their faces masked with a mixture of worry and caution.

"What's wrong?"

"Oh shit, he doesn't know," Major says.

"Know what?"

"You haven't checked your phone?" Talon asks carefully.

"Not yet. Shift ended at seven. Came straight here."

"Check it."

"Why?"

"You need to see something."

"So show it to me."

"No way, my phone is brand new." He tucks his phone protectively to his hip.

I slice my eyes to Major, who's enjoying this too much. A familiar sixth sense kicks in. "One of you motherfuckers better tell me what's going on."

"Stop being a pussy," Major snatches the phone out of Talon's hold, tossing it to me.

Ford is at my side in a second, viewing the image. "Sweetheart, you'd better move along. This won't be pretty," he tells Mia, who I forgot about.

"Ummm," she hesitates.

"Mia, he's taken. Your flirting is useless here," he says gently, trying not to embarrass her.

I assume she leaves, but I can't tear my eyes away from the image of Harley, leaning over a bar serving a beer to a man who's smiling a predatory smile. I don't have to zoom in to see her tits on display in the shirt that reads *'Tom's'*. A throaty growl builds low in my throat, and I clutch the phone so hard the display blurs.

"Shit," Talon complains.

I raise my eyes to his, waiting for an explanation.

"She's working part-time. Jewls says they are saving for a vacation."

"Does Rich know?"

"He's the one who took us there."

"Sly fuck," I hiss. He had the opportunity to tell me, but this is his way of pushing up my timeline. Blindsiding me into knowing that Harley is working in a bar is not a problem.

Harley working at Tom's is.

Then it hits me like a force so solid I swallow down the roar. I met Tom through Rich ages ago. Word is, he retired and opened a bar, and for that, all the guys on the force go there. I haven't visited him since moving back. The last month in the academy I heard rumblings. The guys dropping the name of the bar with the 'hot babe' bartenders. I had no interest.

Now that I'm aware they were referring to Harley and Jewls, my mind has changed.

"She's working tonight at five," Major offers the information breezily.

"Guess that's where we're headed?" Ford assumes.

"Bet your ass."

"Feel obligated to tell you Jay's pretty popular amongst the crowd." Talon takes his phone back.

"No surprise there."

"I'm sure this will fall on deaf ears, but we just started this job. It'd suck to make enemies so quickly."

"No enemies as long as my point is made."

"What point is that?"

"Harley's off-limits."

WE AREN'T five feet in the door, and the hostile vibes are already rolling. "This is going to be a long night," Ford utters under his breath as we make our way to the bar.

It's relatively early, but the place is busy, almost every table occupied and the bar full. I stop a few feet away, taking in the place. It is exactly what you'd expect from a retired-cop-turned-bar owner. Not a typical sports bar with team gear and paraphernalia everywhere. Instead, pictures of cops through the years, patriotic flags, and emblems line the walls.

"It's about time, Rookie." Tom steps in front of me, his hand extended.

I take it, pulling him in for a one-armed hug. "Good to see you, old man."

"Glad you're back home, Ace. Even more glad to know you're in a different type of uniform."

"Good to be here."

"Any reason it's taken this long to stop by?" He puts me on the spot.

"Been busy," is all I offer.

"Rich tells me you had some close calls overseas."

"We made it through." I shrug, not wanting to discuss my operations in the Middle East. It doesn't surprise me Rich shared them with Tom, but the subjects of my missions are mostly classified.

"Glad to have you back, Marine," he repeats, squeezing my hand before releasing it. "Met two of these grunts last night. Who's the other?"

"Ford." Ford offers his hand.

"Rich mentioned you, too. Welcome to the force."

There's a loud roar from the other side of the bar, a half-dozen guys chanting something.

"Shit, I hope this doesn't get messy," Tom complains.

"What?"

"Started a ritual a few years ago. When a rookie makes their first arrest, I buy them a drink."

"Generous."

"Yeah, but this guy's buddies are hell-bent on getting him plastered. Keep bragging about him being the first rookie in his class to get an arrest."

I glance at my three friends and catch the amusement on their faces. Tom doesn't miss it either, his own expression registering understanding.

"You beat him, Ace?"

"Maybe."

"What shift?"

"Doesn't matter."

He looks over my shoulder, cocking an eyebrow.

"Second shift on the job. Pulled over a drunk with drugs and an unregistered firearm. Guy was blitzed, and he tried to fight his way past Ace until he found himself incapacitated. Woke up the next day with a wild hangover, and a face only a mother could love after being intimately acquainted with the concrete. Totally FUBAR," Major fills him in.

"Shit, you fought him?"

"Didn't have to. Once he lunged at me and fell into my fist, he lost balance and went down," I answer.

"Who's your Field Training Officer?"

"Hal Hanks."

"I know him. Bet he loved that."

"He may have enjoyed it."

"Well, why the hell didn't he bring you in here to celebrate?"

"Wasn't a big deal."

He studies me, a familiar grin forming on his lips. "First drink is on me."

"Appreciate it, Tom."

"Let's get you a table."

"Actually, we're headed to the bar."

"Nah, you men need space, and the bar's crowded."

"The bar is fine. We'll make room."

His grin goes to a full-out smile, his eyes lighting up. "It's about time you 'head to the bar'." His meaning is clear.

He leads, taking us to the far side where four stools are empty. In front of them is a folded sign that reads *Reserved.*

"I had a feeling I'd need these seats tonight. But hear me now, Ace. I don't want any trouble. You start shit, you answer to me."

"Got it. No shit," I agree.

"You're a fucking terrible liar, boy. Remember that."

He slaps me on the shoulder and walks away. I swear I hear the faint sound of whistling as he goes.

My eyes scan the area, not finding Harley anywhere. I'm thrown off balance, my ass almost sliding off the seat when a weight hits me from the side. Small arms wrap around my waist, and Jewls' face flashes in view before she buries it in my chest.

"Hey, Jewls." I squeeze her neck and kiss the side of her forehead. "Good to see you."

She presses back, her bright eyes wide and shining. "So good to see you, Ace."

"What about me?" Ford spreads his arms, and she moves into them.

"She's in the stockroom. And you can thank me for those seats. I passed up an offer for two hundred dollars saving those." Jewls turns to me. "You're also late."

"Late for what?"

"We started our shift at five."

There isn't a chance for me to answer before the catcalls sound out, and all the hair on the back of my neck stands.

"Oops, I better go help!"

My eyes stay trained on her as she runs to the end of the bar and Harley comes into view. She's overloaded with liquor bottles, carefully balancing as she slides them to the edge, and Jewls takes them from her.

She laughs at something Jewls says, and then her eyes shift to me. There's a flicker of surprise, her smile spreading as she steps around and comes my way. I do a quick scan over her.

Relief washes through me that her shirt isn't nearly as tight or revealing as last night. Her hair is tied on top of her head, the curls escaping in all different directions. There's a flash of something bright, and I chuckle under my breath when I notice her pink Converses. For all the years, she still loves those shoes.

"Hi, guys," she says sweetly. "Did I miss the apocalypse?"

"Nope," Ford replies.

"Did pigs fly?"

"Not yet." Major laughs.

"Did hell freeze over?"

"Possible," Talon answers.

"So, what's the occasion?" she asks me.

"It was time to check this place out."

"Check it out?"

"Yeah, heard some great things."

She stands in front of me—eyeing me as if she knows what I'm thinking, and looking gorgeous, confident, and absolutely breathtaking.

Even with the distance between us, I hear her breath hitch and her eyes shimmer. My mask falls and she notices instantly, understanding washing over her features.

In a flash, she's in my arms, wrapping herself around me as a small sob escapes. "I'm proud of you, Achilles," she whispers with a broken voice.

My heart stops at my given name. No one refers to me as Achilles anymore. I've gone by Ace for as long as I can remember. But she never cared, always saying how much she loved Achilles.

And like the young teenage boy that met her at one of the lowest points of my life, I curl her into my body and allow myself to feel her pureness seeping into me. Her scent invades me, and my body reacts, hauling her tighter.

"Harley," is my only response.

I don't know how long we stay like this, her in my arms while I memorize the feel of her body pressed close. A throat clears and she lifts her head, one of her curls tickling the edge of my ear. She turns her attention to the guys.

"Congratulations to all of you." She aims her full smile at them, and the jealous motherfucker in me wants to cup her head back to my neck and haul her out of here.

The urge grows when she embraces Ford warmly.

"Well, look at this shit!" Glen Bates steps into our circle, the stench of beer hitting me hard. "The Casanova Club has finally come out. It's about time, Rookies!" He sets his eyes on Harley, raking them over her until they land on her ass. An unmistakable hunger fills his expression. "Can I get one of those hugs, pretty lady?"

Jealousy ricochets to possession, and I stand, putting force into my right side and my bulk pushing him back into a stumble. Major takes my cue, sliding Harley to me, where I tuck her under my arm.

"Watch where you're going." The sloppy grin on Glen's face turns into a scowl.

"I was. You were in our space."

A quiet hush falls between us, not acknowledging the dumbass. Harley speaks first. "Casanovas?"

"Stupid nickname," I answer her lowly, trying not to growl.

"Oh, that's right, it's not discussed." Glen ignores the rising tension.

"It's not discussed because it's bullshit," Talon grinds out.

"The flock of women, the secluded mansion on the hill, the revolving door… You may be a bunch of playboys, but —"

"I'd be careful how you finish that statement, Glen." I tighten my hold on Harley, twisting her to me protectively.

We go into a stare-down, his face heating as his eyes roam over my position and fall on the arm wrapped over her shoulder. My scorching glare tells him everything he needs to know.

"I wasn't aware the Casanovas had favorites."

"That's because you don't know me well enough. But we will get acquainted really quick if you look at her like that again."

"We have a problem, Kingston?"

"Not if you hear what I'm saying… loud and clear."

He takes a step back, throwing his hands in the air. "Point made." He turns to leave.

"Shit!" I hiss, a searing pain shooting through my abdomen. Harley's nails dig harder, then twist right before she pushes away.

"What the hell was that?"

"What was what?"

She glares angrily and opens her mouth, no doubt to blast me, when her gaze travels over my shoulder and she jumps into motion. "Crap!" She scampers away, rushing behind the bar to help Jewls. In the few minutes Harley was with us, the crowd increased massively.

Tom delivers four bottles of beer, waving that he's got this round, and goes to another group of men waiting to be served. I continue standing, sipping the beer, and observing the room. There are a few servers assigned to tables, but most customers have grouped around the bar. It's easy to tell why. Harley and Jewls are the center of attention. No matter what, the men all wait patiently for them to approach.

"Told you she was popular with the crowd," Talon reminds me.

"And I told you I'm not surprised."

My skin prickles with the familiar sensation of being watched. I spot Glen, surrounded by six other men I recognize, glowering our way. Shot glasses and beer bottles litter the table in front of them. I catch the mixture of bloodshot sheen and anger in his expression.

Great, he's drunk and pissed.

He holds my glare until Harley steps in front of him, cleaning the mess and offering another round. His eyes drop to her, then back to me, licking his lips as an evil grin crosses his mouth. He leans in, places his hand over hers, and says something in her ear.

She politely slips her hand away, stepping back and pasting on a fake smile. Her body language screams uncomfortable, and I slam my beer on the bar top so hard the sound echoes enough to get their attention.

It also catches Tom's attention because, in less than a second, he's blocking my view. "No trouble tonight, Ace."

"He needs to go."

"His buddies already paid the tab. They're on their way out the door. He's had his sights on Harley for a while, and tonight, he probably figured out he has no chance. His arrest today added to his already inflated ego."

"He's the one with the arrest?" I snarl, remembering the noise when we walked in.

"Sure as shit is, been bragging for hours. He couldn't turn her head.

You're in here less than two minutes and she's in your arms. I think he knows he's lost this battle."

"If he doesn't know now, he'll know next time he touches her."

"My advice?"

I pull my eyes from Glen. "What's that?"

"Don't let your own ego get in the way. There are many more Glens out there looking for their chance."

It's impossible not to catch the meaning in his words. I glance back to Glen, who's stumbled off his stool and is arguing with the guys trying to gear him toward the door. The thought of him and many like him thinking they have a shot with Harley rolls disgust in my gut. I've always considered myself not good enough, but dickheads like him don't deserve the time of day from her.

"I will say this, Rich describes you as a man of action with one exception."

"I think you've figured out the exception," Major notes matter-of-factly.

"I've known the exception since Ace was eighteen-years-old, but times have changed. I'm looking forward to seeing how this plays out." Tom jerks his chin and walks away.

I catch Harley watching us and shaking her head.

"Why do I think that we'll be spending at least three nights a week here?" Talon asks no one in particular.

"Tom might want to put our names on these stools," Major concludes.

"Well, since Ace works tomorrow night, I'm on duty." Ford takes the task with a knowing smirk. "Guess we found our new hang-out."

4

HARLEY

THIS IS IT… the time I'll look back on my life and realize '*Harley, you are officially a stalker.*'

"Maybe we should rethink this." I try to opt out before it's too late.

"Don't get cold feet now. We're almost there, and I didn't buy these outfits for nothing," Jewls sasses, waving down her body.

We are identical in leggings, Chucks, mock turtlenecks, and beanies —all in black. "Why did you insist we wear these ridiculous outfits? We're not getting out of the car."

"Because we're on a stakeout and this seemed appropriate. If on the off chance we leave the car, we can blend into the night. Being a cop's daughter, you should know the process."

"Jewls, criminals dress in all black when conducting crimes! We're supposed to be doing an innocent drive-by to check the place out."

"Mmmhmm, you keep telling yourself that, Harley, but we both know why we're here."

I snap my mouth shut because she's right and there's no point in arguing. We're here because curiosity has seeped its way into my overly nosy brain. Achilles' visit to Tom's two nights ago left me aggravated and even more confused than ever. I felt more a part of his life during his first deployment to the Middle East than I do with him living in the same city. Then he shows up, looking heart-stoppingly gorgeous, and for a split second the air filled with the same heat we shared from the graduation. The way he hugged me close sent tingles shooting through my body. I wanted to stay that way, never leaving his arms. Those minutes were perfect until dickshit Glen came over and ruined the moment.

He's been trying to get my attention for weeks, but I've politely ignored his advances. To me, he's harmless. The thunderous rage on Achilles' face said otherwise.

I wasn't sure whether to shout with glee or fury at Achilles' caveman attitude. Acting like an overprotective barbarian when he's ghosted me for longer than I want to admit.

The comment Glen made about the Casanova Club stuck with me, but I didn't ask him more because he was drunk. When he brought it up again, warning me to be careful of the *'Club',* while insinuating Achilles was a legend, my mind took off. I mentioned it to Jewls, and she went to work asking around and uncovering the rumors behind the name. Her persistent poking paid off when she hit up a group of cops that enjoyed a few too many and had no problem babbling. According to the tales, the four men earned the name Casanova Club during the first weeks at the academy. They mostly stuck to themselves, which didn't surprise me, considering how close and private they are. They turned down invitations to go out, they never socialized, and the only place they ever hung out was the gym. One lady in the group told Jewls that the gym was where they made contacts. Women flocked to them and word quickly spread. The four of them had private parties at the 'mansion on the hill'. Not one of them had any type of proof, but they all insisted that the whispers were true.

Major, Ford, Talon, and Achilles are considered playboys who don't share the wealth. Hence earning the name Casanova Club.

I planned to mention it to Achilles, but he hadn't been back to the bar. Instead, the last two nights, Talon and Major had come in, sat on the same stools, and stayed until Jewls and I left for the night.

Jewls thought it was hilarious. She's trying to convince me that

Achilles orchestrated this because *"he's finally ready to get his stubborn, bull-headed, ridiculously self-righteous head out of his ass"*—her exact words.

I wanted to hope, to believe she may be on to something. But before I could allow myself to feel this, I needed to investigate the 'Casanova' mansion. Not that I believed these guys were egotistical playboys, but it was my way of justifying spying on them.

We chose tonight because Achilles is working, and I knew if anything about the rumors proved true, at least they wouldn't be confirmed by him bringing a woman home. I'm not sure I could handle witnessing him with someone else. Which is absolutely stupid since he's free to live his life any way he chooses, including hooking up with random women night after night.

"Well, shit." Jewls slows down, pulling off into a small parking lot.

"What's wrong?"

"Look at that." She points to the large stucco sign that reads 'Whitman Estates'.

"Shit," I repeat her earlier sentiment. This neighborhood is pretty well-known and sought after. I've only been back here one time when Jewls and I attended a bridal shower. The houses are mansions on massive lots.

"Are you sure you have the right address?" I question her, unbelieving that the guys live back here.

"Yes, I memorized it off Talon's driver's license. Just to be sure, I snuck a look at Major's, too, when he left it on the bar. This is the right place according to the navigation."

"I don't understand. How can those four afford this? It has to be a mistake."

"Only one way to find out. Let's ride through, then we'll think of something."

She drives down the main road, and I relay the directions from her phone to their address. We hit the back of the neighborhood when their street comes into view. Daylight has turned to dusk, but it's easy to make out the lone house on the hill that is the only one on this street. My jaw hits the floor at the sight.

"Holy fuck, is that a compound?" Jewls reads my mind.

"It looks like it." The enormous two-story brick home sprawls out across the end of the cul-de-sac.

"Considering it's the only house, it's hard to be conspicuous. How do we get close?"

"Good question."

We sit quietly, staring until she jumps, twisting to the back seat and tossing a small bag in my lap. "There's a pair of binoculars in there; grab them."

I hand them over to her. She scans right to left, chewing on her lip until I get nervous that someone may drive up and catch us creeping.

"We need to go." She drops the binoculars in my lap and reverses quickly.

"What happened?"

"One of the guys came out the front door and took off for a run. I think it was Talon, but can't be sure."

"Hurry." I panic, hoping like hell he doesn't see us.

"Calm down. He may be fast, but he can't outrun my car. Hold on." She swerves onto a street where a few lots are being cleared, then pulls behind a dumpster and turns off the car.

"Why are you stopping here?"

"Do you want to watch the house for a bit to see if anything happens?"

"Like what?"

"It's Friday night. Talon, Ford, and Major aren't working. If any speculation of the Casanova Club is true, then surely we will see something."

I flatten my hand to my stomach to ease the queasy ripple, my eagerness to spy turning to shame. "I'm not sure this is a good idea. We can't even see the house, and it's gotten darker."

"I think we can see the house if we go through that small patch of bushes." She waves to a thick brush a little in front of the car.

"We really are stalking, aren't we?"

"Aren't you a little bit curious?"

This is a rhetorical question because she knows the answer. My curiosity is the bane of my existence. I chew on my top lip and peer through the windshield to the brush. "Maybe just a peek…" I trail off because she's already out of her door.

I shove the binoculars and our phones in my hoodie and follow her quietly with the dim streetlights as our only light. When we get to the bushes, we have a clear view of the side of the house closer up. It is much more gigantic and regal at this angle—paved circular driveway, stone columns flanking the front patio, and grand double doors with light shining through. The question from earlier reruns on how these guys can afford a place like this.

We mutter a few words about the house but remain mostly quiet. After what seems like forever, with no action, I finally sigh out loud.

"Nothing's happening. This was a crazy, stupid idea," I whisper.

"I have to agree. This is boring as fuck," a male voice rumbles behind us, and I screech, tackling Jewls as if someone is attacking us. She squeals in response, reflexively pushing back until we're rolling on the ground.

We do this for a few seconds, kicking, bucking, shrieking, and holding each other protectively.

A bright light clicks on, and I am momentarily blinded when a firm hand tugs me to my feet. The flashlight moves to Jewls, whose eyes are wide and face smudged with dirt.

"Talon! You asshole," she yells, rocking to her knees and hauling herself up. "You scared the shit out of us."

He laughs a full, deep-in-your-gut roar that has me cringing. It's bad enough we are busted, but his humor at our predicament is mortifying.

"I couldn't help it. You two were easy targets. Want to tell me why you're sitting in the dark outside our house?"

Neither of us answers, but Jewls is eyeing me for a good excuse. Which I can't think of one because all I want to do is crawl into a ball and disappear. The flashlight comes to me, and I catch the white of Talon's teeth with his wide smile.

"What about you, Jay? You want to fill me in?"

The first time I met Talon, he took my last name and slapped me with his own nickname. Jay stuck.

"Not particularly." I dip my head in disgrace.

"How'd you find us?" Jewls tries to take the pressure off me.

"Wasn't hard. We have the whole place secured. Saw your car on the street and went for a run to check things out. At first, I thought it was nosiness until you pulled by the dumpster and jumped out of the car looking like you do."

"What's wrong with the way we look?" she snips defensively. "We're dressed perfectly incognito."

"Babe, you two couldn't be incognito in Ghillie suits."

She raises her hand in the air to argue, and I speak up. "We know about the Casanova Club," I blurt out.

The smile on his face falls fast and transforms into a dark scowl. "Repeat that."

I shake my head.

"Who the fuck told you about the Casanova Club?"

I don't answer.

"Ace will lose his fucking mind and hunt down whoever spread that shit. He already wanted to rip Glen's head off, but if he finds out that dumb fuck said anything, it's going to be ugly."

"It wasn't Glen," Jewls protects the guy. He may be a nuisance, but he doesn't deserve the wrath of Achilles.

"So, you snuck out here on a Friday night to see for yourself if we have a revolving door of women because those fuckers we work with have nothing better to do than make up shit because we don't fuck everything that moves? I can set you straight right now. None of it is true, but people like to talk."

God, I'm an idiot. I knew deep down these guys weren't that type, but my freaking nosiness got me into trouble again. My shoulders sag, and I rack my brain for a plea to keep this from Achilles. "Maybe we can keep this between us?" I try weakly.

"I'm not sure we can do that," another voice comes from the side. Ford and Major step out, and a light flashes with the unmistakable sound of a camera click.

"Oh my God!" I slap my hand to my forehead. "This is bad."

"Get over it, Harley, we're caught. Now, what I want to know is how the hell you guys are living here." Jewls throws attitude, not caring that our situation is ridiculous.

They don't answer and it dawns on me out of nowhere. "Ford!" I throw my finger his way. "Ford Whitman!"

Why I didn't put two and two together earlier is beside the point. Probably because I was too busy worrying about stupid lies that have no merit.

"Can't put anything past you. My family developed the land in this area. The house belongs to them. We're crashing here for now."

"It's spectacular."

"It serves a purpose." He's not nearly as impressed as we are.

"You ladies want to come check it out? See for yourselves that we don't have a harem hiding inside?" Talon returns to his teasing manner.

"We don't want to intrude. No need to completely ruin your Friday night. This is already bad enough."

"Ford and I have to work tomorrow, and we're meeting Ace at the gym at seven a.m. Besides, this is quite entertaining." He rocks back on his heels, enjoying my distress.

"Jewls, give me your keys." Major holds his palm out.

"Why?"

"I'm driving your car around. Go on inside the house."

"No, really—" I start.

"I'm starving," Jewls cuts me off. "Please tell me you men have some decent food. Being on a stakeout is grueling."

My stomach churns, wondering how she could think about food at a time like this. I glance over at the house, feeling uneasy about going inside when Achilles isn't there. I'd much rather have an invitation from him.

"What's on your mind?" Ford steps close, asking quietly.

"I feel like an idiot. I'm beyond embarrassed, and I'm not sure going inside is a good idea. It's like an invasion of his privacy."

Ford pulls his lips through his teeth a few times, observing me as his eyes go soft with understanding. "I'm seeing what Amanda and Rich meant," he utters so low I almost miss it.

"What do you mean?" The mention of my parents sets my head spinning again. What do they have to do with anything?

"Nothing." He throws his arm around my shoulders and walks us forward. "We're all friends, Jay. And I think you owe me a rematch."

"Rematch of wh—Oh my gosh! How do you remember that?"

"I never forget an annihilation that bad. Waited a long time for payback."

"I haven't played video games in forever."

"That means luck is on my side. I've spent years preparing for a rematch."

Nostalgia washes over me, remembering that weekend. What started as a sad affair with the funeral quickly became a favorite memory. Finally meeting these guys after years of hearing about them helped lift the sadness of the occasion. There was no awkward getting to know you stage; it was like we'd known each other forever.

That meant something to me.

Then there was the kiss… *the kiss* I'd been dreaming about since I was sixteen years old and fell in love with the rugged loner boy with the bad reputation. The same boy who lived a life of hell that he kept hidden in the dark.

The schoolgirl crush I'd held on to all those years evolved into something much deeper.

Then he walked away and left me again.

"Hey." Ford shakes my shoulder gently, bringing me out of my nostalgic haze. "You okay?"

We're standing at the foot of the steps, and I realize I missed most of the walk over. I shake my head and glance up at him, smiling the best I can. "I'm great. Thinking about my best strategy. It may have been years, but I'm not going down without a fight."

He scans my face, his eyes filled with sympathy. "You're a shit liar, but I'll let it pass because I have a feeling what you were actually thinking about."

"Probably," I whisper, hoping he doesn't push further.

"I'm gonna say this, and if you ever repeat it, I'll deny like fuck. But you need to hear it." His expression grows serious.

"What?" I hold my breath, waiting anxiously.

"Ace is my guy, he's my brother, and he's a man I'd die for without thinking twice. There is no question of my loyalty. You know I'm crossing a line by telling you this. But give him a little more time, Jay. Don't give up on him."

"Almost eleven years is a lot of time."

"There's a reason for everything, and it's his story to tell. But mark my words, don't give up on him."

I want to push, I want to stand my ground and demand Ford elaborate, but it would be useless. He's right. Loyalty is the blood vein of these guys and he won't budge.

So instead, I twist into his arms and press my head to his shoulder. "I'll never give up on him," I admit shyly, hearing the pathetic teenage girl make an appearance.

"We doing this?" His fingers poke into my side as his tone changes, the seriousness of the moment shifting.

"Absolutely!"

"Talon!" he yells, and the door flies open. "Fire up the game room. Time for a rematch."

Talon smiles wide, making a sweeping motion with his arm for us to hurry inside.

I return his smile, jab Ford in the ribs, and escape his arms, jogging up the stairs.

5

ACE

"REMIND me not to volunteer for this shit again," Major grunts.

"No one asked you to come."

"No, but considering what happened at the gym, I think it's best you have an alibi at all times."

I roll my eyes and turn onto our street, picking up the pace and leaving him behind as I run the last half-mile. My blood pumps harder, adrenaline pulsing through my veins. He may be exaggerating the situation, but he's not all wrong. When Ford and Talon told me about Harley and Jewls' visit last night, I didn't react. But when they told me the reason for their driving all the way out here to investigate the fucking Casanova Club, I came close to losing my mind.

I'm generally a pretty level-headed man. When I joined the Marines, I learned to control the temper that almost cost me everything my senior year of high school. Since then, it takes a lot to get a rise out of me. I've gotten a handle on controlled reactions. There are few exceptions.

Harley is one of these exceptions.

When I get to the house, I jog in place, slowing down and waiting for him to catch up. His expression is hard and eyes sharp as he approaches.

"We done now?"

"For now." I rip my soaked shirt over my head, tucking it into my waistband, and grab the towel I left sitting on the porch table.

Major does the same, breathing heavily as he wipes himself down. He follows me through the house and into the kitchen, mumbling his thanks when I toss him a bottle of water. I swallow most of the bottle in one gulp and catch his expression as he watches.

"We're in the house now, no need to monitor me."

"I've got something to say."

"If it's about Harley, save your breath."

"Held my tongue for a long time, man. It's time you hear me out. You're a lot of things, Ace. You may have come from a bad situation, but you became a decorated Marine with an intuition like no other person I've ever met. You overcame all the fucking shit and are one of the most badass men I know. I'm proud to call you my brother. But right now, I'm wondering when you became such a cruel son of a bitch."

I stumble back on my heels, not expecting that last blow. "What the fuck are you talking about?"

"Why the hell are you holding back? She's yours, Ace. And I don't mean she loves you like the twenty-one-year-old that has feelings for the boy from high school. I'm saying she's yours in the sense that the woman here last night has feelings for you that run so deep she can't get away from them. Forget the reason she drug her ass out here. She didn't believe the rumors. I clocked that with one look at her. She may have toyed with the possibility they were true, but she knew better. There was another reason for coming here, and that reason was you."

"I was at work."

"No fucking shit. That's why she came. She knew there was no chance of running into you, and since you've blown her off for so long, she didn't have to face another round of disappointment. I think you're a damn fool if you continue this."

"Not having this conversation with you."

"You'd rather have it with me than Talon or Ford because I can bet your ass they're ready to lay into you."

"Highly doubtful."

"You would say that because you're wrapped up in your warped head, and you don't see what everyone else sees. What they told you at the gym this morning was only the half of it. When you went half-cocked and knocked that punching bag to the ground, they knew it was up to me to explain the rest. Jay is confused, and that's not fair. It was obvious last night in her actions. She was quiet and detached, kind of tiptoeing around the place like she didn't belong even though she was invited. She acted the part, but you could tell she was uncomfortable. There wasn't one word of protest when Ford roasted her ass in racing and we know he cheated. She wasn't the same woman. I get your reasoning, but it's time to rethink your plan."

"What do you suggest?"

"Stop avoiding her. Go back to being her friend."

"Her friend?"

"Yeah, simple stuff. Text her, call her, take her to coffee, ask about her life. Stop ignoring her. Keep it simple and platonic. Then, maybe as you carry on with this stupid fucking charade of being aloof, she'll finally clue in that you're not interested and move on. Like I said, be her friend."

Plastic cuts into my hand as I crush the water bottle in an attempt not to take him down. "I don't want to be her motherfucking friend and you know it."

"I thought I knew it by the way you acted at Tom's, but seeing her last night made me rethink my stance. Anyone who loves her wouldn't put her through this. Maybe you don't love her. SITFU and be her friend."

A red film clouds my vision, and I'm about one second away from jumping the distance between us. The air in the room turns hot as I mentally try to control my anger. My entire body tenses, muscles strung so tight I feel my pulse ticking in my jaw. There's a ringing in my ears at his implications. This morning is not the morning to fuck with me about Harley, and definitely not the time to mention her moving on. Telling me to *suck it the fuck up* isn't smart. We don't talk about shit like love and feelings, but these guys have always known, without bringing the emotions into it, how I feel.

And right now, I feel like kicking my best friend's ass.

His lips split into a wide grin and he laughs, the sound grating on my already overactive nerves. "Yeah, that's what I thought."

"Are you aiming for a death wish?" I grind out.

"No, I'm changing my side. As of today, I'm officially on Rich and Amanda's team. Get your head out of your ass and make your move. It's time. And if it was me, I'd find a way to be charming. She may love you, but she's got a stubborn streak that mirrors yours. My money is on her teaching you a lesson." He waltzes out of the kitchen, leaving the words hanging.

They sink in and I throw the crushed bottle across the room. "Son of a bitch!" I yell, hearing his laughter from down the hall.

He knew exactly how to bait me, and it worked. I check my watch, and my adrenaline races for an entirely different reason. Harley's yoga class is over in an hour. That gives me very little time to shower and figure out what the fuck I'm doing.

I LEAN against the front of my truck, taking in the trendy strip mall that looks like all the others in the area. Both ends capped with drive-thru windows, one a dry-cleaners and the other a non-chain coffee shop. In between are small businesses, including a yoga and Pilates studio. The windows are tinted, but once in a while, I catch a shadow of movement.

I check my watch again, thinking that she should have been done five minutes ago. The eerie feeling of being watched prickles at my skin, and my eyes scan the area. A growl builds deep in my throat when I spot the assholes. Major is leaning casually against his driver's side door talking with Talon, Ford, and Officer Randall, who are standing outside of their police SUV.

They're all smiling, eyes on me as I whip off my sunglasses to glare. "Killing them all." I take a step forward right when the studio door opens and a string of women file out. At first, I think the glare must be bad, but after blinking a few times, it's clear. The women are covered in sweat, red-faced, and some of them slow-moving. Harley is in the middle of the pack, and my chest seizes at the vision. Her tank top is plastered to her torso and chest, the red fabric more of a burgundy. Her braided hair is held back with a sweatband that is barely containing a few flyaway curls. She's turned to the woman next to her, talking. As if she feels my presence, her head pops up, and she stops mid-stride.

The woman next to her stops as well, following her gaze to me. I barely pay attention, focused on Harley and taking another step forward.

Her friend nudges her shoulder, and she walks again, this time separating from the group.

"Hey," she says timidly, brushing her hair back absently when she gets closer. "What are you doing here?"

"Are you okay?" I reach out to tuck a stray curl behind her ear, ignoring the question.

"Yeah, why?"

"Because you don't look like a woman that just did yoga."

She giggles, throwing her head back, her chest shaking. "You always have a way with words. I look like a wet rat. It's hot yoga on Saturdays. They set the heat pretty high."

My body jerks. "Why would you do that?"

"Because not all of us are built like a brick house, Ace." She nudges my side.

I'm about to respond about how she's built perfectly fine when a male voice calls her name. She twists to the sound, and I step closer, watching a man in athletic gear coming our way. He rakes his eyes over us, and I don't miss the flash of surprise aimed at me.

"Hey, Erik," she greets cheerily.

"I meant to catch you before you left. I was wondering if you had time to grab a quick lunch. There's something I'd like to discuss." He glances at me uncomfortably and then back at her.

She picks up on this and tilts her face to mine. "Achilles, this is my yoga instructor, Erik. And this is my friend, Ace."

"Nice to meet you." He offers his hand and I take it, swallowing down the acid scorching my throat at the use of the words 'friend' and 'Ace'. I'm always Achilles to her.

"Yeah," I respond, tightening my grip before releasing his hand.

"Did you want to have lunch today?" she asks him.

"Yes, unless you already have plans."

"No, I just need to go home and chan—"

"Actually, I am taking you to lunch," I cut her off briskly.

Her eyes bulge and her mouth snaps shut.

Erik's expression turns to amusement as he crosses his arms. "Maybe tomorrow you could meet Kelvin and me for breakfast?" He speaks to her, but his focus is on me.

I drop my head and bite the inside of my cheek to keep from laughing. He's good. That one statement tells me what I need to know. It also shows he's fishing for information. My hand goes to her hip and pulls her the few inches to me.

"We could probably do breakfast," I say into her ear, but loud enough for him to hear.

She huffs, elbowing me in the ribs, trying to move away. "I know *I* can do breakfast."

He flat-out smiles. "Great, I'll text you later and set up a place."

"What do you want to talk about? Is everything okay?"

"I'm expanding my business. I wanted to get your advice on marketing, promotions, and budgeting. A few facilities around town have contacted me for specialized classes. The short-term goals are pretty simple because I'm contracting with established businesses. It's the long-term plan that needs some crafting."

"That sounds like a great opportunity."

"It is, but I don't always want to be at the mercy of others. Eventually, I want my space and facility. My ideas are overflowing, but the cash flow is tight. Kelvin's encouraging me to start a business plan."

"I'm not a genius, but we could throw some ideas around. My main recommendation would be to focus on building word of mouth for a foundation." Her enthusiasm picks up, and she bounces on her toes, the movement rubbing her full back against my front.

My body comes alive, my cock swelling fast, and I grip her tighter. "Why don't you save the good stuff for breakfast tomorrow?"

She stills, and Erik's smile grows wider. He eyes me knowingly. "Should I request a table for four or eight to include your audience?"

Harley whips her head around, and when she spots the guys, she lets out a squeak. "What the hell?"

"Let's stick with four. Those assholes may not be functioning tomorrow," I answer.

He tips his chin and turns to leave, jogging back to the studio.

"What in the world is going on?" Harley hasn't taken her eyes off the men.

"Ignore them."

She steps out of my hold and shakes her head a few times. "Let's go back to my original question. What are you doing here?"

"I thought we established this. I'm taking you to lunch."

She looks at me like I'm crazy, her hands flying in the air as she lays into me. "Taking me to lunch? Did I miss something? I don't remember setting anything up. As a matter of fact, I distinctly recall trying to get together for months with no interest from you. Did you think to call or message me? Maybe say '*Hey, Harley. Sorry I've avoided you forever, but let's grab a bite to eat and catch up.*' Or '*I'd like to take you out to apologize for being the world's most evasive ass lately.*' "

Here's the fire Major was referring to this morning. Luckily, I came prepared. I pull out my phone and hit send.

I'm taking you to lunch. We need to talk about last night. I'll be waiting after your yoga class.

Less than three seconds later, her phone chimes, and she scowls at me as she digs it out of her bag. "I'm not sure I want to talk about last night." She slumps, her spark and irritation dying out.

"We're talking about it, but I'd prefer we don't do it with the idiot peanut gallery watching on. Knowing Major, he probably has a listening device set up."

"It's embarrassing."

"So jump in the truck and let's clear the air."

"How about we never speak of it again and forget it ever happened? It was not one of my shining moments. It's none of my business what you do in your personal life."

Her voice drops low. I immediately pick up on the hurt in her words, and move into action. In a second, she's in my arms and I'm stomping to the passenger side of my truck. She lets out a little yelp when I haul her onto the seat and slam the door, jogging to my side.

"Buckle up," I instruct, pulling out of the parking lot.

"What about my car?"

"We'll come back for it."

"I'm not exactly dressed for lunch."

She's perfectly dressed, but instead of telling her, I decide to set things straight.

"Glen Bates is an arrogant prick with a big mouth and nothing else to back him up. He's been a pain in the ass since the first day in the academy. His type is straightforward. High-society shithead raised with a silver spoon. Give him the chance and he'll tell you how special he is. My guess is he has no interest in being a cop, but he wants the power behind the title. He doesn't have what it takes to handle the badge.

"He tried to buddy up to us and we edged him out. He didn't like being snubbed. Since he thinks his shit doesn't stink, he became a passive-aggressive pussy. About that time, the rumors started. Unlike a lot of those guys, chasing women and talking about our conquests isn't our gig. We socialize little outside of ourselves and don't feel the need to explain. I can't speak for what Ford, Major, and Talon do every minute of their days, but women aren't parading through our house—ever. Ford's parents are loaded and make their money in real estate. They develop communities all over the place. Having a community in Nashville was a coincidence. Also, a convenience. Hence the mansion on the hill. The four of us moving in together may seem odd to some, but we don't give a fuck. The house is huge, we have our privacy, and even if we had our own places, we'd probably still be together."

"I don't think it's odd," she says shyly.

"Glad to know."

"I think it's outstanding."

I glance across at her and see her eyes are full of sincerity and shining brightly. "You think it's outstanding that a group of grown men live together?"

"I do. I've worried about you for a long time. You've never really had a home. The environment you grew up in wasn't healthy. Then you travelled the world with the Marines, never settling down. I can sleep easy at night knowing you're in a place that's beautiful, safe, and filled with people you care about. That's why I went snooping. A part of the reason was the stupid rumor, but the larger part was to see where you are living. I needed to see for myself."

My gut twists at her raw honesty and the wounded demeanor Major was referring to.

"I'm good, Harley. You never need to worry about me."

"I'm still embarrassed."

"I wish I was there. Talon says the best part was the wrestling match with Jewls."

"Men are ridiculous."

I pull into her complex and turn the corner to her apartment, spying the delivery propped by her door.

She doesn't notice, gathering her things and jumping out. I follow her closely and know the minute her breath hitches.

"What is this?" Her eyes dart between the floral arrangement and me.

I shrug, handing them to her and sliding the card into her palm.

I'm Sorry.

Two words… The most important two words I owe her.

Silence hangs between us, and when she looks up at me, her eyes are shining a deep, bright blue. "You're sorry?" Her question comes out raspy, her voice loaded with emotion.

"I am." There is much more to say, to explain, but the timing isn't right.

She launches forward, throwing her arms around my neck. I return the embrace, squeezing tight.

"The last time you gave me flowers was the night I forced you to take me to your senior prom."

"Having the most gorgeous date at the dance was no hardship." The prom was all her doing, and I hated the thought of attending. But her excitement made it worth it.

"Come on in. I need to clean up and change." She takes out her keys and leads us into the apartment. "Make yourself comfortable. I'll get these in water." She heads to her kitchen.

I've never been in her place before, but know the layout because when she told me she was moving here, I made a call to the leasing office. The security is decent; the neighborhood is safe, and the surrounding tenants all have clean records. Rich and I both agreed it would do for now.

Her stamp is all over the place. I spot myself in a few of the pictures, and my pulse races at the shot of me walking into the arena a few weeks ago at graduation. It's placed right next to the picture of Harley and me the day I left for boot camp. Over a decade separates the two—it feels like a lifetime ago I was that boy.

"Where would you like to eat?" She places a vase on her small table. "How should I dress?"

"Actually, you are perfect. We're going someplace cool, easy, and very casual. Maybe even pack a bag with a suit."

"A swimsuit? To a restaurant?"

"No one said anything about a restaurant."

"Where are you taking me then?"

"A mysterious place on a hill called the Casanova Club." I crook an eyebrow, waiting for her reaction.

Her mouth drops open, and she slaps her hand over it as a loud giggle escapes. Her body vibrates with laughter until a tear slides down her cheek. "That place has quite a reputation," she coughs out.

"Only the best for my sweet Harley."

A beautiful glow sweeps over her expression, and she turns toward her room, calling over her shoulder. "I hope the Casanova Club serves a good lunch because I am starving."

It's my turn to smile.

6

HARLEY

I STARE in wonder at the sight Achilles casually refers to as the 'pool area'. Yes, there's a pool, but that's a minor piece of this breathtaking back yard. It's as if I've transferred to a swanky spa resort and men dressed in uniforms are waiting to offer me a cocktail. There's so much that I don't know where to focus first—pool, hot tub, and a raised fire pit at the edge of the patio made from the same stone pavers. The outdoor kitchen is larger than my entire apartment, and I lean to see what it's backed up to.

Ford, Talon, and Major didn't exactly offer a tour when we crashed on Friday night. I saw the living room, kitchen, and media room upstairs. That's about the extent.

This is incredible.

"Is that a house?"

"Yep." Achilles passes me, grabbing my hand and linking our fingers as he drags me along.

"There's another house next to the pool?"

"That's probably why they call it a pool house." He winks, flashing a sideways grin.

My heart races, and the skin on my palm tingles at the feeling of his hand covering mine. My brain scrambles to think of a smart remark to his teasing, but I can't think straight. It's an insignificant gesture, nothing special to most people. But I'm not most people. A strange wave of something comes crashing down around me, and I draw in a deep breath.

In a second, he's in my face, our joined hands lodged between our chests, and his free hand cupping my cheek. "What's wrong?"

"I-I'm not sure. Is this happening?"

"Is what happening?"

"Are you really holding my hand?" Instead of saying the millions of things running through my mind, this is what I utter like a bumbling idiot.

His gorgeous brown eyes cloud into a deeper shade, and instead of letting my hand go, he tightens his grip. "Yes," is his simple response.

"It's been years since you held my hand," comes pouring out before I can stop it.

"Get used to it." He leans in closer, placing his forehead against mine.

Flutters begin low in my stomach and my heart pounds wildly. For a brief second, I'm transported back in time. Standing in my parents' yard, pressed against him, sucked into the depths of his eyes, hypnotized by everything about him. He made me feel like the most precious thing on earth, the way he held me captive. The warmth of his breath coats my lips, and I fight the desire to move the centimeter it would take to touch my mouth to his.

Something passes between us. Without a word, I know he feels it, too. The tip of my tongue runs along my bottom lip and his eyes grow darker. "Harley," he practically growls, his hand squeezing tighter. In a flash, he steps back but keeps our hands attached. "Let's eat."

I want to scream in frustration that I'm not hungry and yank him back to me. Then I remember what else happened that night. It physically hurts remembering his expression when he broke our kiss and walked away. Taking an enormous piece of our relationship with him.

Achilles has always been beautifully complicated. I knew it the first time I laid eyes on him at fifteen. He doesn't know it, but it took me almost a full year to gather the nerve to talk to him. Loner, bad boy, social outcast… whatever it was, it drew me to him.

Beautifully complicated… and I knew I wanted to be a part of it.

Then it happened. The night before I started my Junior year, my dad got called out on a domestic issue. He and his partner at the time walked up on an obliterated Pete Kingston in a fit of rage, and his wife, Sandy, was being shielded by her seventeen-year-old son, Achilles. In an ironic twist, it was my dad that gave me the courage to talk to Achilles.

On the first day of school, I approached him and never gave him the chance to turn me away. And it's been that way ever since. I've always loved Achilles, and no matter how hard I've tried, I've never gotten over it.

To this day, I don't understand what happened to him three years ago, but I swore if we ever got back to a good place, I'd cherish the friendship and leave the rest behind.

"You hear me?" His question breaks me out of my thoughts.

"What?"

"Did that yoga class mess with your head? I was talking and you went into a daze."

"Sorry." I shake out of my haze. "I was actually taking a trip down memory lane."

His expression goes blank. "Was it a pleasant trip?"

"It was sixteen-year-old Harley and seventeen-year-old Achilles… what do you think?"

His expression changes. "Sixteen-year-old Harley is always an excellent memory."

My heart and stomach do that flipping, twirling, fluttering thing again, and I decide to move to safer subjects because this exchange is giving me too much to think about.

"What's for lunch?"

"Hopefully, still your favorite." He awards me with his heart-stopping grin and goes behind the counter of the summer kitchen. Unfortunately, this means he releases my hand, but when he places a tray on the counter, I debate on what is better. Achilles holding my hand or the unmistakable packaging of my favorite sandwich ever made.

"Oh my God," I sigh as my mouth waters. "How did you do this?"

"Called the shop this morning and had it delivered."

"That's impossible. They don't deliver. I should know. I've tried many times to order delivery, even starting an online petition to change the owners' minds. It didn't work, but they gave me a nice gift card for giving them the publicity."

"They deliver to me."

"Don't be cocky." I scrunch my nose and shoot him a scowl.

"You want to argue about how the food was delivered, or would you like to eat?"

He sweetens the deal by opening one Styrofoam box, and the sight of the sandwich shuts me up. I sit on one of the barstools, take the box, and reach for the plastic silverware. Carefully, I cut each half into halves until there are four equal portions. Then I sprinkle a few of the chips on top of one side and take a bite.

A small moan escapes when the rich mixture of cream cheese, turkey, and provolone coats my tongue. It's the perfect way to distract me from my Achilles and Harley history. A bottle of water slides in front of me, and I glance up to find him watching me closely.

"Thanks."

"What's with the sections?"

"I'll eat one for dinner and save the rest for tomorrow. It's my way of savoring."

"We're having steaks for dinner."

"Since when?"

"Since I marinated them before coming to pick you up."

"Presumptuous much?"

"I call it decisive."

The smart ass in me wants to educate him on the proper etiquette of asking someone to dinner. But the silly, frilly hearts and unicorns Harley wants to keep the mood light. "I guess I could eat a steak. But regardless, there's no way I could eat all this." I point to my food.

"Try," he clips, picking up his own sandwich.

"I don't remember you being this bossy."

This time, when his eyes flare, there's a slight gleam that shines. He shakes his head, finishes chewing, and relaxes his hip against the counter. "Tell me about your job."

I decide to let him have his play, ignoring my comments and changing the subject easily. I launch into my position, explaining that it's a lot more administrative work than actual marketing. It would be nice to have a seat inside the circle of creativity, but my time will come.

He listens intently, keeping his eyes trained on me, and after a long while, I realize he's finished eating and letting me ramble.

"Sorry! I get a little carried away."

"I enjoy listening to you." He takes my leftover food and puts it in a refrigerator that I thought was a part of the stone façade.

"Is that yours, too?" I refer to the other container on the counter.

"Nope, it was for Major, but his stupid ass can eat dirt for all I care." He hesitates for a second, then shoves it into the fridge as well.

"Is he here?" I twist back to the house.

"I'm assuming he's asleep, considering he bitched like a baby during our run."

"You ran? I thought you met Talon and Ford at the gym."

"I did, then I got in six miles here."

"Have you slept at all?"

"Not yet."

"Aren't you exhausted? You should rest."

"I'll be fine. Pool time." He once again ignores my comments, comes around to take my hand, and leads me to a chair where he threw my bags earlier.

I set up my chair and tighten the hair tie on top of my head, knowing it's a hot mess and wearing it down is out of the question. I'd like to think I'm one of those girls that can work out and look like a runway model afterward, but I am anything but. In the quick change I did at my apartment, I was able to partially tame my curls, spritz up a little, and dress in my favorite bikini.

I pull off my cover-up and reach for some lotion when a low rumble causes my head to fly up. My breath catches at the wild expression on his face. But my heart races out of control for other reasons. He's removed his shirt, and I become paralyzed, unable to move anything but my eyes as they travel over him. Achilles has always been well built, and I've seen him in a swimsuit dozens of times. But the man in front of me is almost unrecognizable. My knees wobble and I grip the back of the lounge chair for support. Every part of him is sculpted and muscular, defined much thicker than the last time I saw him.

I zero in on his chest and shoulders, drawn to the massive amount of ink. I knew he had a USMC tattoo on his shoulder blade, but these are new to me. Some of the artwork is recognizable numbers, but most are custom-designed swirls and lines. All of it is remarkable.

I think of his mythical Greek hero namesake. He's gorgeous… Godlike is the word that comes to mind.

The silence stretches on as I continue to soak in and appreciate every fine detail of his physique. When my eyes find their way back to his, an icy chill runs down my spine.

The intensity in his gaze has me frozen. Insecurity takes over and my hand inches for my towel.

"Stop." He reads my mind, stepping forward. His fingertips skim down my arms to my hand, where he links our hands again. "You're beautiful."

The way he says it sends another kind of chill along my spine, this time bringing a full out body shiver.

"So are you," I basically whisper.

His own body jolts, and he tightens his grip. "I fucking missed you, Harley."

"I missed you, too. Maybe too much." I can't control my admission.

"I'm back now."

"What does that mean?"

"It means, *I'm back*."

He doesn't elaborate further and I force myself to look away, breaking the intensity of the moment. I've never been able to hold a grudge for long. It isn't in my character. Someone says they're sorry, I either accept or don't, but always move on. With Achilles, our history is complicated, and I want answers. My heart beats in rhythm with the ringing in my ears, and I swallow down all the thoughts whirling through my head.

'I'm sorry, I missed you, and I'm back' replay over and over. I make the decision that it is enough—for now. It may make me pitiful, but with this man, sensibility flies out the window.

"I'm glad you're *back*." There's no way he can miss the meaning behind my words.

The change in him is immediate. Before I know what's happening, I'm swooped in the air and over his shoulder. His mission is clear when the edge of the water comes into view.

"Don't you dare!" I screech, squirming to get free.

In another swift move, I'm upright, with no choice but to wrap my limbs around him and hold on. He jumps forward, both of us going airborne for a second before the cold water crashes around us.

"You want help moving her?"

"You touch her, I will break your hands," a hushed growl responds.

There's a low chuckle followed by a few words I can't make out, then a cool material drapes over my hips and legs. I curl deeper into a ball and sigh, falling back asleep.

"If you care about him, the best thing you can do is let him be himself. Accept and support him. If it ever becomes too much, know when to walk away."

My dad once told me that Achilles carried the weight of ten men on his shoulders. He bore responsibility that wasn't his and accepted it willingly. I'll never forget his advice. My parents knew that I'd never walk away from him. I took Dad's advice—accepted and supported every step of the way.

Today was different. Achilles has changed. For a few hours, his armor slipped, and he revealed a part of himself that was rare and uncovered.

During the afternoon, Major joined us at the pool. Achilles speared him with a look that would shatter glass, but Major laughed in his face, undeterred, and dove in. I didn't ask, but I assumed the death glare had something to do with the show this morning at the yoga studio.

I slipped out of the pool and discreetly snapped pictures of the two tossing the football in the pool, then sent them to Jewls. Her comments kept me entertained until my phone was snatched from my hand and I was tossed back into the pool and forced to play a game of volleyball without the net. I spent most of the time dodging the ball and being teased mercilessly. It was humiliating, but the smile on Achilles' face made it worth it.

I got a semi-tour of the house and discovered there are six bedrooms and seven baths. Achilles showed me to my own room to shower and change, leaving me alone for the first time since the morning. I called Jewls, gave her a brief rundown of the day, had a semi-freak-out, and then rushed to shower before Achilles wondered why I was taking so long.

Luckily, before leaving my apartment, I had the foresight to pack a few essentials. It wasn't much, but I wasn't a total train wreck.

Achilles refused my offer to help with dinner and instead poured me a glass of wine while he did most of the prep. Ford and Talon came home from their shift and neither acted surprised to see me. Achilles shot them the same glacial stare as Major, and like Major, they laughed in his face and ignored it.

We ate, we drank, and we caught up on each other's lives like old friends. The only time Achilles left my side was to grill the steaks, and even then, he pulled my barstool closer to him. I went with the flow, enjoying the carefree atmosphere.

There was a hesitation in the air when I asked about their obligation to the Marines now that they were in the Reserves. Achilles' jaw got tight, and he sent a look to the others, who didn't speak up. He sort of brushed me off, saying it was basic protocol, and quickly changed the subject. I let it go because the last thing I wanted was to ruin the relaxed atmosphere of the evening.

Mentally, I make a note to not make that mistake again in my next dream. Because now I'm sure that's exactly what is happening. I dreamed the whole thing.

Strong arms circle my middle and haul me close. My hair is swept off my face and soft skin runs along my forehead. I clutch my sheet tighter, throw my knee over my pillow, and readjust my body. There's a grunt, followed by a gentle nudge at my thigh. My leg brushes along something hard before settling. Pounding rushes through my ears and I burrow deeper. The pounding accelerates with my wiggling body.

My eyes fly open and take a few seconds to adjust to the low light coming from the hallway, but when they do, I'm staring at a black serpentine form. The same shape tattooed on Achilles' ribcage. My body goes rock solid when I realize where I am and exactly what I'm doing.

My hand isn't gripping my sheet, it's clutching the waistband of his shorts. My leg isn't settled between my extra pillows. It's nestled between his thighs. And the pounding in my ears isn't excitement from my dream, it's the beat of his heart against my cheek.

My gaze darts across his broad chest and I recognize the fabric of the sofa. I rack my brain, trying to figure out how we ended up this way. The fog lifts and it comes back to me slowly.

I talked the guys into watching one of my favorite cop shows, which they begrudgingly agreed, then tore it apart. Achilles stretched out on the extended lounger next to me, throwing in his own comments at the stupidity of the people on the TV. He looked tired, so I requested an Uber. The wait time was longer than usual. I must have fallen asleep before it got here. But that doesn't explain how I wound up attached to his side.

Ever so gently, I dislodge my fingers from his waistband and reach for my phone lying next to his shoulder. His hand flies up, captures my wrist, and flattens my palm on his chest.

His eyes remain closed, and I take a second to appreciate the view. The dark stubble covering his cheeks and chin, his hair spiked in every direction, the thick eyelashes fanning out. Even unconscious, he's sinfully sexy.

Drool threatens to dribble down my chin so I try to figure out another way to move without disturbing him. His torso shifts inward, and this is my opportunity. I inhale deep and roll the other way. This doesn't work, mainly because his grip on my wrist turns vice-like and his other arm hauls me back. Now I'm full out on top of him.

"Where do you think you're going?" His deep, drowsy voice causes a stir in my belly.

"I didn't mean to wake you. I was trying to—"

"Get away?"

"Give you space."

"Does it seem like I want space?"

"I am practically attached to you."

"Does it seem like I want space?" he repeats, pressing down on the small of my back to emphasize his point.

In this position, I can feel every ridge and plane of his body, including the hardness against my hip. I make the mistake of jiggling sideways, and his eyes grow heated at the friction.

"Baby, you slide one more time, we'll have issues."

"Sorry." I chew on my lip and hold motionless. "If you let me go, I promise to roll off slowly."

"Christ, Harley." It's hard to determine if he's aggravated with me for waking him or frustrated with the fact that I'm sprawled on top of him like a horny teenager. The heat in his eyes glitters and his lips tip upward. "You into slow torture? Cause that's what will happen if you try to get away from me again."

"You're not mad?"

"Why would I be mad when I put you here?"

Now, my stomach does an all-out flip, and a thrill races through my veins. "You wanted me to plaster myself to your side?"

"I wanted you any way I could get you. It's my luck you don't mind contact sleeping."

"Do you like contact sleeping?"

"Never thought I would. Now I know differently."

"I'm usually a terrible bed partner." I didn't know what to say, but apparently, this was the wrong thing. His glittery eyes turn hard, and his hold grows uncomfortably tight.

"That's what Jewls tells me. I steal all the pillows, twist in the bed, and usually kick until she's forced to move," I try to explain.

His hold loosens, and the glimmer returns as he shifts slightly. Signals fire off in my brain and I'm not sure what to say next. Dealing with a bunch of executives and macho-man cops is much easier than facing Achilles right now.

"What time is it?"

"Early," he responds without looking at his watch.

I wrangle my hand free and reach for my phone, only to be stopped —again. "Your phone is off."

"Why?"

"Because I didn't want it bothering us."

"Was it bothering *you*?"

"You passed out watching that fucking awful show. The phone kept dinging with messages. I assured Jewls you were safe and staying here. I confirmed with Erik that we'd meet for breakfast at ten-thirty, and then I intercepted the goddamned Uber and canceled, but only after the security cameras showed him driving up the street." His entire mood changes when he mentions the Uber.

"Oh shit, I probably lost my account."

"Highly doubtful since I gave him a hundred dollars to erase the pick-up."

"You did what? A hundred dollars? That's crazy. Why didn't you wake me up?"

"The only way I was waking you up was to take you to bed, but you seemed comfortable."

"Were you… comfortable, I mean?"

"Best night's sleep of my life."

My breath catches in my throat, and I lock eyes with him. The sincerity of his words sinks in, and like yesterday by the pool, the air takes on a new energy between us. A rush of courage shoots through me, and I make a split-second decision before losing my nerve. My hands press down on his chest, helping propel me the few inches so our faces are close. I say a silent prayer, close my eyes, and gently place my mouth to his.

Slowly, I kiss along his lips, brushing back and forth several times before my tongue darts out to trace across the seam. His chest vibrates with a low throaty rumble, and in a flash, I'm on my side, his fingers threaded through my hair and his mouth covering mine. His tongue slides inside, giving me no choice but to release all control. My thigh goes around his, using all my strength to pull him flush so our bodies are tangled together. He groans his approval, deepening the kiss as his tongue explores with an urgency that makes my body ignite. Blood scorches through my veins, and I lose myself, pouring everything I have back into him.

One of my hands slips free from between us, and I slide it around his neck, clutching his scalp. There's another sound from deep in his chest as his tongue curls around mine, and at the same time his hand begins caressing the back of my head.

My skin tingles, my heart thunders, and my lungs burn, screaming for oxygen. I arch into him, separating our mouths enough to suck in a breath, and then crush my lips back to his. The memory I've held on to for all these years all but disappears. What we shared back then is nothing compared to this moment. The heat from his skin seeps into mine, and I grind my hips into his, feeling his length pulsing against my thigh. A rush of empowerment comes over me, and I moan into his mouth while rocking into him.

He tears his mouth from mine, dropping his face into my neck. "Fuck me." His warm breath floats over my skin.

I fight to regain my breathing, holding tight and trying to tamper the panic threatening to erupt. "Please don't walk away from me again." There's no stopping the words from spilling out.

"Three fucking years… three years I've thought of this. Every single goddamned second was worth the wait." He lifts his face to mine, and I lose my breath all over. "There's no fucking way I'm ever walking away." His eyes have transformed into a glowing shade of caramel. My panic vanishes, and a new kind of heat rushes through me. Passion, intensity, lust, hunger—it shines from him and bleeds directly into my soul.

There are many things to say, to talk about, tons of questions I want answered. But none of it matters right now because, without him saying it, what we just shared changed the course of our relationship forever.

"Totally worth the wait," I agree, running my thumb along his jaw. "Let's not go another three years."

His eyes gleam with amusement and he lowers himself back down. "Never," he says before crashing his mouth back to mine.

7

ACE

"I DON'T WANT to hear shit from you." I slam my locker and come face to face with Talon, who's grinning like a sly cat.

"I said nothing."

"Keep it that way."

He falls into step beside me, whistling all the way down the hall. The sound grates on my nerves and I stop, twisting to face him.

"Go ahead, get it off your chest."

"What exactly do you think I have to say?"

"You're gloating like a motherfucker, and it's pissing me off."

"After what I witnessed this morning, I was betting on a whole day without the broody, pissed off, *Achilles*." He intentionally rasps my name in a feathery, breathy tone.

"Your impersonation is shit."

"She had the advantage of her tongue lodged down your throat and her body fused to yours." Hilarity fills his face, and he wiggles his eyebrows suggestively.

"What are you, fourteen? Were you spying?"

"Nope, went to get water and couldn't miss the sounds coming from the living room at five in the morning. I had to investigate and make sure you hadn't rolled over on her and she was struggling for life." He waves his hands in the air and makes a gasping sound to emphasize his point.

He looks like a fucking idiot, and I catch myself grinning. "She wasn't suffocating."

"I got that. She seemed to breathe fine when you let her up for air."

"You enjoying yourself?" I cross my arms and give him a stony glare.

"Cool your shit, I'm giving you a hard time. I glimpsed at what was happening and went back to bed. But tell me the truth, do I need to buy a new sofa? I'd hate to think of laying where your bare ass was pound—"

"Don't be a dick." I shove him on the shoulder and start back down the hall toward the parking bay.

His laugh echoes in the hallway, and it doesn't take long until he's by my side again. "Man, I'm fucking happy as hell you finally pulled your head out of your pretentious ass. You know I love Harley, but you had this coming. Whatever Major said to you must have worked."

I jerk my chin, not responding. Them showing up yesterday was the first clue that Major opened his mouth.

"Tell me, how was brunch with the boyfriends."

"It was fine. Erik, Kelvin, and Harley covered a lot of ideas."

"You didn't scare them off?"

"I made my point."

"Yo!" a sharp voice booms behind us.

I look over my shoulder and spot Hal Hanks strolling our way. Hal's been my field-training officer most of the time. Unlike some veterans on the force, he seems to enjoy this part of the job. He's a pretty laid-back guy and easy to get along with, but he's also not someone you want to piss off.

"You're with me tonight," he informs us when he's closer.

"I'm with Crews," Talon corrects him.

"He got called out on something. I got the hassle of both of your asses. Let's get to brief and then we roll out."

"Roll out where?"

"It's your lucky night. Tonight's extra security at the stadium."

"Shit," I say under my breath. I've worked one football game, and it was a pain in my ass.

"Sunday night football, seventy-thousand fans, and high-intensity rivals. Not to mention the entire day tailgating. This should be fun." Talon is thinking the same thing.

"After the shift, I'll splurge on mani-pedis for you pansies." Hal cracks a smile, enjoying his own joke.

We follow him back to the bullpen, where the room's packed with other officers. I'm surprised to see Ford and Major heading our way. Hal takes charge, covering the night's protocol while we stay on the outer edge of the group.

"We got the call for extra help tonight," Ford explains.

"Hell of a night to accept overtime," I mutter.

When Hal's done, the group breaks up, and Talon and I follow him to the parking lot. We pile into an SUV and drive toward the stadium.

Out of the corner of my eye, I catch Hal glancing my way.

"What's up?"

"I'm trying to put my finger on it. Something's different."

"Nothing different here."

"Oh, there's definitely something going on. Your intensity is… less intense."

"Not sure that makes any sense."

"You're cooler than usual."

"He's cool, all right," Talon throws back. "I'd guess it was the cold shower he had to take."

Hal doesn't comment, but his mouth splits in a wide grin. "Nice perfume."

Talon barks out a laugh, and I whip my head to him. "Shut the hell up."

He shakes his head and continues to laugh.

"Didn't think the Casanovas had to take cold showers," Hal states.

"Are you shitting me?" I roll my eyes "Don't tell me you believe any of that."

"Not a word."

"I'd like to know who made that shit up."

"Don't get too worked up about it. Anyone with sense knows it's bullshit. I've been on this job for over twenty years and learned early on how to read people. You four caused quite a stir."

"Want to elaborate?"

"Four badass Marines rocket through the application process, kick ass in the academy, and set their sights on SWAT before their badges have time to get dirty? People stood up and took notice. Half of your peers want to be you, the other half want to knock you down a few notches. As for the women, it's not lost on anyone that you all could have your pick."

"I left high school behind a long time ago."

"You'll get used to it."

Something he says stands out, and Talon's expression tells me he heard the same thing. "How'd you know about SWAT?"

"Officially or unofficially?"

"Both."

"Unofficially—told you, I've been around a while. Your names were pinging around the station a long time before you graduated. I got the vibe the first time I set eyes on you. Officially, Boyd told me."

"He wasn't pleased."

"Nope, but can you blame him? You waltzed right into his office and told him your days under him are numbered and you were applying out as soon as your required tenure was up. Ballsy, bold, arrogant. You caught him off-guard, and he reacted. He also realized he was most likely losing four good cops. A lot of men try to walk the path you're traveling, but not a lot make it. That's why Boyd wants your plans kept under wraps. He's not interested in the headaches that come with the tension when egos get torched."

"Is that gonna cause a problem with us?"

His carefree mood shifts, his eyes turning steely as he pins me down. "Do you think I would have requested your sorry ass if it would cause a problem?"

I lean further into my seat, unsure of how to respond.

"Except for the days I'm off, you are with me for a reason. The same with the others." He gestures his head to Talon. "We know talent when we see it, and training you to be a good cop will only transfer to other skills. There's no way you renegades were getting a half-interested veteran that would take you down the lazy route. Like I said, I pegged you before you even walked into the station on your first day.

"And since we're sharing, here's another tidbit. I've seen your file… the real file. I know what you four did in the Marines, seen your missions, and understand your specialties."

Now I'm truly curious. My application to the academy and resume are pretty generic. They skim the surface of what we needed to be accepted. Our real files have almost everything except the confidential details.

"Why? How?"

"Let's just say I have an allegiance to the SWAT teams, and I wanted to make sure you four have what it takes."

"Didn't know your job description was so detailed."

"Never underestimate, learn that quick."

I think about what he's said and the reality hits. "You were SWAT?"

"Was," he confirms.

"What happened?"

"Walked into a hostile situation, took one look at the woman crouching behind the desk, scared out of her mind. I fell hard. At that moment, I let my guard down and got shot. It was a superficial wound, but when I got out of the hospital, I found her. She became my everything. The next hostile situation, I came home and she had a panic attack. The fear in her eyes was enough for me. I couldn't do it to her. So, I asked to transfer back."

"You did that for a woman?" Talon asks in disbelief.

"Not just any woman. Fifteen years and not once have I regretted the decision."

"Police officers aren't exactly out of danger," I add.

"No, but I use my skills in different ways now. I take on rookie asses, teach them the right way to execute the law, and close my cases. Then I go home to the one woman on this earth I can't live without and three kids that mean just as much. I live easy."

"Oh, shit," Talon mutters, his words hitting me in the gut.

"Like I said, I don't regret it, but I know what it takes. And from what I can see, you guys have it."

"We have it," I confirm, glancing at Talon to find him staring at me. "We have it," I repeat for emphasis.

"So, if people make up shit about you to make themselves feel better, let them have that. Don't let it get to you."

I don't care what people say or believe. The only reason it even slightly bothered me was because of Harley.

"In this case, I think Ace needs to be thankful. It worked out in his favor," Talon throws in.

"Think I got that with the scent of perfume lingering through the truck and the twinkle in his eye."

I jerk my head and look at him like he's crazy. "Have you lost your mind? I don't have a fucking twinkle in my eye. I don't even know what the hell that means."

"Look in the mirror, it's hard to miss."

"Ace!" Talon shouts my name, and I wind in time to hear the click of his phone. "Good one." He smiles at the screen. "Totally see the twinkle."

"Erase that."

"Never! This is going down in history, and I have proof. Achilles Kingston with a twinkle in his eye. The guys in MARSOC won't believe this."

"You're a shithead."

He flashes a cocky grin, types something quickly, then puts his phone back in his shirt pocket. "Been accused of worse."

"You boys done?" Hal cuts in, and I realize we're parked in the personnel lot at the stadium.

"Yeah." I shoot Talon one more glare and get out of the truck.

"Try to steer clear of any messes. I'd much rather smell Ace's perfume on the way back than alcohol-induced vomit."

Hal's warning is unnecessary, and Talon mutters, 'That shit is gross,' as we walk in.

THE WOMAN SITTING behind the desk doesn't glance up when I approach. She's scribbling something furiously into a notepad and talking under her breath. I wait patiently for her to finish the conversation with herself and notice the textbook.

"Looks like statistics."

Her head pops up, she lets out a small squeak, and her pencil goes flying my way. I immediately recognize her as the woman walking out of the yoga studio with Harley on Saturday.

"Didn't mean to startle you." I pick up the pencil and hand it back.

"I… um… didn't hear anyone. You… are…" Heat crawls up her skin, and she takes a deep breath, then starts over. "Let's try this again. Yes, it is statistics, which has become the bane of my existence lately."

"I've only met one person in my life that enjoys it. And I'm not sure he's right in the head most of the time."

"I'd definitely question their sanity."

"I do, every day of my life."

She stuffs the notepad into the book and smiles at me perceptively. "You here to see Harley?"

"I am."

"Let me give her a shout." She presses a button and puts the receiver to her ear. "Harley, you have a package in reception." There's a pause, and her eyes light up as she keeps looking at me. "I suppose I could open it up and see what's inside, but I hate to ruin the pretty packaging. Come get this one."

I return her smile and shake my head when she hangs up. This woman definitely knows something about me and my relationship with Harley.

"It's been one hell of a Monday, but I bet you can turn her mood around."

A few minutes later, Harley appears and stops dead when she spots me. I scan her over and force myself to swallow the possessive growl at the sight. The woman standing in front of me is a fucking vision. My eyes rake down the black dress that cuts off mid-thigh and land on the bright red shoes with a pencil-thin heel. When they travel back up to her face, she's smiling widely.

"You have a thing for surprise visits."

I smile back and decide that I don't give a shit where we are. I make it to her in two strides, pulling her into my arms and brushing my lips across her. She has no choice but to fall against me, gripping my arms for support.

"I wanted to see you," I say lowly.

"What about Wednesday night?"

"Fuck of a long time to wait."

There's a dreamy sigh behind us, and Harley giggles, turning to the woman. "Ginger, did you meet Achilles? Or, Ace, to his friends."

"Not officially."

I slide my arm around Harley's waist, tucking her close, and tip my chin in greeting. Ginger's eyes jump from Harley to me and back a few times, her expression confirming my earlier thoughts. She knows exactly who I am, and it's not because of Saturday morning. "Nice to finally meet you, Ace."

"What are you doing here?" Harley tilts her face to mine.

"Can you go to lunch?"

"I should be able to. Let me go grab my purse." She tries to slide away, and I twist us back toward the door.

"You don't need your purse."

"My wallet, my phone," she objects.

"I have both things."

"What if someone needs me?"

"I can cover for you. Anything urgent I can text Ace," Ginger offers eagerly.

I flash her an appreciative grin and rattle off my number, then guide Harley out the door.

"I'm not sure I like this pattern with you," she huffs on the way to my truck.

"And what pattern is that?"

"Showing up unannounced, taking charge, not giving me a say."

I chew the side of my lip to keep from smiling outright. "I asked you to go to lunch."

"Yes, but you rushed me out, and I may need my purse and my phone."

We get to my truck, I open her door, pick her up, and place her on the seat before planting myself in front of her. "You really irked about not having your purse?"

She glances over my shoulder, seeming to think about her answer, holding something back.

"Harley?"

"You have no clue about how this works, do you?"

"How what works?"

"Fine!" She throws her hands in the air in exasperation and looks to the sky then back to me. "I can't believe I'm doing this, but here's how it goes. You show up, looking like you do, totally catching me off guard, and all thoughts of my shitty morning vanish. You ask me to lunch. The proper thing would be to let me run to my office and grab my things. I'd have time to freshen up, fluff my hair, and apply some lip gloss to feel a tinge better about my appearance. That's how women work, Achilles. We like to be prepared."

This time, I don't hold back my grin and step further into her space, wrapping my arms around her waist and nudging my hips between her thighs. "First off, your appearance is perfect. I thought it couldn't get much better than swimsuits and sundresses, but fuck me if the professional Harley doesn't rock me to my core. You're gorgeous, and fluffing the hair and freshening up isn't necessary. As for knowing how this works, no, I don't know how it works. I've never given a shit about how women think, except for you. When I left the gym this morning, I decided I wasn't waiting until Wednesday night."

Her expression softens, the attitude disappearing. "Is this going to become a pattern?"

"Me coming to take you to lunch? Probably, at least until my schedule transfers to days."

"That's good to know, but I'm referring to you storming in, taking charge, and then saying something so incredibly sweet that squashes my irritation? This is the third time in less than a week."

"You'll get used to it."

"So you keep saying."

I tag her closer for a quick kiss before releasing her. She scoots out of my hold, and I go to the driver's side.

"Is Ginger one of the women you mentioned all these years ago?"

"Yes, we started at the company the same day and clicked immediately. She's my age, but flitted around a few years after high school trying to find direction. Then she decided to get her degree. This is her last year. We're actually pretty close. She's the one who introduced me to Pilates and yoga. We brought Jewls one time, but she couldn't hack it."

"Couldn't hack yoga?" I side-eye her. "Seems like an impossible activity to flunk out of."

"Let me rephrase; Jewls is more of the kickboxing while the rock music is blaring type of exercise gal."

"That makes total sense."

"So, Ginger and I try to meet weekly and Zen out. Usually rewarding ourselves with margaritas afterward."

"Tell me where to go." I indicate which direction to turn.

"There's a terrific bistro about two blocks away. You can't miss the blue and white umbrellas. We actually could have walked, but I'm too exhausted."

"The exhaustion goes along with the shitty Monday?"

"The day hasn't been bad, but my patience is thin and the normal first-of-the-week urgency is more annoying than usual. It's partially my fault, though. I was up way too late."

"Did Jewls stay over late?" When I left her at her apartment yesterday, Jewls was pulling into the parking lot, no doubt to grill Harley over our days together.

"Not exactly, we got called into work."

"At Tom's?"

"We had to work the floor because two servers are sick. With the game, it was insane. I didn't get home until after three a.m."

"You went to work last night—alone?" I grind out.

"I go to work every night alone."

"Why didn't you call me?"

"You were working. I didn't want to bother you. Besides, why does it matter?"

Wrong thing to say. "It matters because there was no one there to watch you! What if something happened?"

She whips her head my way with fire building in her eyes. "Watch me? So, it is true? You send the guys to watch my shifts? Is that why Tom saves a seat at the bar every night I work?"

"Hell yes. I'm not taking any chances on something happening to you."

"What can happen? I'm completely safe. You're being ridiculous."

"Call it what you want, but with my schedule, I can't always be there. I hate the hours and I don't approve."

"You don't approve? Tom is a family friend. His bar is a respectable establishment. You know the customers, and get something straight right now. I don't ask your approval," she seethes, the fire in her eyes now fierce.

Anger fills the inside of my cab, and I notice the umbrellas she mentioned. I use the ten seconds to think of how to get her to understand my point before pulling into a spot and slamming the truck into park. "That may not have come out right."

"You think?" Her gorgeous face is now twisted and fuming.

"I'll talk to Tom and explain that when none of us are available, you can't—"

"I'd be very careful how you end that statement," she warns.

"Glen Bates —"

"What about Glen? He's a dick. I knew that before you explained your disgust with him. Any woman in her right mind can spot his type a mile away."

"It's not you I'm worried about. It's guys like him. They want to fuck you. No respect for women, superficial, and have no boundaries."

"Newsflash, Achilles, the Glen Bateses of the world have been around since I was fourteen years old. You only missed it because, in the short period you were around in high school, everyone was scared of you. When you left, I was fair game, and I suffered under the cloud of rumors because no one understood our relationship. They assumed I was the easy girl left behind. My friendship circle was small and tight because of the jealousy among the girls that couldn't get your attention. I could go on and on, but the point is, until my date two weeks ago, I hadn't been out with anyone in six months.

"You've been gone close to eleven years. A lot has changed. I'm a twenty-seven-year-old woman who does not need your approval or your protection. I know how to handle myself and can tell the skeezy jerks with one interaction. You will never be skeezy, but I'm questioning the jerk part." She slings off her seatbelt, opens her door, and spears me with that raging gaze. "Someone from my office is going into the café. I'm joining her and pretending I was out for a walk. Do not follow me, do not embarrass me in front of the people I work with, and do not show up again unannounced with this attitude. If I find out you call Tom, I swear I'll break your fingers! God! I am such an idiot." She jumps out, giving me one last look before slamming the door so hard it shakes the truck.

It goes against every instinct I have not to chase her as she stomps away. My heart thunders in my chest, the blood scorching my veins. You don't have to be an expert to know I fucked that up and took it a step too far.

The last line remains in my brain because it was filled with much more than anger. It was hurt.

I hurt her… again.

"Fucking hell." I dig my phone out, keeping my eyes on her. She'll get her wish and I won't follow her, but I'm also not leaving until she's back in her office.

The first call I make is to the café, instructing them to take care of her lunch. The second call is to the person that will undoubtedly piss her off beyond belief.

If I can't call Tom, I'll settle for the next best thing. Her dad.

8

HARLEY

"I DON'T KNOW what happened. She came in this way," Jewls fake-whispers.

"Well, you need to figure it out real quick. Last night, she was walking on cloud nine, spreading a fucking glittery glow everywhere. Tonight, she's scaring my customers. Dressed like that, I'd expect a packed bar, not a dead zone," Tom advises grumpily.

"Maybe it's a bad day at work."

"You've got five minutes before I get involved."

"I can hear you. I'm pissed, not deaf," I snap, sneering at them. "Stop talking like I'm not here."

"Maybe you should put the knife down and step away from the lemon," Jewls suggests, pointing at the cutting board.

"Maybe you two should mind your business and go back to work."

"I'd love to, but our bar is a desert."

I scan the circle of the bar, and not one stool is filled. Then I glance at my watch and notice the happy hour rush is usually in full swing. "The Monday after a game is usually slow," I offer, knowing it's a lie.

"Bullshit. Maybe it's the tortured, resting bitch face or the '*don't get near me or I'll shank you with my knife'* vibe you're emanating," Jewls snips.

"Don't be dramatic. I'm tired and had a bad day."

"My guess is this isn't about a bad day. This has lover's quarrel written all over it. Ace know you're dressed like that?" Tom refers to the same too tight shirt of Jewls' I borrowed last week paired with black leggings with slashes throughout the leg showing plenty of skin.

I slam the knife down and pivot to face Tom. "No, Ace doesn't know I'm dressed like this because it's none of his business. Like my working here is none of his business. And this is NOT a lover's quarrel in any way, shape, or form!"

My outburst doesn't faze him, and he has the nerve to grin knowingly. "Uh-huh." He slides behind Jewls, going toward the storage room, calling over his shoulder, "I'm bringing the stock up tonight. I want to see some asses in those seats when I return."

I swallow down my frustration and switch my glare to Jewls, who's staring at me curiously. "What'd he do?"

I think about giving her an excuse, but know I'll end up spilling my guts eventually, so I fill her in on the morning and the exchange in his truck. She listens keenly, and when I'm done, instead of showing signs of sympathy, her eyes light with amusement.

"You think this is funny?"

"Not exactly. This happened a lot quicker than I suspected."

"What does that mean?"

"Yesterday was all unicorns and flowers—literally. You were walking on cloud nine. Lunches, dinners, falling asleep on sofas, and waking up to the man of your dreams. Breakfast with Erik, doing laundry, watching TV… You jumped from not talking for years to making out like teenagers at lightning speed. You skipped a lot of details, and I knew reality would hit at some point."

"I'm not sure I like where you're going with this."

"You shouldn't because the truth stings, but from what you told me about his showing up on Saturday morning until he left yesterday, don't you think you avoided some major subjects?"

"What's wrong with living in the moment? Enjoying what was happening? It's called new beginnings."

"Yeah, babe. New beginnings are the fun parts. The giddy, butterfly swarming, hand-holding, stealing-a-kiss type bliss moments."

"Is there a problem with that?"

"There's not if you were experiencing them with a stranger or a man more like the chump you went out with a few weeks ago. You and Ace have a long history, most of that with you being head over ass in love with him."

"I don't think I want to discuss this anymore with you."

"Sure you don't, but straight up, you and he are different people, and anyone that has knowledge of this song and dance knows it will work out. What you're ignoring is that the *decade* isn't water under the bridge. Accept each other as you are today."

"I've always accepted him as he is."

"Yes, but you are a different person. He's got to deal with the bombshell, grown-up version of the girl he left behind. He's got to find his place in your world, and thank God you stood up for yourself today."

"Wasn't it immature to stomp away and slam his door?"

"Maybe, but you sent a message. Achilles grew up in shit. He went into the Marines and saw things we only hear about, and continues his life in public service. He's rough, gritty, and self-deprecating."

"You don't know him like I do. He's deep, thoughtful, loving, and selfless. He fought for his mom, he fought for this country, and now he's building a career around protecting his community. He may be rough, but to me, it's everything," I defend, my anger shifting toward her.

She flashes her perceptive smile and walks forward, grabbing my face and smacking a loud kiss on my forehead. "That's exactly right, Jay. He's your everything. Make sure to keep your spunk while taming his beast."

Her words penetrate deep, and I know she played me a bit. "Sometimes I hate you took all those psychology classes."

"Being a Social Worker requires a lot of mental adaptabilities. I swear to God, as your best friend, he will figure it out along with you. But know you probably can't change his possessive tendencies. There's bound to be a few clashes along the way."

"You think it's real this time?" I almost whisper.

"It's the most real thing I've ever witnessed. If we had last night alone, I could have been a little more thorough in my delivery. But don't become submissive to him. This isn't even close to being over with him. Have your spat, stand your ground, and be strong. Don't lose yourself."

"My barstools are still empty." Tom appears balancing two boxes, eyeing me carefully.

"I have faith they'll fill up soon." I send an apologetic grin.

"Good," he replies brusquely, "get to work."

"You know, Tom, maybe you should consider implementing a ladies' night." I try to lighten the mood.

"Why the hell would I do that? Ladies' nights come with too many headaches. I have enough headaches with you two."

"I take offense to that. What have I done?" Jewls scoffs.

"Give it time. It's only Monday."

"If I remember correctly, we both gave up our Sunday nights to help you out. I'm due to have a bad day once in a while without you accusing me of being a headache." I cock an eyebrow.

"I know all about your damn bad day. Six foot six, powerhouse of muscle, that looks like he'll rip someone apart if they glance your way."

I want to argue that he's exaggerating, but today is proof Achilles has an overprotective streak that I never knew about. "Moving on." I unpack the bottles from the boxes.

"Hey." He lays a hand on my arm, his tone softer. "I've known you since you were a kid and watched you grow up. I'm not blind. Jewls is right. Stand your ground, but don't write him off. That boy has a lot to work through."

It's almost hilarious to hear him refer to Achilles as a boy, but I bite my tongue and nod. Thankfully, a group of men walks in, heading directly to the bar. Glen's in the group, and his eyes go straight to my chest when he gets closer.

"Pissant," Tom growls, aiming his snarl at Glen, then steals the bottle out of my hand and takes it to the far drink station.

Guess that's the end of his unconventional wisdom.

Tom calling Glen a Pissant is too kind. Something comes over me, and I smile openly, ready for anything that he throws my way.

Because tonight is not the night to piss me off.

I'M AT YOUR DOOR.

I snatch my phone off the counter and stare at the message in horror.

"Shit!" I scream, grabbing a handful of bobby pins. Once my hair is secure in a bun, I apply minimal make-up and slide my maxi dress over my head.

It's been two days since my argument with Achilles, and I've spent the time miserable but determined.

Yesterday, I broke down and called my mom at lunch, hoping that hearing her voice would help. The second she answered, it was obvious she was waiting for the call. It took little coaxing for me to unload what was on my mind. She listened to what happened patiently and reiterated what Jewls and Tom said, but told me to go gentle on him.

It was my decision to keep some distance from Achilles. He hasn't called, and his few texts have been generic, asking how I am. Which always gets him the same response.

I'm fine.

I questioned this every second of every day. But it was important for me to figure out exactly what to say. Then the self-doubt crept in. The one scenario no one mentioned was the one that scared me the most. Achilles has always been low-key and no-nonsense. What if my tantrum turned him off? Regardless of his macho-man attitude, my departure from his truck was overly dramatic.

And maybe a little mortifying.

I run through my apartment and cringe at the blankets and pillow balled up on the sofa. "Shit!" I cuss again.

"Take your time. I'll wait for as long as it takes," his gravelly voice calls through the door.

Of course, he heard me. I decide the sofa is the least of my worries and take a deep breath to calm my racing nerves.

"You're an adult, Harley. Act like it. Be natural, not too eager, not too distant. No matter what happens." I pep myself up on the way to answer.

"Good mor—" The rest of the word lodges in my throat when I come face to face with what can only be described as anguish.

He tugs me gently into his arms, crushing me to his hard body, lifting me off the ground, and stepping inside. There is no choice but to hold tight as I hear the door shut. "I know you told me not to show up unannounced, but I couldn't stay away. I'm an asshole. I shouldn't have said the things I did." He buries his face in my neck. His voice is a combination of desperation and regret that pierces me so deep my eyes sting.

"Achilles." My arms circle his shoulders, and my face tilts to his. Once again, words fail me at his tortured expression.

"If you need me to apologize, I will," he offers unconvincingly.

"Are you sorry?"

"I'm sorry for upsetting you."

"What about the rest?"

He glances over my shoulder, the answer easy to read. I place my hand to his jaw, bringing his gaze back to mine. "Are you sorry?"

His eyes slowly close, and when they open, they're filled with guilt, telling me all I need to know.

"You can't dictate my life. If you care about me, trust and know I can take care of myself. This isn't only about working at Tom's; this is with everything."

"When it comes to you, I'm fiercely protective. That will never change. I've seen the way men look at you, the way they crave your attention, thinking they have a shot. Knowing that they go home with a fucking hard on and jack off to the image of you is enough to set me on edge. I can't promise to back off."

"Do you trust me?"

He nods.

"Do you care about me, Achilles?"

The storm in his eyes softens, and he clenches his arms around my waist. "You are my everything." The honesty in his voice rocks me to my core.

You are my everything.

Those four words set my pulse racing and my body melting at the same time. The same words I used to describe him to Jewls.

The last two days of confusion, anger, and internal turmoil go up in smoke, and I'm left with a feeling unlike I've ever imagined. "Then the rest we'll take in baby steps," I tell him softly.

He slides one hand up my back, along my neck, and threads his fingers in the base of my hairline, caressing gently. "Harley, I gave this up for over ten years. If I come on a little strong, cut me some slack."

"I'll get used to it."

At the use of his phrase, the intensity finally seeps out of his body. "Yeah, you'll get used to it."

"It may not always be easy."

"I'm not going through the last two days again."

"Are you saying you learned a lesson?"

The side of his mouth twitches right before he flashes me a playful grin. "I'm saying I'll never watch you walk away from me again."

I decide to let that go and focus on something more important. I lift on my toes and sweep my lips across his. "What do you mean you gave this up for over ten years?"

"We'll talk about it tonight."

There's no way I'm leaving this apartment without an explanation. The last few days, I've spent too much time thinking about what Jewls said regarding overlooking important subjects because I was lost in the moments. If there's any chance of us making this work, I have to know and understand the man Achilles has become.

"I think we should talk about it now."

"Right now, I need to take you to work."

I step away and grab my phone, shooting off a quick email. "I'm working from home today."

"Didn't know that was an option."

"There are some perks to my job. And today, I'm taking advantage of one of them."

"You sure?"

"Yes. Do you still keep a bag in your truck with extra clothes?"

He nods.

"And do you still have the night off?"

"I do."

"How would you feel about hanging out here today? I need to work some, but you could rest, and then maybe we could do lunch?"

He grins and brings his forehead to mine, his eyes melting into the amber hue I love so much. "I do owe you lunch."

9

ACE

My eyes slowly open at the sound of Harley laughing from the other room. I check my watch and see four hours have passed since I laid down. "Shit," I grumble, scrubbing my hands over my face and swinging my legs to the floor. Exhaustion weighs on me, but I force myself to stand, grab my bag, and go to her bathroom.

This was the first actual sleep I've gotten since Saturday night when Harley was with me. My body is conditioned to schedule changes, and I can get by on little sleep, but the last few days it's been useless. My mind wouldn't shut down, and the image of her walking away is branded into my memory.

I smirk at the stack of purple towels laid out for me on the counter. Her shower is significantly smaller than mine, and it takes a bit for me to get situated. The hot water beats down on my back and shoulders, easing the tension away. I relax for the first time in days. The scent of her fills with the surrounding steam, and my dick grows hard instantly.

Fuck! Don't be a fucking tool, Ace. Get your shit together.

I turn into the water, trying to ignore the throbbing in my cock as I wash my hair. There's a knock at the door, followed by a muffled voice.

"Come in."

"Checking to see if you have everything you need."

"I got it."

"I forgot to leave you a washcloth," she says right as a cloth sails over the curtain rod and lands on my shoulder. "Although I'm sure you're a wash your body with your hands type of guy."

I poke my head around the curtain and find her propped against the sink, staring at the shower. "You'd be right. But today, I may break tradition just to say I've used a purple cloth."

"You know there are other colors of the color wheel besides black, white, and grey."

"I'm learning that, seeing as your soap is pink. I didn't even know they made fucking pink soap."

"Stick with me and I'll teach you about the colors of the rainbow."

"Looking forward to it."

She smiles at me, and my eyes fall to the faded USMC lettering on her shirt. Actually, it's my shirt, hanging mid-thigh and revealing her bare legs. She's changed out of her dress. Everything about the sight sends my blood south. My already hard cock lurches, bouncing against my stomach. When my gaze moves back to her face, she's staring at me expectantly.

"Hope you don't mind. You were resting peacefully. Instead of rummaging through my drawers and risking waking you, I grabbed it out of your bag."

"Looks a fuck of a lot better on you."

"I'm thinking of stealing it."

"You want it, it's yours."

"I was hoping you'd say that." There's a flicker in her eyes that quickly grows heated. She takes a hesitant step forward, closing the space between us, then traces her finger along the lines of the tattoo on my bicep.

"Harley, babe, I think you better move back." My self-control is slipping.

"I should, but I can't help it." She leans in, brushing her lips across mine. "Is that bad?"

"Babe, you're testing my self-restraint."

She grins against my mouth. "Testing it how? Maybe I'm trying to show my appreciation for the shirt."

My blood pumps harder when the tip of her tongue trails my bottom lip, teasing back and forth. The familiar desire and need for her races through my veins, and I roughly growl, "fuck it," before shutting off the water. My arm shoots to her waist, lifting her over the side of the tub and twisting her against the shower wall. Her legs automatically link around my waist, and her elbows brace on my shoulders as my mouth crashes to hers.

There's nothing slow and sweet about the kiss as my tongue dives inside, demanding control. She lets out a small moan, wrapping her body tight and grinding her hips downward. The feel of silky satin material sliding along the tip of my cock ignites a ravenous hunger to be inside her. My hands go to her thighs, slipping up the shirt until they come into contact with the bare skin of her ass. Her muscles flex against my palms as she rocks down again.

I temporarily lose my mind, groaning down her throat and surging upward to feel every bit of her along my dick. Her head angles to the side, deepening the kiss. My hips thrust twice more until she rips her mouth from mine and pants against my lips. Signals fire off in my brain to shut this down before I go too far.

My hips freeze, my head drops to her throat, and I clutch her ass to stop her movements. "Babe, we have to stop."

Her pulse races against my cheek as my own beats wildly in my chest. "Are you okay?" she rasps huskily.

I glance up and my heart races for a new reason. Her face is flushed, her lips swollen, and her blue eyes shining so brightly they're blinding. "Jesus, Harley, you're so fucking gorgeous it hurts."

She smiles and asks shyly, "So, I didn't hurt you?"

"How the hell would you hurt me?"

"When you stopped, I thought maybe I'd done something painful."

"No, babe, nothing you did hurt me."

We continue to stare at each other, the air around us sizzling with the heat of our bodies attached. "I should give you some privacy to finish your shower." Her grin grows wicked as she unlatches her legs and slides down my body.

I hiss when she intentionally scrapes along my cock and rubs her chest against mine. She bends to the side, the shirt riding up enough to expose the cheeks of her ass as she picks up the washcloth. I cross my arms and force myself to remain still as her eyes travel over my body and bulge when they land on my cock.

"Oh my God, is that…."

"Yeah, baby, my dick is pierced."

She licks her lips, and my cock twitches, pulsing painfully against my stomach. "You may need this washcloth after all."

Her voice is low and thick with intention, taking me close to the edge that I snap, reaching out and hauling her back to me. "You're playing with fire, Harley."

"Maybe a little temptation is a good thing."

"Get out of the shower. I'm warning you now."

"I'll meet you in the kitchen." She scrapes her nails across my abdomen as she steps out and flashes me a triumphant smile, backing out of the bathroom.

I watch the door for a few seconds, red-hot sensations scorching through my veins. The last few minutes roll through my head and my dick throbs.

"Goddammit," I mutter under my breath, twisting the faucet, and yanking the curtain closed. The cool water does nothing to my overheated skin as I grab myself and stroke.

She did this on purpose. Just when I thought the woman couldn't get anymore perfect, she showed me she is full of surprises. An idea comes to mind as I grip harder and speed my movements. She's going to pay for this one day, and I'll enjoy teaching her exactly how it feels to be teased.

I LEAN against the doorway and watch her flit around her kitchen, oblivious to my presence. She cracks eggs into a large bowl, cursing under her breath and leaning over to scrape what I assume is shell out of the mixture. The shirt rides up, exposing enough skin for me to know she still isn't wearing shorts over the scrap of silky panties. Dirty thoughts flood my head, and the image of her laid out on her counter comes to mind. I adjust myself in my shorts and softly clear my throat. She twists at the sounds of me moving, her lips sliding upward as her gaze lands on my bare chest. "I like," is all she says.

"Seems I lost my shirt."

"I think you may have given it to me."

I go to her, placing my hands on her hipbones and kissing her temple. "What are you making?"

She sinks into me, tipping the bowl forward. "Omelets."

There are half a dozen eggs in the bowl and slivers of shell mixed throughout. I bite my lip to keep quiet, but she catches on, jabbing me in the gut. "Go ahead and laugh. I'm not the best at actually cracking the eggs. I usually boil them."

"Do you even know how to make omelets?"

"Is it hard? I assumed it was a little whisking, some easy ingredients, and voilà!" She snaps her fingers.

I can't stop the bark of laughter. Harley has never been a cook. There are a few things she mastered in her teens, and as far as I know, her skills never improved.

"Make fun. Once I get these shells out, I'll blow your mind with my culinary technique." She wiggles away, reaching for the carton. "Maybe I should start over."

"Let me." I intercept her hand, turn her toward me, and sit her up on the empty counter space. I go through her cabinets and drawers, gathering what I need, and begin extracting the shells.

"You're good around the kitchen."

"I've learned a few things through the years."

"Maybe you can help teach me."

"Maybe," I mutter half-heartedly, hiding my amusement.

"That didn't sound convincing," she huffs.

"If you don't know how to cook omelets, why try today? I would have picked something up."

"Because I wanted to do something nice for you on your day off. Since I'm never here for lunch, all I have is breakfast food, frozen meals, and a few snacks. You seem to like protein. I figured an omelet was better than a frozen pizza. People eat omelets for lunch, right?"

My chest seizes at the simplicity of her explanation. Memories of the screwed-up teenage rebellious loner and the pure beauty that befriended him slam into me. There aren't many people on this earth who have ever given a shit about me.

"Hey." A soft hand runs along my cheek, and I turn to see her eyes filled with concern. "What's wrong?"

"You're one of the few people who has ever given a shit about me. The Marines gave me a family I never had, but until them, it was you."

The concern in her eyes swells with pain, and the air between us takes on a new mood. I recognize my mistake immediately, catching the hesitation before she asks, "Then why'd you shut me out?"

There's a brief second I think about lying to her, but I can't do it. I drop the items in my hands and move in between her legs, scooting her closer to me. "Because I was a piece of shit that didn't deserve you."

Fire flames in her expression, and she opens her mouth to argue before I place my finger to her lips. "I was, Harley. I was an eighteen-year-old punk filled with rage and anger. My dad was a drunk who wasn't fit to hold down a job, and my mom was an enabler trying to keep her job as a teacher to where we could have food on the table. She depended on me to do the right thing, and pulling my dad's ass out of bars got him home before he could cause too much trouble."

"None of that was your fault. You are not your parents. We talked about this many times."

"You don't understand. I kept a lot from you. It wasn't fair to drag you through the ugly side of my existence."

"I wouldn't have cared," she whispers so sweetly, my chest constricts.

"I know. That's why I had to leave the way I did. Your dad saved me."

She stiffens at the mention of Rich. "My dad did what? I think you should explain that."

"April of my senior year, Mom got a call from a bar downtown where Dad was on a bender. By the time I got to him, he'd started a fight with three mean bastards. I walked up to him, getting the shit kicked out of him, and even though he probably deserved it, I had to jump in and help. I was young, fit, and much faster than those guys. Not to mention they were loaded as well. It was a tough fight, but I got them down. By then, the cops had arrived, and lucky for me, Mom had called Rich. One guy on the ground was fighting for his life because my kick to his chest punctured a lung. They rushed him to the hospital, and I was responsible.

"Rich was furious with me for not calling him, but he got my ass out of a sling and I wasn't arrested. He asked me that night what I wanted out of life—what kind of future I could have with a criminal record. My answer was immediate; I wanted to be a Marine. The next day, he drove me to the recruiter's office, explained my situation, and I committed. As soon as I knew I passed high school, I shipped out."

"Why didn't he tell me?"

"Because I made him a promise, and in return, he did the same."

Understanding washes over her features, and the blazing flames in her eyes scorch right to my soul. "You promised to stay away from me… you broke my heart for my dad."

"I didn't break your heart for your dad."

"You did!" she yells, shoving at my shoulders with all her strength. I'm caught off guard, stumbling back enough for her to hop down and shuffle out of my reach. "How dare you? How dare he? I cried for months. My mom thought I needed counseling! They fought at night over me, and I thought it was because I was heartbroken, but now I understand it clearly. My mom was pissed. She wanted me to know so I could love you without the pain. You kept it from me! How could you? Did you think that little of me? The simple, silly, innocent young girl who couldn't handle the truth?"

She's pacing the floor, ripping pins out of hair and flinging them around the room, her face blistering. When she pins me with her glare, I struggle to find my breath. Injured anger, disbelief, and pure, unfiltered rage roll off her. She's looking at me with such betrayal, fear seeps into my bones.

"You didn't trust me?" Her question spears me, and there's no turning back now.

"I made a promise to become a better man before I came back for you."

"A promise to who!"

"To your dad, but mostly to me."

She looks away, tossing the rest of the pins in her hand to the ground, and stomps out of the kitchen. I blow out a breath and wonder how many times I can fuck up with this woman before she finally kicks my ass out of her life.

I'd give anything to go back thirty minutes ago in the shower and have her in my arms.

"That's not it!" she screams, flying back in. "You were a better man when you came back for Grandpa's funeral. You fought wars, saved lives, lived through secret missions. Why'd you leave me then?"

"Because I'd committed to two more years. I had a plan at that point and knew what it required of me."

"You were deployed two more times! Do you know what that did to me? How I died each time I knew you weren't on US soil?"

"Harley, come here." I hold out my arms, and she pierces me with a look so savage my throat burns.

"No! I'm not coming near you because I want to slap you until you understand what you've done. I was a fucking mess! The rest of high school, my years in college, through my first job… all of it, I tried to move on. I felt pathetic! I thought you didn't care about me!"

"You're the only goddamned thing I've ever cared about!" I roar back, feeling the helplessness taking over. "I knew the risks and pushed myself to the fucking limits to be a man you could be proud of. You were not and never will be pathetic. I was the pathetic one. The drunk's son who was destined to end up in jail. I refused to take you to the depths of hell with me."

I know I've hit a nerve when her body deflates and quakes. She's in my arms in less than a second, and I'm carrying her to the sofa, tucking her to me. A sob escapes, followed by another until she is trembling so hard, I'm scared she's crying herself into hysteria. Every one of her tears sears into my skin, and self-hatred boils in my blood.

She rambles on, shaking her head against my chest and making no sense. I catch a few words and realize she's not fighting to escape. Instead, she's wrapping herself around me tightly as if she wants to fuse directly into my body.

I should have been better prepared for this, knowing she would eventually know the truth. Rich warned me on Monday to be ready because Harley wasn't likely to let the past go. She's lived with too many unanswered questions for far too long. The only thing I think to do is keep talking.

"I knew the risk of you moving on, finding a nice guy with a fine pedigree and good family. You'd make the perfect wife and give him beautiful children. I lived with that weighing on my mind every damn day of my life. Then when I came home for the funeral, I was done. The one gift I ever gave myself was kissing you. Then I knew I was fucked. I walked away because it took all my focus to set my plan in action. Coming home to you was my endgame."

"Years!" she wails, another round of tears soaking my chest. "You left me again for years! Then you moved here for the academy and still shut me out. The last six months have been… I don't know what was worse. You being active in the Marines with all the possibilities, or knowing you were in the same town and didn't seem to want me."

Harley's not a crier. She can show emotions without tears. Knowing she's torn up over me is a mark on my soul.

"I may have left you, but you were always in my line of sight. The academy was a necessity to forge the path of my future. Get a job, start a career, be solid so I could offer stability. And fuck me for saying this, but plans for the polished husband and perfect life were never in your cards. Because even if you were involved with someone, I was coming for you."

"I'm thinking an accountant with sensibility and logic sounds good right about now."

I smile into her hair at her remark, because there was no way that was happening.

"There's more, gorgeous, because in order to get what I wanted, I made a deal for the Reserves. I also made a new plan. We left just shy of ten years because of the academy training schedule. We are obligated to the Reserves for two more years. It's a special arrangement, unconventional, and I'm not at liberty to discuss, but it works for the four of us."

"What exactly does that mean?" she utters into my neck.

"A lot of boring bullshit, but we are a team. One weekend a month, two to three weeks a summer, the usual routine. We will most likely never see a desert or special ops again."

"Most likely?"

I cup the back of her head and massage the base of her neck. "That's the least of my worries at this point."

"It should be because I may hold a grudge for the next ten years."

She's full of shit.

"And tomorrow, I'm scouting the local CPA firms for a solid-looking bean counter."

Full of shit again.

"Not a good idea to tell me about your tactics. Gives me more of a reason to monitor you."

She bolts up, giving me the briefest glimpse of her face before trying to scramble away. I catch her under the armpits, throwing us sideways and pinning her to the sofa with my body. She twists inward, hiding her face in my neck, her hands trapped between us.

"Do you understand now, Harley?"

She hiccups, and the tears stain my skin again. "I don't want to. I want to be furious with you, make you leave and never talk to you again."

"But you're not." What I don't say is that she can try to make me leave, but I'm not going anywhere.

"Don't sound so self-righteous. "

"Leaving here and having you not speak to me isn't an option."

She remains quiet for a while. I wonder if she's fallen asleep until her hand flattens over my heart.

"I'm confused," she admits softly.

"Tell me why and I can help."

"I've spent so long feeling rejected, accepting that you didn't see me as more than a friend. It had to be enough to have you in my life. When you walked away three years ago and avoided me, it was like losing you all over again. Then there was Saturday… Sunday… Monday and now today. I'm on an emotional rollercoaster."

"You have never been, nor will you ever be, just a friend to me. I've made a lot of mistakes, Harley. I left you, but my heart was always yours. Everything I've done is for you. For us."

Her breath hitches again, and I brace for more tears. Instead, she sucks in a deep breath and drops her neck back, bringing us face to face.

Every inch of her skin is splotchy from her forehead to her chin, and her eyes are glassy with unshed tears. It takes all I have to not collapse on top of her.

"Is this real now? Are we done playing around? I'm not sure I can deal with the uncertainties and whiplash again."

"For me, this is as real as it gets."

The tears clear from her eyes, and she studies me closely, bringing her hand to my jaw. "Is there anything else I need to know? Any more soul-racking confessions?"

"All my cards are on the table. If you need time, I'll be patient."

She looks to the ceiling and rolls her bottom lip between her teeth as she considers what I've said. Her eyes fall back to mine, shining bright. The sadness and hurt from earlier are gone. "I don't need time."

10

HARLEY

"SPILL IT, I've waited long enough." Jewls rushes behind the bar, dropping her bag in the usual spot. "I can't believe you didn't call me at work today!"

"Keep your voice down." I glance around to make sure the few customers we have are taken care of and tug her out of earshot. Quickly, I give her a run-down of my last two days. When I'm done, she's staring at me in disbelief.

"Say something." I wave my hand in front of her face. There are very few times Jewls is at a loss for words. She's known for her quick wit and snark. I wasn't sure how'd she react, but stunned silence wasn't in my mind.

"Wow," is her only response.

"Wow? My universe took a seismic shift and you say wow?"

"Give me a second, I'm processing."

"Well, process quickly because he'll be here soon."

"I thought he had to work tonight."

"He does, but since he insisted on taking me and picking me up from work, one of the guys is going with him to get my car and bring it here."

"One week, Harley. He walked into this bar one week ago."

"I know it's fast."

"That's one way to put it."

"Do you think it's too fast?"

"For anyone else, I'd say hell yes. I'd even say you're straight-jacket crazy. But with a history like you and Ace, I'll say it's about time and I am damn happy for you."

"Thanks." I jump forward and hug her tight.

"I also want to throw out there that you better not turn into one of those lovesick guppies that makes me want to cut you."

"Never," I promise.

"What the hell is going on now? I pay you two to sling drinks. Please don't tell me we have another lover's spat," Tom complains from behind.

"No spat. Things are great," I assure him, looking over my shoulder.

"Good, because the crowd is coming, and Sylvia's out sick. Get ready." He roams off.

"Holy mother of sweet Jesus," Jewls breathes out.

I twist, my hand automatically going to the edge of the bar. Talon, Ford, and Major are coming our way with Achilles leading the pack. His eyes aimed at me as his lips curl into his signature grin. My heart skips a beat and I forget to breathe, clutching the bar for a lifeline.

The others stop at their usual spot, but Achilles continues walking, coming around the side entry and directly to me. He links his arms around my waist, lifts, and kisses me gently. I'm too shocked to move, and when he places me back to my feet, my knees give out and I sway back to him.

"Is it bad that I'm picturing him naked, pinning you against the shower?" Jewls butts in, and I whip my head to her.

"Shut up!"

"Just sayin'." She shrugs nonchalantly and goes to help two men and a woman that are openly gawking at Achilles.

When I peer up to him, his eyebrows are arched and his lips tipped in a side grin.

"I may have over shared."

"Good to know."

"Although, I didn't share about your… you know… piercing."

That earns me a smile. "Sure you will."

"Unless you're on my payroll, I don't have insurance on your ass back here," Tom booms, hustling by with a tray of empty glasses.

"I have insurance," Ace replies.

"Let me rephrase. Unless you're wearing one of my shirts and busting your ass, then get out from behind my bar."

"You better go sit down before he has a hemorrhage. We're short a server tonight."

"You're parked under the light by the back entrance." He twists my hand and drops my keys in them.

"Thank you." I brush my lips across his one more time and then give an effortless shove to get him moving. "Who's drinking?" I look at the guys.

"Major and me," Ford answers.

"Since it doesn't take all four of you to bring my car, what's the occasion?" I set down their beer and get water for Ace and Talon.

"Major and I came to watch the game," Ford explains.

"You have an eighty-inch television and two refrigerators full of beer at the Club."

"We came for the company," Major speaks up.

I roll my eyes and toss my gaze to Achilles. "What you mean is you two are on Jay duty tonight since my boyfriend doesn't like me working nights."

Talon chokes out a cough, and Ace doesn't flinch.

"Could be something like that, too." Ford's answer is laced with enjoyment.

"I assume you all are eating?" I hand them menus without waiting for a response.

"Hey, Talon, Ford, Major…" Jewls greets them, stopping in front of Ace. "…Usain Bolt."

"Usain Bolt?" His eyebrows go up.

"Yes, you know, the world's fastest man?"

"I know who he is, Jewls. I don't get the connection."

"Since you broke the land speed record for fastest moving relationship, I thought it was a fitting comparison."

"Julianna!" I swat at her arm, scolding with her full name.

"Ten years is hardly time travel."

"Ten long…" Talon starts.

"… Loooonnnggg…" Ford accentuates.

"… Excruciatingly drawn-out years," they all add in unison.

"I will say hearing Jay refer to Ace as her *'boyfriend'* almost makes the torture of living with this guy worth it." Talon winks my way.

Ace slices his eyes to him sharply, and I wonder briefly if Talon will make it through the night alive. The others catch it, too, and a roar of laughter erupts from everyone but Ace and me.

"Fucking jackasses."

"Well now, he's more of a speed king than the shuffling tortoise," Jewls jabbers.

I catch Tom signaling from across the room for assistance. "Be back, Tom needs some help."

He points to a large group waiting by the door, and then to the cluster of high tops in the corner. I do a quick headcount of twenty, pulling tables together and hauling the stacked chairs away from the wall. In a flash, the four men are at my side, taking over until I have no choice but to instruct them what to do.

Sylvia's absence means I work both the floor and the bar. For the next two hours, I run like a maniac, trying to manage the normal bar rush and keep up with the table. When things die down and I get back to the men, I find my mom sitting in the seat formally occupied by Achilles.

"Mom! What are you doing here?"

She shoots me a saucy grin and lifts her highball glass. "Having a cocktail with the guys. Your dad and I popped in to say hi."

"Popped in? You don't like sports bars."

"I do tonight. Look at my company. Can you blame me?" She gestures to the men, which now include my dad and a few of his friends from the force. Hal Hanks has joined the group. When Achilles told me about the conversation Sunday night, I hoped Hal would be his field training officer for all of his shifts. But seeing Hal drink a beer tells me he's not working tonight.

Looking through the crowd, Achilles seems to be the only one missing. I check my watch and know he has at least an hour before he heads to the station.

"He's talking to Tom, sweetie. Stop worrying." Mom pats my hand.

"I wasn't worried, but things got busy, and there hasn't been a lot of time to talk to him."

"Speaking of talking, seems things have changed since our last conversation."

It's then I remember that I'm mildly pissed at my parents for keeping so much from me for all these years. "Achilles told me everything, Mom, including the fact that Dad practically marched him into the recruiter's office to get him away from me." I snatch my hand back and cross my arms to glare at her.

The happiness on her face fades and she leans in closer. "He called us today and explained that he finally told you the truth."

"It's not cool to ambush me at work. I have a few things to say to you both."

"I fully prepared your father for the tongue-lashing. When we have the time and the privacy to sit down and talk, you will hopefully see where your dad was coming from and the guilt he's felt."

"What about you? Do you feel any guilt?"

"Guilt, anger, helplessness… and many more emotions. You do not know the pain a mother feels watching her daughter travel through the stages of heartbreak. But if Achilles told you everything, you know that what your father did had very little to do with you and everything to do with helping a struggling young man find his way in the world. Pete and Sandy Kingston were well on the path to destroying their son's life. It pained me to see you hurting, but I agreed with your father that Achilles needed to find his way and discover who he is."

"He could have found his way with me by his side!" I argue.

"You were by his side, as his friend. Which is exactly what he needed. Things are different now, and we couldn't be prouder of him. Knowing you are finally together makes me a happy woman."

Her words sink in, and I decide to let this go for a time when I'm not standing behind a bar working. "You need a refill?" I point to her drink, and her smile returns as she slides the glass toward me.

"One more thing."

"Maybe your *one more thing* should wait until tomorrow." I pour the vodka and soda, slip a lime on the rim, and hand it to her.

"Weirdly enough, when I hung up with Ace today, I received another call. This one from Sandy."

My ears perk up at the mention of Achilles' mom. To my knowledge, she's called my parents occasionally throughout the years, and I've run into her in random places, but I've never attempted to keep in touch. According to Achilles, their contact is also limited.

"She misses her son fiercely."

"She should have thought of that when she was sending him on errands to pull Pete out of seedy bars and get beat up." I can't help the hatred that spews out. Knowing what she did cut me deep, and knowing she was involved with him leaving hurts even more.

"Pete's been sober since Ace left for boot camp, and Sandy is a new woman. She left teaching and is now in administration with the school system. She works closely with children in troubled homes."

"That's fucking irony at its finest," I snarl.

Mom doesn't blink at my foul language and continues on. "You love him and you're protective, I understand that. But she is his mother and I'm sympathetic."

"Are you asking me to orchestrate a reunion?"

"No, I'm telling you this because you know the truth now. Obviously, you forged past and forgave Ace. You'll eventually forgive your dad and me for keeping things from you. Since the forgiveness is flowing, maybe you could nudge him to call his—"

"Stop right there. Forgiveness isn't like magical fairy dust that is sprinkled from the sky. It's his choice what to do about his parents."

She nods, taking a sip of her drink and sitting back on her stool. "I've said my piece. And you have customers trying to get your attention."

"Crap!" I turn to see the three men with bills in their hands and scramble to them.

"Sorry," I tell Steve, who's been a regular since Jewls and I started. "You want the usual?"

"Sure."

"What can I get you two?"

The other guys order beer and I pop the caps off, handing them over.

"Is that your mom?" Steve asks.

"It is."

"She's as beautiful as you." He's always been flirtatious.

"I'll tell her you said that." I pour his usual, and when I hand it to him, his eyes are wide and geared over my shoulder.

Without looking, I know who he's staring at.

"You guys staying a while?"

Steve nods, pulling his attention to me.

"I'll start a tab."

I step into a wall of steel, losing my balance. Arms wrap around me to keep me upright. "Careful."

The warmth of his breath sends a shiver down my spine, and I link our fingers, dragging him to the end of the bar where Tom is smirking.

"You have ten minutes." He tosses his hand dismissively.

"Ten minutes for what?"

"Ten-minute break."

"You never give breaks."

"Your boyfriend seems to think you need one. And since you saved my ass with that large party, I agree. Jewls and I can handle this for a few minutes."

"Are you feeling alright?" I reach to his forehead.

"Don't be a pain in the ass." He swats the air.

"Babe, you hungry?" Achilles squeezes lightly.

"Kinda, I usually scarf down something when things slow."

"I ordered you something."

"What did you order?"

"Grilled cheese."

I burst into giggles. Last night, I attempted to make grilled cheese sandwiches for dinner, which ended up charred. It was his fault for distracting me.

"Sounds great."

We walk to the crowd, and Jewls pushes a plate my way. "Where's the other half?"

"I was starving." She licks her lips.

"You want more, I'll order it." Achilles settles his arms around my hips and props his chin on my shoulder.

"This will be fine." I offer him a bite and he nibbles a corner.

"Is it better than last night's version?"

"Nothing is better than last night, except for maybe the shower."

Heat creeps up my cheeks, remembering the endless hours we spent making out yesterday. We also talked—about everything. Once Achilles unloaded his reasoning for his distant attitude, a new man took his place. He shared stories from his time in the Marines, places he'd traveled, different missions and assignments they all had. I realized early that he'd given me only tidbits all those years in order to keep me from worrying. For hours, we reacquainted on anything and everything about each other.

Mistakenly, I let it slip about the only guy I dated seriously in college. Well, as serious as it could be with only one party in the relationship that was faithful. Achilles' eyes went scary dark, his jaw ticking as he held me tighter. Possessive vibes radiated from him. I changed the subject quickly to lighter stories from over the years.

It was one of the best days of my life. But the shower will always be a fond memory. That first look at Achilles naked is forever seared into my brain. So strong, so built, so incredibly sexy. And discovering he had a penis piercing… my insides heat thinking about the desire and hunger in his eyes as I backed out of the room.

The noise grows quiet, and I look to find everyone watching us. My mom is beaming so brightly I wonder if she's about to burst into song and dance. I glance at my dad, who's also smiling approvingly. My bit of erotic bliss shatters when I remember his part in Achilles' ruse all that time.

"You and I are having a talk." I point to him.

His grin grows wider, and he tips his beer. "I expect we are."

"Wait a minute… is little Harley the…?" Hal trails off, staring at us.

"She sure is. You can't miss the twinkle," Talon chimes in, holding out his hand in waiting.

Ace grumbles low at the same time I ask, "Twinkle?"

"Shit, I totally see it now," Ford adds, digging out his wallet and handing Talon a twenty-dollar bill.

"Fuck, me too." Major does the same.

"Do I want to know what they're betting on and why Hal is looking at me funny?" I semi-whisper.

"Got that one, too."

I glance at Talon, whose phone is geared in my direction, and Ford is grinning at the screen.

"Did you take a picture of us?" Achilles' voice is low and angry.

"Yes, the guys in MARSOC are loving this. I tried to get a few last time, but there was too much happening. They turned out blurry."

"Are you fucking kidding me?"

"What's MARSOC?" I break in to help ease the irritation coming off of Achilles.

"Acronym for Marine Corps Forces Special Operations Command. We have some buddies invested in this."

"Invested in what?"

"Ace isn't exactly known for his softer side. The romance between Ace and Jay is spreading like wildfire and the guys want proof."

"Does this have anything to do with the twinkle comment?"

"Yep." He perks up proudly.

"Bunch of grown fucking men acting like teenage girls," Ace utters. "I told you they're jackasses. Ignore them, that's what I do."

I shrug, taking a bite of my sandwich and leaning into him.

"I spoke to Tom, and whenever he thinks the crowd has thinned enough, Ford and Major plan to help him move those tables and chairs back to the corner."

"That's unnecessary. Everyone will pitch in. It's our job."

"It's not up for discussion, and they don't mind helping."

He leaves no room to argue, and their help will make it much easier. After a night like tonight, closing will be a pain in the ass. "Okay."

"I'll pick you up at seven-thirty, and I'll bring breakfast."

"Once again, unnecessary. You'll be exhausted."

"Seven-thirty," he states plainly. "And at the risk of seriously pissing you off, it would make me really fucking happy if you could let *Steve* know his flattery is useless."

There's a bite to his request, and I swallow down my laughter. "Considering I've met his girlfriend several times and he openly dotes on her, that is *unnecessary*. He's harmless."

He grunts, kissing the side of my neck and twirling me to face him. "I have to get to the station. But text me when you get home and let me know you're safe."

"I will."

"You think you can pack a bag and spend the weekend at my place?"

"Wouldn't my place be more private?"

"Your place is great, but I'm scared I'll crush your bed."

The image of his huge frame in my bed pops into my head, and I let out a small laugh. "A sleepover at the Club? All weekend?"

His eyes begin to shine that lightened hue, and I understand exactly what Talon was referring to.

"Yeah, a sleepover at the Club, with me, all weekend. I don't work again until Sunday night."

"I think I can handle that." I slip my arms around his stomach.

"Ten minutes is up!" Tom yells from somewhere close, and I sigh, dropping my head to his chest.

"Baby, I know you're itching to lay into your dad, but he's here tonight for a reason."

"What's the reason?"

"To see for himself that I'm done fucking things up."

God, I love you… I bite my lip to keep from blurting it out loud. Instead, I say softly, "You better go before I tackle you."

His eyes flare, and he tips his head to kiss me quickly. "Save the tackles for this weekend."

"Go." I pinch his side and step away, heading back to work. "I'll see you in the morning."

11

ACE

"Oh my God, is this all yours?"

"Yep." I toss her bag onto the bed.

"Achilles, this is enormous. It's three times the size of the bedroom I showered in last weekend." She walks to the French doors leading to the terrace that overlooks the pool and yard. "Are the other rooms like this?"

"Just Ford's."

"How'd you get so fortunate?"

"I won a bet."

She chuckles and spins, her eyes flinging around rapidly. I prop my hip on my dresser and watch her as she explores my space, disappearing down the hallway and coming back a few minutes later with a look of wonder. "This suite is possibly larger than my apartment. Your bathroom is the size of my bedroom."

She's right. "When Ford's parents built this house and staged it, they set this room up like a studio apartment, with a full sitting area in front of the fireplace and an office section in one corner. The only thing missing is a kitchenette. When we moved in, the Whitmans offered the furniture but we furnished our own way."

Her eyes go to my bed, which is the key piece of furniture. "You were correct in your bed being larger than mine. I'm not sure if that would even fit in my room."

"It wouldn't. I measured this morning when you were finishing your hair."

"It's massive, but then again, you're kinda a massive guy."

"Come here." I hold out my arms, and she doesn't hesitate to walk into them, her hands going around my neck.

"I like your room."

"But…"

"No buts, it's very nice."

"My room is a room. I spend little time in here. The bed is for sleeping, the dresser holds my shit, and I bought the nightstands because they came in the furniture package."

"Don't forget about the gigantic television."

"A man's got to have his TV."

"Utilitarian."

"Utilitarian?"

"Basic, bland, no-frills."

"Baby, I know what it means. But what do I do about that?"

She pulls her bottom lip through her teeth and glances around thoughtfully. "We could start with your own set of purple towels."

"These walls may crumble if you add purple anything."

"Hmmm, you're probably right. There are some beautiful shades of grey that may be a better choice until I ease you into the color wheel."

"Sounds like I'm getting a woman's touch?"

"Only if you want it."

"We'll find time this weekend to hit a store."

She jerks, her eyes lighting up. "You'll go shopping?"

"I've shopped before, but bet going with you will be more fun."

"I'll make it fun, promise."

My hands settle on the small of her back, my palms cupping her ass and closing the few inches between us. "Whatever makes you more comfortable when you're here."

The light in her eyes fades, and she tightens the hold on my neck. "I don't need anything but you."

The raw honesty in her voice hits me deep, and my forehead falls to hers, searching to find the right words. "Harley," her name comes out strained and she nuzzles closer.

"We're new and things have been shaky. Maybe it's too soon to say that, but I haven't exactly hidden my feelings."

"We covered this ground. Never keep things from me."

"It feels surreal, standing here in your arms like this." She tilts her neck, sweeping her lips across mine tenderly. "I really, really like it."

We stay this way for a few minutes, kissing gently. A slow burn builds inside, racing through my veins. Her tongue slips through my lips, curling around mine at the same time she arches her back and presses deep into me. My hands slide down, bunching the material of her skirt until my fingertips glide over her silky smooth skin.

"Baby, where is the rest of your underwear?"

"I don't like panty lines." She smiles against my lips.

A new hunger builds inside, and I growl down her throat, gripping her ass cheeks firmly. She shifts her hips, purposely rubbing against the bulge in my shorts, and I rip my mouth from hers, dropping my face to the column of her throat. My tongue darts out to lick the vein racing against my lips. "We need to leave this room." The statement comes out more as a warning.

"Why?"

"You know why."

She sighs. "One of these days, I'm breaking through that impenetrable self-restraint."

I bend my knees, lowering my hands to her thighs, and hoist her up, twisting to sit her on my dresser. She lets out a small yelp, locking her ankles around my hips, and when I pull back, her eyes are glittering wildly.

"My self-restraint is non-existent with you."

The argument forms on her face, telling me what she's thinking. Before she can speak, I continue. "Forget about the years we were apart, because that wasn't as much restraint as it was determination."

"What about now?"

"Now it's about much more. I'm not sure I can explain it."

"Try."

I slide one hand from under her thigh, along her back, until my fingers thread in her hair. "I've waited a long time for you to be mine, Harley. And I'm never taking that for granted. Fucking you against a shower wall or dresser for our first time isn't the way I want this to happen."

She tries to bow her head, but I hold her in place. "Let me do this my way."

"I don't have a choice." Her voice is small, and a tinge of pink splotches her cheeks.

"You deserve to be cherished and devoured by a man who knows how lucky he is to have you. Fortunately, that man is me. Wipe any doubts from your mind and trust me."

"I've always trusted you."

A new high rushes through my system. This is an honor that I've felt only a few times in my life. But unlike those times that were wrapped in tactical and power accomplishments, this is much more. "How about dinner?"

"I am hungry. I skipped lunch today to run a few errands."

"What errands? I had the day off, you could have asked me."

A coy smile tugs at her lips. "The kind of errands a woman does to surprise her boyfriend."

The possibilities of her 'surprises' set my mind spinning. We have to get out of this room before I break every one of my rules. "Let's go."

"Are we going out or staying here?"

"Staying here."

"Then do you mind if I change?"

"No." I set her down and smooth her skirt. "I'll wait."

She throws a wicked glance my way and reaches behind her to unzip the skirt while walking to her bag. Once there, she slides the skirt off. I plant my feet and cross my arms, watching her every move. She unbuttons the four buttons on the front of her blouse and slips it over her head, leaving her in nothing but the deep purple matching bra and skimpy panty set, and strappy silver heels. As hard as I try to keep my eyes straight, I can't stop them from roaming over her.

She bends over her bag, taking her time digging through, and turns slightly to give me a view of her ass. The same perfect fucking view she teased me with in the shower.

I lock my knees to keep from storming to her.

"I can't seem to find the shirt I'm looking for." Her eyes are dancing with delight as she raises them.

"Take your time. I'm enjoying the show. The heels are a nice touch."

She blows out a frustrated breath and tosses clothes on the bed. I press my lips together to keep from laughing as she jerks a tight tee over her head and slips on cut-off shorts, throwing the shoes in her bag. "I'm ready."

I make it to her in three strides, yanking her back in my arms. "I amend my statement earlier. Purple is quickly becoming my new favorite color. And at some point, I plan to take my time undressing you and getting an up close and personal view. If that was a preview of your surprises, I can't wait."

"I'm thinking you have a will of steel."

"I'm trained in patience and discipline. But even the strongest man can break. I said I wasn't fucking you for the first time against a shower or on top of my dresser. I didn't make many more promises."

Her breath hitches, and she glides her hands under my shirt, sliding them up my back. "I'm not hungry anymore."

In a quick move, I have her over my shoulder. "Put me down." She wriggles to get free, and when we get to the kitchen, I plop her on the center island.

"There you go." I kiss her nose.

"You don't play fair."

"I can say the same thing about you."

"Fine! I'll behave."

"Who's behaving?" Talon strolls in, fresh from a run, wearing nothing but shorts and dripping sweat. Ford is behind him in the same state.

I open the wine and pour her a glass, throwing them each a bottle of water and grabbing a beer for myself. When I hand her the wine, I notice her eyes glued to their chests.

"Babe, it's not a good idea to ogle other men in front of me." My attempt to tilt her chin fails.

"Doesn't bother me." Ford flexes for effect.

"Yeah, let her look." Talon smirks.

I follow the path of her eyes and the hair on the back of my neck prickles when I realize what she's seeing. "Baby, look at me."

She snaps out of her daze. "Sorry, I zoned out." She tries to cover, but one glance at Talon and Ford and they know she's put it together.

Our identical tattoos.

"I'll explain later," I mumble softly.

She nods, taking her wine and flashing them a smile. "I'm thinking I could sell tickets to the Casanova Club if this is the way each Friday night kicks off. Achilles serving wine, half-naked men prancing around the kitchen. A girl can get used to this."

"I don't know, I miss the sex kitten sprockets wrestling in the bushes from last week," Talon teases.

Her cheeks flame. "We weren't—" She stops herself and drops her head. "Yes, we were totally dressed like sprockets, but the wrestling was a fluke. You scared the shit out of us."

"Let's do that again."

"Not on your life. My days of spying are over. I can't speak for Jewls, but I learned my lesson."

"Don't be too embarrassed, Jay. It worked out pretty well, don't you think?" Ford goads her.

She peers up at me through her eyelashes and nods. "Yes, I think it did."

"I'm not sure what a sex kitten sprocket looks like," I admit.

"They're exaggerating."

"Somehow, I doubt it."

"Maybe I'll add it to my list of surprises," she says low enough for only me to hear.

The air in the room changes, her words full of much more than just promise. I lean down, touching my lips to hers. "So much to look forward to."

She grins, taking a sip of her wine and turning back to them. "Are you guys eating with us?"

"I'm sure they have plans." My icy tone backfires immediately. They exchange a glance and say "sure" at the same time.

Dipshits.

"We're grilling." I jerk my head to the back door, which is their cue to leave.

When they're gone, she wraps an arm around my neck and runs her fingers through my hair. "You don't mind, do you?"

"That they're crashing our night?"

"It's not crashing if I invited them. And besides, I like this. Being with your friends, joking, hanging out. They're a part of you and know so much that I don't about your life."

"I'll tell you anything you want to know."

She hesitates for a second and I wait her out, pretty sure what's on her mind. "The tattoos. On your left pecs, near your heart, they're all the same. I saw the similarities with Major last week in the pool. I thought it was a coincidence. But it's not, is it?"

"No, it's not a coincidence."

"What do they mean?"

"They're the dates we walked away alive from specific missions."

"You have an extra date."

"I do."

She places her other hand on my chest, covering the spot where my ink is. I can see the question forming in her mind, and my gut tightens, waiting for her to ask the inevitable. "Why?"

"Tattoos are personal for their own reasons. Mine all have importance. The first date in my sequence is a day I'll never forget because it's the day I met you."

A soft shine pools in her eyes, and she sets down her wine, sliding her hand under my shirt and lifting the material. The pads of her fingers trace the date inked directly over my heart. "I love that."

My skins prickles with each swirl over the numbers as she stares as if it's the most important thing in the world.

"Achilles?" My name comes out faint and raspy, making me wonder if she's close to crying.

"What, baby?"

"Since you like to haul me around, I suggest you carry me outside before I wrestle you to the ground and put all my effort into slaughtering your self-restraint on the kitchen floor."

"I can do that." I scoot her forward and she falls into me, kissing the skin on my chest before releasing my shirt.

"SHE'S PRETTY SPECIAL." Ford takes a swing of his beer, watching me closely.

I move my gaze to Harley, who's sitting across from Talon by the fire pit, moving her hands in the air as she tells him something that has a relaxed grin on his face. "If that's how you want to put it."

"How would you put it?"

"I'm not going there. You know what she means to me."

"She seemed pretty excited about us applying to SWAT."

"She's not only a cop's daughter; she also wants me to be happy. Same with the three of you."

"Talon told me what Hal said last week."

I sigh, bringing my attention back to him. "Are we shooting the shit after dinner, or are we pussyfooting around something?"

"Both. I want you to know none of us will think any differently if you change your mind."

I swallow half my beer in one gulp. "We're in this together. I'm not changing my mind."

"This Reserve thing may be hard on your relationship, especially with the deal we made. I'm guessing you haven't told her about that yet."

"I'm working on it. We've had a lot to talk about. She knows we have drills the weekend after next. Since I can't give her details of our commitment, I can't exactly tell her what we signed up for. Besides, it's a long shot we're going back over there."

"Man, you love her, and that's a good thing. If the time comes and we get called back, I'll do whatever I can to take your place. Don't put her—"

"Stop. Don't finish that sentence." My bottle slams loud enough for Talon's eyes to slice my way. "We're a team. Harley is in my life, but that doesn't change the man I am. Never forget that."

"The offer stands. We got your six."

"Do you want me to fuck you up with my girlfriend twenty feet away?" I glare at him.

He stares at me a beat, then finishes his beer, tosses it in the trash, and reaches in the fridge for three more, passing me the bottle of wine. "Nah, we're done shooting the shit. Time to go see if Talon has stolen your woman."

"Not a fucking chance." I follow him to the seating area, and she flashes me a smile. "Hand me your glass, babe."

I fill her up, setting the bottle on the ground and sliding in behind her. She shivers, scooting closer and laying her head on my shoulder. "Did you forget to mention something, Achilles?"

"Can you be more specific?"

"Talon told me about the party next weekend."

I'm not sure I'd call it a party, considering all three of the guys' parents are descending upon us. Talon and Major's parents had made reservations at a hotel, but when Celia Whitman found out, she stepped into high gear, insisting everyone stay here. Last I heard, she and Doug were flying in Thursday night so she could spend Friday stocking the house for what she referred to as a celebration.

"I had other things on my mind when we got here." My lips brush her earlobe.

Talon coughs and Ford openly chuckles.

"But since the subject came up, I want you to invite Rich and Amanda for Saturday night."

Ford nods in agreement.

"Jewls is welcome as well," Major adds.

"She'll love it."

"Tell her to pack a bag. She can stay."

"Oh, no. We'll go home. It wouldn't be appropriate for us to stay. This is a family weekend."

The carefree mood in the air instantly crisps, and my head pops up at the same time the guys hit their feet. Harley scoots back, looking between us. "What's wrong?"

"Nothing, gonna let Ace handle this." Talon flicks his fingers as he walks away.

"I'll come back in an hour to handle the fire," Ford offers before heading toward the house.

"Appreciate it," I call, taking her wine and putting it on the side table next to my beer.

"Did I say something?" She stares after them.

I straighten, hook an arm around her middle, and lay her across my lap. "You aren't going home."

She crinkles her eyes in confusion. "What?"

"Next weekend, the weekend after that, any fucking time you want to be here, you are here."

"Okay, I get that. But between the Simms, the Powers, and the Whitmans, this house will be bursting at the seams with people. Not to mention, this is the Whitmans' home. It's not appropriate—"

"How old am I?" I cut her off.

"Twenty-nine in November."

"Twenty-nine. The other guys are almost thirty. We are men, Jay. Our living arrangements may be unconventional, but it doesn't change the fact that we're men. We have our own space, we pay our way, and the moment we moved in, it became ours. That is a directive from the Whitmans. They know the men we are. None of us plan to live here forever, but it's a convenience we are grateful for."

"What if I am more comfortable going home?"

"Then that's an entirely different conversation. But if you think you're going home because it's inappropriate, forget it."

"I was trying to be polite!"

"You want to be polite, offer them a drink when they walk in the door and welcome them."

"I don't even live here. That would be incredibly awkward."

"Going back to the fact that I live here, and with me comes you."

"That is bizarre logic." She tries to sound strong, but the fire fades from her glare. "These people don't even know me."

"They know me and they will love you."

"That's a lot of pressure."

"No pressure. Invite Rich, Amanda, and Jewls. Like you said, it's a family weekend. Talon's right. If Jewls wants to stay, she's welcome."

"I'll mention it." Her hands move to frame my face, and she scales her nails through the stubble. She remains quiet, her expression thoughtful as the flames of the fire crackle and pop a few feet away. My mind travels back to countless nights on bases. I'd sit with men and women, listening to them reminisce about home and stare into the embers, wondering about her.

"What are you thinking about?"

"The endless amount of times I've sat around a fire wishing I was doing exactly what I'm doing now, holding you in my arms."

She inhales softly, running the pad of her thumb along my bottom lip. "The hidden facets of my Achilles."

"Facets?"

"Intense, bossy, guarded, possessive beyond belief, soft, sweet, reflective, protective… all of them."

"I'm not sure anyone has ever referred to me as soft and sweet."

"That's because you give that to me. Did I mention tempting? Hot? Unbelievably sexy?"

"That describes you."

She kisses me lightly, then settles back, moving a hand to my chest. "You know there's a fireplace in your room."

"I'm aware."

"We could put a fluffy rug on your floor for when it gets too cold to sit out here. The weather's changing already."

"The term fluffy rug hits hard at my masculinity."

"Not sure it's possible your masculinity could take a hit."

"We'll see," I half-commit, nuzzling into her neck so she can't see my grin.

Looks like I'll be buying a new rug tomorrow.

12

HARLEY

"ARE YOU FALLING ASLEEP AGAIN?" Ace's smooth voice rumbles in my ear.

I shake my head.

"Then you want to tell me what's on your mind?"

No, I don't want to tell him what's on my mind. Because what I'm thinking about is exactly what my next moves are to break his will of steel. So far, nothing has worked.

Last night didn't go exactly as planned, considering I fell asleep in his lap by the fire and he carried me to bed. The skimpy silk pajamas I bought remained packed in my overnight bag because I was too tired to go through the effort. Instead, I took the shirt off his back–literally—shed my clothes to put it on, stumbled into the bathroom to brush my teeth, and then into bed. He curled in beside me a few minutes later, and I passed out on his chest.

This morning, I woke up sprawled half on top of him, my calf twisted around his thigh. He was already awake, his fingers weaving lightly through my hair. Even in my drowsy state, I couldn't miss the hardness pressing against my knee. My hand skimmed down his bare chest, and right when I hit the waistband, he stopped my exploration by clutching my wrist and yanking it back to his chest.

That was the first, but not the only time he stopped me today. I know little about the game of seduction, but I am pretty sure I'm failing at it. Years of paying for my Cosmo subscription have gotten me nowhere.

Tonight, he'd suggested the hot tub, and it seemed like the perfect plan. My heart skipped a beat when I walked out of his bathroom and his eyes turned molten at the sight of my barely-there midnight blue bikini.

This was by far my most revealing piece of clothing outside of complete nudity. Truth be told, I am practically naked. Jewls told me about a store that specializes in stunning lingerie and swimwear. I am pretty sure they meant this bikini for an exotic dancer, but I bought it anyway. The look of savage hunger that took over made every penny worth it. His eyes darted from me to the bed, and I knew I had him.

Instead of throwing me on the bed, he threw me over his shoulder and stalked out his side door to the Jacuzzi.

I sighed in defeat, but wasn't ready to give up.

So, now I'm leaning quietly on his chest, trying to figure out a way to seduce my boyfriend without resorting to begging.

"Like your suit, Jay." He breaks into my thoughts.

My head pops up, and I catch the smug grin playing on his lips.

"You noticed?"

"Hard not to."

"Could have fooled me." My reply comes out a little too whiny.

His grin turns into a full-out smile, and in one quick move, he's twisted me to straddle him. He thrusts his hips upward, the hard length of him rubbing directly between my legs. Since the bottoms of the suit are all string except for one scrap of triangle, the friction hits me in the right spot and I swallow a moan.

"And your yoga outfit was sweet, too. It's a good thing Erik is gay and the class is full of women or I'd never have left you there."

A thrill slides up my spine when he toys with the tie at my neck.

"The one-piece thing was hot, too."

"Romper," I croak when his finger traces over the swell of my breast to make his point. The romper I wore today was more fitted than usual, with long flowy sleeves, a deep V at the neck, and a belt that helped me bunch it up so short, the cheeks of my butt were close to showing. At normal length, the shorts would have been decent, but I made it obscene.

"I walked behind you the whole time with my eyes glued to your ass. I was hard as a steel thinking about how perfect that ass is."

He rocks his hips again.

"Ahhhhh," I whimper at the sensation, driving my own hips downward.

"If you thought I was possessive before, you have no idea after watching you strut around all day. Those legs should come with a warning."

He's right. I strutted, pranced, frolicked, and sashayed through the day, hoping to get a reaction. A new thrill washes through me.

"You could have fooled me." This time, the statement comes out throaty and almost breathless because he leans down to trace his lips along the teeny patch of material covering one nipple.

"You were playing a game with me. A game I enjoyed. But you should know something. Nothing you wore today to tease me was as fucking gorgeous as waking up to you in my bed in my t-shirt, your sorry excuse for panties, and having your body tangled with mine."

"You didn't seem too interested in me then, either."

"We both know that isn't true."

"You cock blocked me."

He grins against my breast, rubbing his stubble against the skin that is scorching under his touch. "Not sure I'd call it that, but hearing the word cock come from your mouth is sexy."

"What would you call it?"

"Enjoying your persistence."

"You locked me out of the bathroom!" I'm grateful for the dim light, so he can't see my face blazing at the mortifying admission. During my yoga class, he went for a run to pass the hour. Back at the house, he promptly headed to his shower, announcing he'd hurry so I could have the bathroom to get ready for our shopping trip.

Boldness came over me, and I attempted to join him, only to find he'd locked the door. He came out fifteen minutes later fully dressed, and I was casually scrolling through my phone. Neither he nor I mentioned the locked barrier, and in my mind, it was staying that way to avoid further embarrassment. Until right now when my big mouth blurted it out.

"I cut my run short to come back and watch you at yoga. Only so much a man can take. Even a cold shower didn't help. For the second time in four days, I visualized you while taking care of myself."

I bite down on my bottom lip to keep from smiling. A rush of satisfaction replaces the earlier embarrassment.

"It was its own form of fucking torture waiting to have you alone tonight and see what you had planned for this piece of fabric."

His hands glide over my shoulders, down my arms, and slip into the water, going straight for my ass. He leans up, sweeping his lips across mine until I release my bottom lip from my teeth and give in to his kiss. My arms go around his shoulders, my chest arching into his so almost every part of us is touching. The hot water bubbles around us, scorching my already overheated skin as he grips my flesh and grinds in a rhythm with his hips.

It's easy to lose myself, giving him control of our bodies moving together. He slows the kiss, sucking my tongue deeper into his mouth. He groans down my throat when I score my nails along his shoulder blades, thrusting down harder. The thin triangle of fabric snaps, and the second my skin comes in contact with the soft material of his swimsuit, sparks shoot through me.

I tear my mouth from his and shove my head into his neck, sliding back and forth over him.

"Baby."

"Don't you dare tell me we have to stop."

One hand loosens, sliding over my hip, pelvic bone, and between my legs to cup me. Two fingers run gently along my sensitive skin until one slips easily inside. My muscles instantly contract, gripping his finger as I whimper into his skin.

Every muscle in his body tenses as his hand freezes. I try to swivel my hips, but the hand cupping my butt grips tighter.

"Baby, look at me."

I do as he asks, and my already racing heart threatens to leap out of my chest at his expression.

"Harley, baby…"

Without asking, I tell what he wants to hear. "I'm..."

"You haven't ever been with anyone?"

I drop my head, wishing my hair was down so I could hide my awkwardness at the admission. "Not in that way."

His finger slides out of me as gently as it slid in, and I swear he growls as he stands, crushing me to him. One arm curls under my thighs as the other goes to my neck, cradling me to him like a child. He stalks out of the Jacuzzi, the cool air hitting my body before he snatches a towel off a chair and throws it over my back, rubbing it to dry me. My head pounds with the possibilities of what he's thinking and if I should have shared my information sooner.

He takes us to his room and doesn't stop until he lays me on the bed.

"Don't move," he orders, disappearing into the bathroom.

My anxiety spikes, realizing I'm naked from the chest down. Before I can scoot under the covers, Achilles is back, a towel wrapped around his waist. He goes to one elbow, crowding to my side, his other hand framing my face tenderly. His eyes gleam a shade of amber so deep, I swear they're glowing. I suck in a breath and decide to give it all to him before losing the courage.

"I didn't exactly sit in waiting all these years. I've dated and had my share of flings, but it didn't go anywhere. Every time I'd meet someone, I'd wonder if he'd be the person who would fill the void that was you. That didn't happen. It may make me an anomaly, a twenty-seven-year-old virgin, but in my head, it never felt right."

"Not even what's-his-fuck from college?"

"I walked in on him getting a blow job from a former friend."

Blatant relief lights on his face. "Untouched."

"I'm not a prude. I've been touched—"

A throaty rumble vibrates low in his chest. His jaw gets tight and the air between us thickens. I massage the back of his neck and press up to kiss him quickly.

"I didn't know what would happen, but I always hoped it was you."

"We need to go slow. This doesn't have to happen tonight. I'll wait as long as you want."

"I'm done waiting."

"You saved yourself for a reason."

"And you're that reason."

He studies me intensely, my stomach curling at the possibility he's about to turn me down. Every muscle in my body tenses, and my brain goes into panic mode.

He picks up on my anxiety, his fingers sweeping affectionately across my cheek. "You are my reason for everything."

The ragged gentleness in his tone turns my panic into a whole new emotion. He's staring at me adoringly, his gorgeous glowing eyes piercing mine.

With everything we've shared, it should be obvious. But the need to tell him the depth of my feelings is overwhelming. It's terrifying and thrilling to know I'm laying out my vulnerability. I open my mouth, then his thumb slides to my lips, pressing lightly to silence me.

"I love you." He steals my words.

My heart threatens to shatter at hearing the endearment I've wished and longed for. "I love you, too."

"I feel like I've waited a lifetime to tell you that."

"You have. Took you long enough."

His lips curl in an amused grin.

I shiver at the feel of his fingers gliding along the edge of the fabric of my top, going around my neck and tugging at the tie. "This needs to go." He does the same with the string at the back. Leisurely, he peels the material from my chest and tosses it.

I forget to breathe as his gaze travels downward

"Flawless."

My body lurches when his lips graze over my nipple before gently sucking it into his mouth. His hand moves to my ribcage, traces over my hipbones and between my legs. Instinctively, my knees part, giving him access.

Similar to earlier, the instant his finger slips inside, my muscles cinch tight. He works it in and out, adding another that has me moaning in pleasure. He moves to the other breast, sucking and kissing every inch of flesh.

Nothing in my past lives up to this moment. Any other experience I thought I had will forever be a memory replaced by the way my body reacts to his touch.

Desperate need seers through my bloodstream. I rock my hips to meet his movements, grinding on his fingers and palm.

"In a hurry?" He smiles against my skin, knowing exactly what he's doing.

I want to yell in frustration at his unhurried approach. My body screams for release at the sensations of his soft stubble against my sensitive flesh, the way his mouth closes around me, tugging and playing. His fingers twisting and swirling inside, touching deep every few strokes, toying with me at what's coming.

An idea flashes through my mind, and I yank the towel at his waist. The second my hand closes around his dick, his body shudders.

I've been shamelessly dreaming of this since the tease in the shower. The first sight of him naked was luscious, but actually touching him is far better. Long, thick, hard as steel, yet the skin is smooth and soft. I scrape my nails gently up and down. His cock lurches in my hand when I circle his piercing and rub around the crown and metal.

"Fuck, Harley."

"Hmmmm," I utter innocently, hoping he feels a fraction of my burning desire.

His face comes to mine, a chill racing over my skin at the smoldering lust in his eyes. His fingers move faster, this time testing how far they can go, and my breathing shallows. I try to play his game, stroking him at the same pace, but it's no use. He strums his thumb along my clit, and I convulse in response.

"Come for me." The roughness in his command is all it takes.

The orgasm washes through me as his mouth covers mine, taking my whimpers. He removes his fingers and pulls away when I grab the back of his neck, scared he's about to stop this.

"Condom, baby," he eases my mind.

Condom, of course.

But wait, do I want there a condom between us? I may not be experienced in sexual activity, but we love each other. This is a conversation couples have… even if it is uncomfortable. He reads my hesitation wrong and cups my jaw.

"It's okay, we don't have to rush."

"No, I don't want a condom. I'm on birth control. Are you…? I mean, when's the last time?"

Hell, Harley, get a grip, this is Achilles. We've been in each other's lives far too long, and now's not the time to clamp up with cold feet.

"Are you clean?" The question comes out in a whisper.

"I'm clean."

"Then just you."

Something similar to fascination crosses his expression before he crushes my body to his, lifting to situate me in the middle of the bed.

He braces on his elbows, locking eyes with mine. I wrap my thighs around his waist, feeling his firmness twitch at the contact.

"Any time you want me to stop, you tell me."

"I won't want you to stop."

His finger sifts through the hair at my temple. Holding my stare, he rocks his hips up and down until he's at my entrance, the cool metal pushing through. Carefully and slowly, he sinks in, stopping too soon. Concern and worry show clearly on his face. I shift upward and feel a tight pinch at the penetration.

"I'm fine." The discomfort eases and is replaced by a foreign sensation of him filling me.

He sinks in further, stretching me as my muscles constrict around the invasion. His forehead drops to mine, and I know he's holding back. The boldness from this morning resurfaces and I pivot my hips, taking more of him, and then thrust until he's skin to skin.

"Fuck, fuck, fuck," he bites out, as if in pain. "Goddamn, Harley. Don't move or I'm gonna fucking blow."

The timing sucks, but I can't help but giggle at his glower. He's on the verge of losing control, and it's all because of me. His eyes darken and he moves, his jaw tight with each shallow thrust. His cock pulses, and the barbell scales along my walls with each stroke.

"Beautiful." He braces up on his arms, glancing down in between us before bringing his gaze back to mine.

I move with him, rolling and moaning at the contact. His speed increases, pumping harder. A burst of pleasure ripples through me when he rubs against my clit. I thought it was rare to enjoy your first time and almost impossible to come, but neither is true.

Watching him drive into me over and over, his sexy tattooed chest before me with the date we met inked into his skin, the power on his face—all of it proves my assumption was a lie.

Anticipation and desire build as the friction increases. I tighten my inner muscles, trying to suck him deeper inside.

"Harley," he grounds out in warning.

"You feel amazing." I don't recognize the hoarse, raspy voice that comes out of my mouth. His eyes blaze darker, that control about to tip.

"Come for me, baby. I need you there."

I unlatch my legs and plant my feet on the bed, surging up and tilting down.

"Fucking shit."

A sense of empowerment rises. I am responsible for his strained control. Our hips find a rhythm, meeting and moving together expertly. Need sparks low in my core, and I close my eyes, lost in what's happening.

The pressure is exquisite, and too soon, a wave of pleasure so intense washes over me. I scream his name, my body quaking as I come apart.

"Harley, give me those eyes." It's a ragged plea.

My eyelids flutter open in time to see him drive twice more before slamming hard and roaring my name. His dick pours into me, jerking over and over, threatening to bring me to the brink again.

He closes in, careful not to crush me, kissing me gently as we catch our breath.

"Are you okay?"

"I'm perfect."

"Did I—?"

I place a finger to his lips. "Seriously, Achilles, stop before you say something barbaric and ruin my high."

"Your high?"

"No amount of self-satisfaction comes close to what is floating and zinging through my body right now. If you weren't on top, I'd probably be levitating above the bed."

He grins against my finger before sucking it into his mouth. In a flash, we're up and I'm wrapped around him again.

"What are you doing?"

"Rewinding eight hours and giving you what you want."

He walks us straight into the shower, shielding me from the cold spray and turning when it's warmed. "We're taking a shower?" Confusion bleeds through my question.

"You seem to have a thing for me in the shower."

I slide down his body, grinding slowly when I come into contact with the firmness between us.

"Careful," he bites out.

"Am I hurting you?"

"Savage torture that's fucking perfect." His voice is rough, sending a tremor through me. "I'm washing you, making sure you're really okay, then I'm taking you back to bed so we can explore more of this self-satisfaction theory."

There's an unspoken promise in his words that sends an entirely different tremor racing through my system.

THE BED DIPS right as a strong arm circles my waist and Ace's hard body curls around me. Through the slits of my eyes, I see it's dark.

"Are you okay?" I ask drowsily.

"Yes, go back to sleep." He sounds suspiciously alert for the middle of the night.

"Sweetie, I know you're programmed to function on little sleep and work nights, but normal people sleep when it's dark outside."

He chuckles softly and kisses the bare skin of my shoulder. "I'll have to remember that."

I'm close to dozing off again when the unmistakable aroma of cinnamon and maple fills the air. "What is that delicious smell?"

"Ford made waffles. I snagged one."

The news doesn't faze me until I comprehend what he said. "Why is Ford making breakfast at this ungodly hour?"

He smiles, his stubble tickling my skin. "Baby, it's almost noon."

My eyes fly open, and I jolt. He tightens his hold, throwing his thigh over mine. "Noon! It's pitch black in here."

"Blackout curtains," he explains.

"Achilles! Why didn't you wake me up? Half the day is gone."

"You were sleeping hard. Figured your body needed the rest."

I pick up immediately on the underlying meaning of his words, and my heart melts at his implication. "My body is fine," I assure him softly.

"You were peaceful."

It's on the tip of my tongue to ask him how he could see me in the dark, but I already know the answer.

"How long have you been up?"

"A while."

We lay until I'm fully awake and need to get up. "Will you turn on the light, so I don't break my neck trying to stumble my way to the bathroom?"

He twists, taking me partly with him and switches on a light, then sits us up. "Do you want me to carry you?"

"No, caveman. I think I can make it on my own."

He smirks, laying back and roaming his eyes over my naked body. I cover myself, then remember he's had his hands and mouth on every inch of my skin and there's no use in being shy.

Once I'm through with my routine in the bathroom, I inspect myself in the mirror and half expect to see someone else staring back at me. Besides a few noticeable marks across my breasts, I look exactly the same. Something in the shower catches my eye. When I realize it's the bottoms of my bikini that were left in the hot tub, a giggle escapes. The outfit may have been sexy, but it wasn't very durable.

Which is probably the point.

I make a mental note to buy another one for the mere pleasure of seeing Achilles' reaction.

A loud crash of thunder sounds outside, followed by droplets of water hitting the tile block window. I go to the closet and throw on some clothes, then take my bag back to the bathroom to pack the rest of my things. Physically, there may be no difference in my appearance, but emotionally, I'm floating on cloud nine. In less than forty-eight hours, my world has taken a massive shift. It's not about only the sex; it's about the commitment and the way Achilles treated me afterward. His words from Friday night pop back into my mind. He *cherished* me. I grab my toothbrush and face wash, lost in thought.

"What are you doing?"

I swivel toward his voice and find him leaning against the door. He's completely nude with his arms across his chest, scowling at me. My skin scorches under the heat in his glare and my stomach flips at the sight.

He's nothing short of perfection. My knees go weak, remembering him moving inside me, and I grip the counter for support. When I bring my gaze back to his, I'm pretty sure I'm having a hot flash.

"Harley, what are you doing?" This time, the question comes out smoother.

"Right this second, I'm admiring. You should go nude all the time."

His glare softens. "If you think that, then why the fuck are you dressed and in here packing your shit?"

"I figured since it's raining, we aren't going by the pool and we have to go soon."

In true Achilles' fashion, he stalks to me, throws the items in my hands into the sink, and lifts me off my feet. I wrap around him to make it easier and kiss along his jaw until we reach the bed. He falls against the pillows propped on his headboard, keeping me in the same position. "Arms up," he instructs, whipping my shirt over my head. There's no missing the flicker of appreciation when he sees my baby blue demi-cup bra. Jewls will be pissed when she finds out how much I dipped into my vacation fund to shop for this weekend, but it will be worth the wrath.

"Bra stays, for now."

"I take it we don't have to go soon?"

"Not until I take you home tomorrow morning."

"Ace." I stop his hands from roaming down my stomach until he looks at me. "You know I love the guys, but I'm not sure I'm comfortable staying here while you're at work tonight."

"I'm not working tonight. Made arrangements to work tomorrow."

I'm not exactly up to date on the human resources handbook, but I know rookies don't get to set their own schedules. Achilles and the guys may be hardcore badass Marines, but they are still rookies on the low end of the totem pole at the police department. "Achilles! You can't."

He moves fast, throwing me to my back and situating himself between my thighs. "I can and I did. Major told me this morning when he got home that Hal is sick, and I saw an opportunity to work to my advantage. It's handled. I work tomorrow day shift. Hopefully, Hal's back. If not, then I deal."

"Will you get in trouble?"

"I don't get in trouble."

None of this makes sense, but I store it away for a later conversation. "So, we have all day?"

"Yep, that's why we're going back to bed."

My stomach chooses that moment to growl, and his eyes drop to our joined hands. "Change of plans. First I feed you, and then we come back to bed."

I want to argue that I don't need food, but he doesn't give me a chance, sitting us back up. His phone rings and his eyes shoot to the nightstand in irritation. He ignores it, placing me on my feet and handing me my shirt from the floor.

"Where are your clothes? Did you go to the kitchen naked?"

"I got undressed to slide back in bed with you." He heads to his dresser and grabs some shorts lying on top.

While he's slipping them on, I glance at his phone, and my stomach pitches at the voicemail notification from his mom. Another notification pops up, alerting him that this is the fourth missed call from her. Immediately, I think something is wrong, and turn to see him watching.

"Don't," he shuts me down.

I snap my mouth closed, aware of the ice in the air. His sweet-natured mood has disappeared, replaced with a blank stare. "Okay."

He comes to me, lifting my face to his and brushing his lips across mine. "Baby, whatever she has to say can wait. I woke up today knowing you gave me the most precious gift I've ever received in my life. She doesn't get to cloud that."

"Something could be wrong."

"Nothing is wrong."

"How do you know?"

"Because if something was wrong, *your* mom would be calling."

"You know about her keeping in touch with Mom?"

"Of course I do. I also know she called your mom last week to gather an ally."

"Apparently, she misses you."

"She told me repeatedly when we spoke on Thursday."

"You did?"

"Yes, she's thrilled to death about us. Rambling on about getting together with you and Amanda, wanting to take us out to dinner or any kind of get-together."

"What did you say?"

"That I work mostly nights and you are holding down two jobs, one of them nights. Told her I'd get back to her and plan something."

"You didn't mention it." He picks up on the hurt in my voice.

"Because it slipped my mind the instant I walked into Tom's. And we've had a lot going on since then."

The hurt dies away, realizing he's right. A lot has happened since Thursday night.

"Has she changed?" I can't stop the question from slipping out.

He closes his eyes, but not before I catch a flicker of pain slash through them.

"I'm sorry, I didn't mean—"

"Yes, as far as I can tell, she's changed." The pain is gone when he looks back at me. His expression says it all. She may have changed her life around, but there are scars that haven't healed.

There are countless thoughts running through my mind regarding Sandy Kingston and the mistakes of her past. After Achilles shared with me what happened that night, my heart filled with anger and resentment for the woman who was supposed to protect him. But standing here now, the resentment turns to pity, knowing whatever happens in the future, she may never fully get her son back.

"Call her back when you're ready."

He blows out a sigh of relief and moves his hand to cup the back of my neck.

"Now, if you want me to have any energy to spend the afternoon in bed, you'd better feed me. I'm craving waffles."

"I'm craving something entirely different and a lot sweeter." His voice dips low, his eyes now blazing with sensual hunger. "I plan to spend the afternoon tasting every inch of you."

Lust, desire, need—they all ignite, searing through my veins. "I'll eat fast."

"You do that, baby. But I plan on taking my time."

13

ACE

I STAB the log on the fire a little too forcefully, sending sparks flying in a spray as I try to ignore the loud bursts of laughter coming from the Jacuzzi area. The only thing stopping me from hauling Harley out of the water is the fact that she's practically a beacon of happiness. Like I explained, no one blinked an eye about her staying here. Instead, the web of women embraced her immediately.

I had hoped for a quiet afternoon alone with her, but those plans blew up in my face about five minutes after we walked in the door from her yoga class. Her mom, dad, and Jewls were waiting for us with two unexpected guests.

"If you're thinking about killing them, it's harder than it looks. I've tried and those guys have more lives than a cat," Major jokes, glancing over his shoulder.

My focus goes to his twin brothers, Drake and Sam, who flew in this morning to surprise him. They are typical, good-looking, twenty-six-year-olds. Both are highly intelligent and found success right out of college. They manage all our investments and make us a lot of money.

I've always liked them.

Today, things changed.

"I think they both have a death wish," I relay to Major.

"You know they are fucking around. Drake still talks about that night in the bar when you shut down every woman that tried to speak to you. They never understood why you had no interest. Then you walk in today with Jay, looking like she does, and they saw an opportunity to screw with your head."

"One look at her explains why I wasn't interested in anyone else. But man, beware, looks like your brothers are giving up and moving on."

I take a swig of beer to hide my grin because Major's body stiffens. His own glare becomes lethal. Drake says something that has Jewls in hysterics.

"I'll feel better when I can haul Harley's ass out of the hot tub and back to my room."

He crinkles his eyebrows and shakes his head at my bluntness. "You really are a brute."

"I think we're in trouble." Ford joins the conversation with Talon at his side. "Mom is hinting at bringing back some decorations for the house, and she's recruiting Jay to jump on the bandwagon."

"It's fucking Ace's fault. What were you thinking buying that thing?" Talon gripes.

The rug Harley picked out arrived today, and Celia didn't hide her excitement over the addition. Amanda stared at me with wonder as if I had bought a priceless jewel.

"I think we all know why he bought the damn rug," Ford adds. "Do me a favor. When you build your own house, keep that thing in your bedroom. I don't want to think about you having sex on it every time I walk into your living room."

"Speaking of living rooms…" Talon trails off, his eyes going over my shoulder.

I turn to the headlights of the golf cart crossing the yard. Ford's dad, Doug, drives around the back of the fire pit with Rich, Jim, and Mark piling out.

"You get lost? It's been dark almost an hour," I ask Rich specifically.

"Been riding around the neighborhood."

I think twice about pointing out we could have done that anytime in the daylight.

"I made a call, Ace. My guy will be here Monday before we leave town to walk the property. I'll also get started on the permit portion," Doug informs me, unloading a cooler from the back of the cart.

"Thanks, Doug." I glance at my three friends. "You okay with this?"

"Fuck yeah, but it's not us you need to worry about. Jay is the final decision maker in this scenario. She may have her heart set on a different idea."

"She won't," Rich chimes in. "What Ace had planned will be exactly what she wants."

"What about you? Are you okay with this?"

"Hard not to be, knowing what you're giving her."

"Can I trust you and Amanda to sit on this for a while?"

He shuffles uncomfortably, and I feel slightly guilty for asking him to hide something else from his daughter.

"Give us a heads-up when you decide to tell her so we can disappear for a few days."

"Got it." I laugh, thinking about the tongue-lashing she gave him on Friday afternoon before we came here.

Drake and Sam walk up with their arms full of beer bottles.

"I think I love your girlfriend," Sam comments, handing me a fresh bottle.

"I know I do," I reply icily, watching the cocky grin slip into place.

"Any chance there's a sister?"

"Only child," Rich answers with notable relief. "We knew immediately one Harley was all we could handle."

"How about cousins?"

"We may have some rabid contenders on Amanda's side of the family. Her cousin Shayla is a wild child."

I smile at the reminder of Shayla. I met her several times during my senior year and was thankful Harley had her in her life. She was confident, no-nonsense, and tough. Everything Harley needed to get past the pretentious bitches that judged her in high school. Through the years, Harley kept me updated on her continuous tales of 'debauchery', as she liked to call them.

"How is Shayla?"

Rich arches an eyebrow with a quick shake of the head. "Last I heard, she's bulldozing her way through Europe, driving her parents crazy. No plans to settle down but doing quite well for herself in the fashion industry."

Sam doesn't even blink, instead keeping his eyes on mine. "I'll look forward to meeting her at the wedding."

I smile widely, tipping my beer at him.

"I'm getting the vibe that Jewls is off-limits?"

A low rumble comes from Major's throat.

"Better move soon, man, or else someone will." Drake takes his life into his own hands by poking his brother, whose jaw ticks.

"We're just friends."

The sound of Elton John screeches through the air, followed by a loud cheer of approval. The women are shimmying and twirling, each with a full glass in one hand and the other arm in the air.

"Any idea how much Sangria your mom made?" Jim asks Major.

"Her list of ingredients was triple the usual, if that tells you anything."

"And we've been pouring heavy," Drake provides, with Sam nodding.

"An afternoon of margaritas followed by a night of highly potent Sangria, perfect." Doug sounds pleased. "Now it's time to talk."

"I agree, it's the first time we have you four together." Mark, Talon's father, is an easy-going man. Like Talon, he'd rather crack a joke for a good laugh, but his tone is stone serious.

My good mood vanishes and my body goes rigid. This is not the type of conversation where they razz me about Harley and buying the land to build her a house. This is leading somewhere darker. Somewhere we can't go.

The guys told their parents the same story when we left active duty for the Reserves. I glazed over the details with my mom in the few times we spoke, but I'd told Rich as much as I could. The explanation was simple and easy. Only the four of us, and a few highly specialized officials, know the details of our commitment.

Mark, Doug, Jim, and Rich all share the same serious expression, and I know their trek around the neighborhood wasn't to check out the surroundings, but to give them time to plot their attack. They teamed up, knowing we'd do the same.

"What do you want to talk about?" Ford asks his dad casually.

"Are you going back?" Doug goes straight to the point.

"We hope not."

"What the hell does that mean?"

Talon, Ford, and Major all look to me, silently communicating it's my choice how far to take this.

"It means there are only a few scenarios that would pull us back in. In the event that happens, it's temporary."

"Would you go back into the zone?"

"Depends on the situation."

"Any chance you can enlighten us on the scenarios?" Drake questions acidly.

Our silence is our answer.

"Didn't think so," he mumbles.

"So, you're not out of the woods yet?" Jim speaks up.

"Dad, we can't go into details. The probability is slim, but in the off-chance we get called up, whatever the reason, it'll fall directly under special operations," Major tries to explain.

"This makes no sense. The military has thousands of people who should be able to handle things like that."

"No one similar to us. Like I said, the possibility is slim. We made a deal with the Marines that is highly unusual."

"Why even get out then? Why not stay active?" Mark points the question directly to Talon.

"We left because it was time, Dad. You knew we were preparing for this for a while. If I remember, you and Mom were ecstatic."

"Yes! Because we thought your ass was out of the line of danger."

"Being in the Reserves was never any guarantee not to see action again."

"Bullshit. You're all talking around the core of the issue. What the hell is going on? We deserve to know." Any patience Mark was holding on to vanishes as his voice grows louder.

"Trust us," Talon states.

"The threat doesn't hang over our heads. You need to let it go. We're proud of our service, and in the event we're needed again, our asses will be there," Major says flatly.

"We're fucking proud of you, too, but how do you expect us to let it go?" Sam snaps.

"I'm marrying Harley and building her a house less than a mile from where we're standing. Next year, the four of us are transferring to the SWAT team. Who knows what comes after? On the off-chance we're needed back with MARSOC, we'll go. But I focus on the other things and that's how I let it go." I turn to check on Harley, who's now back-to-back with Jewls, shaking their asses to Bon Jovi. My pulse picks up when she tosses her head to the side and catches me watching. Her smile spans across the distance, and the pressure eases out of my body. "I can understand all your concern, but I promise you that nothing is jeopardizing my life with that woman."

"I'm not lying and saying I'm not concerned, but that promise is good enough for me." Rich tips his chin.

"Well, since my son is taking his sweet ass time finding himself a good woman, I guess I'll take Ace's word, too." Doug raises his glass my way and shoots Ford an amused grin.

The tension clears out of the air, and there are several murmurs of agreement.

"Now that shit is out of the way, can we discuss how the hell you guys got the reputation of Casanovas when you're the lamest group of idiots I've ever met? You wouldn't know how to be Casanovas with an instruction manual. Maybe Sam and I need to relocate and teach you lessons." Drake shakes his head in disappointment, and I know exactly the reason for the cackling earlier.

Harley and Jewls have been gabbing, and I don't give one shit.

"ACHILLES, PLEASE..." she begs, her back arching as she writhes against my mouth. I press down on her thighs to anchor her in place and continue to lick slowly, circling my tongue around her clit every few strokes.

I force myself to slow down, my gaze raking up her body. My cock throbs with need at the sight of her staring down at me with hooded, molten eyes filled with desire.

She's wet and hot against my lips, her legs quivering. I speed up, giving her what she needs, devouring her pussy with each lick. Her hand grips my head and she rocks her hips, her whimpers becoming frantic.

My thumb moves to caress her lightly as I tease her clit again. That's all it takes. She comes undone, crying out my name and tearing at the sheets. I lightly kiss over her a few times before kneeling and pulling her hips up. A knot coils in the pit of my stomach at the sight of her laid out before me. Her eyes shine with pleasure when they open and land on mine.

"Good morning," she breathes out hoarsely.

I bend over, trailing my lips up her stomach, around each nipple, and along the column of her throat until I'm at her ear. "Grab onto me."

Her arms circle my shoulders, and I go back on my calves, shifting my legs so they cocoon around her. My cock pulses between us and she grins, shifting upward, swiveling her hips until the tip slides partially inside her heat and it's my turn to groan. She balances on my shoulders, making circles and rolling motions with her hips, teasing me until every nerve ending in my body feels like a live electric current.

My hands clutch at her hips, urging her to slide, but she shakes her head, fisting the back of my neck, and dipping her mouth back to mine. I sweep my tongue along her parted lips before nipping the bottom one gently. "Sink down, give me all of you."

"In a minute. I've always wanted to play 'just the tip'." She swivels her lower body in a large arcing motion, the action shooting a searing heat through my bloodstream. Most of my blood rushes south, leaving me lightheaded. My dick throbs, swelling thicker by the second.

"Baby, if you wait, I'm afraid I'll split you in two." My balls ache to the point of pain with the need to drive into her hard.

"I'll take my chances." Her voice grows raspy, her grip on my neck tightening as she continues her torment. She lowers a few centimeters, welcoming me into her tight warmth, only to retreat upward again and again.

"God." Her thighs quiver at my waist, and she slides her pussy to the tip, rolling against my metal. "Feels so good."

My spine prickles and every muscle in my body contracts. Beads of sweat trail down my neck and back, and the familiar coiling begins at the base of my spine. If she keeps this up, I will fucking blow before I get all the way inside her.

She reads my body, and her lips twitch against mine. "I can see why you like the slow tease."

Her taunting spurs the possessive caveman inside. My heart thunders in my chest, and I know she feels that, too. "I'm about to lose my advantage, aren't I?'

"You want to tease me, baby, have at it. But know there's only so much a man can take."

Her hips roll twice more before her muscles loosen and she glides down, torturously slow, taking all of me. Her breath hitches a few times, a small whimper slipping out, and her eyes flutter closed as she stretches around me. I grind my teeth to stop from exploding.

It would be easy to throw her back, take control, and pound into her until she's screaming again. But I cling to the last ounce of willpower and run my hands up her back, pressing her fully against me. "You okay?"

Her thighs flex and her inner muscles spasm right as she moans. "Yes." Her eyes open lazily and shine bright blue, piercing into mine. "I'm pretty used to you by now."

That barbarian reemerges, and a throaty rumble vibrates in my chest. Heat and desire flicker in her gaze, and she skims the tip of her tongue around her lips. "I can feel the light twitch of you pulsing inside me."

"My body goes on hyper-drive every time I sink into you. It's like a drug that fuels an addiction." I twist my fingers in her hair, holding her in place as I thrust gently.

Her body responds instantly. I will never forget the feeling of sliding inside her for the first time. My lips trail from one corner of her lips to the other. She has a quick intake of breath, and her heartbeat speeds against my chest.

"I know," she whispers shyly. "I love you."

My movements speed, driving into her over and over. She tilts, taking me all with each stroke.

"Arch up, baby."

She arches back, and my lips close around her nipple, sucking hard. Her hips buck wildly, and her muscles clench harder, taking me even deeper.

"Oh my God, I can't… It's too much, too good."

My hand glides down her side, fitting between us where my thumb circles where we're connected

"Oh, fucking…" she pants loudly, her nails now digging into my shoulders.

My balls tighten and signal a warning of what's coming.

"Your pussy is fucking soaked. My piercing scraping against your walls, feeling you throb." I bite softly on her nipple and move to the other, repeating the action.

"You can't… need you…"

The desperation in her voice tells me she's almost there. "Come for me, baby."

She moans a no.

Her body is strung so tight it quakes.

The knot at the base of my spine unravels in one last warning. I stop massaging and flick over her clit until her walls clamp hard and she screams out my name. That's all it takes and I explode, my dick pulsating with each stream it shoots into her until spots fill my vision and I'm forced to release her nipple to catch my breath.

"Shit, Jesus. Fuck me." I hammer up into her a few more times, feeling the heat and slickness of our mixture. "Never fucking get enough."

"Hmmm," is all she replies, her head hitting my shoulder.

When our breathing evens out, I lay her back, keeping us connected. "Say it again."

"I love you."

"It never gets old."

"Over the years, I wanted to blurt it out, hoping it would make a difference, but I was terrified it would scare you even farther away. It wasn't worth the risk."

"I knew you would own me if I ever got my shot. Fate gave me a chance at something incredible and wrecked me in the best possible way."

"What if you become unwrecked?" Self-doubt creeps into her question, turning my gut.

"I'll never become unwrecked. You know the man I am, and even if I didn't always have a clear plan, everything I've done has been for us. You're getting everything you want in life."

A shiver rolls through her right before she begins to tremble, moisture building in her eyes. "I told you before, all I want is you."

"You have me, and I'm working on a way to make sure we can wake up every day like this." My hips buck, and the shine in her eyes sparkles with approval.

"Does this have anything to do with why you, the guys, and Mr. Whitman took off yesterday afternoon? Or the intense conversation around the fire pit last night?"

"The conversation was an attempt to keep me from pounding the twins."

"Your jealousy is outrageous. Sam and Drake are harmless flirts—"

"Don't fucking care." My fingers sift through her hair, rolling it into a thick knot. My mouth goes to her ear and trails along the column of her neck, down her shoulder, and across her collarbone. "But we aren't talking about them in this bed." Her skin heats against my lips and she drops her head, arching her chest and giving me exactly what I want. I skim my mouth over her hardened nipple at the same time I surge upward.

She gasps, rocking with me. "You can't still be hard."

"Not exactly, but I don't have to be for what I have planned."

Her eyes light with curiosity.

"You mentioned never playing 'just the tip'."

I brace over her and slide out, leaving only the crown in her slick folds. "Now I want to play."

"It's a little late, considering what we just did."

"It's never too late, especially when I demonstrate why I pierced my cock with you in mind."

Her eyes sparkle with approval. "I love demonstrations."

14

HARLEY

"Will you sit down?" Jewls complains, inspecting her freshly polished nails.

"I can't sit."

"Your nervous energy is exhausting me."

She's got a point. Since the guys took off on Friday morning, I've had a nervy knot taking over my stomach and tried everything to keep busy. Achilles warned me it was unlikely he'd be able to call, which turned out to be true. Tom mentioned he wanted to take the weekend off, and I jumped on the chance to pick up the bar shifts on Friday and Saturday night. Jewls offered to work with me last night, and we didn't get back to my place until after three a.m. I filled the rest of the time cleaning, grocery shopping, taking a double Pilates class yesterday with Ginger, and then spending two hours with Erik discussing marketing and promotions. Achilles was less than pleased with my decision to pick up the shifts, so it did not surprise me to see a flood of familiar faces at the bar, including my dad and Hal. I'd stayed busy, but it didn't keep me from checking my phone every chance I got.

"If you don't slow down, you will not have the energy left to bang your boyfriend when he gets back." She snorts at her own joke, falling back on my sofa.

"Don't be crass."

"Don't play stupid. It's the truth. Anyone around within ten miles can feel the sexual pheromones coming from you two."

"You're ridiculous."

"Nope, seriously. I'm pretty sure the moms made predictions last weekend when the first baby is coming. Amanda looked like she won the lottery."

"You're kidding!"

"Not at all. Ace rarely takes his eyes off you and doesn't hide what he's thinking. You two don't know the meaning of the word discretion."

"We're not talking about my sex life." I scrunch my nose and try to shake the idea of my parents knowing.

"Why not? At least you have one."

"Is that jealousy I detect?" I tease, running a dust cloth over the picture frames on my shelf for the second time.

"Yes! Who in the hell would have thought I'd be envious of your sex life? You'd never even been to third base and now you're a freaking minx."

"Minx? Should I take offense to that?"

"No, own it with a badge of honor. Many women would give anything to be in your position, and I'm one of them. Fully fucking worshipped by a hot man who thinks you hung the moon. Not to mention, he's a man in uniform."

"Are you saying you have a thing for men in uniform?"

"Don't make this about me."

"Why not? You and Major aren't fooling anyone with this little dance."

"It's not a dance."

"What is it then? He also doesn't hide the way he looks at you."

"A full roadblock. He's got me spinning in circles, and I'm not sure I like it. He may look at me like he's interested, but his actions say different. His choice is staying in the friend zone." There's an edge to her tone that sends a wave of familiarity through me.

I drop my cloth on the shelf and go to the sofa, poking her hip until she scoots enough to make room for me. "You know these men are intense, Jewls. They're not like the guys we've dated."

"I am aware, but I don't want to wait ten years."

Her words sting, but they weren't meant to intentionally hurt me. "I don't want you to wait ten years, either."

"I'm not interested in playing games, Jay, but I can't get him off my mind. It's not only his looks, but his complete personality. He's funny and smart, protective and loyal—all of it is a great package."

I bite the inside of my cheek to hide my surprise. Few people get to see this side of Major. It seems like Jewls has been holding out on some serious details about their friendship. I did not know their spark had even hit the 'talking' stage. Silently, I make a mental note to pay more attention to my best friend.

"Maybe he needs a nudge."

"Like what?"

"I don't know, but we'll think of something."

"Why do men have to be difficult?"

"Wish I knew."

"At least you had the whole virgin thing going for you."

"How did we jump back to me?"

"Because men think that's hot."

"Need I remind you that Achilles didn't know I was a virgin until I was practically humping him in a stripper bikini in his hot tub?"

Her face twists in a disgusted scowl, and she shudders dramatically. "I'm glad you didn't do it in the hot tub. That would have made last weekend awkward."

I press my lips together and hold in my laughter until it bursts out. She's right. It was awkward enough to sit with the moms in the Jacuzzi knowing that I'd rubbed up against Achilles like a dog in heat.

"And don't even get me started on your damn rug. Everyone who's seen any kind of porn knows a rug in front of a fireplace screams *bow-chicka-bow-bow.*"

My giggles grow louder and I fall into her, cackling until tears are dripping down my cheeks. "That's… not… why… we…"

"Oh, please, you're totally going to pound town on that thing."

"Stop!"

Her own laughter turns into snorts, and we're both gasping for air when the two-second tune for 'Bad Boys' sounds from the ottoman. I jump so fast, my butt slips, and I hit the floor, wincing as my ankle twists and my hip slams into the ground. Even in pain, my heart flips, knowing Achilles is finally in contact.

We have a late meeting but should drive in around ten.

I read the text with my giddy mood slipping. The first question that comes to mind is what kind of meeting would keep him four hours later than he expected? The second thought is, why so impersonal? I shake it off and quickly respond.

Okay, sweetie. I'll wait up for your call.

I think for a split second and add, *Missed you!* Before I can press send, the phone rings with his picture.

"Hey," I cringe when another pain shoots through my hip as I move my legs in front of me.

"What's wrong?" he barks out harshly.

"Well, hello to you, too." My attitude kicks in.

"Baby, I have about forty seconds here. What's that noise?"

"If you must know, I fell off my sofa trying to reach the phone. Jewls is laughing at me."

"Are you okay?"

"Of course. Are you okay?"

He blows out a loud sigh. "I'm fine, ready to get the fuck home and back to you."

It's embarrassing how quickly my girly side perks up with his statement. "You want me to come over when you get home?"

"I want your ass in our bed when I get home."

"Achilles, won't it be weird for me to be there when you're —"

I'm cut off by a loud yell in the background and a rustling on the line. "Baby, pack your bag and get to the house. The code on my private entrance will automatically unlock the door and disable the alarm."

"Maybe you could call me when you're close and I can meet you there."

"We all have the security monitoring on our phones, and I can re-alarm it when you get inside." He ignores my suggestion.

I don't scare easily, but the thought of being in his house by myself in the dark sends a chill over my skin. Even knowing they have a state-of-the-art security system doesn't help. Plus, it feels weird being there without him.

He picks up on my quiet anxiety. "Take Jewls with you so you're not alone. I'll be there as soon as possible. God, I fucking miss you."

Something's off in his voice. Exhaustion, irritation, worry… all of it mixing and sending a fresh chill slithering uneasily through me. "If you want me there, I'll be waiting."

"I want you there all the time, and we're talking about that soon. Not going through this shit again." There's a finality in his words. The emotions from his previous statement vanished. I don't have time to reply when the unmistakable sound of a siren blares in the background, followed by Major shouting his name.

"Gotta roll. Get over there soon so I can lock it down."

"I love you, too, babe. I miss you, too, babe," I say sarcastically to the dead air and drop the phone into my lap.

"Uh-oh, trouble in paradise?" Jewls tsks.

"That was possibly the oddest call I've ever had in my life. Ace is getting a lesson in phone etiquette when he gets home."

"That should be interesting."

I stare at my lap with our conversation rolling over in my brain. He did say he was ready to get back and wanted me in *our* bed.

"I can already tell where this is going. Get out of your head and let's get you packed." She heaves herself off the couch and yanks me up.

"What are you talking about?"

"I heard most of what was said and am not letting you internalize it to the point of ridiculousness."

"If you heard what he said, then you know he was bossy, short, and direct enough to be on the verge of demanding."

"Clue in, Jay, the man sends people to observe when you work a night shift at a low-key bar. He's possessive, protective, and borderline Neanderthal. Of course, he was bossy. Think about where he is. Not playing golf with the guys. He's at an active drill weekend with the Marines. He had something to say, said it, and moved on. You need to do the same."

She drags me into my room, waving her finger in a circular motion for me to '*get moving*'. It doesn't take long for me to pack the few items I need and for her to gather her bag from last night.

"I'm totally down for hanging at the Club tonight."

A COOL BREEZE hits my skin before strong arms lift me as I nuzzle closer. My eyes feel like lead, but I pry them open and find Achilles staring at me. "You're home."

"Finally."

"What time is it?"

"A lot later than I wanted. Go back to sleep."

"What about Jewls?"

"Major's got her. He'll get her to a bed."

"I hope it's his bed. She'll love that."

One side of his lip curls into a half-grin, and his eyes flick over my shoulder. I don't have to turn to know Major's behind us.

"We fell asleep watching a movie," I explain unnecessarily.

"I got that."

"We made you guys quesadillas."

"We found them."

"Is everyone here?"

"Yes."

"Good, I'll sleep better now."

I inhale deep, and the scent of his soap fills my nose. "You showered without me."

"I was filthy."

"But we always shower together."

"I'll take another one in the morning."

"That's good because I love it when we—" His mouth closes over mine, shutting me up.

"We have an audience," he whispers to my lips.

The soft chuckles fade away as we move, and I'm too tired to be embarrassed. The feel of his soft sheets and warm body curling into mine puts me right back to sleep.

Sometime later, I wake to sweat trickling down my neck and back.

Achilles' arms are like bands of steel, and his thigh is thrown over mine, cocooning me so close his body heat is blistering into me. His heart is racing, but his breaths are shallow and steady against my throat. I wiggle slightly, trying to pry loose and get one arm free enough to toss the covers to the side. The cool air hits my damp skin, and an uncontrollable shiver travels through my body.

"Am I suffocating you?" His voice is deep and drowsy.

"No." *YES!!!*

"Liar." He unlatches his grip and gives me a few inches of space.

"Is everything okay?" I find his hand in the dark. "You're burning up."

"My adrenaline crashed. It was a long weekend."

"Do you want to talk about it?"

"Not much to say except, mentally and physically, my body went through the wringer."

"Is that normal?"

"Sometimes, but never this bad."

He doesn't have to say it for me to understand. "You worried about me."

"I worried about you," he agrees.

"Because of Tom's?"

He doesn't answer, but his hand clasps mine tighter.

"You can tell me," I urge him gently.

"Last time I told you I didn't like you working there, it didn't go well."

"Last time you tried to dictate my life, blew off the grid, and I didn't know you loved me. Let's try to have the conversation again."

He rolls to his back, bringing my hand to his mouth and running his lips across my knuckles. "It wasn't only Tom's, even though I fucking despise you getting off work at three o'clock in the morning on the weekend shift. Me being away didn't help that."

This does not surprise me because he told me before he left, so I wait for what's coming. "I want you here all the time but know that's impossible. For my sanity, I'm asking you to stay here next time I have a drill weekend."

"Why?"

"Because this place is secure and safe. One of us gets an alert if even a raccoon crosses the motion detectors. Knowing you are locked up tight at night in our bed gives me peace of mind."

I don't remind him I've lived alone for years and never had an incident, nor do I point out that he's been gone for a long time and I can take care of myself. "Okay, but the guys have to agree."

"Already done."

"Then I'll stay here next time. To me, it's overkill because my place is safe, but we'll compromise. You won't lose your mind when I work late, and I'll come back here."

His chest vibrates with a rumble, but he doesn't comment.

"Compromise, Ace. I'm not giving up my job at Tom's."

"Not yet."

"Never if you don't lose the attitude. I'll be his longest-running employee."

He grins against the back of my hand, and I scoot closer, laying my head on his shoulder. "I'll have to get your drill schedule in my calendar in order to make sure Jewls is available to be my weekend buddy. This place is kinda scary to be here alone."

"That can be arranged, but babe, I got to warn you. When we walked in tonight, we got less than three minutes of whatever shit you girls were watching, and Ford is having the channel removed."

"He can't! It's the Hallmark channel in October! Next month is the countdown to Christmas, and there are forty new movies airing."

"You'll find something else to do." I pick up on a hint of insinuation, right before he hauls me on top and shifts so I can feel every hard inch of him. "Since you're awake, why don't you finish telling me more about what you love when we shower?"

A different heat creeps up my cheeks, and I'm glad it's dark. Achilles is bigger, strong, and much more experienced than me. Outside of a few stolen moments, he's always taken control when we make love. He's an expert at commanding my body. Only twice have I seen him on the verge of losing his cool, and somehow, he always reels it in, scared he's going to hurt me. I've willingly given in to him, knowing he needs it. But this morning, I want to give him what he gives me and feel the ecstasy of anticipation.

I unlink our hands and brace on his chest, rocking up to find his mouth and sweep my lips across his. "Usually, it starts with you carrying me into the bathroom, wrapped around you. When you set me on my feet, your eyes always roam over me with a look I can't describe."

My lips move to the column of his throat, traveling down until they're right over his pec muscle. The tip of my tongue licks around his nipple, then traces the tattoos I've memorized.

"You hold me close if the water is too cold until it is just right."

I continue to move lower, covering every inch of his torso with my mouth.

"I love it when you place me under the spray of water, running your hands through my hair, kissing me gently until we're both soaked."

My legs slide to the side of his thighs, and I grind over his cock before continuing my descent and leaning back on my knees.

"I love it when you insist on lathering every inch of my skin using your hands." I mimic the action by skimming my hands across his chest and down his torso, feeling the ripple of his muscles flex under my palms.

My lips finally reach the tip of his crown, closing over it. The first taste of him is incredible. His skin is smooth and hot, firm and silky… his length pulsing at my touch. I whimper, running my tongue up and down the length, gently kissing the flesh.

"Baby, get your ass back up here," he demands harshly.

I shake my head and make a 'Nuh-uh' sound, sucking him slowly in, then circling with my tongue. His hands go to my shoulders, pressuring me to come to him, but I resist, continuing with my story. "You watch me wash my hair, still touching me, not taking your eyes off. So intimate and personal, knowing I belong to you."

"Fuck me," he hisses, his hands gone as he twists and the lamp clicks on. My eyes adjust quickly, and when I raise them up, a flood of craving and lust races through my veins. He's staring at me with a savage hunger, his face set in a way I know too well. He's on that verge, and the look intensifies when I suck him deeper, my throat opening to allow his length as far as it will go.

I say no more, dropping my eyes and concentrating on getting all of him. Before Achilles, my limited experience with make-out sessions gave me an idea of the guy's size. None of that comes close to comparing. He's exactly what I'd imagine with a man of his stature—long, thick, and the skin like silky satin on my tongue.

My knees press into the mattress, and I shift, sliding a hand between us to lightly caress his balls before gripping the base. His hips jerk and twist, a low rumble filling the room. The sound sets something off inside—something primal and illuminating. The need to be in control. I move quicker, worshipping him as he's done to me countless times. I angle to the side and swirl my tongue around his hot flesh, gliding through the tip.

"Jesus… fuck…" he draws out, swelling thicker.

I peer up and instantly feel my skin scorching. He's still watching me. His eyes are smoldering with glittery specks of shimmering gold. His chest is rising quickly, his muscles rippled and strained.

My nipples tingle, my stomach clenches, and my knees threaten to buckle at the electric current between us. I've wanted nothing so much in my life as I want this right now. The power of knowing he's at my mercy drives me harder. I break the stare, close my mouth once more, hollow my cheeks as much as possible, and swallow him until he hits the back of my throat. It's easy to find a rhythm and take cues from the way he responds.

The memory of the other morning comes to mind, the way he devoured me mercilessly. Never slowing until I was begging.

Now's my turn. I suck deep and then slide my tongue up his hard length to twirl it around his piercing. He jerks and growls out, "Harley, baby, give me your pussy."

I shake my head, swallowing him again and picking up speed. His hand threads through my hair, his hips surging up.

"Going to fucking blow. Feels goddamn good."

I savor everything about this. His taste, the velvety smooth flesh, the trembling against my lips.

When I think he may be close, I press my fingers gently into the tender flesh under his balls and feel them tighten.

His body tenses and hips thrust upward twice. I barely feel the first jet of his release before he knifes up and I'm flying backward, his arms circling me.

"Holy motherfucking shit," he roars, his chest heaving as he cradles me close. Warmth seeps through my shirt, his cock pulsating.

I'm too stunned to speak, shocked at how fast he moved. His face goes to my shoulder, and his teeth graze my collarbone, nipping along the tendon at my neck.

"Achilles?"

"Quiet, Harley," he clips starkly.

The electrifying joy from a few minutes ago dies. My heart jumps at the anger in his tone. I have no choice but to hold tight until his breathing slows.

"Tell me that was only for me."

Confusion clouds my brain, and I try to wiggle free. It's useless, especially when he cups my chin, bringing my face to his. My stomach twists and plummets at the ferocity of his expression.

"Please, tell me that was mine," he repeats somberly.

His statement cuts through my brain haze, and I want to beat him and kiss him at the same time. He knows he's the only man I've ever been with, but it never occurred to me he didn't know the extent of my inexperience.

"That was yours."

"Good answer, baby. Because the thought of you on your knees for anyone else makes me insane."

I suck in a deep breath, count to five, then blow it out to stop from screaming my head off. "It may be the last time *you* ever see me on my knees if you don't stop being a barbarian."

All anger vanishes, and his lips curl into a sly grin. "You give great fucking head. Two minutes and I was ready to blow."

My sense of jealousy roars in my blood, and I squirm to get free—unsuccessfully. "I don't even want to know how many women you can compare—"

"None," he cuts me off, sweeping his mouth over mine.

My body jerks and all the air seeps out of my lungs. "Really?"

"Never."

"How is that possible?"

"I waited for you."

"How can you say that? You weren't a virgin our first time."

"No, I wasn't a virgin."

"But you've never had a blow job?"

"Until a few minutes ago, I'd never had a blow job."

"I can't believe that."

"Because of you."

"Me? That makes little sense."

He lets out a breath, his beautiful face filling with something I can't read.

"Tell me," I breathe out in awe.

"Senior year of high school, Dana Meers' party. She'd been working me all night, flirting her ass off, shooting me looks that said it all. I went to take a leak and she caught me from behind, yanking me into what I guessed was her brother's room. In less than a second, she was all over me, grinding herself on my dick. She dropped to her knees, pulled my cock out, and then I heard your voice. You were with some chick in the hall, and you were looking for me. My name on your lips filled my brain, and all I could see below me was your gorgeous face. I couldn't let her suck my cock. It was too intimate. I stood her up, righted my clothes, and told her it wasn't happening. I went to find you."

A nasty taste fills my mouth at the memory. "She told everyone you slept together."

"She wanted to save face, and I didn't care to embarrass her further."

"You took me to prom two weeks later."

"I did. Figured that sent a message."

"That explains why Dana Meers hated me from that night on."

"It makes me the worst kind of asshole, but Dana's not the only one. I've had my fair share of women, but I was always removed. That piece of intimacy was yours."

My throat closes as his words settle over me. I'm thrilled and sad at the same time. I try not to think of the times he pushed me away, but this is another reminder of all the years we lost. He picks up on my change of mood, his arm slanting across my back to press me close.

"You'll always have that, Harley."

I barely nod, dropping my gaze.

He tilts my chin, ducking into my line of sight. "Right, more proof

I'm an asshole. Never had sex without a condom, sometimes doubling up until you. Never made love to a woman in my life until you. Never understood the appeal of eating pussy until that first taste of you. Now I crave your taste on my tongue. Tits and ass never caught my attention. The picture of you bending over that bar in Jewls' tight shirt changed that. You don't even have to be near, and my dick gets hard thinking about the way your body fits to mine. That fucking scrap of material you wore the first weekend here… fuck that. Full-on need to jack my shit to get beyond it."

"So, you like sex with me."

"It's more than sex. We've fucked hard, baby, but each time I come inside you, I slow it down, savoring what a lucky fucking bastard I am. Waited a lifetime to have this, and I'm not stupid enough to miss it."

My eyes pop wide, understanding washing over me. He does that, every time. We can be wild, but in the end, he always turns gentle. "I love that."

"All that hair, tits, ass, those legs wrapped around my waist as I pound into you. Never want to come, want it to last forever. See you fly apart as many times as possible. Then you clench around me, pulling me in, and I know I'm the only man that will ever get this. It's a fucking gift. Hopefully, you understand that when you suck my cock into your mouth, no woman will ever have that from me."

A weird sense of empowerment comes over me, and I lean in to pull his bottom lip through my teeth. "That's a lot of pressure. You'll never know if I'm good."

"I'm fucking lucky you're an absolute natural."

My skin blushes at the compliment. It's one thing to be in the heat of the moment, but things didn't go exactly as planned. "Thanks," I murmur.

"You do not know how hot it was—"

"Stop." I try to look away but I'm trapped.

"Don't be embarrassed."

"You ripped me off right as things were getting good. Then you acted like an insane lunatic."

"Let's say I temporarily lost my mind with jealousy. Baby, you worked me like a pro. Looking down and watching you swallow my cock was one of the sexiest things I've ever seen. Dreams came true."

That was sweet, but I'm still shy. "Can we not do a play-by-play?"

"Sure, the mental image is enough to keep me hard as a rock." He's full out smiling now—amused, happy, playful. His legs go out from behind me, swinging over the bed as he stands, easily adjusting me. "Since we're both dirty, it's time for a shower."

15

ACE

I TAKE the corner to our street, slowing my pace to a jog and checking the time. The southern rock music blaring in my ears is interrupted with the familiar tone notifying me someone's at our door. I don't recognize the newer model Yukon in the driveway, but the form of the man waiting on the porch is unmistakable.

He turns, watching me running his way. I use the minute to take him in. One thing to say is sobriety has been good to my dad. When he limped away from the bottle, he turned his life around and got healthy and fit.

"Dad, what are you doing here?" I grab the towel on the rail and wipe my face.

"Jesus, Ace, look at you."

"I'm aware of what I look like," I growl the response under his judging eyes that are gaping at my tattoos with disapproval.

His chin juts out, and his expression changes. "That's not what I meant. You're jacked, like seriously built. How much time do you spend a day working out?"

The irritation slides away, and I hook the towel around my neck. "You saw me a few months ago. Nothing has changed."

"I haven't seen you without a shirt. The clothes cover it up. Knew you had a few tattoos, but not to this extent. Nice ink."

"Thanks, but again, what are you doing here?"

"Can we talk?"

"About what?"

"It would be nice to take this inside."

The last thing I want to do is have a chat with my estranged father, but I punch in my code to the door and motion for him to follow me.

He whistles loud, undoubtedly impressed with the house. "This place… wow."

"You like my house, my body, and my tats. Now what do we need to talk about?"

He stops looking around, his gaze locking with mine with the familiar regret staring back. Shit, here we fucking go.

"Achilles, I'm sorry."

"We're past this."

"Are we?"

"Yeah, seeing as I've accepted your apology the last nine years."

"It doesn't seem like you accept it when you're keeping this massive wedge between us."

"There's no wedge."

"You've been back in Nashville quite a while and seen your mother twice. You graduated from the Police Academy without as much as notifying us. I can understand you having resentment toward me, but this is killing Sandy. She'll do anything to have you back in her life. Please stop making her pay for my mistakes."

Guilt slams into me full force. "I'm not making her pay for anything."

"Then why won't you at least take your mother's calls?"

"We text." It's a stupid comeback, but it's the truth.

"You're not a parent, but when you are, you'll understand. I'll stay away if it means you'll give your mom the time of day."

Dad was a drunk. A stupid, sloppy drunk unable to beat back the disease. And I've held it against him even when others could forgive.

"I'm a different man and wish you would give me a chance to prove it." There's desperation in his voice that stirs deep inside.

"I almost lost everything by stepping in that fight to help you out."

"I'll live with that on my soul forever."

"Could have gone to juvie, or worse. Fucked up my chance at a future. If it wasn't for Rich, I don't know what would have happened. Where I'd be right now." Acid bleeds into my words.

"Fucking finally."

"What?"

"Fucking finally, you're ready to hash it out. All these years, you've kept the rage and bitterness inside. I've been waiting... no, I've been praying for this chance since the day I went to rehab."

"You don't know what rage is."

"Then tell me." He throws his arms wide to his sides. "Unleash that Achilles temper. Give it to me, I can take it. I deserve it. Shit, I welcome the anger just to be in the same room with you."

"I'm not unleashing."

"Respect."

"What about respect?"

"That respect you carry is one of many badges of honor. Even before the military, you knew the meaning of respect."

"Kind of an odd time to notice that."

"You won't unleash on me out of respect. And, in turn, we can't get past it until you let it all out. Right now, forget I'm your old man—unload the hate and anger."

Years of pent-up anger roll through my head, my body stringing tight. Dad's look is a mix of expectation and fear. He's prepared for the worst. I prop my hands on my hips and glance to the side.

My eyes instantly zero in on the sports bottle on the counter filled with pink liquid. Harley's energy drink. I inhale, smelling the faint scent of her perfume. I check my phone, and there are no notifications from my alarm app showing how she got in.

I shelve that for later; knowing she's close wipes out the anger. Her face flashes in my mind. How I avoided her, letting my stubborn streak win out. Years lost with her suffering at the result of my actions. No games, no drawn-out resentment, no time wasted. She forgave me. Let it all go. Accepted me as I am.

Something inside me shifts, and a sense of peace settles. All the things I've wanted to say to him no longer seem relevant. It's over. I'm my own man with my future planned out. A future that includes the woman down the hall undoubtedly working her way to a nervous breakdown.

I look back, and he's clearly preparing for the worst. "Since the day I enlisted and hit the road to boot camp, I've been around people who have courage. So much fucking courage it's a part of their soul. I'd like to be half the person some of my brothers are. Especially the ones who didn't make it home."

He drops his eyes to the floor, but not before I catch the glistening. Then I hear a tiny whimper from the back of the hall.

It's time to give it to him straight and move on. "You were sick with a disease. I hope like hell I never know what that feels like, but at the end of the day, you got help. That takes a special kind of courage. Courage is something I respect more than anything. I've spent years trying to work my resentment out of my system. And you're right, I may have accepted your apology, but there was a deep-rooted animosity that lingered. Dad, I'm not unloading on you. That's not the answer and won't solve anything. I'm forgiving you and wiping the slate."

The word *slate* is barely out of my mouth when he's in my face, yanking me into a hug. I can't remember the last time we did this. Twelve years ago? Fifteen? It's been a firm handshake between us for as long as I can remember.

"Goddamn, son, you don't know how long I've waited to hear that. Fucking proud of you."

I may be a grown man, built solid and mentally tough, but the feel of his arms tightening and hearing his statement touches deep inside.

There's another whimper, this time louder, and he releases me, glancing down the hall. "You have a dog back there?"

A half- laugh escapes while I shake my head. "Nah, more like a five-foot-five, auburn-haired firecracker."

His eyebrows shoot up. "Harley is here?"

"Apparently. Give me a second, be right back."

I head down the hall, catching a flash of white before it disappears into my room. When I hit the door, Harley's standing in front of my fireplace with tears streaming down her cheeks.

My gut screws uncomfortably at the sight. As long as I've known her, I've only witnessed her crying a handful of times.

When I left for boot camp.

When her grandfather died.

When she discovered why I avoided her for those years.

Now she's crying for me.

"Baby, why the tears?"

"Do you really forgive him?" she asks hoarsely.

"I do."

For the second time in a matter of minutes, I'm engulfed in a tight embrace. She hoists herself up, wrapping her legs around me. Her hands cup my jaw and she peppers my face with kisses.

"I'm proud of you too, Achilles. You're amazing."

"Not sure about that."

"Seriously, letting it go must be a relief. Carrying that kind of weight all this time isn't healthy."

"I didn't think about it much."

She pulls back, her eyes scrunched in disbelief. "You didn't?"

"Not really. It was what it was."

"But today you forgave him?"

"Seeing as you heard everything, I meant what I said about him getting help. That takes courage. I've always felt that way, but today it was time to tell him."

"I didn't mean to eavesdrop, but I was in the kitchen when he rang the bell. Then I heard you approach him on the porch. When y'all came inside, I stayed close in case it got out of hand."

"Appreciate you having my back, but it wasn't getting out of hand."

"Another reason you're outstanding." She plants a hard quick kiss on my lips, then loosens her hold. "I should get dressed to go say hello."

I don't let go, hitching her up and sliding my hands to her ass, feeling the bare skin under the oversized shirt. "Let's talk about what you're doing here."

"I knew you were running, so I came over to surprise you. With our work schedules, we haven't seen each other in days."

"Baby, I see you every night at Tom's before my shift."

"You watch me run around during the rush and settle for bits and pieces of conversation between slinging drinks. That's not seeing each other."

My cock stirs, knowing exactly where she's going with this. "You telling me my dad showing up cock-blocked me from a booty call?"

Her eyes pop, and she slaps her hand over my mouth. "Shhh! He'll hear you!"

"He won't hear me, babe, but he'll clue in when I tell him reunion time is over. My woman wants to get laid," I mutter to her palm.

"Stop!" The splotches flame pink. "It's not a booty call. I set up to work here so we could have the day together."

I glance over her shoulder and spot her laptop and a stack of folders on the bed. "How'd you expect me to fuck you when your office is on the bed?"

"Oh my God, can you stop?"

"You're in my arms, wearing nothing but my shirt. I haven't had you alone in four days. If it wasn't for my dad, that laptop would have been a casualty."

Her eyes flare, sparkling in a crystal glimmer. "Noted, next time I plan a surprise mission, I'll place my things in a safer spot."

"Why don't you do that now and I'll get rid of him?"

"No! He knows I'm here, and it's rude not to go talk to him."

"Pretty sure his interruption is what's rude. I could be inside you right now."

She chews on her bottom lip, scanning over my face. "Good point. But I still need to say hello. This is an important occasion."

"Your idea of important and mine are vastly different." I thrust up to prove my point.

"Achilles." She tries to sound strong, but there's a wispiness in her tone.

"As much as I want to back you into the wall, there's no way I can fuck you like I want with him waiting in the living room. Get dressed, we'll go speak to him, and then when he's gone, you'll get your chance to carry out your booty call."

"Quit saying that or your day of surprises will take a drastic turn."

My hand slides lower, my fingers skimming along the folds of her pussy. Her breath hitches and thighs clutch tighter. "Look forward to what you have planned."

I lean in, crashing my lips to hers. She whimpers low when my tongue sweeps around her mouth. That sound, her taste, the warmth of her wrapped around me, has my dick hard as steel and throbbing. I tear myself away, easing her to her feet.

"This is not fair. I'm supposed to be seducing you."

"I'm about four seconds away from kicking him out. Get dressed or I can't be held responsible for what happens next."

She shuffles away, digging in her bag on my dresser and rushing into the bathroom. My cock is no longer an issue as I stare at the bag. She comes out dressed in frayed jean shorts with my shirt tucked in the front, hanging low in the back.

The familiar sense of possessiveness rears up. Before I can say anything, she takes my hand and pulls me along.

Dad's in the kitchen, staring into the back yard. When he hears us, his head swings our way, his gaze dropping to our joined hands, and it's impossible to miss the warmth in his smile.

"Harley, sweetheart, you are a vision."

She releases my hand and moves to his outstretched arms. "Hey, Mr. Kingston."

"Pete, honey. Call me Pete."

"Okay, Pete. How are you?" She braces, holding on to his forearms and giving him her blinding smile.

"I'm great. Didn't know you were living here."

"I'm not." She shakes her head rapidly, stepping out of his embrace. "I parked around back. Achilles has a private entrance to his room. My job allows me to work remotely, and today I set up my office here."

The timing sucks, but I don't hold back what's on my mind. "The dresser has three empty drawers. You need more, I'll go through and clean out. I can rearrange the closet any way you want to fit your things."

She jolts, her eyes crinkling. "Pardon?"

"I hate your bag." I reach out and tug her back to me.

"You hate my bag?"

"I hate what it stands for. You shouldn't have to pack your things to come here. I want you to have a stash of things here, so you always have what you need. Not only the soaps and shampoos. I want you to walk in my door and know you have everything here without packing a fucking bag."

"I-I… ummm, packing doesn't bother me. I never know what I'm in the mood for. And three empty drawers and a portion of your closet is more than a stash."

"The more the better."

"We'll talk about this later."

"Nothing to talk about."

"Now is not the time. We'll discuss it when your dad isn't here to see me lose my mind at your absurdity."

"Doesn't seem absurd to me," Dad pitches his support.

Her eyes flame, swinging between us. "Shacking up with my boyfriend in a house of four bachelors is not sane!"

"Three bachelors. As you mentioned, I'm spoken for," I correct her and fight my grin when her nails dig into my side.

"It's going to be four if you don't shut down this ridiculous, and very private, conversation."

"Is this the first time you've mentioned it?" Dad asks me, ignoring her.

"Yes."

"Is she close to blowing up?"

"Quite possibly."

"Maybe you should finesse it better, explain the benefits."

"With my shifts, we have three nights a week together. I'd hope she understands the benefits."

"Hello! I'm right here, hearing everything you're saying. And I don't need finessing. Achilles has a way of telling instead of asking."

At the mention of my name, his chin jerks. "She still calls you Achilles?"

"The only person in this world who does. And honestly, the only person I want to."

The intensity of her nails ease, and her hands flatten on my chest. "Don't try to sweeten your way out of this."

"Either you do it, or I'll go over and load a suitcase."

"You can't get into my apartment. I have a security system."

I cock an eyebrow, not hiding my grin anymore. "I'm a cop and a Marine. I have my ways."

"I can skate out of work tomorrow if you need help," Dad adds, and that's what pushes her to the edge.

Her hands fly in the air, and she drops her head back, screaming at the ceiling. "MEN!"

Dad chuckles. I take the opportunity to run my lips along the column of her neck. Her head pops back up, and she shoots me an evil smirk before twisting to Dad.

"Don't—" is barely out of my mouth before she intercedes.

"Pete, we'd love if you'd stay and join us for a late breakfast."

His smug grin is his answer. Fucker is enjoying the hell out of this.

THE HARD SLAM of the locker ricochets around the room, and a few veteran cops turn my way, giving me 'the look' that they've been in my shoes.

"What did that locker do to you?"

I spear Ford with a hard glare, not in the mood for his shit. He ignores it, slinging his gym bag across his chest and shutting his own locker.

"You were there. She needs to get out and leave his ass."

"I'll gladly take drunk and disorderly and barroom brawls over a domestic. At least D&D's get the sober tank and usually have remorse when they dry out."

"We need to talk to her again. Let's swing by on our way home."

"No," he deadpans, his expression hard.

"No?"

"No, Ace. There are countless reasons that's a bad idea."

"Did you miss the marks on her arms? They'll be bruises by now."

"I didn't fucking miss them, nor the already fading bruises on her legs. But we can't make her press charges. Shit, Ace, it was the neighbors who called it in. That woman isn't in the right headspace."

"She's being beaten by that low-life motherfucker."

"Yeah, she is. And that's exactly what he is—a motherfucker. But she has to be the one to take action. Unless we catch him in the act, or she presses charges, we're at an impasse."

"It fucking blows."

Hal walks up, a file in his hand, his eyes angry. "Do I need to remind you two of protocol?"

"Nope," Ford affirms.

I blow out an angry breath as my answer.

"Good, because regardless of being badass soldiers who have experienced more action on the ground than most the cops in this department, you're rookies."

Something in the way he says it puts my instincts on alert. "Rookies are still cops."

"Yes, but there's a difference. You're my rookie, under my guidance, and I won't stand for skating lines."

"Jesus, Hal. A woman's being beaten; some lines need to be skated."

He casts a glance over his shoulder to check if we are alone. The other guys are ghosts.

"You bet your ass lines need to be skated." His voice goes low and acidic. "This wasn't an isolated event. One look and it's obvious that man married up. Seen too many like him in my career. Wealthy, spoiled, and thinks his shit doesn't stink. Bad combination. Don't know how he landed her. My guess is he used money and influence enough to sway her, then put that rock on her finger the first chance he got. Punk ass like that needs to be taught a lesson."

"That sounds more like a protocol I'm familiar with." Ford rocks back on his heels.

"What are you suggesting?" I cross my arms, scanning Hal's face.

"Officially, all paperwork is processing. I signed off that it was a false alarm domestic and the neighbor misunderstood the shouting. Unofficially, I have a new file with that woman's name on it." He waves the folder.

For the first time since we received the call-out at midnight, the tension in my shoulders loosens. "What ya got?"

"Not much yet. The good news is her medical file is clean. Except for a nasty case of pneumonia last year that put her in the hospital, there've been no reports of abuse."

"That doesn't mean dick."

"No, it doesn't. But interestingly, there also isn't a record of her marriage, either. My gut tells me we're dealing with a narcissistic SOB that's put a phony symbol on her for control."

"What can we do?"

"Nothing."

I open my mouth to argue, but he points the corner of the file my way. "Nothing yet. Seen women like her before, and she is mortified. If the abuse has just begun, she may process and, in her own way, figure out how to leave the asshole. But I'll be digging more into this guy."

"Keep us updated," Ford requests.

"Yeah, you're not officially under my guidance, but I'll keep you in the loop."

Ford's phone chimes, and his eyes slice my way. The little tension that seeped away ricochets back up my spine. I grab my bag from the bench, ready to move.

"Thanks, Hal. Catch ya on Thursday."

"Actually, you'll see me tomorrow night. Amanda's been on the line, calling all the wives. Tomorrow night, ladies' night at Tom's. Reba arranged for her parents to take the kids, which means she plans to blow it out. Last time my wife blew it out proved in my favor. My ass will be at Tom's with Rich and the other men watching the game while the women do whatever they do."

I can't help my lip twitch, knowing exactly how a drunk Reba 'proved in his favor'. Jewls and Harley finally wore down Tom on the ladies' night concept, and tomorrow is the official kick-off. Harley's been promoting like crazy.

"See you then. We need to go," Ford breaks in abruptly.

I flick a hand and follow Ford to his truck, not speaking until we're on the road. "What's up?"

"Nothing good. Talon got a message from Willie. He's calling in thirty."

At the name Willie, my entire body strings solid. All thoughts of the past shift disappear.

Willie is one of our guys. Well, technically, he was our Lieutenant Colonel. And is currently our connection to MARSOC. When we all left, he was the one who came to us with a proposition. A proposition we agreed to without a second thought. No questions, no hesitancy, no delays. Department of Defense, the Secretary of the Navy, and who-the-fuck-ever step in to take care of the details, and we do the mission.

So, him calling in thirty means something is up. Something that requires briefing the four of us.

"Fuck." I scrub a hand down my face.

"Exactly."

There's no time to question further when my phone rings with Harley's morning call. "Baby—"

"You're upset."

"I'm fine. Rough night, but it's over."

"Did you get shot at, chased, threatened, or hit on?"

I chuckle lightly at the last part. "None of the above."

"Just bad shit?"

"Bad shit," I confirm.

"Do you need me?"

The answer is yes, but she has to work, and even though she can set up in the space in my room, there's Willie's call to deal with.

"I always need you, but I'm good. Got a few things to handle, then gonna crash for hours."

"You're not heading to the gym?"

"Running then bringing you lunch."

"Right… soooo…" she trails off in a way that rouses my already hyper-alert mind. "My mom asked me to lunch."

"Cool, hang with her. I'll be over around six to drive you to Tom's. You're at my place tonight."

"Well, that's not all," she stalls.

"Harley, what's up?"

"We're solid, right? Like super solid, more than the iceberg that sunk the Titanic, volcano rock, and the price of the fall collection of Louboutins?"

I don't even know what the fuck that is.

"Baby, get to the point. I don't even know what a Louboutin spring collection is."

"Fall collection! And it's fabulous with a price tag that rivals anything else. They don't budge on their pricing. It's *solid.*"

Well, shit, I'll need to learn about this lo-bu-ton and find out what she wants in this collection. "We're more solid than that."

She exhales loudly. "Okay, your mom *calledmymomandsetupadatefor-lunchtodaybecauseshe'sgoinginsanewithouthearingfromyou.*"

I hear her but swallow hard again, attempting to drive down my irritation. "What the fuck?"

"My mom…" she explains, and I cut her off.

"I get it, but what the fuck? Mom knows better than that."

"She says you're dragging your feet on planning a lunch."

"She's playing dirty trying to force my hand on this."

"Didn't you talk to her last week?"

"Through text. She asked me again to meet up, and I told her we'd plan something."

"And then you didn't follow through."

"It's only been a week."

"Sweetie," her tone is gentle, and I know what she's about to say before she says it. "You've been back in town a lot longer than a week. She's your mom. She is curious about your life. And she knows you've made amends with Pete, so she's impatient."

"Christ," I gripe.

"I'll cancel."

"No, keep the plans, and I'll be there."

"You will? Don't you need to sleep?"

"I'll pick you up at eleven-thirty. Choose a place that serves more than salads."

"Okay, I'll see you in a few hours. Love you."

I grunt my response before disconnecting. "Lunch with my fucking mom today."

"Picked up on that. Cunning play. First your dad waylays you; now your mom's sneak attack on Harley."

"My family is a pain in the ass."

He lets out an exaggerated laugh, his amusement grating on my nerves.

"They better not make this a fucking habit."

"You don't have to tell me about pains in the ass. Remember, I have two sisters—that adds to four people always wanting to know my business."

I grunt again, this time less irritated. Ford's sisters are exactly like little mother hens. Always in his business.

"Ace, you forgave them, right?"

"There wasn't anything to forgive, but essentially, yes, I let them know it was all good."

"You are back in the same town, with a new career and a new woman. A woman they adore. Be prepared for more ambushes in your future."

"Fuck. Between Harley working two jobs and me working mostly nights, now I have to add my parents in the mix?"

"Looks like it."

"I'm taking her away. As soon as we get time off, we're off the grid."

"You have that wing of the house to yourself, and you already demanded she practically move in."

"A few drawers and closet space doesn't mean she's moved in."

"Just saying, you may want to save that cash for the house. When you do finally tell her, depending on if she kicks your ass, she's likely to go wild."

He drives through the neighborhood and pulls into his regular spot on the outside of the other three trucks.

I hop out, looking across the back, and seeing the piece of land I'm buying in the distance. All four of us purchased a lot from Ford's dad when he offered. I'm the only one who's actually thinking about building soon.

The thought flees when the back door opens and Major's steely expression brings me back to the dark cloud hanging.

The three of us go upstairs to the media room where Talon has his computer hooked up to the console. His usually relaxed disposition is gone.

No whistling. No jokes. No easy-going attitude.

We don't wait long until his phone chimes, and he types in a code on his computer, the TV screen springing to life. Willie comes into view, looking every bit the soldier and one-hundred-percent the badass I remember.

"Men."

"Miss us already?" Ford's attempt at the joke comes out dry.

"Whitman, wish like hell this was a social call. We got a situation brewing."

"Figured that with the cryptic message," Talon mutters.

"Chatters heating about new players on the scene. Word is they're nasty motherfuckers. Hands in everything. Right now, we have a team doing special recon."

"What's this got to do with us?" Major asks what everyone is thinking.

"Nothing yet. Black Shell team is in the mix. But if this moves, I want my men. My men being you," Willie clarifies.

"We have a deal. Our involvement only happens in three instances," I point out.

"If I call you, it's one of those three. Rescue and Recover to be exact."

"Fuckity fuck, fuck, fuck. I just got the taste of that goddamn sand out of my mouth." Ford blows out a breath in disgust.

"No sand, Whitman, at least not the sand you're thinking. This is happening on our side of the world."

"Can you give us more?" I push, knowing it's useless.

"Unfortunately not, Kingston. This is your head's up. Hopefully, it's unnecessary."

Head's up. Meaning he's telling us to get our affairs in order. The man wouldn't do that unless he had a gut feeling. He's not an alarmist.

"You men stay tight. I'll be in touch." Willie ends the call, the screen going black.

The room is quiet with all eyes on me. This is us.

My brothers.

Our commitment and service are non-negotiable.

None of us are backing down.

Our affairs are in order.

But we have a new member of our crew. Harley means a lot to these guys, but she's my world.

Their silent question hangs in the air.

"Tonight. When Harley gets off work, I'll tell her tonight."

16

HARLEY

"JESUS, HARLEY, TAKE A DEEP BREATH."

I try, but the air doesn't reach my lungs and I grow lightheaded. My hands go to his shirt, clutching tight, not able to get close enough.

"Baby, I need you to breathe. You're shaking like crazy."

I take in quick breaths, finally getting my head together, and the panic sets in.

"You're going back." It's barely audible, but his whole body goes solid.

"We don't know that yet." His hand strokes through my hair gently. "We know little."

"Can you tell them no? I mean, say '*nope, I'm done. Let the other guys handle this*'?"

His already solid body turns to steel. "Baby…"

He doesn't have to finish because I'm scrambling out of his hold across the bed.

"Forget I said that! I didn't mean it. I mean, I meant it, but it's something I say to Jewls, Mom, or Dad. Not you. That was shitty and unsupportive."

"It was honest."

"It was still shitty. This is you, who you are and what you do. I'm in shock. Give me a minute to let it penetrate and my senses will return."

"Get back over here."

I shake my head, pulling my knees to my chest and curling around them. "Tell me again what this means."

"There's nothing to tell. Like I said, we know little. If the time comes we're needed, we'll be briefed and brought in the fold. But, baby, prepare yourself. If that time comes, I can't—"

"Tell me," I finish his sentence. "You can't tell me what the situation is."

Regret and guilt fill his features. "No."

"Why would Willie do that? Is it normal to drop that kind of bomb and leave it hanging out there? Giving nothing to go on and worrying you all to death?"

He reaches over, lifting me effortlessly back to his lap. "We're not worried. Like you said, we are who we are and this is what we do. We're trained for many circumstances."

"You said there are only three reasons that would call you back?"

He nods.

"Can you share those?"

His beautiful, thoughtful eyes fill with remorse, and this time he shakes his head.

"Is this like a mission to kill Bin Laden?"

"Baby, that was the Seals. We're pretty awesome, but we're not Seals."

"See? That's where my imagination automatically goes."

"Nothing like that. We're more Special Operations in certain skill sets."

"And Willie can't get another group of badasses?"

His lips curl, the regret changing to amusement. "He's partial to our brand of badass since he trained us."

"Of course, he's partial," I mumble.

"You going to uncurl yourself from this ball and let me get us into bed? It's late and you have to work in the morning."

"I can't think about work knowing every minute of the day I'll wonder if you're being shipped to God knows where to do whatever it is you do." A spark of irritation replaces the shock, and I loosen my arms, releasing my tight hold on myself. "I can't believe you held on to this information all damn day and night. You should have told me right after lunch with the moms."

"You had to go back to work. And you were in such a good mood."

"I was in a good mood because lunch was great. Our moms are nuts, but they are hilarious and fun nuts. Sandy was so elated she was beaming. When you hugged her goodbye, I swear she sagged with relief and wanted to hold on to you forever. It was special."

"It was fucking lunch."

"To you, it was lunch. To her, it was much more."

"Everyone was happy, and that's what matters."

"You let me go back to work like nothing was happening. Then to Tom's!"

"I wasn't disrupting your life with this."

"Disrupt my life?! Tell me you didn't say that!" My screech is a little overdramatic, but I don't have time to check my sass because my blood is now boiling. "Don't you think that being called up on a 'special operations', super clandestine mission disrupts my life?"

I wiggle my way back, roll the opposite way, and jump off the bed.

"Harley—"

"Don't Harley me. I swore to myself that if I ever had you in my life, I'd accept whatever you gave me. From the first day we met, I accepted everything that makes you who you are. For those ten years, I lived in constant fear of losing you."

"You aren't losing me."

"You don't know that! You're a cop eyeing SWAT. Every shift you're on is a risk that could steal you from me. And I've come to terms with that because it's a part of you."

He moves to get up, but I throw my hand in his direction, stepping further back. "I've waited over ten years for you to love me. We don't discuss your time in the Marines because it's yours to share. But this is huge. You've been holding on to critical information. I don't care how much it hurts; we will not work if you keep things from me."

Lightning fast, I'm in his arms. He throws me on the bed, bracing above and bringing his face less than an inch from mine. I'm caged in and immediately under his spell. A chill runs down my spine at the pure power in his eyes.

"You took it all away. Every mission, every risk, every man lost—it was engrained in my life. With you, it's all a blur. I'm not in denial. It's bearable because I have you. You didn't need to wait over ten years for me to love you because it happened the day we met. And every day since then, no matter where I was in the world, you were with me. I didn't withhold critical information. In my mind, nothing will take me from you."

"It all makes sense now. Why you left active duty but stayed in the Reserves. They didn't want to lose you. But I don't, either. Promise me, Achilles. Promise me you will always come home to me."

He pauses, the torture evident on his face.

"Never mind, don't make promises you can't keep. Can you promise to be careful and try to come home to me?"

"I promise. But it may be a moot point."

"You may not have to leave for this, but there is always the chance. Plus, you work in law enforcement."

"Harley, me and my guys know what we're doing. That's why we are who we are. We recon, assess, make split-second decisions that are meant for the greater good. Trust in that. Trust in me."

"I trust you with everything. But I'm also selfish." Guilt slithers through me.

"All the sacrifices and decisions I made, you were in my motivation. Now that I have you, do you think I'd risk losing this?"

I run my fingers along his cheeks, memorizing the beauty he's giving me. The possibility of him being called up and leaving makes our time together more precious. "I'll talk to Tom and try to change my schedule. He'll be cool about me having the same nights off as you."

"I already said this doesn't disrupt your life. Although I will say the purpose of saving for a European vacation is pointless. You aren't going."

"Don't piss me off when I'm in the throes of drama."

"No drama."

"I'm traveling Europe with my best friend, and we're spending a week with Shayla."

"Then I'm traveling, too."

"Achilles! It's a girls' trip."

"Not anymore." He swallows hard. "My sweet Harley isn't roving across the world without me."

His perfect English accent leaves me breathless. "Achilles," is all I can wisp out.

"Don't change your schedule at Tom's unless you want."

"You've never liked me working there."

"I'm a jealous bastard."

"I'm in a committed relationship with a man who can incinerate flesh with a slice of his eyes. Not to mention, your brethren have taken your place when you're not around. The intimidation game is effective."

"It's not a game."

Telling him it's ridiculous is a waste of breath. He's not changing his ways anytime soon. Our conversation from the other day replays in my head. After Pete left, he pushed further for me to fill up his room with my stuff. I told him to give me a few days to think about it. He didn't agree, and I tried a new tactic.

I'd bring some things over after I spoke to the other guys and got a sense about how they felt about it. It's easier to read their personal opinions when we're face to face.

With us spending all of our time here when we're together, it makes sense. "I'll talk to the guys tomorrow."

He understands without explanation. "You do that."

"And I'll bring over things to fill at least two drawers and a few feet of the closet if they agree."

He closes in on me, his cocky grin loaded with purpose. "I'll help you pack."

MAJOR'S HUNCHED over the kitchen island with his back to the room when I enter. Without warning, I plaster myself to him.

"Jay?"

"Promise me, if you get the call to leave, promise me you'll be careful."

"Kingston told you," he states grimly.

"He told me."

"We're always careful."

I tighten my arms on his ribcage, using all my strength to hug tight, pressing my face into his shoulder blades. Like Achilles, his solid frame is like steel against my hold. His hands cover mine and squeeze. "Promise."

"Fuck, I'm not in the mood to go head-to-head with Ace when he sees his lady attached to you." Talon's voice sounds from behind, and I spin, releasing Major to find him and Ford standing at the edge of the room, still in uniform. Talon's amused expression barely registers before I take off and launch myself into his arms.

"Promise me you'll be careful!" I squeal, holding tight as he rocks back.

"Jay—"

"Promise," I cut him off.

"Man, she's got a wicked grip," Major informs him.

Talon's arms go around me, and he nods against my head. "Promise."

I twist and reach for Ford, tugging him close. "Ford?"

"Promise."

"I needed to hear it from each of you." My forehead drops to the edge of their shoulders. I know they are sharing a look right now that says I'm emotional and overacting, but I don't care. Hearing them confirm their commitment to stay safe helps my nerves.

"Harley, you know we dig you, but Ace's eyes are blazing," Talon utters in my ear, and I let them go.

My feet are barely on the ground when Ace folds around me. "That's the last time you get coffee without me."

"Stop being a brute."

"Don't enjoy walking in to find you clinging to other men, even if they are these dipshits."

"I'm actually surprised she's resisted me this long," Talon goads him with a smug grin.

I giggle as a low hum rolls from Ace's throat.

"Take it from that greeting, Jay's been briefed?" Ford changes the subject before Talon can't spur him more.

Ace jerks his chin.

"Actually, it's good you all are here at the same time. We wanted to talk to you about something."

My fingers lace with his, waiting for him to take over. His eyes meet mine and dance with amusement.

"You wanted the big production, this is your show."

"No, you need to ask. It's the gentlemanly thing to do."

"When did Ace become a gentleman? This should be good." Major leans against the island, crossing his arms with a wide grin.

They all stare at me until my stomach rolls in a knot.

"For fuck's sake, should we put her out of her misery?" Ford chuckles.

"Nah, let's wait her out," Talon suggests with his own lip-splitting grin.

Prickles crawl across my skin before the embarrassment hits. "You all know, don't you?"

"That Ace is moving you in and making that wing a love nest?"

At Ford's statement, the four of them burst out laughing, and my embarrassment turns to a rush of heat through my veins. "It's not a love nest!"

"Sin Den?" comes from Major.

"Lover's Lair?" Talon adds.

"Play & Stay?" Ford finishes them out.

I half-twist into Achilles to find him enjoying this a little too much. "Stop laughing!"

"They are fucking with you."

"I'm trying to be polite in checking with the occupants of this house before I practically move myself in."

"A few drawers and closet space doesn't mean you're moving fully in," he corrects me. "But I'm totally game if you're offering."

"Achilles! Stop being ridiculous."

"I'm not the one sweating over asking a bunch of grown men if they have a problem with you staying here."

"I'm being respectful of your home," I grumble, turning back.

"The Casanova Club needs a new member. You'll do." Talon winks. "Besides, I liked this morning's greeting. Next time, let's shoot for fewer clothes."

"Why do I try?" I aim my eyes at the ceiling, feeling foolish.

"Anytime you want to have your chick clique, I'm okay with that, too."

I swing my gaze to Major, seeing my opportunity to butt in. "Anyone in particular?"

His eyes flare before he shakes his head. "Nice tits, hot ass, low maintenance, and not looking for more than a good time."

"If we're throwing out preferences, I'll take the tits and ass, too. Attitude's not a deal breaker, but ditto on the good time. Nothing more."

"You guys are pigs. With those expectations, this will turn into a Casanova Club."

"This place is a drama-free zone. They need to have their own place. Easier to get away."

Achilles's mouth comes to my ear. "They're still fucking with you."

"It's too early in the morning for me to deal with your antics." I glare at the three of them.

"Noted. Jay's not a morning joker. Good to know when you move in," Talon continues to goad.

"I'm not moving in," I argue.

"We're not going over it again or we'll be here all morning. We have somewhere to go before you have to work." Achilles steps to the door.

"Somewhere to go?"

I attempt to pull him to a stop, but it's useless. He drags me toward the garage.

"Wait, I planned to make breakfast."

He halts long enough to twist his head. His lips tip in a confident smirk. "Babe, really?"

"Don't say it like that. I can manage eggs and toast."

"You burnt the toast last weekend."

"That wasn't my fau—" The words die because it was totally my fault. The kitchen and living room smelled the whole day.

"Achilles, I can't go anywhere like this." I try a new tactic.

"You're perfect."

His eyes glint in that wickedly possessive way. I'm wearing one of his sweatshirts over a loose pair of pajama pants with my hair in a sloppy bun. Basically, I look like I just rolled out of bed. But beneath the clothes are his stubble marks covering my skin.

The memory of his wake-up fills my mind, and heat courses through my veins. I bite my lip and drop my gaze to his groin.

"Harley," he grounds out in warning, and a throat clears from behind.

He yanks me forward and guides me out. We pass the row of motorcycles and he stops by the golf cart, urging me to sit. As soon as the garage door opens, a blast of cool air hits us.

"Shit, didn't expect the temps to drop this much."

As if on cue, the door swings open, and a ball of green flies into his hands. "Thanks, man," he tells Ford, draping the blanket across my legs.

"Good luck, Kingston." He leans against the doorframe with a sly grin.

Achilles flicks his fingers, then drives us around the back of the house.

"Where are we going?"

"Over to Holmes Court."

The name sounds familiar, but I can't figure out why until he rounds the pool house and the area comes into view. Then it hits me. Holmes Court. The side street Jewls and I swung into that first night thinking we were camouflaged from Talon. The bushes we hid behind with those stupid binoculars, waiting to see if women paraded in and out of the house.

We bounce across the property, and he pulls onto the street, following the road to and stopping in the cul-de-sac.

"This is the last street of lots to sell out in the development," he tells me, staring at the lot in front of us.

"I thought they sold out last year."

"Every lot but the ones on this street. Doug and Celia held on to these for a reason."

"What's the reason?"

"They offered them to us."

My eyes bulge, and I can't stop the squeaky reply, "They what? Is this..." I swallow to help my dry throat, "...is this yours?"

He shifts his gaze to me. "It is."

"Oh, wow... you own a piece of property—here?"

"Is that a problem?" He crooks an eyebrow. "You don't like the neighborhood?"

"It's not that at all, but it's an exclusive neighborhood with enormous homes. Like mansions."

"Not all the houses are like the Whitmans'."

"No, they are mini-mansions."

"Celia recommended some builders. We can review them together and go with what style you like."

There's a ringing in my ears, and my heart races double time. I open my mouth, but nothing comes out. My mind is racing with scrambled thoughts. There's no way I heard him right. My eyes close and I rewind his words.

"Celia recommended some builders. We can review them together and go with what style you like."

He said it.

He said 'we can review them'.

"Harley, look at me."

My eyes pop open, and he reaches out, scooting me to him. "Say something."

"You want to build us a house? Here? In one of the most exclusive, high-end communities in the area?"

"If the community bothers you, we'll go somewhere different."

My head shakes so forcefully my bun tumbles out. "I don't want different."

His fingers thread through my hair, and he brings our faces close, his dark eyes glimmering bright. "Do you understand now?"

He's assuring me in his own way. He's not making a promise because promises can be broken. It's a different vow. The kind of vow that gives me insight into our future. The double-beat of my heart bursts with so much love, my body trembles.

I nod, laying my forehead to his. "I understand."

We stay like this for a minute, sitting and staring until my brain clears and Ford's statement comes back to me.

"So, all the guys know?"

"Doug gave us all a deal. Talon is on the right." He points to the adjacent property. "Major is two over, and Ford hasn't picked yet."

"We're all living on the same street?"

"Unless you tell me differently."

"Achilles, I know you have money put away, but can we afford this?"

"The Whitmans plan to retire in a few years and move to Nashville. When Doug was here last month, he offered to sell us the lots. The price was too good to turn down. Even if we don't build, we have his permission to sell at the market rate."

"Why would he do that?"

His face softens and lips touch mine. "We're brothers in arms. Doug knows what that means."

"I think I love Doug."

"The feeling is mutual. He's been good to me over the years. Like your dad, he knows to call me on my shit. When he was here, he told me to stop fucking around or I'd lose you to someone better."

"He doesn't know me well."

"He knew prodding me with the possibility of another man would set me on edge."

"We've been dating for a short time. Granted, it's moved fast, but this is unreal."

"We've never dated, Harley. Our story started a long time ago. You forgave me, and that was the beginning of our here and now."

I kiss him, lacing my hands around his neck, and whispering, "I love it. I love you. And it's a shame you have to work this weekend."

"Why is that?"

"We could camp out here and christen our property the right way."

He slants my head and growls against my mouth before slipping his tongue inside.

Making out with him isn't exactly the same, but it will do. For now…

17

ACE

"Another beer?" Jewls is already sliding it my way.

"Where's Tom? Isn't there an occupancy limit in this place?"

"Yes, officer, and we're still under capacity. This happens when men find out ladies' night is happening. They flock to the hopping joint. Lighten up."

I glare at her for a split second before going back to watching Harley across the bar.

"She worked hard on this. The girl is a marketing genius. You should look at the bright side."

"What's the bright side?"

"She continues to bring in crowds like this, we will fund our European vacation before we know it and she can cut back her hours. You get more of her."

At the mention of the vacation, I pin her. "Jewls—"

"Zip it, Ace, she already told me you're crashing. Surprisingly, I'm okay with that. She also told me about the lot of land. I'm proud of you for finally proving you're the guy she waited all her life for."

There's no time to comment before Tom's hustling back with his arms full of bottles. "Jewls! Stop nattering and get these women drinks. They're savages."

She rolls her eyes and goes to help him.

"Son."

At the voice, my head snaps to the side to find my dad with Rich and Hal.

"Dad, you shouldn't be here."

"I've spent a decade working my way into the sober life. Your mom wasn't missing this. She's at the table with the women, but Rich told me what's going on."

I glance at Rich, who's worried. Harley called him earlier, and he must have shared with these men. "Dad, it's not something I can discuss."

"No, but know I'm here."

"All of us fucking are," Hal agrees gravely.

"You're jumping the gun. Nothing's happened." I tip my chin casually. They're not deterred.

"You get the message to go, you call me. My Harley is a strong girl. She'll be encouraging, but she'll need support," Rich demands.

"Done."

"Goes without saying, we're all around," Dad pitches his support.

"Appreciate it."

A loud squawk sounds from Jewls, and Harley pivots quick, squealing as excitedly.

"Rowan!" they both scream.

My head jerks, and I catch the woman standing there smiling wide, leaning over to hug Jewls. A prickle runs up my spine, recognizing her from the call out the other night.

In a flash, Ford is with us. "Shit, shit, shit."

"That's her," Hal notes.

"Who? Rowan?" Rich questions.

"Fuck me, you know her?" Ford narrows his eyes.

"Yeah, she's a great gal. Been around a few years. Hairdresser, I believe. Harley, Jewls, Ginger, and her are a crew. Or, at least, they were. Come to think of it, I haven't seen Rowan lately."

Hal interprets my move, gripping my arm before I can leave my stool. "Wait, there's a good chance she'll recognize us."

"Doubtful." My eyes go to Ford, who's dressed similarly in jeans, a thermal, and a black ball cap. Out of uniform, we blend in. "She walked into a cop bar. It's not a secret club."

"Trust me, I'm an old man and easy to forget. But you and your pretty boys aren't. She'll recognize you. Plus, the way you look right now will scare her off. She's here, surrounded by women and smiling. This is a good thing. Let's see how it plays out."

"If she's facing a situation, I don't want Harley anywhere near it. Jewls either."

The words hang in the air and the mood instantly changes. Rich and Dad don't need further explanation to understand.

"What kind of situation are we talking about here?" Rich asks with an edge to his tone. "Harley's got a good sense of character and reads people well. Let's rely on her judgment."

Rich has been doing this for so long, he feels the same burn in his gut at the possibility of a woman being abused. He's not fooling me. He can spew that shit, but we both know he doesn't want Harley anywhere near it.

"I trust her judgment. I don't trust the pompous ass we met blaming a nosy neighbor for a disturbance call."

"Well then, use this to your advantage. Harley and Jewls know her."

His message clicks loud and clear, and I settle back on the stool, sipping my beer. The girls laugh and serve Rowan and her three friends drinks before they wander to a table.

Talon and Major come through the doors, heading our way. Their eyes go over my shoulder before meeting mine. This will be the first time they've been around my dad in many years. The last time was when we came home for Harley and the funeral. They stand on the edge of the huddle, picking up on the tension and waiting for me to make the first move.

"Dad, you remember Talon and Major?" I jut my chin, sending the sign things are fine.

They relax, shaking his hand.

"Jesus, been a while. How are you boys?" Dad's use of 'boys' has Rich and Hal chuckling.

There's another round of squeals, taking our attention back to where Harley is over at the bar again, this time hugging Erik. Kelvin and Ginger from her office are also there.

"Shit, do these girls have to squeal every time someone they know arrives? It's freaking my customers out." Tom hands two bottles across to Talon and Major.

"Your customers are multiplying by the minute. It's fazed no one," I correct him.

"Your woman is down there hanging on a guy much prettier than you. You going to let that happen?" he snaps back.

"Considering his partner is standing there, I think it's passable."

This earns a chorus of rough laughter from all the men.

Tom's scowl tips into his own grin. "Harley did well."

"She did."

"We get this kind of crowd and turn out, I'll have to do it again."

I gulp a healthy swig to keep from telling him it would be stupid not to take advantage.

"How's my favorite group of men doing? Can I get you anything?" Harley pops over, her face glowing with happiness and accomplishment.

"Despite you and Jewls' opinions, I can handle my bar," Tom grouses.

"We know you have bar skills; it's the people skills that are lacking," she teases. "And before you get any grumpier, we have a large party headed in. The girls on the floor are in the weeds. Get back to the service bar and warn the kitchen."

"Watch it, little missy, I'm still the boss around here."

"Can't help if I love the fact that—even you can't deny—ladies' night rocks!"

He does a poor job hiding his approval, giving her a nudge before walking away.

"Hey there." She props on her elbows.

I lean over the width of the bar and cup her head, running my lips across hers. "Great job, beautiful."

Her breath catches and she whispers, "Our dads are right behind you."

"And?"

"And our moms are right behind them."

"Baby, we loaded my dresser and closet today with your things, and I'm building you a house. They all know we kiss." I don't whisper, not caring who hears.

She laughs lightly, her lips vibrating to mine. "You have such a way with words. But I'm too happy to be embarrassed."

"Good, because you should be." I kiss her again and slide back. "Looks like you have a lot of friends showing up."

"You saw Erik, Kelvin, and Ginger."

I nod. "Who was the other group of girls?"

"That was Rowan and the crew from the salon. Rowan is a hairstylist and skin care technician extraordinaire. She's been taking care of Jewls and me for years. It took me forever to find someone who can work with my curls. She's taught me my tricks."

"What tricks are those?"

"Things like how to blow out with the right styling tools and air dry without resembling a chia pet."

"We call her the chia pet tamer," Jewls calls as she rushes by.

"It's cool she came. We miss hanging out with her."

"Surprised you haven't mentioned her before," I push gently, wondering how close Harley and Rowan are.

"She's in a weird position and cut back on socializing. She was engaged to this guy for a long time, and things seemed to break apart. Story on the streets is he was stressed, and she was trying to help him through whatever was bothering him. I figured that's why she didn't take us up on our offers. But since she's here, maybe things are turning around."

"Engaged? Not married?" I ask a little too eagerly, remembering the way the asshole called her his wife, and she didn't correct.

"No, she never married him, which was also odd. But I got the impression she had some reservations. We never met the guy."

Hal clears his throat, indicating he's picked up on this, too.

"Harley, be a dear hostess and send another round of those ladies' night special martinis," Amanda shouts from her table.

"Mom, I'm a bartender, not a hostess," she hollers back.

"Make it sex," Amanda replies, and the table howls.

"Please, God, tell me she meant make it six." Horror fills Harley's expression.

"I'm hoping she meant sex," Rich delivers with a straight face.

She drops her head and bangs it against the bar.

"Mix 'em up, baby, and we'll deliver them." I lift her chin and shoot her an encouraging smile.

"Next time, remind me not to tell her about ladies' night."

She rolls her shoulders and pulls out six martini glasses.

"While you do that, did your mom tell you about the dinner this weekend?" Rich asks.

Harley preps the drinks and nods. "Grandma's seventy-fifth at Giovanni's, right?"

"That was the plan until she found out about your new beau."

Harley's head snaps, her hand losing grip, and the bottle almost crashing before she saves at the last minute. "You promised to let me tell her myself! She adores Achilles and was heartbroken when he left me. I needed to ease her into us."

"Things change."

"Dad!"

"I called her." Her eyes fling to mine, squinting in irritation.

"You," she points, "are in trouble! She'll eat you alive!"

"I'm good, especially since we moved the party to the house."

She pales, looking away and finishing the drinks, adding the orange garnish and placing them on the bar. "Deliver these."

Rich, Dad, and Hal take the drinks. Talon, Major, and Ford settle into the bar stools. She eyes Ford first.

"You approved this?"

"My parents are driving in from Chicago for the occasion, with my sisters."

"They don't know my grandma!"

"My parents are coming from Louisiana," Talon goes on.

Her gaze moves between us, and she straightens, realization taking over. She takes a second, but she breathes deep, knowing everyone is coming for the same reason. "Grandma will love it."

"My parents are heading in, too. My jackass brothers are most likely crashing," Major informs with a frown.

"Everyone will be together." There's a sense of melancholy to her tone.

"Jay…" Ford drifts off, not sure how to finish.

The sadness disappears. She delivers a cunning smile to Major. "Drake and Jewls seemed to hit it off."

Major slams his beer down, but she's already floating off with a wave of a hand.

I watch her ass, slugging my beer.

"We didn't even get a fresh round," Talon whistles out, and Tom swings his head our way.

"Y'all badasses here for the night?"

He knows my answer, but the other guys tip their beer in confirmation. Tom fills a bucket of beer, sets it in front of us, and props on the bar. "I know what's going on. Pray to God your services aren't needed, but if they are, you have my eternal gratitude for continuing to protect this country. Drinks are on me tonight." He shoves off and goes back to the service area.

Talon, being Talon, can't let it go, whistling loud to bring attention his way. "We love you, too, Tommy."

Tom scowls, shooting him an 'eat shit' glare before flicking him off.

"Aww, look at that. He loves us more."

I glance at my friend shoving bar nuts in his mouth and can't help the smile on my lips.

Surrounded by friends and family and watching Harley shine under the success of her pet project, I have a new appreciation for my life.

18

HARLEY

"It's not too late to go to a restaurant."

"It is too late, considering the catering staff is almost ready to open the buffet," Mom replies. "Plus, there's no way we can move this crowd to a restaurant."

"The Bar-B-Q Barn can hold all of us."

"Do you want to tell your grandma she's getting the Bar-B-Q Barn for her seventy-fifth dinner instead of Italian from the city's finest restaurant?"

I think about Grandma Lucy's reaction and the wrath of hell we'll face. "No," I mumble, slinking back.

"It's not that bad."

"She's had Achilles in that corner for fifteen minutes and pointed at his face twice. He looks like he's about to blow."

"No, he looks like a man who will gladly stand in that corner, taking hell as long as it takes for her to get it out of her system. She loves you like crazy. And to him, you're his world." Sandy sighs with unmistakable joy.

"Can't Uncle Michael or Dad intercept?"

"They know better than to wade in," Mom advises.

"I think it's hilarious. Waiting for him to break a sweat," Jewls chimes in.

"You're no help."

"Not when the situation is so entertaining." She shoves a margarita glass in my hand. "Here, have a slug and lighten up. We all know Ace can't be scared off."

"I agree. Doug and I always considered Ace the lone wolf of the bunch. We only met him a handful of times, but each time, he was quiet and standoffish. He had this edge about him that was dangerous and mysterious. Then we come here, meet you. That weekend, when he cornered me about helping you find a builder, I almost fainted. He is a different man," Celia tells our group.

"Agreed, Jim and I noticed the change in Ace that weekend as well," Cindy, Major's mom, pipes up. "We should all be thanking you."

"Why?"

"Our sons have a solid, impenetrable connection among them. They decide as a group. When Major told us they were getting out and moving on, I didn't know what they'd do next. Then, when he told me they were all coming to Nashville with Ace, I felt relief. The choice to come here was driven by Ace's determination to get back to you. You helped find them a home."

"I'm not sure that's how it went. Ace and I weren't exactly on the best of terms. Giving me credit is a stretch."

"She's right, sweetie. And we're all thrilled they are closer. Nashville is the perfect location. It's a simple drive and flight, which is nice." Talon's mom, April, toasts her glass in the air. "Plus, we get you in the deal, which is a bonus."

My skin prickles and heats with the praise, and I flash her a crooked smile. "I'm pretty fortunate, too."

I glance at Sandy, who's barely holding back her emotions. Tonight has meant a lot to her. Meeting the other parents after all these years and being able to share this with Pete and Achilles finally at peace.

"I hate to bring it up, but can we address the elephant in the corner?" Celia's attention lands on me. "Have you heard anything new?"

"No, as far as I know, there has been no more communication. Achilles promised he would tell me."

"Ford's sisters made him promise the same. They wanted to be here this weekend, but it didn't work out. They'll be crashing in soon."

"Maybe Willie's original team uncovered nothing and the head's up call was unnecessary. He got everyone worried for nothing," Jewls voices her opinion.

"I'd love for that to be true, but Achilles says these things take time."

"These men are the best at what they do. And God forbid they are called back, we will band together to support each other."

"We sure will." Mom reaches for the pitcher of margaritas, topping mine off before hers. "Now, let's talk about houses. Do you have any idea what you want?"

"Hold that thought—Grandma Lucy has released her prey," Jewls updates us eagerly.

Grandma heads our way while Achilles joins the men by the fire pit. His eyes meet mine, and a slow, sexy grin forms on his lips. Whatever she said has him amused.

"Do I still have a boyfriend?" I ask Grandma when she sits.

"Hopefully not for long."

"What did you do?"

"I'm a hip old broad. You millennials like to go against the grain, but there are a few traditions that should withstand time."

A knot forms in the pit of my stomach at the implication. "You didn't…"

"Told him he can build you a fancy house, but there better be a ring on your finger before any great-grandbabies get here."

"Oh, God," My chin falls to my chest.

"Harley, why do you act surprised?"

"Because we've been dating a short time."

"He's Usain Bolt," Jewls proudly relays her ridiculous name. "Ace went from lone wolf to speed *king*."

"He is rather fast when he gets going, but considering this has been in the works for over ten years, he's not quite that fast." Grandma pins me with her deep blue eyes full of wisdom.

"You knew how he felt?"

"Of course, I did, sugar plum. It was obvious. I also know why he did what he did and walked away. The eighteen-year-old Achilles Kingston was carrying too much on his conscience to be good enough. Now, he's ready to atone for that time lost."

A lump forms in my throat, and I avoid peering at Sandy.

"So, what did I miss?" Grandma changes the subject, pouring her own drink.

"Talking about the house. I'm getting my own guest suite," Jewls informs them. "And I'd like it to overlook the pool deck."

I roll my eyes, take a large gulp, and say a silent thanks Mom was generous with the tequila. "I picked up a few magazines to get ideas. This whole thing is surreal and hasn't hit me yet."

"Do you have any idea what style you'd prefer?" Celia asks.

"Not at all."

"What does Achilles say?"

"He has four demands. A three-bay garage, a media room, a sizable back yard with an outdoor kitchen, and a large master suite. That's all I have to go on."

"They can definitely save room on the kitchen, considering Harley can't cook shit," Jewls snickers, throwing me under the bus.

"I'm learning!"

"I will never know how you are my daughter and can't cook," Mom adds to the ridicule.

"We'll handle that, starting with lessons this weekend," April offers.

"And maybe tomorrow we can ride around to look at styles of homes."

"I'm not sure what we can afford. Achilles won't give me a budget. He says anything I want."

Celia shares a look with April, Sandy, Cindy, and Grandma. The knot in the pit of my stomach coils tighter, and I swallow another large gulp.

"What?"

"Well, I don't know what his budget is, but you can have almost anything you want. Doug spoke to a few contacts, and the houses are being built with a very generous discount." She blows me away with this news.

"Wow."

"All the guys have done well with their investments. Drake and Sam have been involved," Cindy advises.

"Awesome! I'm getting my suite!" Jewls shimmies in her chair.

"I think we need more." I take the empty pitcher to the sidebar.

The next second I'm screeching like a madwoman as I'm snatched off my feet and hanging parallel to the ground.

"Harley Bell!" My cousin spins around before tipping to the side and shaking me like a rag doll.

"Put me down!" I beat on his forearm, which has an iron-clad hold on my waist.

"Not yet." He slings me up and tickles my side until I'm squirming and squealing.

"Stop… no… please," I beg, knowing it's useless.

His body goes static, and all the playful activity stops. He places me on my feet and leans in to my ear. "The way his lethal laser rays are shooting at me, I'm guessing this is your new beau?"

My eyes fly to find Achilles' fiery gaze aimed at my cousin. Aunt Tina stands close, her mouth slightly parted.

"Tone it down," I hiss-whisper. "It's Mike. Don't you remember my cousin?"

The blaze lessens, and his stance relaxes. "No, never met the guy manhandling you."

It hits me that Mike didn't make it home for Grandpa's funeral because he was in Europe.

"Achilles, this is my cousin, Mike Jacobs, and you met my Aunt Tina." I do the introductions, hugging both newcomers.

"Hey, man, heard a lot about you these last few weeks." Mike makes the first move, offering his hand.

A giggle escapes and I look at Mom. She's beaming brazenly. "Mom, you're shameless."

"What? Am I not allowed to share about your new boyfriend with the family? I'm proud of Ace and wanted Tina to know the scoop."

"More like she wanted to brag," Mike mutters. "Although it wasn't the first time your name was floating around. Nice to finally meet you."

Achilles shakes his hand, wrapping his arm around my waist and folding me smoothly to his side. "Yeah, I've heard your name, too."

Jewls throws herself in the mix, hugging Mike enthusiastically. "Mickey!"

"Julianna Banana!" He lifts her off the ground and shakes her much gentler than my greeting.

I cast my gaze over to the fire pit, zeroing in on Major, who's scowling only slightly less protectively than Achilles was.

"Seriously, you are aware of the reason you're attending this soiree, aren't you?" Grandma's disapproving tone cuts through the patio.

Mike sets Jewls on her feet and moseys over to the table, crouching to hug her. "Grandma, you don't look a day over eighty," he sings teasingly.

She scoffs loudly, pushing him off. "Michael Wayne Jacobs Junior! You're lucky you make your own money because that remark got you cut out of my will."

"But I'm your favorite grandson." He clutches his chest, wounded.

"Not anymore, Dee's boys are knocking you out of the club."

He scans the yard, around the area, and bends backward to peer into the house. "Where are Aunt Dee and her three heathens? I don't see the wreckage."

I bite the inside of my cheek and try to hold back, but a snort escapes, and I press my face into Achilles' chest to cover my hilarity. "Our Aunt Deanna, we call her Dee. Her three sons aren't bad, they're just wild."

"I remember meeting them. They outta college yet?"

"Two are out and 'finding themselves'. The youngest is in his fifth year, testing out majors that suit his lifestyle."

Achilles chuckles.

"Seriously, Grandma Lucy, you are a sight. Happy birthday." Mike quits his teasing and hugs her affectionately.

She melts into him, kissing his cheek. "Always my Mickey."

He straightens and goes to my mom while Aunt Tina moves to Grandma. After he introduces himself to the other ladies in the group, he joins us again. "Not to be rude, but where's the alcohol?"

"We have a bar set up out here, and the cabana is fully stocked."

"How about a beer?"

"That would be the cabana. Come on, handsome, I'll show you around and introduce you to the men." Jewls offers her hand and he takes it.

"We'll meet you down there after I finish the margaritas."

They head out and I tug Ace to the bar.

"I'll make them." He surprises me by reaching for the pitcher before I can.

"Do you know how?"

"I may not drink this girlie shit, but doesn't mean I'm clueless."

He expertly whips up a concoction using ingredients I didn't know were here. When he pours me a sample, I moan in appreciation. "This is fantastic."

"Groan like that again and you'll get something else fantastic."

Swarms of little tingles take flight in my stomach, and I glance up to find his eyes boring into mine. Just like that first time, he continues to take my breath away. So ruggedly gorgeous.

He jolts, his gaze turning heated and hungry.

"Did I say that out loud?"

"Yeah, and baby, fair warning. You give me something that sweet again, everyone at this party will witness me hauling you to my room with my intentions clear."

I ignore his warning, curl my hand around his neck, and tip up on my toes, urging his face down. "I'm glad Grandma Lucy didn't scare you away."

A smile plays at his lips. "She called me on my shit. Knew I loved you all those years ago and thinks I was reckless by risking the chance of losing you. Then she told me she expected our house to fill with babies as soon as we're married. She's completely on board."

My jaw drops and a bubble of a squeal gets out before he crashes his lips over mine. His tongue sweeps through, twirling with mine briefly before breaking away. "Don't tempt me, Harley. My room."

A collective sigh sounds out, and I swivel my neck to find all eyes on us. Mom and Grandma are grinning approvingly, Aunt Tina a mix of happiness and envy.

"Drink your drinks, enjoy your family, and tonight, I'll show you my appreciation for that sweetness."

"We have a house full of people sleeping everywhere."

"We'll deal."

I sigh in appreciation. "Can't wait."

"Baby, really? You got me halfway hard just being around. Now I'm solid."

"Sorry." I push back and motion for him to fill my glass. "Let's head down where they can gossip about us without embarrassing me to death."

He folds my hand in his and leads us to the back yard. "So, you probably picked up that Mom has been running her mouth."

"Hard to miss."

"I forgot you hadn't met Mike before. But we're close, well, as close as his schedule allows."

"He's the one with the record label?"

"Yes, the man is the definition of a workhorse. He's also a master entrepreneur. The label that started small has grown into an internationally recognized name. He'll humbly argue the success is a result of his team. But we all know the truth. It's his own hardworking sweat equity. He's married to his job, and his clients are a part of his family. Aunt Tina is scared he'll never slow down enough to find a woman and fall in love."

"He will."

He says it with such confidence, I stop and glance up at him. "You think?"

"I'm familiar with hard work and sweat equity. Sometimes a man needs to lay the foundation, so when he finds the one, he can balance it out. Sounds like his foundation is solid. He needs to find the one that takes his breath away with the first glance."

I melt into him, memorizing the way he's staring at me with such love it's a miracle my heart doesn't burst from my chest. "God, I love you."

No matter how many times I've repeated the words, his expression always grows thoughtful. He steals a quick kiss, then guides us to the circle of people, positioning us close to Mike.

"Not to sound like an ass, but I didn't believe Dad when he told me they moved her party because your boyfriend offered. I called Uncle Rich to see what the hell was happening."

"Mike, that's tacky."

"Harley, I have clients that live in this neighborhood."

He doesn't have to explain further. Mike represents some of the best musicians and hottest musical talent in the country. He's had full bands relocate to Nashville to work with him and his team. He's made many people very wealthy.

"When Uncle Rich explained the situation to me, it made total sense," Mike finishes.

"It's still tacky."

"I disagree. I see it as looking out for my baby cousin. Seems like my worry was premature. Heard you bought a lot to build her a home—congrats, man." He tips his beer in Achilles' direction and warmth fills me inside.

"How is the glamorous life of jet-setting with the rich and famous?" I tease, moving the subject along.

"Not nearly as glorious as you may think."

"Must be tough."

"Would be less tough if you'd come work for me."

My stomach drops to my feet, and I swing to face him in disbelief. "What?"

"There's an opening in my marketing department that sounds perfect for your expertise."

"How do you know my expertise?"

"Jewls' been filling me in."

"Launching a ladies' night and creating an upstart campaign for an exercise studio isn't exactly your level."

Achilles squeezes my waist with a low grunt. He's not a fan of me dismissing my efforts.

"Rumor has it you pitched for the recent Lamborghini account."

"Yes, six weeks ago, with no word yet. Not exactly a glowing recommendation."

"The reason it's taking time is that they've asked one of my headlining groups to be the face of the ad. They took the proposals to them.

They chose their favorite, and I agreed. Then I asked around and found out my dear, little, sweet cousin was the one behind the gritty, edgy, and advanced idea."

"Ummm, Mike, you're freaking me out. I've waited weeks for any word on follow-up. And you've been sitting on it?"

"It wasn't my decision or call. I gave creative input only."

Anticipation and excitement bubble to the surface and I bounce like a girl. "Tell me who the band is."

He studies me, enjoying my impatience and drawing this out. "Sayge."

I quit bouncing and sway, my ears ringing. "Oh, my."

Jewls lets out a yelp. "Holy shit, Jay!"

"They liked my idea?"

"They liked it," Mike confirms. "You'll hear more on Monday."

"The office will go nuts."

"You did that, baby," Achilles announces proudly, kissing along my temple.

"It was a team effort."

"I may have a source that's on the inside who said a certain junior marketing executive added the most value to the multi-million-dollar campaign."

"What? Who?"

"My lips are sealed. But after seeing for myself, I want that power on my team."

"Isn't it frowned upon to leave my current company and work for a client? I don't want an unfavorable reputation following me."

"That's the beauty. MJ Labels isn't your client. Sayge's business team is the client. They outgrew my boutique business services years ago. Raven heads the business team, and she has four children under the age of nine. Declan wants another one. She's always been hands-on, but she's stepping back. Without her, we are creating a long-ago needed new position."

"Holy shit," Jewls repeats.

"Raven? Is that the smokin' hot model in the video from years ago?" Drake questions.

"Shit, yeah, it is. That woman is fucking stacked," Sam agrees.

"She's also married to the lead singer, Declan Collins, and he's a slight step down on the protection scale from Ace. This comes about and you meet him—word to the wise—don't ogle his wife. He'll pummel you." There's a hint of humor in Mike's reply.

"You should think hard about this. I don't get the impression your cousin is showering you with familial compliments. He sees your worth," Achilles says low enough for only me to hear.

"How about we meet for lunch next week?" I throw out, excitement fluttering through me.

"Text me and we'll make it happen."

I look across the fire at my dad who's standing between Pete and Uncle Mike. All of them are grinning with pride. Then I catch Jewls' eye and see she's smiling bright.

Could I go work for my cousin?

In an internationally respected record label that works with mega-superstars?

Possibly one of the biggest opportunities in my life?

My mind screams the answer so loud it's a wonder it doesn't fly out of my mouth.

Hell yes, I can.

19

ACE

I FIST HER HAIR, tugging up. "Harley, get—" The words die on my lips when she opens and swallows, my cock hitting the back of her throat. She increases her suction and speed, stroking my shaft in the same rhythm.

Every muscle in my body tenses as the familiar flame ignites. My last bit of willpower is on the brink, ready to snap. She senses the change, and her gaze comes to mine, daring me to stop her.

"Shit, you look like a vixen taking me."

She holds my stare, savoring my dick and working faster. She knows what it does to me to watch her. My instincts scream to haul her up and fuck her senseless. She shifts, rubbing her legs together.

Fuck yeah. Two can play at this game.

"Because I'm feeling generous, you have two options. Climb on and ride my dick, or twist around and ride my face. Either way, I want your pussy."

Her eyes widen and fill with desire. She tightens her grip and laps her tongue over my piercing.

"Now."

She crawls over my leg and around to straddle my face. Without even touching her, she's soaking wet. I hold her hips, running my tongue along her slit. She moans her approval, the vibration pushing me closer to exploding.

I wasn't lying when I told her she was a natural. This woman is an expert at everything.

The primal brute rears up, needing to hear her scream. My tongue thrusts inside, devouring her roughly. She grinds against my face, her assault slowing. I use the distraction to my advantage, altering between licking and sucking until she's panting.

Her nails scrape the underside of my shaft before she rolls my balls in her palm. My dick lurches, getting her attention. She catches on to my play and begins mimicking my actions.

Fucking temptress.

It's time to play dirty. My mouth closes over her clit, and I suck hard before flicking it over and over with my tongue.

Her thighs tighten around my head, trembling. My mouth moves mercilessly, one goal in mind. She bobs up and down, increasing her suction.

My hips flex, my balls tightening. Warnings fire off in my brain. I can't stop what's coming.

I lick, suck, and tease until she's all out quaking. When my teeth graze over her clit, she bucks, squeezing my balls and crying my name. I lose her mouth, but it's too late. I shoot off, warm liquid dripping down my shaft.

In a second, I flip her to the bed and kneel between her thighs. She grins smugly, pleased with herself. "Happy Birthday." Her finger trails down my chest, circling the tip of my dick.

Since our first time, I rarely need much downtime. But this morning, my cock throbs, ready to go instantly.

"Shit baby, can you take me?"

She smiles wickedly, sucking my cum off her finger and moaning in appreciation. That's all it takes. I slam into her, filling her in one thrust.

"God, yes!" she arches up and yells.

I grip her hips, driving into her relentlessly. She locks her ankles around my waist, angling in a move that takes me all the way with every stroke.

Her body relaxes back into the bed, giving me a full view of her below me. Her auburn curls spread out wildly on my sheets, her tits bouncing, nipples hard and pink—teasing me. The flush that covers her skin every time she comes.

Twenty-nine fucking years old and finally have my fantasy lying here, taking my cock, while looking like a goddess.

She licks her lips, her eyes glinting with desire and challenge. My cock spasms when her muscles clench and retract over and over, sucking me deeper than I've ever been. The ball of my piercing hits soft flesh, and she lets out a racy, raspy whimper.

"Harder," she begs.

I hammer into her roughly. "Do you have any idea how goddamned sexy you look right now?"

"Mmhmm, I'm enjoying my view much more." Her gaze travels over my torso appreciatively.

The greedy bastard inside needs her wrapped around me. "Come here." My hands go to her lower back, hoisting her to straddle my lap.

"Ahhhhh," she grinds down, sending a spark of pleasure shooting through my system.

As soon as she's seated fully, she glides back and forth, getting used to the position.

"Careful, baby."

"I can't get enough… God, will it always be like this?"

Pride and possessiveness roar to life. "Yes." I drive up, placing my mouth on hers and absorbing her moans.

Her hips pivot, her eyes close, and the rasps become pants.

"I love having you inside me."

"It's an addiction. Like watching you come apart."

"More…" Her breathy whisper spurs me on.

Beads of sweat slide down my back and chest as I fuck her mercilessly. She holds on, taking everything without inhibitions.

"Achilles, I need you." Frantic desperation bleeds through her words.

"Get there."

Her eyelids fly open and fire blazes. She moves her hand between us, her thumb grazing her clit and pressing into my moving cock.

"Oh, fuck, Harley."

My thighs burn as I drill into her from below and lose my mind when her walls close in like a vice, and she screams into the room. My dick erupts, pulsating in sync with her pussy and emptying into her.

All the energy leaves her body, and she sinks into me, muttering incoherently. I slow my movements, kissing along her neck.

"I can't move," she wheezes after a minute.

"Then don't move." I savor each second, realizing the outside world is about to crash in.

"Sweetie, I'm leaking all over you."

"Don't give a shit."

Her head tips my way, and she scrubs a hand through my hair. "You okay?"

"Want you right where you are."

She studies me, her eyes assessing then fading into a heart-stopping shade of pale blue. "It's a big day."

"It is."

Today is a birthday-celebration-slash-Thanksgiving preparation, and for the first time in forever, I'll be with my family. But that's not what's bothering me.

"You're not happy."

"It's my birthday. I have the woman I love in my bed. For the first time in my life, I got a fucking fantastic birthday present. Now we gotta get up so you can cook all day with a bunch of women instead of staying our asses in this bed."

Her face falls, her lips twisting. "You peeked."

"Peeked at what?"

"Your present."

"No."

"Then how did you know it's fantastic?"

"Because you're my fucking present."

She gives me her smile, placing her lips on mine. "You have such a way with words."

"Did you hear the rest?"

"I did. I also heard you every time you griped about it this week."

"So, cancel."

"Honey, I'm not canceling."

"Thanksgiving is tomorrow. Why are you cooking today?"

"Because we're making three separate meals. There's a lot to cook."

"Whose idea was it to feed the station?"

"My mom and the ladies have delivered a Thanksgiving meal to the station for years."

"Fine, but why do you have to help?"

"I want a gourmet kitchen in our house, which means I need to know how to cook. These ladies are teaching me. Maybe next year we'll host Thanksgiving in our own home."

"Publix caters."

"We're not ordering our Thanksgiving dinner from the grocery store."

"Why? It makes perfect sense to me. Less mess and stress."

She grins, her eyes lighting with amusement.

"Something funny?"

"You're adorable when you don't get your way."

"Harley, puppies are adorable. I'm a grown-ass man."

"Oh, I'm well aware of that. A very talented, sexy, phenomenally hot grown-ass man. But you're also adorable."

I clasp her hips, thrusting up. Her grin and the amusement fade. "Oh my God, how can you be…?"

"Always, baby. But especially right now. Your tight, wet heat gripping me. Feeling your tits pressed to my chest."

"But aren't you tired?"

She's right. Last night, I worked, and with it being a holiday week, the streets of downtown Nashville were crazy. But when I closed out my shift, the only thing on my mind was getting home where she agreed to spend the night. "Not when I need to convince you to stay with me."

"I'll be back before you know it. Plus, the guys are taking you to lunch."

"The minute you climb off me, I'll know it." It makes me a bastard, but I'm willing to play dirty to get her to stay. "Harley, it's my birthday.

The only thing I want is you, all day, with no interruptions and no sharing."

Her eyes move over my face, and I know I have her when she fists my hair.

"I have big plans to spoil you."

"Spoil me by letting me have you all day, in bed, and mostly inside you."

"What about lunch with your dad and the guys?"

"I'll reschedule. They'll understand."

"Dammit, Achilles, you're ruining my surprise!"

"I hate surprises."

Her face falls, and a tinge of regret fills me, so I'm quick to cover. "Unless they included stripper bikinis and hot tubs."

"That was the grand finale," she murmurs.

My cock goes rock hard. "That we can leave this room for."

"Stop it. We don't have time," she says unconvincingly. "I really want to give you your present this morning. It's important."

"We'll compromise. I'll let you go to give me a present, and you agree to another hour in bed."

She pulls on her lip, her eyes casting over my shoulder and mentally calculating something. "I can compromise."

"Fine, hurry." I swat her ass lightly and loosen my hold.

I miss her heat immediately, my cock thumping on my stomach when she scrambles to the bathroom. A few minutes later, she comes out with my t-shirt on and carrying a large bag.

"Clothes were not an option in this compromise." I position against the headboard.

She smiles, climbing back on top and placing the bag on my stomach.

I recognize the hard feel of a frame. When I pull it out, I'm drawn to the large picture in the middle of the collage. It's a sketch of a house. Our house. A motorcycle, a landscaped yard, a generous-sized kitchen, and a few other shots make up the smaller pictures surrounding the collage.

My heart picks up speed. "I assume you've decided?"

"I did. This is it, Achilles. This is our home."

When Celia was here, she followed through and took Harley to view homes around the area. Then she took her to builders to get an idea of what the options and process will entail. Harley wanted me involved. She toiled over them endlessly, overwhelming herself. I took one look at the dozen choices she laid out on the floor and narrowed it down to three.

All three offered my requirements.

She pushed me on a budget, hung up on costs. I didn't blame her, but the apprehension was getting old.

Now, looking at her ultimate choice, it's settled. This is exactly what I want to give her.

"I'll contact the builder today and set up an appointment next week. Then I'll call Sam and Drake and get some money transferred to my bank."

There's a flicker of disappointment, and a split second of sadness crosses her face.

"Harley, what's wrong?"

"I called my bank yesterday and spoke to a loan officer," she tells me hesitantly. "It wasn't good news on my end."

I set the frame to the side and circle her waist, urging her closer. "First off, you don't need to discuss anything with a loan officer because I have this. But what did they say?"

"It's not a smart idea to change jobs right before applying for a loan. Even though Mike's offer is fantastic, and MJ Labels is an incredible opportunity, my work history needs to be steady."

I tamper the frustration and force my voice steady when I reply. "That's bullshit."

"Yeah, I've been with the same company for almost five years and make a decent salary. And Tom's income helps, too. But—"

"Stop right there. I don't give a fuck about the shit they spewed, which is probably true for most people needing a loan. What's bullshit is you rethinking Mike's offer. It's not only fantastic, but it's exactly the step you need to be thinking about at this point in your career. Better benefits, better salary, more excitement, getting full credit for your ideas —all of it blows your current position out of the water. Do not think of turning it down because of apprehension about a goddammed loan."

"Achilles, I'd like to help."

There's no way to tame the irritation now. "Baby, I have money. I can afford this house."

"But how?" she blurts out, then flinches. "Sorry, that was rude."

"It wasn't rude, it was honest and you've been holding on to that question for a long time, so here it is. I've been smart with my money. Living a simple life and saving. Years ago, when Drake and Sam got established, we all invested with their firm. They took risks that paid off. That money hasn't been touched, and they've grown it significantly. My savings are padded, and my salary itself isn't bad. Even being a rookie, I'm solid."

She melts into me, but not before I spot the wave of relief.

"Take the fucking job, Harley."

"Mike offered me the opportunity to work from home whenever I want."

"Even more incentive."

"Our new house has a beautiful space for an office."

"Good."

"With my raise, I can put purple towels in every bathroom and still afford kick-ass office furniture."

"Fuck." I cup the back of her head and slant her face to mine. "We're not putting purple towels in our bathrooms."

She smiles, a small giggle escaping. "Pink? Blue? Yellow? Tangerine? Aqua? Azure?"

"You can go through the whole rainbow and the answer is no. I don't even know what an azure fucking shade is."

"You'll learn soon enough." She crawls up my body, placing her lips to mine. "You mentioned something about an addiction."

"Didn't even slow down last time, baby. You broke my fucking control."

"Think we can do a replay?" Her voice drops low and sultry. My dick, already anxious, goes straight to steel. "Something to get you through the day without me."

"Have at it, baby."

I TOSS the washcloth into the hamper and catch my reflection. The small bandage over my ribcage with the recent addition of ink stands out. It's nothing special, just a kick-ass scroll to add to my already elaborate design started years ago. My frame is normal, with a little added bulge in my shoulders, chest, and arms. Nothing about me has changed, and at the same time, there's a glaring difference

Motherfucking Talon and his twinkle bullshit. Even I can't deny the shine in my eyes. I switch off the light and go straight to Harley, tucking her close.

"I think we broke a record."

"Record?"

"Not sure if there's a section in the Guinness book for most sex, most positions, most orgasms, and loudest screams in a day. But if there is, we should claim it."

I chuckle, kissing the side of her neck. "You saying I wore you out?"

"No, I'm just glad I have time to prepare for your next birthday." She rolls onto me, her hand caressing my jaw. "You enjoyed it."

"Best one ever."

"Then it's good I have a year to top it."

"Baby, I'm not sure anything can top today."

After she left this morning, I got a few hours of sleep before heading to lunch with the guys. Dad and Rich met us at the restaurant. For years, if the situation allowed, the guys and I did something low-key on our birthdays. It's another day. But today, Rich and Dad didn't hide their happiness to hang out, chat it up, and occasionally jab me for something. Usually about Harley.

After a while, I settled in and enjoyed it. We all went back to the neighborhood where Celia and Doug had flown in for the holiday, and they met us at the lot to discuss the next steps.

At four, Talon, Major, and I headed to the gym. Which was a total ruse. They drove me to a Tattoo Studio in East Nashville. When we arrived, Harley was waiting.

They shot me shit-eating grins before bolting, leaving me with my bumbling and excited woman. She was ready for her first tattoo. When she explained what she wanted and where, I was glad I was there.

She chose a small section of my design that she wanted placed in the same spot as mine, scaling her ribcage.

A piece of my art inked on her skin forever. I decided to duplicate the design lower on my skin, linking the design further.

When we got back here, our parents and Jewls were waiting. Then Harley dropped her last surprise. She hadn't been with the women preparing Thanksgiving most of the day. She was preparing a meal for tonight.

Not any meal. A meal of my favorites.

I didn't care the house was full of people, and I had to share her, because she was the star of the show.

And she was perfect.

After dinner, Talon, Major, and Ford went to work. Celia and Doug went to a hotel close to the airport to pick up their daughters in the morning, and the rest went home.

The last person was barely through the door when I attacked.

The kitchen, the hallway, the living room… everywhere I could. We never got to the hot tub because I'm a greedy son of a bitch and couldn't get enough.

"We finally christened the rug."

"Good choice, baby. Remind me to thank Erik next time he's around."

"Why?"

"Because this morning, you whipped your body around to sit on my face without ever losing my dick. Tonight, I fucked you hard in almost every position. I'm thinking his conditioning on Saturday mornings is the reason for your flexibility."

"Isn't it awesome?"

I smile against her hair. "It's awesome."

"Who do I thank for your stamina?"

"You're irresistible. It's impossible to control myself."

She lets out a little purr, snuggling close. "Give me a few hours and we'll test that theory further."

"Looking forward to it."

20

HARLEY

Breathe in, breathe out… deep breaths… You got this, Harley.

"You okay over there?"

"Yes," I lie.

"Sounds like you're doing those lamaze exercises," Mike teases as he swings into the driveway already loaded with vehicles.

"Nope, clearing my head."

"Do me a favor and don't hyperventilate or faint. Knowing these guys like I do, they'll beat each other to give mouth to mouth. I don't think Ace would approve."

"I'm not fainting!"

"Then get your ass out of the truck." He eases out, waiting for me.

I grab the gift bag and join him. "I still don't understand why you insisted I come today. These people don't know me, and it's a birthday celebration for the hostess. How awkward."

"That's exactly why you are with me. We're breaking the ice, and you'll understand nothing is awkward. They are down-to-earth people."

"Yeah, if you consider world-famous, high demand, multi-millionaires down-to-earth."

"Can't wait for my little Harley to eat her words." He opens the door without knocking.

A loud chorus erupts when he steps inside and immediately dies as all eyes come to me.

"MJ, man, didn't know you were bringing a date," someone yells.

He shakes his head at the same time a brunette rushes my way with an adorable toddler racing behind her.

"Harley," she greets me with a dazzling smile.

I'm speechless. Words don't form as I am face to face with Raven Collins.

She's stunning. Anyone in the music scene knows the love story of Raven Hayes and Declan Collins. Their pictures and stories were plastered everywhere when Declan's band, Sayge, started making it big and being recognized. Mike told me most of the stories were pure rumors, but there was some truth to the hardship their relationship endured.

To prepare for my new position, I've been studying Mike's clients. There's rarely a mention of Sayge without Raven. She's termed the fifth member of the band.

Mike's hand brushes my back and I snap to attention, all eyes on me. "Hi," comes out more as a squeak, and I clear my throat to try again. "Hey, Mrs. Coll—"

"Do not finish that statement. We're practically the same age. I'm Raven, never Mrs. Collins to you." She shocks me again by throwing her arms around me. "I've been dying to meet you!"

"Meet me?"

"Absolutely. And not because Mike's been gushing non-stop. I've seen your work, and you are likely to become my godsend."

The toddler slams into us, screeching in baby girl glee.

Raven lifts her and blows a raspberry on her cheek, which sets off another round of squeals. "Let's introduce you to Miss Harley. This is our youngest, Rayne," she tells me.

"Hello, Rayne, you certainly are a cute little thing." I tickle her belly.

She squeals in delight, and Mike takes the bag in my hand quickly so I can get her. Rayne nuzzles in my neck and yanks my hair.

"I have got to get me one of those. Chicks love the littles," the same voice from before states.

"Nate, you are a dumbass. You don't just get a baby," someone else replies.

Raven rolls her eyes, shaking her head with a regretful expression. "Let's get this over with. You should meet the guys."

She points to each man as she introduces them. "Nate, Blake, and Cooper are all in the band." They wave, and I recognize each from their pictures.

"Jay is our go-to man for everything." She motions to another man lounging on the sofa.

Mike had also mentioned a man named Jay and his role at the record label. I'll be working somewhat closely with him. Someone steps into Raven's side, and I fight standing.

His pictures don't do him justice. My eyes burn at the hotness factor. Facial piercings have never been my thing, but I'm rethinking my stance. Then again, I never thought I'd date a man with a penis piercing. He's not Achilles, but I appreciate every bit of his lusciousness.

"And this is my husband, Declan." Raven introduces him unnecessarily. Because really? Who wouldn't know him?

"Hey, Harley. Welcome to the team." He flashes me a grin, his green eyes glimmering. The velvety smooth baritone of his voice washes over me.

I sway and Mike chuckles.

Jesus, get a grip.

"Hi, ummm, nice to meet you."

"Wait, you're banging your new employee? Isn't that against the ethics code?" Nate speaks again, and Raven's eyes bulge.

"I swear they're harmless, but all my years of training fly out the window when a gorgeous woman walks in," she admonishes him while looking at me.

Gorgeous? She thinks I'm gorgeous. Whoa.

"She's my cousin, you idiot," Mike clarifies our ties.

Nate bows up, clearly happy at this news. "Awesome."

"Hey, everyone." I give a half-wave and gesture to Mike. "This is for you. Happy birthday."

He hands over the bag, and she glances inside, smiling warmly. "I love champagne! Thank you."

"And I'll take this one." Declan lifts Rayne from my arms. "You girls go enjoy."

Raven hooks her arm through my elbow, guiding me forward. "My parents and father-in-law are coming to get all the kids. They left after the cake portion of the afternoon to prep my parents' house. The children think it's a cousin's sleepover, but it's a huge birthday present for me. I get the night to let loose. My sisters-in-law get a night to party. Sleeping in tomorrow is a luxury I plan to enjoy."

Her warm and gentle reception eases all my nerves, and I smile back at her. "My boyfriend's birthday was this week, too, and it's been crazy. I can imagine that extra rest will be bliss."

"You do not know. Now let's go to the back yard. There's a whole other crew for you to meet. And most importantly, the bar."

"Sounds great."

She leads me through her house, and when we hit the kitchen, my feet freeze mid-step, jerking her back.

"Oh my God," I whisper in awe.

She shuffles uncomfortably, glancing around.

"I'm in love with this kitchen."

"Thanks," she responds apprehensively.

"I'm building a house soon, and this is exactly what I'd design."

"I can't take credit for it. It was designed when we bought the house."

"It's perfect."

Her unease loosens, and she grins proudly. "Declan and I love to cook, and we spend a lot of time in here as a family."

"I can see why. I'm learning to cook. Now this can be my inspiration."

"The developers definitely chose high-end builders for this neighborhood."

"That's the truth. Celia set me up with several of them to help decide on my choices."

"Celia Whitman?" She leers at me quizzically.

"Yes."

"You know Celia and Doug?"

"Yes."

"Are you building close?"

"Mike didn't tell you? My boyfriend and his friends bought the group of lots on Holmes Court. It's in phase three of the development."

"No, Mike didn't tell me. We'll practically be neighbors."

"It's close. Our home will be a little more... um..." I search for words that don't sound insulting.

"Traditional? Humble? You can say it. Everyone in our lives has teased us mercilessly since the day we signed the contract about the size of this place. But no one complains when it's time to party and there's a game room, a theatre, a pool, and enough privacy for the band to jam without neighbors complaining. Plus, Declan keeps wanting more children, regardless of my protests. I have help with a nanny and our parents with the children, but no one helps when it comes to wrangling the four boy-men in the band. They are worse than all my babies combined."

I press my lips together, but a small sputter escapes. "Believe it or not, I can understand."

"Come on, we need a drink. As soon as the parents grab the kids, the party really goes off. But I need to warn you," she pauses, twisting her face in thought. "Some of my friends are highly blunt and inappropriate. Ignore them."

"I'll introduce you to my best friend, Jewls, and you'll see that's not a problem."

"How about we save this bottle for a night it's only us?" She places the gift bag on the counter and drags me out the back door.

Once again, I'm stunned. The sizeable crowd of people all turn our way. The outdoor set-up resembles a normal birthday party. Streamers and lights hang high. Multi-colored balloons are tied to chairs and posts. A brightly colored cake that is half-eaten sits in the middle of a table.

All the guests are dressed casually. Even in the chilled weather, a few of the women are barefooted with their legs propped on the stones of the fire pit.

It's not the glamorous, high-society birthday celebration for the wife of a lead singer in a world-famous band.

It's informal, comfortable, and sophisticated without all the glitz. Completely down-to-earth.

Mike has earned his right to gloat like a fool when I eat my words.

A loud cheer has me swirling in the other direction, and I gasp. Loads of kids are playing some kind of game. Boys and girls run in different directions, and my quick count adds up to ten.

"Everyone, this is Harley Jacobs. Harley, this is everyone." Raven waves her hand in a semi-circular motion. "Three of those kids are mine, two belong to my brother, and the rest are nieces and nephews from Declan's sisters."

"Hi there, I'm Ember." Another beautiful lady introduces herself, handing us a cup of pink liquid. "And I'm in charge of keeping the birthday girl's drink filled all night. That's kind of our signature drink. If you'd like something else, we have a full bar stocked. Let me know."

I take a sip and groan in appreciation. "Are you kidding? This is one of my favorites. I haven't had a pink panty pull-down in forever."

She beams proudly. An incredibly handsome man comes up behind her, wrapping his arms around her waist. The resemblance to Raven is unmistakable.

"This is my husband, and Raven's brother, Robbie," Ember carries on.

The floodgates open and the introductions are endless. Declan's sisters and their husbands, Raven's best friends and their husbands or significant others. There's no way I'll remember all their names, but I try my best to keep up.

Declan and the rest of the guys join us with another round of guests that are obviously the parents. After a few minutes, they gather the overly excited kids and leave.

"You good?" Mike comes to stand next to me.

"I'm eating my words."

He grins around the rim of his beer bottle.

"Yo, boss man, I'm stealing your cousin." This comes from Charlie. She's not only married to Blake in the band, and one of Raven's best friends, but she's also my soon-to-be co-worker.

"Behave," he warns her.

"We're not at the office, so you can suck it up," she snips, dragging me to an open chair amongst the other women. "For the first time in for-fucking-ever, no one is pregnant." She lines up eight plastic shot glasses on the side table and fills them with a yellow liquid, then scans the group. "Right? No one is pregnant?"

There's a quick chorus of 'no'.

"But since I'm nursing, shots aren't a good idea," a lady named Harper pipes in.

"Pump and dump that shit like the rest of us did." Charlie passes the shots around to us and goes to shoot it then stops, pinning me with her eyes. "Wait, I heard nothing from you."

"Me? I'm not pregnant. I've been drinking this." I show the cup Ember gave me earlier.

"Yeah, but you could be fake sipping. And since I don't know you, I can't tell."

"I'm not even married, so no, I'm not pregnant."

"I wasn't married either," she replies.

"You were engaged," Raven points out. "And your wedding was in less than a month when you found out."

"Very true. Okay, bottoms up, girls."

We all shoot back the tangy, citrusy concoction.

"That was delicious." I lick my lips and get the aftertaste of sweetness.

"Of course, it was. I make a perfect lemon drop," Charlie brags. "Now that the pleasantries are done, time to get real. Please tell me you know how to whip ass."

The hair on my arms prickles under the heat of the curious stares. "Whip ass?"

"In the office. I've spent a lot of years in several positions at MJ Labels, whipping that place into shape. The staff and clientele know very well what happens if they step out of line. I need a wingman and hope like hell you'll fit the bill. Mike assures me you have it in you."

I stare at this woman, understanding exactly why Mike refers to her as a wildcard. A bubbly giggle escapes before I slap my hand over my mouth. When it's under control, I answer. "I bartend three nights a week at a bar geared toward cops. My dad is a cop-turned-detective, and I frequently spend time with four macho-type men. You can count on me to hold my own."

"Good to know. But note—giggling is not good. Badass bitches don't giggle," she chides.

"Charlie, stop harassing her. If she changes her mind about joining the label because of your mouth, I'll strangle you." Raven cuts her eyes in warning.

"I'm resigning on Monday. You can rest assured Charlie isn't chasing me off."

The back door opens again, and Raven squeals like a little girl at the group walking through.

"Max!" She leaps up and rushes to a dark-haired man whose arms are outstretched.

"That's Max Roberts, and the couple is Finn and Presley Black. Max, Finn, and Robbie are best friends and served in the Marines together. Max is the only one still active," Ember leans in, informing me quietly.

Hearing the word Marines, I twist to her. "Your husband is a Marine?"

"He and Finn did many years and now work in security."

"My boyfriend was active and is now in the Reserves."

"Wow, small world. I have a feeling our guys will have a lot in common." She toasts her cup to mine and flashes me a mega-watt smile.

It's then I realize these people aren't only down-to-earth, they're cool. My earlier trepidation disappears. I say a brief prayer that the other clients of MJ labels are equally as awesome and easy-going.

I return Ember's smile. "This is quite a mix-matched crew."

"Yeah, it's hard to believe, but we all fit. I have a feeling you'll be right in the mix, too."

The compliment washes through me, and I take a large sip to keep from giggling with glee and earning a nasty glare from Charlie.

Raven and Presley wander back to our group. Finn gets a chair and slides it in the circle before kissing his wife and joining the other men.

The girls immediately jump into conversation. It's easy to follow along and keep up, even with several side topics ricocheting around the group. Every few minutes, a man comes over to refill drinks and check in.

Eventually, the entire crowd migrates to the area. I don't know how much time passes, but as the night goes on, the party gets rowdier. My cheeks and sides ache from laughing.

"Sparkle, are we expecting anyone else?" Declan's eyebrows furrow together as he studies his phone.

"Tripp and Reese are coming."

"Got it, I'll let them in." He disappears inside the house, with Cooper following.

"Sometimes that front gate annoys me. It's a necessity, but I prefer for family and friends to come and go easily," Raven says to no one in particular.

"I'm ready to give up my title as the hottest eligible rocker in this world for you. Just say the word," Nate flirts shamelessly, drawing attention our way.

"She has a boyfriend, Nate," Raven informs him.

"Boyfriends don't scare me, Rave."

"He's a Marine," Ember chirps.

"Hmm." Nate rubs his hand over his chin, rolling his teeth through his lips. "That's problematic, but I'm not discouraged."

Mike clears his throat at the same time Nate continues. "We would make beautiful babies and live out the world's greatest love story."

At this, I lose it, doubling over in a howl. "I'm flattered… r-r-r-eally flattered," I sputter, "but I'm already—"

"Taken," a rough voice finishes for me and I whip around to find Achilles standing beside a highly amused Declan.

All the laughter dies. He's changed out of his uniform and into my favorite jeans and a black shirt with MNPD stretched across his chest. With his hands propped on his hips, his tattoos snake out from the sleeves. My stomach dives and flips at the look of possessiveness on his features.

"I'm guessing Five-O isn't here about a noise complaint." Robbie chuckles under his breath.

"No! No way! I'm losing out to a cop?" Nate cries out in mock disbelief.

"The way he's glaring, you're lucky he isn't carrying his gun," Mike chuckles.

I go to him, wrapping my arms around his stomach and tipping up to kiss the underside of his jaw. "Hey, sweetie."

His arms circle me, and he lowers his mouth to mine, licking along my lips before a quick kiss. "You taste like lemonade."

"Isn't it awesome?"

His eyes glitter in the dim lights, and his lips tip at the edges. "It's awesome."

I twist to the crowd, who's silently watching intently. "Guys, this is my boyfriend, Achilles. But he goes by A—"

"Ace." Max weaves around the fire pit, stopping in front of us with a huge smile. "Ace motherfucking Kingston. Can't fucking believe this."

They've obviously met before.

Robbie and Finn are instantly at his side with their own grins.

"Max? What the hell, man?" Achilles holds out a hand, which Max tugs, and I'm smashed in their man hug.

Max releases him and glances between his two friends. "You got to remember this guy."

"Abso-fucking-lutely."

Robbie and Finn repeat the same greeting, and I try not to flip as all these hot guys crush me with their bodies.

This is definitely a story for Jewls.

"Can't believe this shit. What are the chances?" Max goes on.

"Wild, man. Was in almost ten, moved back, graduated the academy, work on the force. Aiming for SWAT." Achilles covers the high points of his life in man-speak.

"Ford, Major, and Talon?"

"Same."

"Out of the Marines?"

"Signed to the Reserves."

There's something in the tone of his voice that sends the same look across the three men's faces.

An understanding, a non-verbal explanation. It's a split-second, but I don't miss their reaction to this news. Luckily, the powwow is broken up by Raven.

"Hi, I'm Raven, and I think you met my husband at the gate."

"Sorry to bust in on your birthday party," he apologizes politely, but not sincerely. "I got off shift and Harley wasn't home yet."

"You're not busting in on anything. We're about to jam. How about a beer?" Declan offers, and Achilles juts his chin.

"Excuse me, can we all meet the extremely hot cop that has dashed all of Nate's dreams?" Charlie waves from her perch in Blake's lap.

I glance up at him, wrapping my hand around his neck. "Extremely hot cop doesn't do you justice."

"How badly do you want to stay?" His gruff question takes me off-guard.

"Are you mad? Nate is harmless."

"Nate, the guy who told you that the two of you would make beautiful babies?"

"He's harmless," I repeat.

"This has nothing to do with Nate. Looking as gorgeous as you do and tasting the sweetness on your lips—I want you on my bike."

"You brought the bike?" I love his motorcycle. We've only been riding once, but I was hooked. The power, holding him tight, feeling the wind whipping around us. At first, it was terrifying, but then it was exhilarating.

"I did, and right now, I want to drive you to our property and fuck you on it."

Between our work schedules, we have had little time together since the night of his birthday. With it being a holiday weekend, he picked up overtime to let some of the other men be with family.

A white-hot tingle races through my bloodstream, and I grip him to remain standing. "One hour?" comes out breathy, and his eyes turn molten.

"One hour."

He pulls my bottom lip between his teeth, plants a quick kiss, and tucks me to his side.

"Whew, I need a private room after that," Charlie announces, fanning her face. "Didn't even have to hear what they said to understand it. The sexual energy is thick. I'm pretty sure the new girl has Raven and Declan beat. That was smoking."

Heat flames my face at all the knowing looks aimed at me.

"Warned you. We have a muzzle somewhere around here since she has no filter." Raven winks at me. "And, so you know, we may be laid back, but we're still rock and roll. You need some privacy, down the hall, last room on the right. No questions asked."

Ace's mouth twitches. "Appreciate that, but I have a bed close."

"Suit yourself, but the offer stands. It wouldn't be the first time."

"He's taking me home on his bike," I divulge for no reason.

Her blue eyes pop and then fill with appreciation. "Ahhh, the bike. I love riding on the *bike*. Harley, babe, I have a feeling you and I will be great friends." With another wink, she walks away.

"I think she knows we're having motorcycle sex tonight."

"Yeah, pretty sure she clued in. But gotta say, the way her husband is looking at her, they may be the ones needing the private room."

His chest vibrates, and I fold into him, bursting into laughter.

21

ACE

I SWALLOW a large gulp of beer, staring out the window. A loud wolf whistle cuts through the room, my eyes staying trained on the darkened back yard.

"Oh, shit, we have the broody Kingston." Talon gauges my mood instantly.

"He's pissed. I feel for the jeweler if he fucked this up." Ford's statement is laced with sarcasm.

Major steps into my line of sight, assessing me warily. The flash of recognition in his eyes is like looking into a mirror. "Fuck, you too?"

"I feel it, man. It's coming."

The air in the room turns static, the other guys closing in

"Yeah," Talon agrees, his jovial mood gone.

"Knew it last weekend. Felt it during drills," Ford admits what we all picked up on.

When we reported to our monthly drill last weekend, there was an intense vibe around the four of us. We were under a microscope. Expectations are always high, but this was different.

It was physical and mental. We were being evaluated.

And there is only one reason.

"I spoke to a few of the guys at MARSOC. The atmosphere is hyper-alert and the information scarce." Talon drops the news.

"I called Dad today." Ford opens his own beer and takes a long swig. "No specific reason, had a nagging feeling I needed to."

"Shit, you mean we're all in the zone and said nothing?" Major sounds pissed. He has the right to be.

There's a reason we work well together and we're all standing here alive. We trust each other, we share what's on our mind, and we don't fucking hide behind the shadows of 'what ifs'.

"I'm ready for whatever comes." Ford's matter-of-fact attitude applies to all of us.

A silence fills the room, and I know what they're waiting for.

"I haven't told her. She's been looking forward to this party tonight."

Tonight is the MJ Labels holiday celebration. But Mike didn't limit the invitation list to staff only. He extended to clients, friends, and family. "Harley and Jewls have been excited all week, and hell if I wanted to ruin it."

"We got this, Ace, no matter what comes our way," Ford speaks low. "We don't fail."

All I can do is nod.

"I don't mean to add to the fire, but did the jeweler fuck up?" Talon attempts to lighten things.

"No, he didn't fuck up." I take the box out of my pocket and chuck it his way.

He pops it open and gives a low whistle. "Nice. When's it happening?"

"Soon as possible."

"Then why are you in here staring at your reflection in the window?"

I slice my eyes to him. "I'm banned from my room. Unless I wanted to pick her up at her apartment, Harley insisted she and Jewls have privacy."

At the mention of Jewls, Major's attention shifts. "They almost ready?"

"Hell if I know. She sprung this shit on me today, telling me they had some appointments and then would be here. They rolled in around five, and I was ordered to get ready in the guest room. I've been waiting."

Talon hands the box back. "I assume you spoke to Rich about this?"

"Yeah, and Amanda is about to burst at the seams."

"You gonna try to get it on her finger tonight?"

"If I had it my way, she'd be wearing it right now. But seeing as Jewls already announced she's spending the night, it's not happening."

"You could always wait until Christmas. I hear chicks go nuts for Christmas proposals," Ford suggests.

"Too cliché. I'm not waiting almost three weeks."

"Just saying, you could kill two birds with one stone. The ring could double as her present."

"Ford, for a guy so loaded, you're one cheap motherfucker." Major lays him out.

For the first time all day, I crack a smile.

The clacking of heels on tile pulls my awareness down the hallway, and my smile dies.

Talon whistles again, this time a low-pitched siren.

I barely give Jewls a glimpse, my gaze zeroing in on the vision strolling my way.

Her hair is sleek and straight, hanging over her bare shoulders. The blue hue of her eyes is glistening under heavier than usual make-up. Tiny sparkles glitter on her exposed skin. The black and silver dress hugs her body with a deep slit down the front that crisscrosses at her tits. That's as far as I get.

My arm reaches back, someone taking the ring as my bottle hits the counter.

Harley's eyes go wide, and she stops mid-stride, throwing her hand up. "No, no, no… stay back. I worked all day on this!"

Her words do nothing to stop me from stalking to her. She backtracks, but I'm already on her. She squeals as she goes over my shoulder, beating on my back. "Put me down!"

"Nope."

"Achilles…" Her voice is drowned out by Jewls' yell.

"I'm opening a bottle of wine. Try not to wreck her too much."

We hit my room, my foot kicking the door shut and jostling her so she has no choice but to wrap her legs around my waist. I slide a hand to the back of her neck and slam my mouth to hers.

She whimpers down my throat as the taste of mint and peaches coats my taste buds. I hum in appreciation, slanting her head for better access. Her tongue tangles with mine, meeting me stroke for stroke, driving me insane.

Her fingers dig into my scalp, her thighs tighten, and she rotates her hips, coming into contact with my throbbing cock. Her scent, her taste, and the feel of her body pressed close ignite my sense of possession and send it into overdrive.

I slide my hand under her dress and along her ass, my fingers slipping inside her panties.

I tear my mouth away, growling against her lips. "Fuck, Harley. I need you now."

Without a word, she reaches under the dress, and the silky material releases, giving me full access. "They clip at the sides so you have easy access."

"You have a split second to make a choice. Here or the bed?"

Her mouth splits into a provocative smile. "Here."

I make quick work of my belt, button, and zipper, freeing my cock and stroking it along her slit. Somehow, I find the will to hold back, knowing she needs to be ready. My piercing rubs back and forth, grazing over her clit until her breath hitches and her gaze grows hazy.

She traces the outline of my lips with her tongue, swiveling slowly with my movements. "What are you waiting for?"

"Getting you ready, baby."

The haze clears and her eyes light up. She slants up and then drives down, taking my dick all the way. Her body shudders in response.

"Jesus, fuck, are you okay?"

"Oh, God, yes." She rocks into me.

That's all it takes for my will to snap. I back her into the wall and ram up hard. Her muscles contract, and she moans, dropping her head back. "Please…"

"Please what, baby? What do you want?"

"You. Harder. More."

Fire scorches inside as I hammer into her over and over. With each stroke, her pussy clenches tighter until sweat rolls down my back.

"Don't stop. Feels too good." Her voice is hoarse and dripping with need.

Fiery sensations pulse along my cock as the piercing scrapes along her soft flesh. "Your pussy's pulling me deeper, baby. Can you take more?"

She lifts her head, bringing her eyes back to mine, and my cock threatens to explode.

I pound harder, the sounds of us filling the room. Her lips part as her breath comes in shallow gasps and she grinds down, her fingernails digging into my scalp.

"Achilles, so close."

"Come for me."

"I want you."

"You'll get me on the next one." I grip her hip, rotating slightly, and slam up.

She lets out a small cry, dropping her head to my shoulder and moaning into my neck. My cock swells at the flood of wetness making her slicker.

The walls of her pussy contract and release as she chants my name, flying apart.

"My dick is fucking ready to blow." I shift, slowing for her to adjust to me at this angle.

"Oh, shit. The tip of your… the ball…" she can't finish, her breath shallowing out.

"I know, baby, I feel the metal twisting inside you."

"More." Her hoarse whisper is a plea.

I drive up harder and faster, animalistic need coursing through my veins. "Let me see your face, gorgeous."

She brings her face to mine. Her eyes are wild and frenzied, cheeks flushed with small patches of pink from my stubble.

"So fucking perfect. Taking me hard, riding my dick, driving me insane. "

"I love the rough and untamed, Achilles."

Electric jolts rip through me. "Get there again, Harley."

Her hips roll, sliding into my strokes until we're both on the edge. She arches, groaning in appreciation, and that's all it takes. I thrust up hard and explode, crashing my mouth to hers.

I savor the sensation of her pussy pulsating, taking everything and sucking me dry.

My lips kiss a trail to her ear, feeling her chest rise and fall against mine. "The hair, the face, the dress—all of it adding to perfection."

"I want to be mad, but that was hot," she mumbles. "So much for hours of preparation."

"Baby, you walked out looking like this, you should have expected me to pounce."

"I thought maybe you could conjure a little control."

"Not a fucking chance."

She giggles, lifting her face to mine and scaling her nails lightly down my neck. "I take it you like the dress?"

"Yeah, I like the dress, but you're not wearing it. Your tits are practically hanging out."

Her eyes narrow and mouth pinches in a scowl. "They are not. It covers everything."

"Plastic clasps hold your panties together."

"Only you and I know that."

"Harley—"

"Swear to God, Achilles, don't piss me off after scorching hot wall sex. I'm wearing this dress."

I think about throwing her on the bed, but before I can move, her fingertips dig into my skin. "Don't you dare."

"Dare what?"

"Whatever it is you're thinking of doing that has your eyes reeling."

"Shit." I lay my forehead to hers. "It's impossible to deny you."

"It's not denial. The thrill of anticipation is good for you. Think about what happens when we get home. It'll be worth the wait."

My cock lurches at the comment, and she bites her lip, squirming.

The diamond ring pops in my head, and I wish like hell it was on her finger.

Like right now.

With me inside her, the combination of us coating my cock, and her staring at me this way… Trust, love, a devotion so deep it hits me solid in the chest, rocking my foundation.

"Sometimes, I look at you and can't believe my luck. I've been dealt a lot of shitty hands in my life. Seen things, done things, made decisions that literally meant life or death."

Her face grows pensive, her eyes filling with understanding. She opens her mouth, but I keep on.

"Every minute of every day since you gave me a chance has been worth the wait. I'd go through it all again to have you and know you're mine. Tonight, when we get home, I want you like this as I take my time and show you how much it means to me."

"We aren't talking about scorching hot wall sex, are we?" she whispers.

"No, baby, we're talking about forever. You want to talk about that while I'm balls deep inside you against the wall, we can."

Her lips quiver as a tear slips down her cheek. "Dammit, Achilles, you're not allowed to make me cry and ruin my make-up."

"That's impossible. You're exquisite, Harley, always."

"You can't have this incredibly sentimental and heartfelt conversation when I don't have the time to show you *how much you mean to me.*" She twists my words.

I walk us into the bathroom and set her on the vanity, immediately missing her warmth while I fix my pants. "Want me to clean you up?"

"I've got it. I need to touch up my face."

"Your make-up is fine."

"I had to up my game. My date is the most gorgeous man in the world. I'm taking a colossal risk bringing you to this party. You may replace me with some famous musician."

"Never gonna happen." I kiss her quickly. "Meet you in the kitchen."

"Everyone knows we had sex, and I don't even care."

"It was a given when you walked down that hall."

She smiles giddily. "I love you."

"If I don't leave this bathroom now, we're skipping the party."

She releases me and slaps my chest. "Go, I'll be out in a minute."

I head back to the kitchen where Jewls is perched on a stool with a glass of wine and talking to Major. He's freshly showered and wearing an outfit similar to mine. I cock an eyebrow in question as I pour Harley a glass of wine and grab another beer.

"We changed our minds on the invite. Talon and Ford are getting ready," he explains.

"Gotta say, Ace, you don't disappoint," Jewls pipes up. "And I'm not talking about the whole savage beast throwing his woman over his shoulder to go screw her senseless. Even though that was entertaining. Never thought I'd see the day where Harley would embrace her sexuality."

"Jewls—"

"Nope, I'm talking about something much more impressive and timeless." She taps her ring finger. "Nice job. It's classy, stunning, and one-hundred percent Harley."

I swing my eyes at Major, who's grinning. "She zeroed in on it before you even shut your door."

"Jewls— "

"Don't worry. I'm a vault. And you're fortunate."

I'll regret this, but I ask anyway, "Outside of the obvious, why am I fortunate?"

"Because I'm a fabulous best friend. Since my girl loves you like she does, that means my fabulousness spreads to you. Tomorrow, when we decorate this place for Christmas, I'll make sure you have several choices for the most romantic backdrop for your proposal. Unless, of course, you plan to pull the whole savage beast-slash-boorish act and slide the ring on her finger while banging her."

"Knowing Ace, that's more his style." Talon strolls in, with Ford following.

"Yeah," she agrees, "and Harley would probably gush until the end of time about how romantic it was."

The scene from a few minutes ago replays in my head, bringing forth the feelings that rocked me. I don't tell Jewls that's exactly how I plan to get the ring on her finger. Instead, I reply, "Anything you do is appreciated."

She flashes me an approving smile.

This time, when I hear heels on the tile, I turn to fully appreciate the view.

A blush fills her cheeks when she joins us, taking the glass of wine I offer. There's a hushed silence as the guys each have shit-eating grins on their faces.

"Thank God he didn't ruin your hair," Jewls blurts. "And, Jesus, I need my sunglasses. You're radiant."

The grins turn to low chuckles, and Harley lays her head on my shoulder. "Stop being dramatic. And, no, he didn't ruin Rowan's work."

At the mention of Rowan, my gaze shoots to Ford, who's looking at me.

"Rowan is the hairdresser, right?" I play coy.

"Hairdresser and cosmetologist extraordinaire. She was at ladies' night last month."

"I remember, didn't have time to meet her."

Harley straightens and focuses on the guys. Her eyes light with excitement and mischief. "Rowan is our sweet, fun, and newly single friend. You guys should meet her. I have a feeling she'll be around a lot more now that she dropped the loser she was dating."

"Dating? I thought she was engaged."

"Turns out he was a complete douchelord. Didn't ask her to marry him, but manipulated her into wearing the ring for appearances. He wanted other guys to *think* she was taken, even though he wouldn't commit. She deserves to find a good guy."

That last part was meant for Talon and Ford since we all know Jewls and Major are dancing around some heavy attraction behind the muse of being friends. I can also tell they're not fond of the possibility of being set up, regardless of Rowan's situation.

"She's shed two hundred pounds of useless weight and has a lot to offer someone."

"Baby, kinda harsh to try and play matchmaker when the woman recently got out of a relationship."

She peers up and shrugs. "Nothing wrong with making friends with really hot Marines-turned-cops. Especially when they're members of the exclusive Casanova Club."

"Fucking ridiculous name," Ford sighs.

"I think it's awesome." Harley winks.

"Let's get out of here. Jewls, you're riding with me," Major declares. I know exactly what he's thinking. They may not be a couple, but he's walking in that room with her close and sending a message.

She slides off the stool. "Let me get my coat."

"Ford and I will ride with Ace," Talon states, also picking up on Major's intentions.

"Finally, we may get somewhere," Harley says low enough for only me to hear. "He needs a push."

"We're not getting involved."

"I can't help it. I'm full of love, and I mean that literally."

A throaty growl rolls up my throat. "Jesus, Harley."

"MAN, NAME YOUR PRICE."

"Still a hard pass," I reiterate to Cooper.

"Coop, give it up. The guy has declined the offer three times." Declan jabs his bandmate and friend. "Have some respect."

"Nah, money talks. Surely, he has a price. We can sweeten the pot and get all of you." He waves between Ford, Talon, Major, and me. "You join Sayge as security, no one's fucking with anyone. We'll be crushing it on the stage and know we're safe."

"You have a reason not to feel safe?" I raise an eyebrow.

"Nah, but you guys will add to our team."

"What he's saying is you'll bring in the chicks." Blake hands me a fresh bottle of beer.

"Thought you rockers had that angle covered."

"We do, but with security looking like you guys, it wouldn't hurt. Although, I'm off the market, and my lady is taking yours under her wing. Brace, man." He motions to the dance floor where Charlie is in the middle of a circle, twerking while expertly holding her martini glass without spilling a drop.

Harley catches my eye and struts over, adding a little sway. She's also drinking some kind of martini. "What are we talking about?" She leans in, kissing the underside of my jaw.

"Kill me now, I can't handle it!" Nate grips his chest dramatically.

She shoots him a smile. "If I hadn't fallen ass over heel in love with Achilles at sixteen, you'd totally be my type." There's a giggly slur in her words.

"Baby, the saying is ass over elbow," I correct.

"Whatever."

"We're trying to talk these guys into joining our security team," Cooper throws out.

She shakes her head, her sleek hair swishing in the air. "Not happening. Achilles is becoming an accountant."

A couple of throats clear while Ford outright laughs.

"I'm not becoming an accountant."

"If you change your mind, I'm always in need of a good tax guy," Mike eggs me on.

"See, you can be a part of the family business." She pokes my side. "It's a perfectly safe occupation."

"Ace as a bean counter." Talon tilts his head, studying me. "Not sure it fits. He's a little too edgy."

"Gotta agree, Harley. Ace is the type of man that would rather shoot at targets than click away on a calculator," Mike prods her.

"You make it sound frumpy. Achilles would make a sexy accountant."

"How about we give it a rest?" I slide my hand around her waist and tuck her close.

She gives in. "Are you having a nice time?"

"I am drinking a beer, shooting the shit, and watching you strut around while sucking down martinis. It'd be hard not to have a nice time."

"Do you work next Sunday?"

"Not sure, why?"

"We are invited to a Christmas party."

"Another one?"

"This is more of a family event. Santa's popping in to surprise the kids."

"You're all welcome to come," Declan extends the invitation.

"Appreciate it, but we're working overtime at the football game," Talon answers.

"You may get the better deal. It's a nuthouse. The chaos is off the chain. But these women always find a reason to have a party." Declan glances at his wife with admiration, clearly not caring.

I peer back down to Harley, feeling the same. She enjoys a party, loves people, and is a natural hostess. When we have our own home, I expect to have family and friends invading often. Which means I'll need to curb my voracious need to have her alone most of the time.

It's not happening.

But I'll pretend to try.

She sips her drink, eying me knowingly. "Whatever you're thinking is naughty."

"Not to me."

I lean in to kiss her, but only get mid-dip before my phone vibrates in my jeans.

It's on my mind to ignore it until Talon's low hissing snaps my attention. The three of them are looking at their phones, and their expressions say it all. The four of our phones getting a message can only mean one thing.

We're up.

Time to head out.

Ford's gaze meets mine, silently explaining.

Someone has made contact. And it's not good.

"No. Please, God, no." Harley clutches my shirt, her voice a desperate plea.

A heavy darkness settles in the air, and the crowd around us closes in. Mike's the only one to speak.

"All okay?"

I drop my eyes to Harley, my heart cracking at the raw pain etched on her features.

"We have a situation." He steps closer, aware of what our *situation* has to do with.

"What can I do?"

"Take care of my girl."

Harley shivers, and a little cry escapes. To the side, I catch Jewls moving close to Major and him squeezing her hand. There's a similar pain on her face. Mike notices, too, nodding.

"We'll take care of them."

"I'm guessing this isn't a cop call-out," Declan assesses correctly. "We're here for whatever you need."

I jut my chin in appreciation and wave at the others. "We need to get to the house."

"Go out the side door, easier access to the elevators and less chance of getting mobbed." Mike takes Harley's glass and kisses her cheek, telling her he'll check on her soon. I guide her around the room, the others following, and get her to my truck before she loses it.

She whimpers when I try to put her in the passenger side, tightening her clutch. I toss my keys to Talon, climbing in the back seat with her and not bothering with a seatbelt.

"Please, please, please let this be a false alarm."

My hands scrub through her hair, holding her gently.

Because there is no false alarm. This is as real as it gets.

One of our own is in danger. Deadly danger.

And our job is to get him—or them—back.

22

HARLEY

I STAND IMMOBILE, staring into the open bathroom, but not seeing anything. Achilles is in the closet changing, and the silence is deafening. My gaze drifts to the wall where we had sex earlier tonight.

It seems like a lifetime ago.

South America…

Going in hot…

Two dead….

Team and three civilians missing…

All of this jumbles in my mind, replaying until my stomach turns.

Achilles asked me to stay with Jewls and let them take their call with Willie. But I couldn't handle the wait and listened outside the door. Most of what they said didn't register, except these that stuck.

Four of the most important men in my life, one of whom is my everything, are about to head into treacherous territory and save their own.

My emotions are on shaky ground, the dam ready to break. Self-preservation is my only lifeline.

They called Achilles and his friends for a reason.

A reason I hate, but important nonetheless. They are heroes.

He comes my way, and I suck in a breath.

Gone is my casual-slash-sexy-as hell-Achilles Kingston.

In his place is a full-on military man.

Black cargo pants, tight black shirt, black boots, and carrying a matching large duffel that's stuffed. His big, powerful body is strung so tight his muscles bulge under the fabric of his shirt.

He digs in the top drawer of his dresser and pulls out a watch, snapping it on his wrist, and I immediately recognize it as the one my dad gave him at his boot camp graduation. His stature is sharp and focused, his mind a million miles away.

I memorize everything about this time, knowing he's leaving me any minute. On the thought, a lump forms in my throat, threatening to choke me.

His beautiful eyes lock with mine, and the harshness in his features wanes.

"Baby, come here."

I don't delay lunging the few feet to him. His bag hits the floor with a thud, and he gathers me tight.

"It will be okay."

"How can you be sure?" My voice cracks over the lump.

"Because I know us."

I peer up at him and ask another question that's picking away at me. "What are the other reasons? You told me there are only a few reasons you'd return. It was in your agreement. What are those?"

His eyes flash with conflict, and I know he can't share. "They aren't specific reasons. It's more like hostile levels. Once a situation hits a certain level and it falls under our skills expertise, we could get called."

Involuntarily, my body does a top-to-toe shiver. "Hostile levels? How bad?"

"I can't say."

"I heard him—Willie. He said two people are dead and others are missing. That's pretty fucking hostile!" I unravel.

"Baby, you shouldn't have listened. It adds useless worry."

"Worry? I'm fucking terrified. My heart is on the brink of splintering apart with fear."

Pain slashes through his features.

Guilt claws at me for being so selfish. "I'm sorry. I'm trying to be strong, but the uncertainties are making me irrational."

"It kills me I'm the cause."

"What if this was me, and I was being called away on some highly confidential and undoubtedly dangerous assignment? What would you tell me?"

His grip tightens fiercely, his gaze turning lethal. "Nothing, I wouldn't tell you shit. Because it would never happen. Any thoughts of you in danger make my blood run cold. Whatever it took, even if that meant cuffing you to me."

My feminist side takes a cruel hit, but the vice around my heart loosens. "Tell me what to say. You already know I support, trust, and love you, but it doesn't seem like enough."

"It's everything." He drops his forehead to mine. "I need you to do me a favor."

"Anything."

"I need you to stay here. Not only tonight, but while I'm away. Jewls can stay as much as she wants. Invite any friends if you get lonely."

I open my mouth to argue it would be weird, but he places his lips on mine. "We have top-of-the-line security, and you already know about the cameras and entry alerts. It'll give me peace of mind to know the doors are locked and you are tucked away safe at night."

I nod my agreement because the lump is forming again. Being alone in this massive house may be intimidating, but if it helps ease his worrying, I'll do anything.

"And tomorrow, decorate the house. Rich and my dad will help. Pick out a tree, and Rich can use my truck to pick it up. If you need, I'll call some guys from the station, and they'll hang the outdoor lights."

"It won't be the same without you guys." Panic sets in at the thought flashing in my head. "Oh, God, what if you're not back for Christ—?"

The question dies because the sorrow in his expression brings my guilt back to the forefront. "Never mind. Christmas is a few weeks away. You'll be back."

He reads through my false bravado but encourages me. "Hold on to that. Know we're doing everything to get through this and get home."

The warmth of his breath coats my lips, and I tip up, opening to give him access. His tongue sweeps through my mouth slowly, touching everywhere before tangling with mine. His hand travels up my back and winds in my hair, caressing my scalp as he angles to go deeper.

I follow his lead, the kiss turning greedy and desperate. Both of us needing more. The hand at my hip slides lower, tucking up the top of my thighs. I give him what he wants, bracing so he can lift me.

I kiss him harder, pouring every emotion into my strokes. He growls, taking over again, sucking on my tongue and breaking away enough to get a breath.

Electric heat spreads through my body, taking over, and I force all thoughts out of my head except this moment and how I feel in his arms.

Too soon, there's a loud rap at his door followed by two softer ones, indicating it's time. Achilles slows, placing sweet kisses across my lips.

"I love you, Achilles."

"I love you, too, Harley. More than anything."

"Come home to me and give me my forever."

"Forever isn't enough time, but it's yours."

I press my lips together to keep from bursting into tears. "It's ours."

He places me on my feet, lacing our fingers together, and grabs his bag.

When we get to the living room area, the guys are dressed identically to Achilles. A coldness slithers through my veins and I move in closer.

Then I notice my best friend and see she's barely holding it together. She is not plastered to Major, but she's standing at his side with her hand wound around his elbow. Whatever is happening has spooked her.

Talon comes over, jostling me into a gentle hug. "Take care of my plants, Jay."

"You have plants?"

"A few. Mom's doing. They're in my room."

"I'm not very good with plants."

"They're easy. If you can take care of Kingston, you can do it."

I kiss his cheek, cupping his chin. "Love you, Talon. Please take care."

"Always. Made you a promise, Jay-Jay. Not breaking that."

Ford steps in, taking his place and lifting me as much as he can with my hand still in Achilles'. "Do me a favor and don't turn our house into a Hallmark movie set."

I giggle, remembering that first time they went to drill weekend and found Jewls and me watching the Hallmark channel when they got home.

"No chance, but it will be beautiful."

"Know it will."

"Love you, Ford Whitman. Take care."

"I also made you a promise." He gives me a gentle look, his grey-blue eyes full of sincerity.

There's a buzzing followed by a ding, and all their heads go to the door. I recognize the sound and glance at the clock. "Who could be here? It's almost midnight."

"Rich and I'm assuming Amanda," Achilles answers.

"You called my parents?"

"Didn't want you two alone."

My beautifully complicated man always thinking of me.

A flash of headlights lights the circular drive outside, and four shadowy figures walk up the steps.

"Oh, fuck," he hisses under his breath, his grip turning painful.

I understand why when Ford swings the door open, and Pete and Sandy stand with my parents.

Pete is composed. Sandy is a full-on mess, her face swollen and splotchy, tears falling freely.

"Mom," Achilles is interrupted when she throws herself around him.

"Don't, Achilles. I am your mother and this is my right. At least, this time, I can tell you how much I love you in person."

"Son, those deployment calls took years off our lives. This is something she needs," Pete interjects warmly.

Achilles drops his face to her neck and gives her a one-armed hug back, refusing to release my hand. She's so close, I detect the vibration of her body.

She gathers her composure and steps back, Pete folding her to his side.

"Can you boys tell us anything?" Dad asks boldly, but I catch the worry in his tone.

Achilles wiggles my hand, sending the message to keep quiet. I wasn't supposed to hear what I did earlier.

Major slices his eyes to Jewls, sending the same message. I don't know what happened while I was with Achilles, but Jewls must have admitted to eavesdropping, too. She bites her lip and leans her head to his shoulder.

"We'll be briefed soon." Achilles' answer is non-committal.

"First stop?" Pete presses.

"North Carolina. Camp Lejeune. There's a plane waiting at the airport."

Pete dips his head and blows out a breath. "Praying for you, son. Praying for all of you."

At this, tears build and threaten to fall. I untangle my hand and urge him toward his dad. He goes and wraps both of his parents in a hug.

The guys all get their bags, and the sullen mood hangs low around the room.

"Take care of her, Jay," comes from my left side, and I twist to find Major leaning in. He brushes my cheek with his lips and pins me with his eyes.

"We'll take care of each other," I reply hoarsely. "Take care of my Achilles."

"Made the same promise."

"Love you, Major."

My heart physically aches to the point of pain as they make their way to the garage. Jewls moves in, Mom and Dad closing in behind me. Achilles stops at the door and turns. His eyes are dark and troubled. He prowls back to me, lowering his head and crashing his mouth to mine.

It's a closed-mouth kiss, but my knees wobble and the dam breaks. Tears roll over and pour down, covering our lips. He pulls away, giving me his most beautiful grin, and gently pushes me into my dad's waiting arms.

I watch him leave through tears, holding my breath and hearing the garage door go down. When the dings beep, indicating they are down the driveway, I exhale loudly and collapse. Dad gets me to the couch, and uncontrollable sobs rack my body. Jewls crawls in behind me, holding tight, her own whimpers audible.

I find her hand and squeeze, giving us this because we need it. But after the jag is over, we have to be strong.

She squeezes back.

She knows.

I have a feeling my best friend has fallen for a badass Marine-turned-cop.

I try my best to pull her to me but fail because all I can think is that the man I love with all my soul just walked out the door into imminent danger.

23

ACE

It's time.

The phone feels like a hundred-pound weight, pulling me down.

Find your balls, Kingston. You're a fucking Marine. Act like it.

My subconscious mocks me, painting me as a coward.

"You need me to dial it for you?" Talon comes to my side.

"Nope. You make your call?"

"We all did. Waiting on you."

"Sam and Drake have all our paperwork and know what to do?" The rhetorical question is another excuse to stall. Sam, Drake, and all the dads—except mine—know our wishes. It's Sam and Drake that have our financials.

"You know they do."

"Fuck." My head falls, and I grip the back of my neck to release some tension. "How do I do this?"

"This isn't new, we've all been through it before."

"Yeah, but I called Rich." That's the truth.

Before every mission, we make one last call. The guys called their parents. I called Rich. He knew the significance of those calls and always told me how proud he was and reminded me there were people that loved me at home. Each time, he'd drop in something about Harley. It was what I needed to hear. We'd hang up, and I'd go straight into the zone.

Tonight, my call isn't to Rich.

"Kingston, my guess is she needs to hear your voice, too."

Kingston.

The second we stepped foot off the plane and were greeted, we were no longer the casual Ace, Talon, Ford, and Major.

We were back to Kingston, Simms, Whitman, and Powers.

"Want me to hang with you?" Talon offers.

"Nah, I'm good."

He slaps me on the shoulder, and when the door shuts, I dial her number.

"Achilles." Harley draws out my name, setting my pulse racing.

"Yeah, baby, it's me."

"I've been worried."

"I called you when we landed in North Carolina."

I leave out the part that stint only lasted twenty-four hours before we were wheels up again.

"That was four days ago! Are you okay? Is it over? Are you coming home?"

My chest aches at her hopefulness. "We're working things out."

"Have you…? Did you find…?" She doesn't have to finish the questions for me to know what she's asking.

"Not yet."

Her breath hitches. "You're not in Carolina anymore, are you?"

"No."

"Are you in South America?"

My silence is my answer.

"Oh, God, Achilles." Horror and fear bleed through her voice.

"That right there is why I didn't want you to hear what you heard. You already know too much."

"I know nothing and it's driving me insane."

"How'd today go?" I gear the conversation away from my whereabouts, needing to get a read on her state of mind. "It was a big day."

"I was an emotional wreck. My co-workers have no idea what's happening with me personally, so they thought it was remorse. My boss pulled me aside and repeated his counteroffer. I had to decline a-freak-ing-gain, which made me feel like shit. They threw me a big to-do with a cake and champagne. My parents surprised me, and it was nice to have Mom take the attention off. Dad loaded my boxes while I said my goodbyes. They followed me back here, and Mom worked with me on my cooking skills while plying me with wine. She's convinced it will help me sleep."

My ears perk up at this. "You're not sleeping?"

"Ummm… well… it's just… been difficult." She trails off.

"Jewls around this weekend?"

"She's coming back tomorrow night and spending the weekend. Tom offered Spazle to keep me company."

"Who's Spazle?"

"His German Shepherd. She's a spaz, so he named her Spazle."

"Tom has a female German Shepherd?"

"Why wouldn't he?"

"Because he's a hard-knock ass. Good to know I can give him shit."

"He rescued her. But she's full-bred German Shepherd. Sweet to those she likes and protective. He brings her to the police picnic every year, and she definitely picks her favorites."

Suddenly, I like the idea of Harley having a little extra protection in the house. "Take her to the house anytime. We don't care."

"I'll think about it. Right now, I'm trying to keep sane by cleaning, decorating, and working. But as of today, I'm officially unemployed."

"Only for three weeks."

"Yes, but this was a much better idea when I thought you'd be home every day. Now I'm afraid I've broken my promise to Ford."

"How's that?"

"His parents' house is resembling a Hallmark movie."

I chuckle, thinking of the dozens of pictures she sent. "It's beautiful, baby. We all agree."

"Jewls and I are stringing garland around the living room columns this weekend."

"Go for it."

"Sweetie, I know what you're doing, and I appreciate it. But I'm okay. You don't need to agree to everything."

"That's not exactly what I'm doing. If you want Spazle to come, get her. If you want to get us a dog, go for it."

"Achilles! I'm not picking out a dog without you. Plus, we haven't decided on our back yard landscaping. What if we can't have a fenced-in yard?"

"I've always wanted a dog, and we're getting a fence. Speaking of that, carry on with the house plans. Anyone pushes back, you call Celia, Doug, Dad, Rich—whoever and set their asses straight."

"I can handle it."

"Then use this free time to get things going."

"Hal came to Ladies' Night last night. He told me about your text."

"Sucks the way we left him hanging. Felt like I needed to explain."

"You didn't have a choice. But that was considerate. He was cool, but I could tell he's concerned about you guys."

"We're all good."

"Are you really?" Her voice takes on a serious undertone.

"Yeah, why wouldn't we be?"

"Would you tell me if you weren't? You're a fearless, brave, untouchable badass, but would you tell me if you were uneasy?"

"Yes," I lie without skipping a beat.

"You're lying." She catches on. "I'll let it slide since you're doing heroic acts to serve our country. However, know you can talk to me."

"I know."

"And I'd like to take this opportunity to point out that accountants have little to be troubled about."

I laugh outright at her own change of subject. "I'll point out that accountants also don't participate in heroic acts to serve our country."

"You can work for a non-profit you feel good about."

"No accountant I've ever met nails beautiful auburn-haired, blue-eyed bombshells."

"You can be the exception."

"I changed my mind."

"About what, being an accountant?"

"No, about you picking out our dog."

"You worried your masculinity will be shot by tooling around the neighborhood with a Chihuahua? Don't worry, I'll put her in my purse."

"You even mentioning a dog that fits in your purse shows you can't be trusted with the breed."

There's a split-second of silence before she bursts into giggles. "Oh my God! If you're scared of a small dog, imagine how you'll be with a baby."

My heart stops, and I swear, the image of Harley with our baby flashes in my head. At this moment, she can have ten fucking Chihuahuas if it makes her happy.

"When you have my baby, he won't fit in your purse."

"Not if he's anywhere near your size!" Her cackles bring a smile to my face for the first time since we left home.

Behind me, the door creaks, and Talon whistles, signaling it's time.

"Fuck if it doesn't kill me but, baby, I need to go."

"Okay," she replies sadly. "When will I hear from you again?"

"I don't know."

"Texts?"

"You send them, I'll eventually get them."

Her silence stretches the thousands of miles between us, and I picture her curled in a ball, getting lost with the thoughts in her head. A muffled sniffle comes through the line.

"Don't cry, gorgeous."

"How did you know?"

"Because I can feel it. Go back to that place you were a few seconds ago. Giggle, think about ridiculous, overpriced dogs that are puff pieces."

"I'll try."

"Do me a favor. Are you close to the mail?"

"I can be. I've stacked it on the counter."

"There should be something from my bank. Open it. It's for you."

There's movement and then the sound of paper ripping. "You got me a credit card?"

"Seeing as I'm out of touch, there's not a lot of time for shopping.

Need you to be my personal shopper for Christmas gifts for our parents."

"Shop? You want me to shop while you're across the world risking your life?" she questions incredulously.

"I do what I do in order for you to do what you do."

"That's the mo-mo-most selfless and selfish thing I've ever heard. Selfless on your part and selfish on mine. I'd gladly never step foot in a store again if it meant you were here safe with me."

"I will be soon. And it would be great if you had presents under that massive tree for me to give. Plus, it will keep you busy. Spend what you want."

She mutters something under her breath. "I can't believe we're even discussing this, but okay. What about the guys?"

"What about them?"

"Gifts?"

"We usually take turns picking up the tab on dinner or something."

"Not this year. I'll take care of them, too. How are they? Talon's plants are thriving."

"They're fine. He'll be pleased to hear."

"You need to go."

"Yeah."

"I love you, Achilles. More than anything."

"Same, baby. This will be over soon. I'll touch base when I can."

"Be safe. Come home soon."

"Always." I hesitate, then add, "Love you," before disconnecting.

The guys are standing around waiting for me in the office, all our gear laid out. I flick a finger to them to give me another minute while I shoot off texts to Rich and Dad.

A series of beeps sound, and they all look at their phones, their lips curling.

"Shit, that woman is turning the place into the Biltmore." Ford flips his screen to the circle. Harley is standing in front of the tree, holding up a personalized stocking with his name on it.

"She's moved my plants." Talon's screen is a picture of his house-plants staged around my fireplace.

Major's eyes are glued to his phone, and he slowly curves it to us. It's a picture of Harley and Jewls at their first ladies' night. They're in Tom's shirts, arms around shoulders and lips puckered at the camera.

"You called Jewls?"

He shakes his head. "I sent her a text. She's been busy, and I don't want this bleeding into her life."

I know exactly what he means.

"Here." I hand over my phone to Willie and take the specialized one he hands me in return.

"You know the drill. The drop is at twenty-one hundred."

"We'll be ready."

Willie steps up, slapping a hand to my shoulder and applying pressure. "Take care of our men."

"Goes without saying."

"I'm gonna keep this brief. Simms has been keeping us in MARSOC entertained with tales of you finally landing your lady. Twinkle in the eyes and all that shit. I need you focused and in the zone, which has never been a problem. But it's nice to know you now have someone waiting at home to add to that momentum."

Willie knows the history with my parents and our relationship. He learned long ago I would rather take leave with these guys than go home. My gaze goes to Talon, who's grinning without shame.

"You couldn't help yourself."

"Not a chance. The guys wouldn't believe it without continual photographic proof."

"Payback is hell."

"We'll see."

"All right, Marines, gear up. It's almost go time," Willie orders, and all humor dies.

Search and Rescue is our mission.

It's what we're trained to do.

We're some of the best for a reason.

Now, it's time to prove it.

24

HARLEY

"Honey, Ace will understand if you come stay with us. You staying here alone is unhealthy." Mom frets, continuous in her persuasion for me to go home with them.

"I appreciate it, but Achilles specifically asked me to stay. It puts him at ease."

"Yes, but it's so…"

"Lonely?" I finish for her.

She twists her fingers in mine, nodding.

"It's not that bad. Promise. Jewls is staying with me on the weekends. My schedule and staying busy have helped."

This is partly true. Jewls has been staying the last two weekends. And I picked up as many shifts as Tom would give me. Days at the bar aren't nearly as busy, but I've been handling inventory and waiting tables where needed. I've popped into MJ Labels a few times and set up my office, so it's ready when I start after the holidays. And our massive tree in the living room has tons of presents stuffed under it.

Working, shopping, wrapping, decorating, and exercise classes have kept me busy. But at night, when I crawl into Achilles' bed, the loneliness hits hard.

It's been a week since Achilles' call.

A call I learned was his 'last' call before heading out. Dad let it slip that Achilles had called him over the years before disappearing on his missions. Every time I think about it, a chill settles in my bones.

I knew he wouldn't be in constant contact, but this silence is torture.

The security camera alarms, and the monitor on the end table shows Jewls' car approaching.

"Now you don't have to worry because my partner in crime is here." I jostle Mom's hand and get up to open the wine. "Let's watch a movie."

"God, please, no more sappy selections," Dad groans from the other side of the sofa. "I'm tapped out."

Jewls lets herself in and drops her overnight bag, openly eyeing the wine with appreciation. "Thank God, I need my own bottle tonight."

"There's plenty."

"I'm officially off until after the holidays."

"When are you going home?" Mom asks.

"Christmas Eve."

"You don't have to stay around here for me." I serve them their wine, grab my own, and scoot next to Dad.

Jewls' family lives two hours away in Kentucky. She goes home for the holidays each year and comes back with the best stories of her rowdy family Christmases. I've been to her home and met her family—all the many generations living there—and know her stories are one-hundred percent factual.

Backwoods bootleggers, Law Enforcement, Educators, High Society Equestrian farms—they have a little of everything mixed into their group. One thing they have in common is they're crazy.

"Are you kidding? You're the perfect excuse to miss out on the Eve-before-the Eve bash. Last year, my uncle's fight was the talk of the town for months. Mom is still mortified to go to the grocery store. She calls it the scene of the crime."

I snort, my wine burning down my throat at the memory of her replay. "Maybe they can agree on a turkey this year."

"Didn't happen. Dad went to Costco, picked out three birds, and told everyone else to screw off. If they want to eat, they'll deal with it."

"Oh my, I love your parents," Mom gushes. "They're so colorful."

Jewls barks out a laugh, taking a large gulp. "Yeah, colorful." She glances between me and Dad, her smile waning. "Any word?"

I shake my head, expecting Dad to do the same.

"Jim has no news either, which is actually a good sign."

His statement surprises me, and I twist his way. "Jim? Major's dad? When did you talk to him?"

"Us dads have a chat going."

"But why Jim specifically?"

"The boys made a choice to have one emergency point of contact. That person is Jim."

"Why?"

"Collective decision. He served over twenty years and knows the process and protocol. He's connected to the uniform."

"I meant why only one contact. Don't they have emergency contacts in their records?"

"Yeah, but this is a unique situation."

I don't have a chance to get into what is different about this situation because my phone rings with Mike's name on the screen.

"Hey."

"Hey, Jay-Jay, what are you doing?"

He's taken to calling me Jay-Jay since hearing it from the guys. It also keeps things clear when the other Jay is around. "Sitting with my parents and Jewls, drinking wine and thinking about a movie."

"You up for company?"

"You want to come by?"

"Not only me. I have a few people with me."

I assume he's with Declan and a few of that crew. "I mean, sure, but we're super low-key."

"This isn't a social call. Don't worry about entertaining."

"Mmm, okay. Come on."

He disconnects, and I relay the news he's on his way.

A few minutes later, the security camera picks up two cars coming up the drive and parking. I open the door to Mike, followed by Declan, Raven, Robbie, Ember, Finn, and Presley.

Mom and Dad get up, making their introductions. Presley gives a short wave but comes straight to me, yanking me into a hug.

"How are you?" Her voice is so warm and kind, a stinging pricks my eyes.

"I'm okay."

She leans back enough to assess my face and smiles gently. "You're lying, but it's acceptable at times like this."

"He's been gone eleven days and silent for seven. My heart hurts."

Jewls is at my side, Raven and Ember all joining the embrace. I try to hold it together but a stray tear drops.

"Girls, give her some room," Robbie instructs, and when they step away, Mike steps in.

He kisses my cheek. "Is it okay with you if I help myself and get everyone a drink?"

"Of course, I'll help."

"No, you sit. Robbie and Finn want to talk to you."

My eyes go to Robbie and Finn, who are standing back, cautiously observing. Jewls remains at my side as we sit, my gaze never leaving the two men.

"She's white as a ghost. Stop being scary." Raven points at her brother. "Tell her."

"Tell me what?"

"We've heard about your situation. We may be able to help." Robbie's answer confuses me. It's unlikely Mike would share my business and label it a 'situation'.

"I'm not sure what you've been told, but I'm not in a situation."

"We work in security."

Kind of a weird thing to announce, so I cast a glance at my dad, who's visibly perplexed. "That's great."

Finn's mouth splits in a wide smile, and my heart does a flip. The man is gorgeous. Totally opposite from Achilles, with his lighter hair and piercing aqua-eyes, but I can still appreciate his looks.

"Robbie's not great at finessing things. I'll jump in. He and I work with Hayes Security at top-clearance levels. Our jobs aren't about installing systems and alarms. Our job description is more high-profile. We also know how to assess threats and get information."

At the words 'get information', the realization crashes down. "You're Marines! You get information and you're Marines!" I squawk out, waving my finger wildly like we're playing a game of charades.

"She's getting it now." Finn chuckles.

Mike comes in, passing out bottles of beer. Ember closes in on Robbie's side and shoots me an encouraging smile. "Robbie and Finn are very good at their jobs."

"Can you do it? Can you get information on Achilles and their team?"

"Can we do it? Yes. Can we share it? That's up for debate."

The small amount of hope crashes and burns.

"There's a good chance we can't share anything we find due to national security and protocol. We have confines. But any updates or information outside of that, we can relay."

"Is seven days with no contact normal?"

They exchange a look that sends my stomach diving. "I just want to know he's alright."

"He's alive. They all are. We had Max make a call before we came over here."

Relief floods through me, and I slouch into Jewls. "Thank God."

"With that call, we also got a picture of these men. Exceedingly revered, people in high places respect them. They are missed in active duty. That says a lot."

"They're heroes," Dad chimes in.

At the description hero, Presley leans into Finn, and Ember gazes at him gratefully.

"We know and we're putting this on our radar."

I think about what I know and if it would help them. My mind is volleying back and forth, and I notice too late that Finn's studying me pensively.

"Thank you. This is kinda my first time going through this. Well, not actually. It's always been terrifying when Achilles was deployed or out of touch. But this is different. It's like a piece of my heart is dangling from a high cliff."

Presley breaks away and comes to squat in front of me, taking a hand. "My brother was killed while serving. He was also a Marine. It was rough, and I'm not sure how to explain that sort of pain. But years ago, Finn was shot while on an assignment. That pain was gut-wrenching and paralyzing. When I tell you I understand, I truly understand."

"Presley, I'm sorry about your brother."

"Thanks. He was a great guy. He left behind the most precious daughter that reminds me every day of what a beautiful soul he was." She peeks over her shoulder at Finn, and he gives her a crooked smile. Her face comes back to mine. "Even in death, he was still wringing miracles. He brought Finn into my life."

"I want to hear that story," Jewls mutters low.

Presley squeezes my hand and stands. "We'll plan a girls' night. But now you have to keep the faith and believe in the best. You need someone to talk to, I'm here."

"That means a lot."

"Not to make light of this, but now that the heavy is out of the way, can I say how stunning this house is?" Raven gushes. "Next year, you have to help with my decorations."

"I'm more interested in the security system. Any way you can walk me through what the guys did?" Finn gestures to the screen on the table.

"Yeah, sure. I can show you how the entry system works from Achilles' entrance, but I know little about the front security or how it feeds to the monitor."

"That'll work."

I motion for him to follow me and lead us to Achilles' room. "Achilles and Ford have private entrances. All the guys have individual codes that send messages to their phones when the codes are used. Same with all the other doors, too. The motion detectors and alarms also feed to their phones."

"Hmm." His disinterested reaction takes me by surprise.

When I glance his way, the same contemplative stare is back, but in this proximity, it's lasering into my skin. He remains quiet, as if he's waiting for me to explain more.

"I'm not really sure of the nitty-gritty details on the motions."

"Robbie and I tested the prototype and ended up putting this same set-up in our homes."

"Then why did you want me to explain?"

"Because I needed to get you alone. Talk to me."

A sense of uneasiness washes through me, and I lose his gaze, focusing on the rug under my feet.

"Harley, babe, don't be afraid. I'm not trying to scare you. I need to know what you know about Ace being called up."

"Ummm," is all that comes out.

"You can trust us."

"I heard their contact—or whoever—and he mentioned South America, two people dead, others missing, and going in hot."

The words spill so rapidly, it's a wonder if he heard me.

He rocks back at the same time his crystal aqua eyes fill with sympathy and care.

"Jesus, that's confidential intel." The way he says it indicates he already knew this.

My hands fly into the air in frustration. "I know! Achilles already told me that. I was supposed to wait for him to come to meet me in here, but I couldn't stand by and do nothing. So, I listened to their call."

The sympathy and care glints in a show of amusement. "Damn stubborn women. Yeah, if I told Presley to wait in another room, she'd have done the same thing."

"It's not stubborn, it's astute."

"She'd agree and she'd love the fact you used the word astute."

I grin, remembering Presley does something in editing.

"Jewls seems solid."

"She is."

"Anytime she's not available or you feel down, call Presley. She's genuine in her message. When our boys return home, the offer still applies."

My heart hammers and I swallow hard, mustering up the courage to ask a question that has been tearing me up. "Is it a bad sign that it's been seven days with no contact?"

"No." His swift answer comes out abrasive.

"Why don't I believe you?"

It's then I see right through him. He knows a lot more than he shared earlier. Which means Robbie knows, too.

"Talk to me," I repeat his words.

"Ace and the guys rescued three missing Marines. Got them out alive."

Relief, gratitude, pride, love—every emotion bubbles to the surface and threatens to spill over. I'm torn over wailing or cheering. My hand goes to the wall to steady my shaking legs. "Thank God."

"That's what going in hot meant. Once their team had all the tactical security in place, they got to our men."

"They're coming home soon."

He flinches, and my excitement fades. Then I remember he probably doesn't know about their deal with the Marines.

"They have some kind of arrangement, and there are only a few instances that put them back in duty. If they saved those men, they accomplished their mission. They'll be coming home."

"Fuck." He cups the back of his neck and studies his boots before glancing back at me. "Harley, I know nothing about their arrangement, but when we heard of it, Robbie and I agreed it was highly unusual. Then we saw their service records and know why they are there."

"You don't think they're coming home soon?"

"Something else is happening. The Marines have an abundance of capable and bravura rescue teams. For some reason, they reached out to these men. My gut tells me they're highly skilled in other areas that are needed. I hope like hell I'm wrong."

"No, no, no…"

"They're all okay. According to Max's intel, they're with others in a secure location."

"Can you get a message to him?" I plead desperately.

"No, because that would mean someone finds out we had this conversation. Which is not happening. You already know too much."

"Jewls knows, too."

"Of course, she does."

"I didn't tell her. She overheard."

"Right… think you two can keep this quiet?"

"We haven't told anyone so far until a few minutes ago."

"And you need to continue to keep the information to yourselves."

"What about Dad and the rest of the families?"

"Right now, it needs to stay quiet. In my experience, things will shake up or shake out in a day or two. Robbie and I will keep checking, too. If anything happens that we can share, we will."

I nod.

"Maybe my instincts are wrong and he'll call tonight with news he's on his way home."

"I wish."

"Harley, he's alive, with his team, and currently not in danger. That's a win."

The resolution in his voice and the facts at hand put clarity on what's happened. "You're right, it's a win."

25

ACE

"They're on the move." A brusque voice comes through my earpiece. "Six in the SUV, armored and outfitted. This is it."

"We're rolling in two."

"Got your six. See you on the other side, Marines."

Talon pulls out a handheld, punches in a few codes, then presses the button that will scramble the security system of the compound in front of us.

Ford and Major move ahead through the dark, ready to go.

Days of surveillance and hundreds of aerial shots gave us the details on every inch of this place. The underground tunnel on the other side of the building leads to the private beach where the other teams will wait for us to flush any stragglers trying to get their equipment out.

Our team has one goal—find our man and his family and get them out alive. The other teams will handle their side and do a sweep to get the information.

That's it. Then we're headed home.

When we landed in North Carolina, it was like the last nine months were a blip. We were back in the fold without a hitch.

First up, rescue the guys captured in the initial attempt that went south. Two Marines were already dead. It was our job to get the remaining three out.

No one knows who got the kill shot. There was no hesitation, no discussion. We came in from the shadows, seeing our guys hanging from chains with multiple stab wounds and lacerations from other methods.

The sick motherfucker from the cartel was alone, taunting them about whose dick was going first. One look between us and we shot. He went down without a clue he'd been infiltrated.

Good fucking riddance, you piece of shit. Talon spit on his dead body.

Less than a day later, a Marine on vacation with his family in Costa Rica was abducted and brought here to Colombia. Not just any Marine, a high-ranking Marine with specialized communication skills.

This cartel has upped their game.

A naval ship out of San Diego with Marines on board is their target. They're planning an attack on the ship with a man on the inside to relay communication back to them. With attention on the attack of a U.S. Naval ship, and speculation of who was responsible, the cartel could move shipments without eyes.

I'll give it to them. The mastermind behind this operation is slick. They've been under the radar until two days ago. While interpreting the ship's communication system, MARSOC picked up an anomaly inside the message.

It was the coordinates of this location. That was our sign.

At exactly one-hundred and twenty seconds, we all move in. The exterior motion lights are disabled, but the house immediately flickers to life and shadows fill the windows.

"I've got four," Ford calls through his mic.

"Same." Major aims at the second level.

We each take a window and wait. Talon throws a rock at the door and the shadows move, shooting through their glass. I bust through the door with the others close.

There's a millisecond to assess the room. One man's eyes widen in shock, taking in our military status, and then he shouts as gunshots erupt. We return fire, taking them down easily.

"Bet those cocksuckers wished they volunteered for the dinner run with their buds." Talon's voice comes through my earpiece.

Major leads us down the hallway.

Our intelligence of the property told us the rear of the house is all windows with a view of the water beyond a small cliff. The tunnel runs under that side of the property.

We've been warned there are rooms hidden along the tunnel that aren't on the plans. They could hold areas for almost anything—drugs, ammunition, artillery, whatever.

Our only concern is getting the family. The rest of the teams can recon the tunnel.

We round the corner and Major stops, signaling our prediction is correct. These guys are using the library as their command center. The only sound is the clicking of fingers typing. Then a man barks in loud, rapid-fire Spanish.

Out of all of us, Major is the expert in linguistics. We can hold our own with the basics, but Major has spent the last few days studying the Colombian-style Spanish dialect.

The man barking orders is getting more frustrated, his words coming too fast for me to pick anything up.

"The others are less than five minutes out. He thinks we're local government," Major expertly relays the information in his mic without making an audible sound. "They'll surround the perimeter."

Talon sends a message on the handheld, alerting the others to get ready. Ford catches my eye and tugs on his ear. I listen closely and pick up the ticks and clicks of the typing now in a pattern. Immediately, I make out the Morse code and start deciphering the message.

This has always been my area.

Two men, three o'clock and nine. Two covering my family in back. Armed.

As the words come together, I convey them using hand signals. Talon and Ford take off toward the back, and Major silently communicates with me he's got the lead-in. I nod and wait.

"We've got eyes on the wife and kids. Going to flush them out," Ford mutters in our ear.

A few seconds later, the unmistakable explosion of the flash bang echoes through the house followed by four shots.

The Spanish begins again, and this time, I recognize a few words. He's threatening our man while yelling at his cohort to find out what's happening.

That's all we need. Major crouches, raises his gun, and edges in.

Both men spot us at the same time, aiming our way.

We take our shots and they go down.

"Bayer?" The man's been worked over. Black eyes, lips split, dried blood on his temple.

"Kingston and Powers." I point between Major and myself.

"My family?" He winces, a dribble of blood pooling at the corner of his mouth.

"All clear!" Talon yells from the back of the house.

"Let's get you to them."

"Hold on." Bayer twists back to the computer, his fingers flying across the keyboard. He then slams the laptop shut and shoves it under his arm, standing. "You have a piece I can borrow?"

"We need to worry about anything?"

"Nope, but I want to shoot that motherfucker that touched my wife and kids."

My lips twist as I hand over my pistol, jerking my head to the hallway. "We're headed out the tunnel."

"Tell your men to get my family out. We're coming."

"Move out. We have Bayer, and we're right behind."

"Roger that," Talon whistles in the mic.

Bayer takes the lead this time. When we pass the bedroom, he veers in, and two gunshots ring out.

"This is my kind of guy." Major voices his approval.

Bayer returns. Even with his features swollen and bruised, it's easy to see his satisfaction. "Wasn't the kill shot, but it'll do."

"Let's roll." I move to the open doorway off the hall and motion for Bayer to go down first. Ford announces in our ear that they're out and teams are surrounding the perimeter. "Your family is out safely."

"We've got company," Talon warns in our ear.

The three of us move, Major and I keeping our guard up, edging down the stairs and the hall backward with our eyes alert. Shouts from the men get louder when they find their friends dead.

"As soon as you asses care to join us, they're ready to go. On the double would be nice," Ford tells us unnecessarily. Asshole has the nerve to sound bored. We're all aware of the plan to ambush and capture any remaining kidnappers for interrogation.

"About twenty yards and they can have it," I mutter.

Right as the words leave my mouth, the door at my side slams open, and three men burst out, firing frantically. I duck and roll, shooting as I go, knowing Major's doing the same.

"What the fuck is happening?" Talon roars.

"They're coming in from the tunnel! Taking fire now!" Major barks while firing and taking one down with a bullet to the chest.

"Bayer—get out of here!" I order, firing and hitting my target.

"Fuck that shit," Bayer raises up, aims, and shoots directly into one of their temples.

"All down!" Major announces, still in position.

"Get the fuck out here," comes from a voice I don't recognize.

"Are there other access points?"

"We don't know."

"Watch that shit." I do a scan over my shoulder. "We have three more doors before we hit the exit."

Together, the three of us form a circle, moving cautiously.

It's quiet, almost too quiet, and I'm listening for any kind of sign. We're almost to our destination when Major stops. The next few seconds are tense before he shoves me to the side.

"Kingston—get down!"

The force of his body sets me off-balance, and I lose my footing, stumbling back. Everything goes in slow motion. A blast shakes the building at the same time the last door flies open and more men file out.

Plaster and dust fall around us, and bullets soar through the space. The air is thick, but I fire back, ignoring the searing pain in my arm and thigh.

There's another shove, and Major's in front of me, taking the brunt of the gunfire. He jolts back and my heart stops, knowing he's been hit.

"Goddamn motherfucker!" I aim and fire furiously, wrapping my arm around my brother. "Hit! Major's hit!"

I'm pulled from the back. Bayer may be a communications expert, but he's a trained fighter. Regardless of being in civilian clothes with no bodily protection, he's shooting over my shoulder until the gunfire stops.

"We're there, Marine," rings in my ear.

I position myself, slinging Major's arm over my shoulder and hauling him out of the tunnel. As soon as the fresh air hits, we're surrounded. Talon slides into my side, taking my weight, while Ford does the same on the other side of Major. We drag him to the waiting vehicle.

The van roars to life and we're moving, bouncing roughly over rocks.

"Major, man, you with us?"

His response is a weak mumble.

"Shit, get us some light back here," Ford orders.

Light bathes the space, and my eyes roam over him.

"Here let me look." A harried but attractive woman sidles close. I recognize her from her picture as Ada Bayer. "I'm a nurse practitioner in the ER and pretty skilled with gunshot wounds."

"Your husband may need your attention. He's been beaten hard."

"He's good."

My attention goes past her to where Bayer's two kids are clutching tight to him. His arms are circled protectively, shielding them from what's happening.

We give her some space as she presses her fingers to his neck and leans to his mouth. "Breathing shallow and heart rate erratic. Most likely, his adrenaline is carrying him. Do you know where he was shot?"

Ford takes Major's weapons, and Talon makes quick work of removing his protective gear. Each of us conducts our own assessment. Blood oozes from under his armpit. I point to it, lifting his arm.

This time, he groans.

Ada gently skims her hand along his back and side. "I don't feel a point of exit. The bullet is likely inside his chest cavity somewhere."

The pain in my thigh radiates, spots filling my vision.

Major's eyes open and dart around, focusing on me. "We get them?" comes out hoarse and ragged.

"Bet your ass."

"Everyone good?"

"Yeah, and you will be soon."

The spots return, and I sway forward, dropping his arm.

"Kingston?" Ford dips into my line of sight.

I shake off the dizziness. "Good."

"Where's all the blood coming from?" He jostles my legs, and I fall backward, the pain firing up my spine and down to my feet.

"Jesus, fuck, fuck, fuck! Ace is hit. Looks like his thigh. He's in a pool of blood. Too much blood for a leg wound."

Bodies shuffle all around me. Someone cuts the material from my pants, and a tourniquet is secured around my upper leg. Ada's fingers press into my throat, her concerned eyes holding mine. Without her saying it, I know the bullet nicked an artery.

My eyelids grow heavy, and I suck in a deep breath. A rough hand closes around mine as the guys shout.

My mind clears, and for the first time in days, I let myself drift to Harley.

Then it's black.

26

HARLEY

I'M IN SHOCK.

That's the only explanation for what's happening right now. Goosebumps pop on my skin at the same time a violent quake rocks through my body. Achilles' face fills my head right before little dots take over my vision. The weight of my head becomes too much, and it falls into my hands.

Jewls curls around me, her tears soaking through my shirt. "We should call Rich."

A whimper escapes as my stomach rolls. "Harley, take a deep breath. I'll make the call if it's easier. Or maybe we could ask Finn to—"

"No, I'll do it. Dad needs to hear it from me."

Before I can dial Dad's number, an incoming text buzzes from Finn.

We're in the driveway when you're ready.

Even in my grief and worry, my heart flips. "They came. Finn and Max are here."

"It's two-thirty in the morning and it's snowing."

I don't know Finn well and don't know Max at all. But those two men don't give a shit about the time or the weather. They're worried, and this is their style.

"We need to let them in."

She releases me and moves to her suitcase, slipping a hoodie over her flannel pajamas. I go to the bathroom and flinch at my reflection. My skin is pale with splotches snaking down my neck, eyes are blood-shot, and lips swollen and chewed. My hand goes to the wall for the set of hand towels that hang there, and I freeze.

Bright aqua.

Not white, or grey, but a shade of blue I thought Achilles would agree to.

They were meant to be a Christmas present, and lead into telling him my plans for our bedroom scheme in the new house. But I couldn't put them under the tree. They gave me a sense of comfort by being in here where I see them every morning.

Jewls walks in and takes in my struggle. She lifts the towel, wets it, and presses it to my neck and cheeks. "How about some tea?"

"That would be great. Not sure my stomach can handle coffee."

"What can I get you?"

"Achilles' black sweatshirt on the closet shelf."

She purses her lips, her eyes glassing over, and kisses my forehead quickly. "Wash your face."

I do as she says, brushing my teeth, too, even though I wasn't sleeping when Finn called a half-hour ago. It makes me feel a little more put together.

The cold water does a little to help, although misery remains clear on my features. It is what it is. Jewls tosses me the sweatshirt, and I slip it on as we go toward the main room. She veers off in the kitchen while I turn off the alarm and switch on the outside lights, opening the door.

There's a second of shock when I see Presley standing there flanked by Finn and Max. She pounces, embracing me tightly, and I melt into her, smelling the fresh scent of baby powder. My insides shake, but I don't let myself break down.

"Pres? You want to move her inside, or should I lift you both and haul you inside the house?"

"Max, you pick up my wife, I'll level you."

At Finn's reply, an unfamiliar feeling of hilarity creeps in, and I giggle into her shoulder. She shuffles us back while muttering, "Men are so stupid."

At this, I openly laugh, pulling back to look at her. "Achilles threatened Talon once when he offered to lift me off the sofa."

The memory crashes into me of that day and night. The flowers, the apology, the lunch, swimming, falling asleep on Achilles' chest… that kiss.

It wasn't just a kiss… it was *THE* kiss.

The kiss that started it all.

The memory is too much, and to my horror, my laughter turns into a wail. My knees give out, and before I crumble, two strong arms circle me from behind, getting me to the sofa and holding me close. Loud sobs rack my body, and I cling to Max with all I have, pouring my unthinkable fears into his chest.

There's no telling how long he holds me like this, but eventually, my sobs die down to quiet cries and sniffles. I swipe at my cheeks, my skin hot and clammy against my fingertips. A wad of tissues is shoved into my hands.

"Thanks." I take them gratefully.

"Harley, drink some tea. It's cooled."

I take the mug from Jewls and swallow a large gulp, hoping it will soothe my throat, instantly realizing my mistake. Tears spring to my eyes—this time because of the potent taste of whiskey. I choke and sputter, gasping like a fool.

"What the hell?"

"My fault." Presley grimaces. "I told her it needed a little spike."

"Little?" I cock an eyebrow at Jewls.

"Don't give me that look. You're exaggerating. Next time, don't chug."

I take a much smaller sip and try to push back the awkwardness of my breakdown in the arms of a basic stranger.

Presley's hand squeezes my knee. "Don't do that, Harley. Don't be embarrassed."

My nerves start to settle at the gentle sincerity in her tone. "I don't mean to sound ungrateful, but what are y'all doing here?"

"You needed to be surrounded by friends," she says warmly.

"What about your kids? It's the middle of the night."

"My brother and niece were already spending the night. They are with them."

Then it hits me, what tomorrow is—Christmas Eve.

An hour ago, I hoped that Achilles and the guys would walk through the door. Now, even a miracle won't make it happen.

"Have they informed the families yet?" I glance between Finn and Max.

Max gives a quick jerk of his head. "Not yet, but it won't be long."

"I need to call my dad. He'll know what to do."

"How about you call your dad and let Finn talk to him?" Presley suggests.

I nod, dialing. He answers on the second ring, fully alert and worried. "Harley?"

"Daddy," my voice cracks, and I close my eyes, sucking in a deep breath.

"Amanda, get dressed!" he bellows, and my mom's own whimper echoes through the line.

"Daddy, there's been an accident. Finn's here and will tell you what we know."

Finn takes the phone gently, his blue eyes loaded with sympathy and understanding. He goes to the middle of the room, Max joining him.

I listen intently as he relays the same news from earlier.

"Max got a call from a contact who knew he was interested in any information that may come in related to this team. Achilles' crew was involved in a rescue and recovery mission. The details are minimal, but after their original mission, a Marine and his family were kidnapped…"

My stomach rolls when Finn's eyes slice to me and he delivers the worst of the news.

"Kingston and Powers were shot. Help was en route to get them from a remote location. Reports on their status are unknown."

Jewls and Presley sandwich me between them, forming a protective ball.

"Right, we'll be here. See you then." Finn hands me back my

phone. “Rich is notifying the other fathers and putting Jim Powers on notice. Then he’ll be here.”

“Do you have any idea where they were in South America?”

“No.”

“I’m not an expert, but we don’t have the best relationship with some of those countries.”

“Doesn’t matter.” Max is quick to throw in.

“How can you be so sure?”

“Because they’re Marines.”

This makes me feel slightly better. “You’re right. They’re Marines. Do you think Talon or Ford will call soon?”

They exchange a look that gives me my answer.

“Never mind.”

“There are protocols and procedures in place that aren’t defied. Certain ranks and personnel do notifications,” Finn explains comfortingly.

“I’ve been in the same position when Robbie and Finn were in their accident in the Middle East. It fucking sucks. This isn’t about what they want to do; it’s about obeying the system. It’s also about national security,” Max adds, his gaze on Jewls. “You and Major a thing?”

“Ummm.” She squirms, casting her eyes between them and me. “Not exactly in the way you mean.”

Achilles and I promised each other we’d stay out of whatever may be budding between our best friends. Of course, I haven’t always stayed true to my promise, prying a little here and there. But in this situation, I’ve completely gotten involved. They really are in the friend zone.

But it seems like an odd question to ask right now, especially from a man she’s only met once before.

“You seemed tight at the Christmas party,” he continues.

“We’re friends. Kinda getting to know each other better. He thinks I’m a little wild.”

“Aren’t you a Social Worker?”

She perks up, squaring her shoulders. “Are you saying Social Workers are dull?”

“Never personally met a wild Social Worker.”

Oh, shit, here we go. Presley nudges my side, and I return the gesture, biting my cheek.

"He thinks I'm wild. I don't agree. But for your information, I'm great at my job. However, my philosophy is there is too much heavy and serious in the world. I've been known to cut loose and kick it up a notch. Plus, I work part-time in a blue bar. It's a requirement to sling drinks and snark."

"So, you know how to hold your own?"

"Hell yes! I have two brothers and nine cousins who *thought* they were my brothers. I was born knowing how to hold my own. It's a science putting a grown country bumpkin in their place. I perfected the art early in life."

The corners of Finn's lips curl.

"Good to know. Powers will need that when he gets home. You too, Harley. I was there after both Finn and Robbie's accidents. They were surly, temperamental bitches."

At his insinuation, my mouth pops open.

Finn shakes his head, dropping his chin. "You have no shame. My case was a little different."

"Yeah, Presley dumped your bum ass."

"Is this your tactic to lighten the mood? Drag my ass through the mud? If so, it sucks."

"Just telling the truth. Plus, I'll do anything to make a beautiful woman smile again." He spears me with a glance, his lips tipping.

My insides turn and cheeks flush at his statement. Like all the other guys, Max is extraordinarily good-looking. Tall, built, sharp facial features, and deep, stormy blue eyes that can make a heart swoon. Knowing he's such a good guy adds to his already oozing sex appeal.

If I didn't think my best friend was hiding her true feelings for Major, I'd encourage her to go after Max.

"In case you didn't know, Ace and Major are surly and temperamental bitches already. But if you're advising us to have thick skin, no worries," Jewls responds causally.

"I've grown up surrounded by law enforcement. The good, the bad, the devastating—I've known it all. At sixteen, the bad boy with the raging temper stole my heart. Now he's a tattooed, fiercely protective, badass that carries a badge and serves his country. When he comes home, I promise I can handle anything."

Both their faces mask with approval. Presley pats my thigh. "Of course, you can."

Max's phone beeps and I sit forward. He scans the message, Finn reading over his shoulder.

"My source is reporting Ace and Major are in surgery."

"Where?" I ask anxiously.

"Don't know, but this is good. It means they are likely in friendly territory."

"Thank God."

My phone rings, Cindy Powers' name on the display. I dislodge from between Jewls and Presley, standing to take the call.

"Hey, Mrs. Powers."

"Harley dear, are you okay?"

"Yes, are you?"

"Oh, honey, a mother is never alright in these circumstances. Every time Major is out on these missions, I barely breathe right. But we just received some promising news. Jim is calling the others now. I wanted to share with you personally."

"What news?" All eyes swing at me.

"The men are in a Costa Rican hospital. They took Major and Ace to surgery."

I slump against the wall in relief, relaying the news out loud. "They're in Costa Rica."

The guys give chin jerks in acknowledgment. My phone beeps with an incoming call. When I catch who's calling, a fiery pain pierces my chest.

"Sandy's calling."

"Take her call. We'll be in touch if we hear anything."

"Thanks, Cindy, same here."

When I click over, Sandy's sniffles fill the line.

"Sandy—"

"Harley, are you alright?" Her teary voice is hoarse and broken. The pain in my chest intensifies.

My eyes go to Max, remembering earlier, and I pull myself together. She needs my strength right now.

"I'm okay, terrified out of my mind, but keeping up hope. These guys are pretty invincible."

"You're right. Are you really okay? I hate to think about you being alone."

"I'm not alone. Friends are here with me."

The security alerts us to my parents driving up. Finn and Max go to greet them. The next few minutes are a blur. I finish my call with Sandy, promising to call if we get any information. Then my parents pounce as soon as they get in the door. When they're assured that I'm far from a breakdown, they give me some space.

Mom immediately turns on the Christmas lights around the rooms, giving the house a brightness that shifts the intensity in the air.

"I don't care about the time. This old man needs a drink." Dad lobbies to the liquor cabinet. "Anyone else?"

"Yeah," Finn and Max reply together.

"Harley?"

"No thanks, Jewls sauced my tea."

"That sounds wonderful! Jewls, whip me up one of those hot toddies," Mom orders as if she's here for cocktail hour.

Jewls grins, hopping over the back of the couch, Presley following her to the kitchen.

"Guys," I try to gain the attention of the area. "I appreciate all your support and love, but it's late. You don't have to stay with me."

Finn and Max are identical in stature, staring at me over the synchronized slugs of their scotch. Neither says a thing, turning back to my dad.

It may have been a silent scorn, but it was a scorn nonetheless. They aren't leaving.

Then it hits me. This is my life.

My future.

I've been practically living with Achilles, Major, Talon, and Ford for months. Their bond is impenetrable. They have become a part of me.

But more importantly, I'm a part of them. Which means I'm part of this. It doesn't matter if they just met Finn, Robbie, and Max. There's a bond.

My throat tickles, and my mom catches my eye. She's watching close and easy to read.

Get ready.

When it's time, Dad will make a call. And then we will be swarmed with police and other members of law enforcement who know and respect my guys.

It won't matter that it's Christmas. This is family.

As it sinks in, I think of what we can do to keep busy. I may not be a great cook, but I can bake.

"Mom, want to make some cookies?"

"Do you have what we need?"

I gesture to the pantry.

She smiles wide, a slight shimmer in her gaze. "That's perfect."

"Jesus, all these sweets, and I'll be diabetic when this trip is over," Max grouses.

"You love it!" Presley calls.

"I'll make you an oatmeal cookie," I shoot him a sarcastic reply, "with raisins."

"Turn those raisins into chocolate chips, we're golden." He pats his firm stomach.

The next hour flies by as we work side-by side, Presley keeping the conversation flowing. I force my mind to stay in the present, trying not to remember the reason we're all gathered in the middle of the night.

My brain is calculating the timing of baking the rest of the cookies with the brownies when I vaguely hear Max on the phone. He comes to me, his eyes alert, his mouth barking into the receiver, and his body strung tight. "Can you get me into the secure network in the house?"

"I think so."

He gestures to show him, and I lead him to the media room where Talon and Ford have an elaborate set-up. It doesn't take long for me to get into their system using Achilles' log in. He scoots me out of the way and does fast work of getting into wherever he's looking for. Finn steps in, tapping a few keys and blocking my vision of the screen.

"Holy fucking shit." Finn scrubs his hands through his hair.

"You seeing what I'm seeing?" Max prompts.

"Obviously."

"This means…"

"Sure as shit does…"

They speak in clipped, unfinished thoughts until I am coming out of my skin. "Guys! What's happening?"

They turn my way, their expressions almost unexplainable.

I've seen this expression before. The night the guys were called away.

"Those sons of bitches are bonafide fucking heroes. They not only saved the Marine and his family. They helped stop the attack on a naval ship in the Pacific. Then they took out thirteen members of one of the largest drug cartels in Colombia."

I fight standing, a whimper gurgling in my throat.

"Grab your phone, Harley." Max grins wide. "You should get a phone call from your guys any minute."

27

ACE

"His vitals are good. Don't worry, he should wake up anytime now," a female voice says in a thick accent.

"I'm not worried. I'm waiting on this dipshit to wake up so we can go home," Talon complains.

"I'm pretty sure we can handle his patient care and you can go home."

"You don't know his woman. If we arrive without him and Major, we'll be the ones in hospital beds."

The female giggles. "Is she the spitfire who calls my station several times a day?"

"Most likely. She's blowing up our phones."

"It's Christmas, she's anxious. There's nothing wrong with hoping for joyous news."

Christmas?

The word resonates in my brain, and my pulse races. Jesus, how long have I been out?

A monitor beeps and a cool hand compresses my wrist. "Something has him rattled."

"Fuck, Ace, if you can hear me, open your damn eyes," Talon demands.

I fight through the sleepiness, twisting my neck and groaning at the stiffness.

"Stop the growling. It's overrated."

The first thing I see when my eyes slit are his haggard eyes that fill with relief. A sterile odor of antiseptic and antibacterial cleanser hits me next. My gaze darts around the room and immediately tells me I'm in a hospital.

The hand at my wrist squeezes, bringing my attention to the nurse staring down at me with a kind grin. "Mr. Kingston, can you hear me?"

My throat is like sandpaper and I croak, "Water."

Talon brings a straw to my mouth, and I sip greedily, the cold liquid helping me find focus. It all comes back. The raid, the rescue, the ambush, the helicopter…

"Major?" My voice is rough.

"Next door. Alive, awake mostly. Bullet caught him under the armpit and punctured a lung. He'll make a full recovery."

"Harley?"

"She's ready to talk to you."

"Give me a phone."

"I need to do a full assessment and alert the doctors you're awake." The nurse gently nudges Talon away from the side of the bed.

"That can wait. Get me a phone."

"When I'm done."

"Talon—" I snarl.

She shoots me a threatening glance, her eyes narrowed and unyielding. "When I'm done," she repeats curtly.

He raises his hands, backing away. "I'll let Major and Ford know you're awake and let her do her thing. I've seen enough of your junk the last two days to give me nightmares for life."

"Jealous jackass," I mumble with irritation to his back as he leaves.

"You and Mr. Powers are lucky. The bullet that hit him missed his spine. Fast action on their part helped save your life. Your blood loss could have been fatal."

She doesn't need to elaborate for me to know the danger of a bullet to the spine. Major's recovery will suck, but the alternative of a spine injury is much worse. Then I realize her freely sharing this information is highly prohibited in the United States.

"Where are we?"

"Costa Rica. Obviously, in the hospital."

I move to sit up, wincing at the pain radiating from my bicep and leg.

"Be careful. Here, let me help." She holds her arms out, and I hesitate. "I'm a mother of three boys, wife to a Fire Chief, and a nurse. Don't underestimate my strength."

She helps me into a comfortable position and goes about her assessment, all the while explaining my injuries.

Bullet graze on the bicep that needed a few stitches. My nicked femoral artery was repaired, but my blood loss was significant. After surgery, they've kept me loaded on drugs, and I've been out for thirty-two hours.

When she pulls the blankets down and lifts my hospital gown, I instinctively cover my cock and block her hand.

She doesn't raise her face to mine, but her amused grin is visible. "Three sons, macho husband, and a nurse," she reminds me with humor in her tone.

"You're a little close for me to feel comfortable."

"You were shot near the groin, Mr. Kingston. Not much I can do about it."

I know what Talon meant now about seeing my junk. Then I think about how many people have seen my naked ass in the last thirty-two hours.

My fingers skim the piercing and hit a tube at the tip of my dick. "I want this out."

"The doctor has to make that call. You haven't exactly been alert and functioning."

"I am now. A catheter isn't necessary."

"Regardless of your thoughts on who has the authority here, the doctor will decide."

I glare at her, flinching when she pokes at the row of sutures on my thigh. The skin is shaved, red, and angry. Even I can see the swelling around the wound needs attention.

She cleans it, chatting away about nothing in particular. Finally, she redresses the wound.

"I'll allow your friends to come in. Hopefully, talking to Harley will make you amenable to our healthcare protocols," she chirps, enjoying my discomfort entirely too much.

As if on cue, the door creaks, and Talon waltzes around the partition, Ford pushing Major in a wheelchair. It's hard to miss the exhaustion on his pale features.

"You shouldn't be out of bed."

"You look like shit, too." He reads through my statement.

My lips twitch and I shake my head. "You good, brother?"

"Yeah, you?"

I dip my chin as an answer. "Be better when I can talk to Harley and get this catheter out."

"We need to talk before you talk to Harley." Ford's serious reply has me sitting up straighter.

"What's the deal?"

A quiet settles over the room, and the nurse catches the hint, slipping out.

They each take turns telling me parts about the success of our mission. Apparently, the last thing Bayer did after we killed his captors was get a secure message to the Commander on the ship. The cartel liaison was apprehended, and the rest fell into place. The men who came at us from the hidden tunnel accesses are all dead.

Except during our surgeries, Ford and Talon have been with us since arriving at the hospital. Switching back and forth every few hours.

"Ace, we all know you're made of steel, but that was close. You lost a lot of fucking blood. Scared the shit out of us." Major pins me with steely eyes.

"I didn't—"

"We know, man. The adrenaline, the chaos, the focus, we all get it. But shit, I hope we never have to go through something like that fucking ever."

"You were shot, too."

"And your mind was on me."

"My mind was on the objective, and that includes you," I correct him.

"We've been talking while you were taking your nap."

"I was drugged."

"Drugged, asleep, resting, however the hell you want to phrase it."

"Want to get to the point?" Irritation stirs in my gut. They're stalling.

The look they share is the giveaway. "You want out."

"Weighing the options," Talon says breezily.

"All of you?" The question is pointed at Major, who gives a non-committal shrug.

Something is off. An uneasy feeling curls in my chest, slowly making its way through my body until I'm practically shaking. "What the fuck is happening?"

Talon rolls back on his feet, crossing his arms. "You flat-lined. For nine seconds, I didn't know if you would pull through. Major's lung flooded with blood, and he couldn't breathe. We watched helplessly, not knowing if either of you would live."

The news blows me away, and my gut turns at the reality of the situation. We've all seen death. Too much death. But the fact that they witnessed us in the same position at the same time would rattle even the strongest of men.

"Can we give it up?" I'm unsure it's possible. "Being Marines is in our blood. It's who we are."

"We'll always be Marines. Shit, Ace, think about it. We've stood side-by-side battling the worst of the worst, including our recent annihilation of members of a Colombian drug cartel." Talon takes a breath, visibly struggling with what comes next. "I'm proud of my service to my country. I'm proud of everything we've done. It will always be in my blood. Us leaving the Corps won't change who we are, what we've done, or what we are to each other."

"I don't think of it as giving up. We moved on a year ago when we became cops. When we agreed to this special gig, we got our years of service, and things were a lot different. You're marrying Harley. We've bought land to build houses. We had no idea where we'd be today," Ford adds solemnly.

"Major? You okay with this?" Of all people, this decision has to be weighing heavily. Being in the Corps is in his blood. His dad, grandfather, uncle—all served.

"Ace, you have to admit, this was a close call. Closer than ever before. Face the facts. You and I are out of commission for a while."

He's right. Without talking to the doctor, it's obvious our prognosis will have us out for weeks, possibly months.

"Think about it. We don't have to decide now."

"We're a team. I stand with you guys. No matter what." It goes unsaid they feel the same.

"So, more news. We didn't tell Harley the depth of your injuries. Thought it was for the best," Ford tells me.

"Good."

"She already knew the details of everything else."

"How?"

Talon's jaw ticks, his eyes sharp. "Finn Black, Max Roberts, and Robbie Hayes are in the mix."

"Fuck, how'd that shit happen? We're buried under the radar."

"Apparently not to those three. Max is well connected."

"If he's that well connected, then he knows what happened."

"He does. I spoke to him. He's on board with keeping the medical details vague."

"But we were too late to stop the moms," Major speaks up.

"So, Harley knows," I surmise.

"Yes, and she's not happy with any of us, including Max."

"If someone will give me a damn phone, I'll take care of it."

Talon hands his over after pulling up her contact. It goes directly to voicemail. I disconnect, pressing send again, getting the same result.

"She's not answering."

"Maybe she's at her parents'. We haven't heard from her in a few hours."

Worry sets in, and I scroll to find Rich's number, which also goes unanswered.

"Where the fuck is she?"

"I'm right here." She materializes from behind the partition with Rich and my dad at her back.

Every thought in my head and everyone in the room vanishes. My pulse races hard, setting my monitor off again.

She's wearing shimmery black leggings and a red sweater that's open to reveal a simple white shirt. The leggings and shirt are molded to her tight body. Her hair hangs in soft waves with rhinestone clips holding it back on one side. The color of her eyes is a blazing bright blue.

Unbelievably fucking gorgeous.

Sheer perfection.

And incredibly pissed off.

"Harley, what are you doing—"

She throws her palm in the air and strolls my way. "It's obvious these men can't be depended on. I've spent the last seven hours between airports and in the air. Checking my phone like a madwoman when I had service, knowing my darling, dear, beloved friends would call me the minute there was a change in your condition." She swivels her head to the guys, who are a shade paler. "Then I get here, only to find out from the perky personality nurse that he's been awake an hour?!?"

Major slumps in his wheelchair, while Talon and Ford drop their eyes to the floor.

She gets to my side, doing a once-over, and after a beat, flings herself at me. I wrap my arms around her waist, hoisting her onto the bed. Her body quakes, her breaths coming in short rasps.

"I've never been so scared in my life."

"Baby, I'm good. Even better now that you're here."

She tilts back, covering my face with kisses before crashing her mouth over mine. My hand moves to cup the back of her head as I savor the feel, touch, and taste of her. She angles to give me better access, opening wider.

A throat clears, followed by another, and I grunt, breaking away.

Dad and Rich are looking around in avoidance. Major and Ford are smirking.

"Just to say, that's not sanitary. The purified air and antiseptic are the only things covering his stench. Plus, remember your *condition.*" Talon's gaze goes to my groin.

He's not referring to my wound. It's more about the firmness growing between my legs. A throbbing pain shoots up my shaft.

"He's right. I don't even remember my last shower or when I brushed my teeth."

"I don't care," she insists.

"Beautiful, I've got a piss tube lodged in my dick. It's not gonna go well if I grow hard." I whisper this for only her ears, and she shifts, her eyes wide in surprise.

"Sorry."

"It'll be gone soon." I wink and get a grin in return.

She slides out of my hold and goes to Talon, shooting him an annoyed scowl. He sweeps her off her feet, shaking her like a doll until she's giggling. "Knew you couldn't stay mad."

She gives Ford a quick but tight hug, then crouches in front of Major, taking his hand.

"I have an excuse for not calling. There's a hole in my chest."

"You're excused." She kisses his cheek and stands. "I'm thankful you're okay."

Dad and Rich come to my side, both looking ragged and exhausted.

"Son," Dad's voice breaks, and Rich lays a hand on his shoulder.

"Good to see you awake, Ace." His own tone is heavy and grave.

"Good to be awake."

"Your mom and Amanda will be here later. We couldn't all get on the same flight." Dad speaks clearly this time, his gaze on the square bandage on my arm.

"Flesh wound." I run my hand across the gauze.

"And the other?"

"Nurse said it looks good."

"I'd like to hear that from the doctor. He'll be here soon." Harley crawls back on the bed carefully, situating herself at my side. "I know it sounds silly, uber-girly, and sappy, but walking in and being here with you guys is the best Christmas present ever." She looks at everyone before locking eyes with me.

"Are you saying we're your version of a Red Ryder, carbine action, two-hundred shot range air rifle?" Talon jokes, helping to keep the mood light after her confession.

Her nose scrunches adorably.

"A Christmas Story, babe."

"That's still on?"

"Twenty-four-seven marathon every Christmas."

"Well, if there is any silver lining to spending Christmas in a hospital in Costa Rica—we won't have American television."

"Oh, contraire, Jay-Jay. We've already chatted with the staff, and Talon's streaming it tonight," Major informs her.

She shakes her head rapidly. "The moms are bringing the bag with the presents I packed. When they get here, we're having Christmas."

"You showed up here planning a Christmas party?"

"Told you I had plans to wake you up. Between the food, fun, and present exchange, I figured there was a good chance. If that didn't work, Plan B was more drastic."

"Drastic how?"

She chews on her bottom lip, casting a glance sideways and shrugging. "Doesn't matter."

"Why do I get the feeling Plan B would have had consequences?"

"Because her hock-eyed scheme was to push your subconscious into a fit of jealousy using the guys as pawns." Rich throws her right under the bus.

"Dad!"

"Sorry, honey, been listening to your babbling for long enough to know that wasn't smart."

"It would suck to save his life, only to have Ace slay me," Talon complains.

"Well, I was desperate to try anything. My research pointed toward inciting an emotional reaction," she defends. "Like I said, it's unnecessary now."

Jealousy spikes in my system, even though nothing happened. "Glad it didn't come to that."

"Merry Christmas, Achilles." She nuzzles into my neck.

I curl her to me, kissing along her forehead, and rolling my thumb around her bare ring finger. There's no question about it. When we get back to Nashville, this woman will be wearing my ring.

28

HARLEY

MAX ROBERTS HAD IT WRONG. Way wrong.

If Robbie and Finn were surly, temperamental bitches, he got off easy. I'd welcome surly and temperamental. Instead, I have pig-headed, stubborn, cantankerous grizzly bears who are resolved to defy the science of modern medicine.

The five days in the hospital grew increasingly tense as Achilles and Major tested their limits. It was no surprise they were rebellious patients. Achilles was successful in convincing his doctor to remove the catheter, and both men were required to move around. Achilles made it three times with the walker before he refused to use it again.

Not that he didn't have mobility, but because of his bulk and stature, we had to make sure he didn't put too much stress on his wound. Each day that passed, he and Major grew more impatient. Finally, the doctors agreed they are young, healthy, fit men with extremely strong wills, so they released them. But their release came with strict orders. No strenuous activity, no overexertion, and no work for at least a month. Then a reassessment. Gunshot wounds are no joke.

One good thing that occurred was I got to meet the infamous Willie.

My first instinct was to be angry with him, but it was impossible. He may have been some kind of big-wig in the Marines, but he walked in like a normal man and won me over. Luckily, he was there when the men were discharged and reiterated their orders with strong authority.

It irritated Major and Achilles, but they didn't argue when he told them he'd be in touch with me. Either they follow directions, or he'd be making a trip to Nashville. I'm not sure if that's normal protocol, but I hoped he was serious.

We were discharged and had one night in a Costa Rican hotel courtesy of the U.S. Government. Once again, not sure this was protocol, but I wasn't complaining. Since I'd arrived, I'd spent every night at Achilles' side in the hospital. The parents went home two days after we got there. Talon and Ford had a hotel but spent all day at the hospital.

Once again, they displayed the depths of their brotherhood, refusing to leave unless the four of them were together. Well, five, including me.

The early flight out this morning couldn't have come soon enough. Now that we've touched down in Nashville, I'm facing another battle. They are refusing the wheelchair service to get through the airport to baggage.

"Jay-Jay, I handled it. Trust me," Ford says lowly in my ear as we leave our seats.

"Not sure you gained my trust back yet."

"Aww, sounds like a challenge."

We exit the ramp and are assaulted by clapping, howls, and deafening cheers. People we don't know and will never see again are welcoming us.

I stop dead, my heart in my throat and Achilles' hand tightening around mine painfully. He glares at Ford. "You couldn't help yourself?"

"May have flirted with that flight attendant a little too much. I asked for waiting transportation." He's not sorry at all.

"Payback is hell." Achilles pulls me into a protective hold and gets us to the waiting airport trolley. He gives a few chin dips in appreciation, Talon showboating to all the attention.

Jim Powers is waiting in baggage claim, his eyes scanning through us and lighting with relief when they land on Major.

By the time we are off the trolley, Jim has his son in one of those dad-type bear hugs that has my eyes stinging. He takes turns with each of them, welcoming them home. Our bags are out first, and I suspect this has to do with Ford sweetening up the flight attendant.

Jim's Escalade is parked curbside, which is usually prohibited, but the traffic attendant waves as we load up.

"Your mom and brothers are eager to see you—all of you," Jim announces.

Major's spoken to his parents daily and assured them he's fine, but they insisted on being here when we arrived home.

Rightfully so.

I lay my head on Achilles' shoulder and listen to the men carry on conversations about nothing in particular. Ford and Talon may have kept up a good front in the hospital each day, but they didn't fool anyone. Sitting around with spotty television, playing board games and cards was boring. It didn't bother me as much because my days were filled with phone calls, emails, texts, tons of Facetime sessions, and even a few impromptu meetings with Raven regarding an upcoming charity event that MJ Labels is sponsoring. My cousin Shayla got a hold of me on Christmas, hysterical that she was in the dark about everything in my life. We had a serious showdown about what was more important—her jet-setting around the globe, or my newfound love life.

I lost, and now she's been in daily contact.

So, I've been busy.

But these are action men, and being cooped up drove them all crazy.

When we turn onto their street, my stomach goes into a flurry.

"What the fuck?" Achilles grinds out. "Is that my dad's SUV?"

"Yes." My answer is low, testing his next reaction.

"Why?"

"Because your parents want to see you."

"Are your parents here?"

I peer up, nodding.

"We spent three days with them earlier this week. They know we're all good. Why are they invading our home?"

"Ummm," I glance in the rearview mirror, and Jim's eyes are dancing with humor.

"It's New Year's Eve."

"Oh, shit," Ford draws out.

"Harley, what's going on?"

"We're kinda doing a *homecoming-slash-Christmas and New Year's Party*." The last part is lightning-fast and I brace.

The four guys share an expression that sends an icy chill down my spine. Jim's shoulders bunch, and a low hiss slithers through the cab of the truck. "Ace—"

"No problem, pull around back," Achilles instructs him gruffly.

"Honey, if you're tired, they'll all understand."

He doesn't answer, hopping out before we're stopped. One arm goes under my knees and the other around my waist as he whisks me out of the truck. "Luggage," he barks.

"We got it, Ace."

"Put me down! You're not allowed to lift heavy objects." I squirm and wriggle.

"You're not heavy." He pounds his code and slams open his door.

"Why are you acting like a lunatic? We have a house full of people."

"That's a problem for me right now." He stalks to his bed, setting me across it. "Don't move." His demand is curt and terse.

I'm stunned stupid at his anger and the whiplash of the last two minutes. He disappears into the closet and comes out clenching something in his hand.

Is that a box?

It is.

As soon as my brain makes the connection, all the air whooshes out of my lungs. My heart races to the ringing in my ears. I barely register him situating me to straddle his lap.

"Get us home, bundle you up, and drive us over to our lot with a bottle of champagne. Take you to where our bedroom will be. Tell you, you aren't only the love of my life, but *everything* to me. I didn't want to be rushed or cliché. You, me, all the time in the world. In that hospital room, every night while you slept beside me, I'd think about it, perfecting it in my head. I had a plan. A plan that did not include a house full of people invading before we even got here."

"Achill—" His name comes out scratchy around the boulder in my throat.

"I love you, Harley."

"I love you, too. Always have."

His beautiful dark eyes go molten, his lips skimming over mine. A cold metal pushing on my finger brings my focus to our hands.

He slips a ring to the base, and my breath comes in short, shallow pants. The center diamond shines and sparkles a brilliance so bright my eyes burn.

"Marry me, Harley." He kisses along my knuckles.

Words escape me as I stare at the exquisite ring that may never leave my finger.

"Baby?"

I throw myself forward, tackling him back on the bed.

His grunt turns to a groan when my mouth crashes to his. My tongue plunders around clumsily, wanting to taste and touch everywhere I can. His fingers thread through my hair, angling my head and taking over.

Our tongues swirl together, finding a rhythm.

I kiss him with everything I have, growing lightheaded as the reality of the situation settles deep inside. Emotions bubble to the surface, tears threatening to fall. I push them back and frame his face, soaking in the way he kisses me greedily.

His hips grind into mine, the hard, thick length fitting perfectly between my legs. I moan down his throat, pressing down.

My brain screams for oxygen, and warning bells go off when his hands slip into my waistband, cupping my ass.

"Sweetie, we can't." I break away, regretting my words. His eyes are now smoldering with hunger and lust, sending a tingling all the way to my core.

"Fuck the doctor's orders."

"It's only one more day."

He frowns but doesn't argue. "Is that your way of saying yes?"

"You didn't ask a question."

"Marry me," he repeats.

"As a matter-of-fact, since the day you showed up at my yoga studio all those months ago, announcing you were taking me to lunch, you don't ask many questions when it comes to your plans."

"I'm decisive when it comes to you." His smirk melts my insides.

"Yes," I breathe out.

His smile radiates as bright as the ring now resting against his cheek.

"Now, that's something to celebrate."

I forgot about the house full of people down the hall ready to celebrate homecomings and holidays.

"They already know." He reads my thoughts.

"They do? How?"

"Had the ring a while now. Since before we were called away. Jewls gave her approval."

"Of course, she did. It's the most perfect ring in the history of rings."

"Glad you like it."

Something hits me. "Wait, is this why you've been in such a bad mood?"

"One reason. I wanted to get home and get it on your finger. But that hospital was boring as fuck."

I giggle, sitting up and flashing my hand in the air.

"Baby, you straddling my dick is not helping my condition."

I wiggle purposely, smiling at him. "You'll live."

He glances at his wrist. "You're right, because in about eight hours, I'll be buried deep in your pussy with you wearing my ring."

My body does an all-over shiver, and I refrain from commenting on how barbaric he sounds.

"We're engaged."

"Yeah, and I'm guessing there are about twenty people outside that door waiting to hear the news."

I bend in for a quick kiss and roll off of him. He stands, adjusting the bulge in his pants. "Give me a second." He goes to the back door and hauls in our bags, then takes my hand, pulling me to his side to guide us to the living room.

Celia is the first person to spot us, her gaze dropping to our joined hands. Her face splits into a wide smile, and she lets out a cry of happiness. The entire room erupts and we're surrounded.

Achilles kisses the side of my head and gets away from the swarm of women.

At some point, Pete and Dad step in to steal a quick hug, but otherwise, it's a huddle of women gabbing over rings and wedding stories. Now that the families are assured the men are okay, the attention rains down on me.

"I totally approved that ring," Jewls announces proudly as if she picked it out herself. "Personally, I couldn't believe the big oaf had taste."

"Jewls!"

"Then again, he finally got off his ass and made a move on you, so he has some sense," she covers.

"He's been in love with Harley since he was a teenager. This is like a real-life fairy tale," Sandy states wistfully.

"That damn husband of mine, he should have kept his mouth shut and we could have had grandbabies by now." Mom drops that tidbit without even blinking.

My eyes pop, and I search for Achilles across the room.

'Babies,' I mouth, and his lips curl up.

The door opens, and Mike strolls in carrying a spray of holiday flowers and a case of beer. I slip through and go straight into his waiting arms.

"Heard there was a homecoming celebration. Hope you don't mind my crashing."

"I'm glad you're here."

His gaze travels over my shoulder. "Hey, man, damn good to see you."

I edge into Achilles while they shake hands. "Good to be home."

"Harley, goes without saying, due to the circumstances, we can push back your official start date and give you more time here."

This is not a surprise; I suspected Mike would offer. It's not because we're family, either. He's that thoughtful, and it bleeds into his professional decisions. It was obvious when I called him from Coast Rica to fill him in on the guys' recovery, he was pushing me to take all the time I needed.

"That's unnecessary. Achilles and I talked about it. I'm starting next week. He's agreed to take it easy and follow all instructions on his recovery." The last part isn't exactly true.

"Don't remember agreeing to anything except you should start your new job as planned," he utters.

"Okay, I'll amend my statement. At least, if I'm at work, I'll be in denial that he's actively disobeying medical advice on his rest and recovery."

Mike chuckles, jerking his chin in approval to Achilles. "We'll make sure IT gets you outfitted with everything you need to work from home pretty quickly. In case you need to be here and supervise."

I smile in appreciation.

The rest of the guys idle over, shaking hands and greeting.

"Ahhhh!" I squeal when my feet leave the ground and I'm swept in the air.

"Jay-Jay!" Drake's deep voice booms in my ear as he shakes me.

I've been so wrapped up with the ladies, I haven't made my way around to see everyone. He places me down, and I twirl to hug him.

"He may have had a life-threatening injury, but he still could pummel me," he murmurs.

I shoot Achilles a warning look and step over to hug Sam.

The group gets quiet, and I note all eyes are on me. "What's wrong?"

"Jay? My house?" Ford quirks an eyebrow.

"I sent you pictures."

"You left out quite a few details."

"Told you it was over-the-top."

"Wait until it gets dark and you see the outside," Dad pipes up. "Harley had us old men hustling."

"If any of the guys at the station still believe the Casanova myth, they should see this place now," Talon adds.

"Oh no! We can't have that! I have the best thing going as the scandalous and sordid woman who frequents the Club."

Achilles yanks me to his chest, lifting my chin and brushing his lips across mine. "The house is beautiful, baby. You did well."

"Thanks. Hope you feel that way when we take it down."

"Those presents under the tree? Who are all those for?"

The pile under the tree has tripled since I left on Christmas. "The moms added. We're doing a real Christmas tomorrow with everyone."

His eyes darken and jaw ticks. "I agreed to share you with these people tonight. Not tomorrow."

"They're not here for me, honey. They're here for y'all."

"Jesus, is this our life?"

"Isn't it awesome?"

"Next year—our house, my rules."

I smile wide, giggling a little. "We'll see how that goes."

"I don't care that it's technically afternoon. It's time to pop the champagne! Rich, come help," Mom directs from the kitchen.

"I'm guessing that rock on your finger isn't an accessory." Mike lifts my hand and inspects it.

"No, I'm getting married." The words tumble out gushy and girlie.

"Congratulations, you two." He slaps Achilles on the back. "Now let's celebrate."

Feeling like I'm floating on cloud nine, I repeat his sentiment. "Let's celebrate."

"Harley." My name comes out as barbed and predatory.

"Patience," I urge, rolling my hips.

"Been fucking patient for over a week. Give me your pussy or the deal's off."

"Tsk, tsk, tsk... This is my show. Doctor's orders."

"Doctor's orders are no excessive exercise. Fucking you is not excessive."

I brace on his chest and feel the surge of empowerment at his expression. His jaw set firm, his eyes wide and hungry, his muscles flexed and defined. He's on the brink, ready to throw me back and take control.

I pivot my hips again, taking the tip of his cock and teasing him. "I disagree. It's very excessive. And we have to be careful of your leg wound. No need to take any chances."

Fire blazes in his eyes, singeing over my skin. I heed his warning and drive down, impaling myself. My body quakes with a pinch of pain at the sudden invasion. I moan at the intense pleasure radiating all over.

"Shit," he hisses, "so damn tight."

"Hmmm," I mutter, rocking slowly.

"Babe, you gotta move faster."

"Patience," I repeat.

Irritation flickers in his gaze before his lips curl naughtily. "You're right. The view from down here is fucking incredible. Watching you ride me. Your hot, tight pussy is drenching my dick."

My stomach flips at the new hunger staring back at me. His cock pulsates and twitches, heightening my already shaky resolve. My plan to draw this out is backfiring.

I move, rocking back and forth, the electric sensations already tingling. Since our first time, we've never gone this long without sex, and my body reacts to the sensation of his thickness stretching me. "Feels so good."

He grips my thighs, encouraging me to speed up. "You're torturing yourself unnecessarily. You want to come. I can see it on your face."

He reads me expertly, but I refuse to succumb yet. His hips surge up, once, twice, and on the third stroke, the metal connects with the place that makes me crazy. I drop my head back, giving in and quickening my pace.

My heart races and skin sizzles at the sensations building.

"Give it to me, Harley." His thumb circles my clit and I come apart.

In a flash, he knifes up, cocooning me between his hard body and knees, his face coming to mine. "My girl was needy."

"Not fair," I rasp out hoarsely.

"Baby, you want to be a badass and own the control, you gotta be able to take my dick for more than a few minutes."

"It's not my fault. You went off to play G.I. Joe. It's been too long."

His lips twitch with amusement. "That's why I jacked my junk to the image of you in that nightie before coming to bed. Knew I wouldn't be able to last."

"Now, that's really not fair."

"Had to take matters into my own hand, literally. What'd you expect with that get-up?"

"I thought it would last through one use." The silky material now lies somewhere in tatters.

"Appreciate the effort."

"Apparently, I suck at the provocative part of seduction."

"No, baby, like everything else, you're a natural." He drives upward, gaining a moan of appreciation. "It's hot watching you come apart and using my dick to get the edge off."

"Don't be cocky."

"It's true."

"It's still crass." I wiggle a little to get loose.

All movement stops when his fingers twist around my nipples. I bite my cheek to keep from purring.

"You wanted control, take it now."

I use his shoulders as leverage, rising and slamming back down.

"Fuck yes." His mouth goes to my chest, licking around my breast before sucking the nipple roughly.

My stomach pitches, and the uncontrollable need to have him returns. I angle my hips and drive back and forth, clenching with each stroke. His face raises to mine, and I fight to breathe. Unmistakable savage power is written all over. He heaves up, driving so deep I cry out.

Over and over, he hammers me from the bottom while I hold on and meet him stroke for stroke. We both move in sync.

The sound of our bodies slapping and heavy breathing fill the room, and my brain fires off warnings.

"Achilles—"

"Get there, Harley," he grinds out through gritted teeth.

I refuse to come without him this time. My lower body tenses, my inner muscles clenching as hard as possible. I move on him frantically, knowing what's coming.

"Jesus, fucking aaaahhhh—" He drills me harder.

A frenzied force hits hard, and I call out his name. My body takes flight, shattering as fierce waves of pleasure roll through me.

He doesn't let up fucking me until he lets out a roar. I barely hear him over the ringing in my ears. His cock convulses, inciting another orgasm from me. Through it all, he never stops moving.

His gentle caress on my clit has me wheezing. Ecstasy rushes through my veins, threatening to drown me.

His mouth goes to my ear. "Give me another one."

I thrash against him, holding on for dear life, unsure I can take anymore. "Can't." The ragged and hoarse word is almost like a plea for mercy.

He continues to drive into me, his thumb brushing between my clit and where we're connected. Electric heat races up my spine, and I grow dizzy.

His dick jerks, and I fly apart again, melting into him and moaning incoherently.

His lips trail down the column of my neck, both our hearts racing together. He removes his hand from between us and takes my left hand. His fingers circle my ring, pulling our hands to his chest.

"Seems like I have a lot of lost time to make up for." His voice is laced with smugness.

My last bit of energy is used to clench around him. He goes rigid, hissing his reaction.

"Shit, baby." His knees drop, placing me back on the bed and kneeling above.

My pulse races again at the smoldering shade of amber in his gaze. A renewed sense of verve stirs in my system. His eyes go to my chest, and it's impossible to miss the glint of satisfaction.

"You marked me, didn't you?"

"Yes." He traces over the area around my nipple. "Fucking beautiful."

"I just had mind-blowing sex with a complete Neanderthal."

"You'll get used to it." He grins slyly, not caring in the slightest.

29

ACE

Tom's the first person I spot when we walk in. His arms crossed, legs planted firm, and wearing his signature scowl. "I've been waiting for you to get here," he belts out, and my eyes fly to the bar.

Harley and Jewls are busy, but nothing they can't handle, and the clientele is mostly women.

"What's the problem?"

"Your woman's a mess. Came in here today hyped to the max. Won't shut up. Jewls said it's some kind of nervous energy, worried about you. She's driving me fucking nuts."

"I'll talk to her."

"You better. I agreed to a monthly ladies' night. Now's she's pushing for nightly drink specials, more theme nights, and mentioned booking some local rock band. Apparently, her new fancy job has her hobnobbing with the rich and famous. She ain't turning my blue bar into a millennial hotspot. Snap her into shape. Shut down this crazy talk."

He may have a tough exterior, but it's easy to see he's concerned about Harley.

When word got out about our injuries, Tom was one of the first people to show at our house. Since it was Christmas Eve, Harley forced Jewls to go visit her parents and keep her original plans. Tom and Rich didn't want Jewls driving in her state of mind and going on no sleep. They planned to meet Jewls' parents at the state line, Tom following behind Jewls and Rich in her car.

He then came back and sat with the family while they arranged their trip to Costa Rica. The night of our homecoming, he stopped in to confirm for himself we were all okay.

Harley refers to him as a moody, gruff, irritable man with a heart of gold. I'm getting her point.

"I'll take care of her."

"Good. Customers love that bubbly bullshit, but I'm on the verge of tearing my hair out." He looks across the group of us. "It's about time all four of you get your asses back here. Figures it's ladies' night."

"Why come for the ladies when we have your charming personality?" Talon harasses him.

"Screw you." His gaze lands on Major and grows thoughtful. "You good?"

"Yep, start desk duty next week."

"You too?" He points to me.

"Yes."

His face grows serious, his eyes working through something before he speaks. "My older sister got engaged to her high school sweetheart at twenty-one. She was in college, he was in the Navy. A month after he proposed, enemy fire killed him. I was there the day his parents called. I was at her side at the funeral, and I've been there every day after. Anything she's ever needed, no questions asked. Took her years to move on, and she found a great guy to marry, but he never filled that hole. Not sure I can comprehend that level of loss. Then, a few weeks ago, déjà vu soaked me to the bones. Being in law enforcement is no cakewalk, not even close. But this old man can't live to see that level of loss again, no matter how strong our Harley is."

Jesus. Fuck. That's the most the man has said at one time ever. And he lays the heavy shit out there. The message isn't lost. He's aware of our meeting today. "I'd like to talk to Harley first before the news gets around."

"Respect. Drinks on me tonight—for all of you. Especially when you get that bubbling babble-head to calm herself."

He hustles away without another word, barely avoiding taking out a passing waitress that yelps. He glowers at her as she shoves him aside without a care of his disdain.

"Oh, shit, incoming."

I hear Ford's warning in time to catch a full glimpse of Harley before she slams into me, leaping into my arms. Her torn jeans are skin-tight, hugging her everywhere. The Tom's shirt tied tight under her tits shows skin and the edge of her tattoo snaking out of the hem.

"You're here," she breathes out like I've been gone for days.

"Babe, told you we would be."

"It's been hours since you called. Is everything alright?"

"All good." Talon steals a kiss on her cheek. "See you at the bar."

She wriggles to get down, but I hitch her higher. "Let's talk in Tom's office?"

"Oh, dear God, do we need an office? You're going back, aren't you? Those people won't let you go. You're in for life, every month a drill, every day a chance to be called back. We can't have a wedding because you can't plan. I'll have children alone in a hospital because you'll be saving lives in foreign territories…" She rambles on with improbable jabber, demonstrating what Tom was referring to. I start toward his office.

When we get there, I realize she hasn't taken a breath. I shift my hold, lacing a hand in her hair and bringing her mouth to mine.

"Breathe and calm down."

She inhales deep, her eyes wide and filled with worry. "Sorry, I've been a little wound up."

"Heard."

She takes another deep breath, grips my neck, and exhales. "Okay, sock it to me. How'd it go?"

"It went as we knew it would go."

"And those people agreed with your decision?"

"Harley, those people are Marines, same as me."

"I pictured you sitting in front of a panel of suits, and they'd disagree with your decision."

"We talked about your imagination running wild. Plus, you've met Willie."

"Couldn't help it. Tell me what happened."

"We went and had a beer. Willie and the others weren't surprised and understood. Knew this was coming. Major and I won't be released for any type of action for a while. The process is extensive before being sent on our missions. We've amended our original arrangement. No more missions. We're still in the Reserves, but now, we're moving to less active roles."

Her mouth splits into a celebratory grin. "Told you they wouldn't let you go. You men are too valuable."

"Guess you were right."

She melts into me, nuzzling my neck. "A thousand pounds are off my shoulders."

"Told you to trust me."

"I trust you, but you're an American hero. You saved lives, thwarted an attack on our US Navy, and exposed a cartel transporting drugs and sex slaves into our country. No one in their right mind would want to lose that kind of talent. Even I don't want to lose that protection."

"Baby, we have skills, but we're not the only specialized four men in the military."

"Let's hope those other guys are as exceptional as you."

A warmth glides through me at her words. All those years ago, when I left her behind, it was to become the man she deserved.

I may never truly be good enough for all the beauty and graciousness that is Harley Jacobs.

For the first time in my life, here, with her in my arms, saying those words, it hits me she sees me as good enough.

"You okay now?"

"Meaning, am I over my spastic hyperactive energy that's been driving everyone crazy?"

"Yeah."

"Then yes. And as much as I want to make out with you in my boss's office, there's a crowd out there."

I brush my lips across her head and set her down, linking our hands. Immediately, I notice her bare finger. "Where's your ring?"

Her smile fades, and she glances away nervously. "In your safe."

"Why isn't it on your finger?"

"Tonight's busy, and I'm scared it would get dirty or damaged."

"If it does, I'll handle it."

"Achilles, everyone knows we're engaged."

"That's the point. You're not available to any shithead that thinks differently."

A fire ignites in her eyes, blazing bright. "Don't ruin our awesome moment by being an irrational Neanderthal."

"An irrational Neanderthal would drive his ass home, get the ring, and come back to plant it on your fucking finger."

The blaze flares, and she tries to yank her hand away. "You know, with your line of work, you'll take your ring off, too."

"Not if I don't wear a ring."

Her body deflates. "You won't wear a wedding ring?"

"What's the point?"

"What's the point? The point is, it's a universal symbol of commitment and love."

"It's a piece of metal that can be easily discarded."

"Wow, aren't you a romantic?" she snips.

"I want something more permanent. Ink lasts forever. Your initials inked in my skin shows a commitment that can't be mistaken."

"Oh my God." Her hand flies to her mouth, the fiery blaze transforming into a bright blue hue. "That's so much cooler than a ring."

"Babe."

"Now I want to get a tattoo, too."

"Why don't we talk about it later?"

"Right. I have to go make a lot of women happy and chirpy with fabulous drinks, hot guys, and my fabulous specialty martini. Plus, we don't want Tom to walk in on me jumping you on his desk."

My cock twitches, the image of her on that desk filling my head. "Don't tempt me. But before we go back out there, you need to adjust your shirt."

"What's wrong with my shirt?"

"It's tied up under your tits, showing everything."

"It's tied at my midriff and completely appropriate."

"Every man in that bar will zero in on your tits."

"Hello! Every man in the universe zeroes in on tits. It's in your DNA."

"Harley—"

"Achilles, shut it and lighten up!" She bounces up to kiss me and yanks me out of the office.

When we get to the bar, the place is packed. She squeezes my hand and rushes to help Jewls and Tom, who's working service bar. He takes one look at her and juts his chin at me in appreciation.

I go to our regular spot, shaking hands with a few of the guys from the force. Major slides a beer my way and clinks his with mine.

"How'd that go?"

"Good."

"Then why's her shirt still tied below her tits?"

I pause mid-sip and glare at him at the same time a roar of laughter comes from the others.

"Shut the fuck up," I grumble.

"Preppy blonde across the bar is sizing her up. Just saying…"

Anything else he mutters drones out as I stand, ready to deal. My head whips across the way to find Erik waving her down. Major laughs, punching me in the arm. "You make it too easy."

"Wouldn't get too cocky. Jewls has an admirer."

His eyes fling to the end of the bar where Jewls is chatting with a well-dressed guy who's clearly interested. She's dressed similar to Harley in tight, ripped jeans and her Tom's shirt. But instead of her shirt being tied up, she's cut the bottom off, making it a crop top. Considering it's also tight, she's showing more skin than Harley.

There's a flicker of irritation in Major's glare before he turns, shaking his head. "He's out of place in this bar."

"She doesn't seem to mind."

"Not her type."

I want to correct him that the guy is exactly her type, but think better of it. "So, still just friends then?"

"Yep, friends."

Her head turns our way, and she flashes a flirty smile.

Jesus, my best friend is a true dumbass if he thinks that's a smile aimed at 'just a friend'. But I decide to let it go. Whatever is happening between them seems to work.

Major waves his beer in the air, signaling he's ready for another. Which is bullshit, since he's only had a few sips. She pulls four bottles out of the tub of ice, bringing them over.

"It's a good thing you arrived when you did. Tom was milliseconds away from tying Harley to a chair and taping her mouth shut," she teases, passing out bottles.

"She's settled."

"That means your meeting went well?"

"Went the way we expected."

"I'm shocked they let you go. All those lines they crossed to keep you in the loop, and they cut you loose?" She makes a scissor gesture with her fingers.

"Not exactly, we're staying in the Reserves in a more training and development role," Major informs her.

"I dig that. At least, now, you guys only have one dangerous job we need to worry about."

"You don't need to worry. We can handle ourselves."

"You can keep repeating that and I'll do the same. *We worry.*" She emphasizes the last sentence.

"Aww, little Jewls. You saying you love us?" Talon makes a kissing sound.

"Yeah, you asshat. Don't know why, but I guess I do."

"Jewls! Get back to work. You two wanted this damn themed night. Go take care of these women," Tom barks brusquely.

Like everyone, she's unaffected, patting his cheek and sashaying away.

A quick glance, and I note Major's eyes glued to her ass.

"You guys know anything about Hayes Security waltzing into my bar?"

The name gets all of our attention. Casting a glance over Tom's shoulder, I catch Robbie and Finn with their wives and another couple, Jimi and Abbi. Max is hanging to the side.

"My guess is Harley and Jewls invited them, and their husbands are checking this place out."

"They friends of yours?"

"Guess you can say that. Only been around them a few times. Why, something I should know?"

"Robbie Hayes and Finn Black are bad mothers. Max Roberts works with them occasionally. Robbie's dad owns the security firm, and his reputation is hailed far and wide. Over the years, we worked together a few times. When I retired, thought about hitting up James Hayes for a side gig, then changed my mind. That team has skills."

"We know that first hand," Ford relays.

Talon and Ford called a few friends in MARSOC to get backgrounds on Finn, Robbie, and Max. Their military and professional records are impressive.

Finn, Robbie, Presley, and Ember came by a few days after we got home. The guys didn't share who relayed the intel of our mission, but gave us a rundown of the news that came in. Max had already left town, but a few days later, I called him to thank him.

While we were in the hospital, Harley filled me in on the night she learned we were shot. The jealous bastard in me reared up, knowing another man had her in his arms, but I forced myself to hold it in, knowing how torn up she was.

Max took care of her, and that is something that she'll always remember. So, I sucked up my pride and let him know how much it meant that he was there.

"They're good people to have relations with. Remember that. Word on the street is they're always recruiting." Tom's parting words hang in the air after he walks away.

"Hey, guys!" Harley notices them, jumping up and waving.

With each bounce, her shirt goes higher, and I dip my chin to my chest to keep from losing my mind.

"Hey there." A hand lands on my shoulder, and I tilt to see Presley sliding in close. "You alright?"

"Trying to keep from catapulting across this bar and yanking that fucking knot out of my fiancée's shirt."

Her mouth splits into an amused smile. "Yeah, you're okay."

"Better man than me," Finn mutters, offering his hand.

"I'd have Ember over my shoulder and out the door," Robbie adds.

"Hardly, I've had two kids and miss the days my stomach was that toned and sexy," Ember speaks up.

"Amen, sister." Presley salutes her with a flick of her fingers.

Both men roll their eyes.

"You ladies get the signature drink of the night on the house!" Harley chirps, pushing three martini glasses across to them.

"Oh, thank God. It's been a day from hell. I've been jonesing for hours." Abbi steps in, swipes a glass, and finishes half in one swallow. "This is divine!"

"Oh, fuck." Jimi drops his chin, much like my move earlier, and shakes his head.

"Four IPA's, whatever you have," Finn orders from Harley.

Major, Ford, Talon, and I offer our seats to the girls.

Harley delivers the drinks and hustles to the end of the bar where a crowd has formed.

"Damn good to see you guys," Max repeats the sentiment we've heard over and over.

"You too, man." I slap my hand in his, bringing him in to bump shoulders.

"Did you get it done?" he refers to our meeting.

"We're not out, but this team is retiring from covert operations." I describe our new arrangement.

"Knew they wouldn't let you go."

"They were happy to let both these thugs go. It was Ford and me that were the losses. Thought Willie would weep the way he took the news," Talon jokes.

"More like weep with happiness your pain in the ass isn't his responsibility anymore," Major throws out.

"What did I miss?" Harley props her elbows on the bar.

"Oh my God, I totally understand why you live at the Club. These guys are fun," Abbi chirps, finishing her drink.

Apparently, the Club rumor has made its rounds.

Harley looks to all of us, her eyes landing on me last. "They're a mess, but they're the best."

"Did Jay ever tell you about her and Jewls' first visit to the Club?" Harley's grin vanishes at Talon's question.

"No!" she cries out.

"Oooh, this sounds like a fun story." Presley does a little shimmy. "Tell."

Talon tells the story with Ford and Major interjecting parts of it. All the while, Harley's cheeks blister into a deeper shade of pink.

"… then she and Jewls went flying. Screeching like banshees, all arms and legs tangling up as they rolled around. Had to be the worst attempt at being undercover. The only thing they had going for them was the matching black sprocket attire. Funniest fucking shit ever."

Jewls hears the story and grins proudly, shouting, "Good times," as she passes.

Everyone gets a laugh at the remark except Harley. She shoots Talon an evil glare and goes to serve a group of guys. They measure her up, one of them openly gaping appreciatively at the edge of her tattoo.

If they're on the force, I don't recognize them. I sip my beer, lasering in on the guy who's now bent over closer, his mouth moving. When his hand covers hers, I'm on the move.

"Shit," Major hisses at my back.

Instead of heading around, I march straight behind the bar to her side. My hand circles her waist and squeezes possessively. "Baby, the girls need more of those drinks. Do you want me to help you here?"

The guy's hand retracts, and he jerks his chin in acknowledgment.

She tilts her face to mine, eyes fierce with irritation. "No, bayyybee, I'll handle it." Her tone's a mix of saccharine and sarcasm, her fingernails biting into the skin through my shirt.

She shunts me to the side and grabs three highball glasses, filling them with scotch.

The guy gives her a card to start a tab, then steps out of the way to make room. I dip my face to find her glaring.

"Can you try to not be bullheaded and overprotective?"

"I'm pretty fucking restrained, considering your shirt is still tied. The guy didn't need to lay his hand on you to order a drink."

"I'm riding the high of my-initial-being-inked-on-your-finger." She pokes me in the chest. "Get over my shirt."

A throat clears, pulling our attention to Rowan and Ginger standing there. I've seen them regularly over the last few weeks.

Harley explained Rowan was finally coming out of her shell. She joins the girls for Saturday morning Pilates and a few after-work gatherings.

Like all the times I've seen her, Ginger is smiling brightly. Rowan is a more reserved, quiet type.

During one of their happy hours, Rowan confessed her ex was a controlling asshole who stepped over the line by using force. The morning after our callout, she began kicking him out of her life.

The night after that outing, I received a text from an unknown number with two words.

Thank you

Simple and direct.

Since then, when we see each other, she's more comfortable, but still shy.

"Y'all came," Harley chirps eagerly, her agitation forgotten. "Try tonight's specialty drink."

"Sounds great to me. This week has been hell. I swear this last semester is killing me," Ginger replies dramatically.

"I remember that last semester at Vandy. So nerve-wracking," Rowan chimes in. "At least you already have a job waiting."

Part of her statement surprises me. I knew they've offered Ginger Harley's vacant position when she graduates, but I didn't know Rowan attended Vanderbilt.

"What did I tell you about being behind my bar? Unless your ass is wearing one of my shirts and working for me, you're a liability!" Tom yells. "Get your ass out and over to the customer side."

Harley passes their drinks over the bar. "Grab Erik and come around to the other side. I want to introduce you to our friends."

"And you need to go before Tom has a conniption. He's had his fill of me tonight." She pokes my stomach.

"When I get you home, I'm getting my fill of you tonight." My thumb scales across her midriff, goosebumps popping at the touch.

Her eyes flare with heat, and she pulls her bottom lip between her teeth.

I brush my lips over hers. "Behave."

She backs out of my reach.

Tom grunts when I pass him, slapping his shoulder. There's a fresh beer waiting, and Jimmy hands it over.

"So, I guess you and I should talk about my job."

The surrounding murmurs quiet, and the hair on the back of my neck prickles. My eyes slice around before coming back to him. "Your job?"

"Yeah, Harley says you're making a career change. Interested in becoming an accountant."

I freeze, beer lifted mid-air, completely caught off-guard. The silence lasts a few beats before Talon howls, followed by the rest. Jimmy's lips twitch, revealing he's aware of the inside joke. My gaze travels to Harley, whose hand is covering her mouth while her body vibrates.

"Bunch of smart asses," I mumble, not able to hold in my amusement.

Oh, the ways Harley will pay for that later.

30

HARLEY

"Where are you?" Achilles barks in greeting.

"Hello, how are you? How'd your afternoon with the girls at the spa go? Are you excited about tonight? Don't be nervous, you'll kill it," I snap back sarcastically.

"Baby, I'll ask all those questions when I see you, which was supposed to be ten minutes ago."

I check the time and realize we're cutting it close. "I'm at the house, where you told me to meet you."

"I meant this house, so we'd ride over together."

"I misunderstood when you said 'our house'!"

"Don't go in without me. I'll be there in two." The line disconnects, and it's my turn to huff.

"Ridiculous manners." I get out of my car, tightening my scarf as the frigid wind bites in the air. My frustration fades when I notice the progress of the house.

Tonight is my first big event as a marketing partner with MJ Labels, and I've been working late every night for two weeks. It's a charity event tied to three of the label's rock-based bands. It has been in the works for months and became my responsibility when I started.

Achilles and Major only lasted one week on desk duty before Hal took pity on them and pulled some strings, getting them on a unit assigned to a special investigation. Since Achilles and I were both working long days, it was too dark to see the development of the house when we got home. Achilles checks with our contractor every day, and the guys have given updates, but this is the first time I've seen it.

My heart hammers in my chest, my breath catching.

This kind of progress is nothing short of amazing.

And I have my overbearing fiancé to thank for that.

The night after ladies' night at Tom's, Achilles came home and informed me my lease was up mid-March. This was something I knew since I lived there for years. The leasing agent had already agreed to month to month.

I thought this was forward-thinking, responsible, and organized. Since Christmas in Costa Rica, Achilles and I had spent every night together. Except for the nights at Tom's, we had settled into a domestic routine. When the guys were home, we had a great time, all fitting together. But I didn't feel right living at the Club full time.

Inevitably, Achilles was going back to working nights at some point. Which meant I would return to my apartment.

He disagreed whole-heartedly. He wanted me to give up my apartment and move in until the house was complete.

Actually, he didn't want it; he demanded it in his impatient, stern, and no-nonsense way. I lost my temper, refusing to even discuss it, and pitched the mother of all fits. My threats to pack up my stuff and leave that night until he could have a two-way discussion ended up with me naked and screaming for many different reasons.

It wasn't my fault. The instant he threw me on the bed and ripped off my clothes, my body betrayed me. He was relentless in his sexual persuasion, fucking all the fight out of me.

With my one functioning brain cell that remained, I offered a compromise. I'll give up my apartment and move my stuff into storage if the house is completed by my birthday on April twenty-fourth. In my mind, this was clever because there was no way he could make it happen. It was the middle of winter, and it snowed in Nashville frequently. Construction delays would hold up the completion.

He knew it was all but impossible to ensure me that, but he took the challenge.

Achilles called our builder and told him our aggressive timeline. I expected a pissed-off brute when the man laughed at the demand. But instead, I received a call the next day asking to finalize all my special requests and customizations.

They were also taking the challenge to finish. Probably because Achilles didn't give them a choice.

Today is the day. Based on what we see inside, we will know if they'll meet the deadline.

A blur of blue and the faint sound of an engine gets my attention. Achilles is speeding over the empty lots in the golf cart. It's barely stopped when he's out and in my space.

My stomach does a roller-coaster dive, spreading the flutter of excitement throughout my body. The heat and hunger I know well form in his eyes as they rake over me. Rowan outdid herself with today's makeover.

"Fuckin' A."

"Please don't maul. I have to meet clients tonight, and I can't look like a sex maniac."

He smiles at the reference of the episode before the Christmas party. "I make no promises."

"The only thing I have to do when we get to your place is get dressed and do my lipstick."

His gaze drops to my mouth, and he leans down, pulling my bottom lip between his teeth. "You are stunning."

The sexy roughness in his compliment sends a flood of heat everywhere. "Wait until you see my dress with the new Louboutins my fiancé surprised me with." I press up, touching my lips to his.

The kiss starts slow, his tongue moving lazily through my mouth. I brace on his shoulders, giving him most of my weight. His hands sift through my hair, tenderly caressing my head.

A purr bubbles from my throat, and he increases his speed, curling his tongue with mine. A low, possessive groan vibrates in our mouths as he walks us backward. My brain fires a weak reminder of why we're here. I try to slow our kiss, but his fingers dig into my scalp.

"I need you now." The warmth of his breath coats my lips and my knees buckle. He takes advantage of my lust-induced state and lifts me off my feet. His mouth stays on mine as he carries me through our future front entrance.

"Sweetie," I try to get in a word, but his tongue delves back in and does another sweep.

"I've waited all day, Harley, knowing exactly what this afternoon would bring. Don't deny me a second of this."

All rational thoughts vanish.

The schedule, the limo, our friends riding… none of it matters. Outside of his possessive ridiculousness, Achilles asks nothing of me. This means something to him, and I'll give anything to make that something special. Even if we show up late and I look thoroughly disheveled, none of it matters.

"Whatever you need." I scrub my hands through his hair.

He keeps walking, our eyes locked.

"All plumbing and electrical done and approved by an independent inspector today. They'll be back to approve the final walk-through with us when it's time. Framing done, the remaining windows installed tomorrow, insulation starts Sunday. Kitchen appliances are ordered, delivery date of four weeks. Tile, wood, brick…"

It all drowns out after he mentions the kitchen appliances, and my spirits drop.

"Appliances? They were a surprise." They are the only items I picked alone since I was designing my gourmet kitchen.

"They still are."

"Then how did you order them?"

"I didn't." His lips curl slyly. "Mom and Dad bought them for us."

My eyeballs threaten to pop out of their sockets.

"Pre-wedding present."

"We can't accept that. I upgraded to top-of-the-line choices. Thousands and thousands of dollars."

"Baby, they can afford it."

"It's too much."

"I'll let you tell Mom that. When I tried, she blathered on about lost time."

I grimace. Sandy and Pete are a big part of our lives and frequently express how much it means to them. They take every chance to rectify those years we were estranged. Mostly by over-compensating. The few times we've tried to intervene, Sandy has been close to tears.

"I don't want to hurt her feelings."

"Then say thank you, like I finally did to shut her up."

I agree.

"Baby, look around."

My gaze travels around our master bedroom in wonder. The frame-out brings the large space's dimensions. I can picture the finished product. My line of vision goes past his shoulder, and he reads my mind, walking us to the bathroom.

My breath hitches at the sight of the huge spa shower. I visualize the free-standing tub on the raised platform at the back. "It will be phenomenal."

"It will be complete on April sixteenth."

My face twists back to his. "They can finish in seven weeks?"

"They will."

"How can you be sure?"

"The builder knows Ford, Talon, and Major are building next. He also knows Celia and Doug plan to use this design as a reference in their new development. That's strong motivation."

"It's surreal."

"Baby, you picked the design and customizations back in November."

With everything that's happened, November seems like ages ago, and also like it could be yesterday. "Wow."

"I filled my end of the bargain, now it's your turn." His lips go back to mine, his voice soft. "Move in with me."

I have no control over my answer; my heart speaks up. "Okay."

"Fuck, I hope there's a solid surface somewhere in this place."

Desire mixed with need floods my body, my hair and make-up forgotten. I yank my scarf and sweater off, flinging them over his shoulder. His eyes drop to my red lace bra, and a deep rumble echoes from his throat. He goes down to his knees, setting me on the ground and whipping his shirt over his head. The chill in the air instantly warms.

Instinctively, my mouth waters at the sight of his bare chest and abdomen. My stomach pitches at the same time a thrill speeds through my veins. It's a sight that never gets old. "When we move in, you're never wearing a shirt."

He grins, easing me to lie back, then places his shirt under my head. His fingers skate along the edge of the lace and down the valley between my breasts, flicking the clip open. "So fucking sexy. Unbelievably gorgeous."

"So are you."

His thumb slides to trace one nipple, which pebbles immediately at the sensation. "I know we're in a hurry, but shit if I don't want to take my time. Run my mouth over every inch of skin, savor and devour you. Didn't get enough this morning. I want the taste of you on my tongue, knowing you're full of me as you work the room tonight."

An intense craving throbs in my veins. "Achilles?"

"Right here, baby," he answers, leaning in to suck my nipple into his mouth.

"Ahhh." I arch up, gripping his head.

He sucks harder, tilting so his cheek scrapes against my skin. A fleeting thought crosses my mind that my dress is low cut, but I don't dare tell him to stop. His mouth moves to the other side, mimicking the same actions.

He trails lower, licking his way down my stomach, his destination clear. I grip his hair, trying to lift his face to try again. "Achilles?"

"Hmmm?" His hand moves between my legs, playing with me through my leggings. Electrifying sparks flame at the friction.

"Oh, God." I grind into his touch.

"All night, the taste of you on my tongue."

"Don't rush," I finally get out.

His head comes up, the heat in his eyes scorching. Savage, raw, unrelenting. He's in the mood to own me. "What about—"

"They can wait."

His grin turns wicked right before his mouth crashes to mine.

"YOU HAVE SAWDUST IN YOUR HAIR," Jewls announces brazenly, not bothering to lower her voice.

The bubbles of champagne get lodged in my throat and I choke.

"Oh no! I thought I got it all," Rowan frets, sweeping my hair over my shoulder and fanning it out.

"Would you keep your voice down?" I sputter, looking to see if anyone is staring at us. "This is a sophisticated event."

"Sophisticated?" She cocks her eyebrows. "Not sure Mike would have let you in the door with these socialites if he knew you were romping in a construction zone."

"Why did I invite you again?"

"I'm the yin to your yang and you can't get rid of me," she replies. "Besides, wouldn't you rather me point it out than Charlie?" Her eyes go over my shoulder as Charlie materializes at my side.

"Thank God for you. This is fan-fucking-tastic." She also doesn't lower her voice, and this time a few heads turn our way. She carries on without a care. "Event planning is not my forte. I hate the intricate details. Who the hell cares if the tarts are gluten-free, the chicken is free-range organic, or the bar is stocked with alkaline water? I mean, it's water! And this is a rock n' roll stacked event. No one's drinking water."

Two couples beside us outright laugh, tipping their glasses in her direction.

"Charlie, me helping wasn't exactly grueling work."

"You took it off my plate, which thrilled Mike. Somehow, when we do these events, I become the office bitch and he's always scared the whole thing will go down the shitter."

I hang my head, unable to stop my lips from curling up. This woman is a total mess with no filter. Mike loves her, but she tests his last nerve.

"Well, you have me now."

"Oh my God, they just walked in," Ginger squeal-shrieks, bouncing like the energizer bunny.

"Be still me heart," Rowan breathes out.

We all glance toward the door, and the guys from Sayge are sauntering in, followed by another rock band with the label, Knights Dream.

"Pretty sure the saying is 'be still my heart'. Unless you're a pirate," Jewls corrects Rowan, whose face flushes.

"Yeah, that too."

"I love this chick." Charlie throws an arm around Jewls' shoulders. "She's got the kind of snark I respect."

"Touché." Jewls clicks her champagne glass to Charlie's.

"Sorry, not sorry," Ginger states without an ounce of remorse. "No matter how many times I dealt with musicians, I'd be Starstruck."

"Honey, I am married to one of those men and have little monsters exactly like their dad. Sometimes, I question my sanity over him more than them," Charlie replies with her eyes on Blake. She may act like a hard ass, but when he glances her way and winks, it's apparent they are crazy about each other.

"That wink would make me pregnant." Rowan shocks us all with her comment.

Our heads swing her way. Her usual quiet and modest demeanor is gone. She's openly gaping at the now large group of guys, which includes my soon-to-be roommates and Achilles.

"It's not the wink. It's the promise behind the wink. My man has been looking forward to this night for weeks. Alcohol or not, when I watch him play, I get drunk on the sound, so he knows he's getting lucky."

I snort at her bluntness and dip my chin again. The other ladies agree with their hums of approval.

She pivots back to us, pulling her arm from Jewls' shoulder, and points her finger in the air. "Listen up. This is how this usually goes. Right now is the conservative portion of the evening. Open bar before the buffet, then we'll hear a few testimonials from the men and women who have benefited from the services of the cause. The silent auction can get wild. But after the auction, most of the older crowd leaves, and the party gets started. This venue has a noise ordinance rule that hits at midnight. We've already decided to head down the street to The Steamroom. Pace yourselves."

Raven walks up looking like a goddess in a simple blue dress that pops with her eyes and makes her look like the supermodel she is. "She's right. Pace yourselves."

A quick glance at Rowan and Ginger tells me they are freaking out with her joining. They've met her once before, but it's obvious they are in starstruck phase.

To be honest, I can't believe my once small circle of friends now involves these world-famous rockers and their crew. A waiter steps in carrying a tray of fresh champagne. We all take another flute and clink them together.

Raven gushes over Rowan's hairstyle, which makes her blush.

"I work in a salon in Brentwood," Rowan offers meekly.

"She's being humble. Rowan's part-owner of a kick-ass salon. She did all our hair and make-up for tonight," Jewls brags.

Raven's gaze does a sweep of us, her head nodding her approval. "You all look phenomenal. Full-service salon?"

"Yes, we do it all."

"Why am I just now learning this? First, I miss the coolest ladies' night around town, and now I miss spa day? You're falling down on the job." She wiggles her finger at me.

"Next ladies' night is coming soon, and we can go see Rowan anytime. Being pampered at her place is special. She's amazing."

"I think she should fire you as a client after your apparent lack of respect for her time. That's twice now she's created a masterpiece of you and you've let your sexual—"

"Jewls!" I whisper-hiss, cutting her off.

"What?" she answers innocently.

"Yes, what? We don't have secrets." Charlie arches her eyebrows expectantly.

"Well, some of us keep secrets, especially from Charlie. She has a big mouth," Raven advises.

"Ace and Harley had sex on the ground of their new house after she agreed to move in with him this afternoon," Rowan divulges freely.

"Oh my God," I whisper, my face flaming.

"I think it's hot, wild, and sexy. Wish some guy wanted me that bad."

My jaw pops open. *Who is this woman?*

She takes a gulp of her champagne nonchalantly. "Don't look at me like that. I'm not a prude. I love sex but hated it with my ex. He was awful." She does an exaggerated shiver. "Terrible."

"Bad sex is the worst. Thank God Blake knows what he's doing."

"He had a lot of practice," Raven throws out unapologetically.

"Declan wasn't a choirboy," Charlie sasses back.

They stare at each other, then both scrunch their faces, parroting the word, "gross."

"Anyway, if I wasn't married, and Ace wanted to fuck me on the ground, I'd gladly strip, lie down, and let him have his way. Anytime he wanted. That man strikes me as knowing exactly what he's doing."

"Charlie! You can't tell a fiancée that you would fuck her man," Raven scolds.

Charlie side-eyes me. "Did you understand where I was going with that?"

"I'm not offended. I've been in love with him since I was a teenager. He's always had an irresistible sex appeal."

"So, you've got an ex who was bad in bed. I'm guessing that's why he's an ex." She speaks to Rowan.

"One of many reasons." Her newfound boldness seems to shrink.

Jewls catches my eye, silently communicating what I'm thinking. We're ready to jump in if needed. Whatever abuse Rowan suffered is not something she discusses openly.

"Good riddance. It sucks to go through the bad to get to the good, but when you find that guy, you'll appreciate it in spades."

"I'll also have the experience to see the flaws clearly. Something that took way too long last time."

"Amen." Charlie raises her glass in approval, not prying further. "And if you spot a fine-looking guy you want to meet tonight, come to me. I'll be your wingman."

"I'll keep that in mind," she answers politely. Even though her expression reads terror at the thought of Charlie helping her land a guy.

"Let's check out the silent auction," Raven suggests. "I'm eyeing a weekend getaway to Florida."

"You have the money to go anywhere you want. Why would you bid on a trip?"

"Because, Charlie, Veteran's Suicide Awareness is one of my favorite charities. The money goes to a good cause."

"Ember and Presley have arrived." They're at the bar with their husbands.

"I'm holding a grudge against Ember. She told me she was too busy to make me a dress for tonight. Then the bitch goes and outfits Presley. I'm her sister-in-law. Where's the loyalty?" Raven's words don't hold an ounce of irritation.

At the news, I scan Presley head-to-toe and my jaw almost drops. The form-fitting, ice-blue cocktail dress hugs all her curves and cuts across in an asymmetrical line that showcases her legs. It's fantastic.

"I knew Ember was into clothing design, but had no idea she could do that," I mutter in awe.

"Yes, she's talented. You should see her wedding pictures. Designed her own dress and swore it was a one-off. Then she broke her rule and helped design Presley's. Now she does custom dresses through referral only. The demand for her grew too much. Having my brother, two kids, being part owner of a retail store, and designing, she's too busy. I begged her to do a quick work-up tonight, but Presley had already gotten to her."

"Your dress is sensational."

She tosses her hair over her shoulder, grinning wide. "Thanks. Declan picked it out." She purses her lips, her eyes scanning over me. When she brings them back to mine, they are shining with mischief. "You should talk to Ember about your wedding dress. She is a genius with a keen sense of style, and she likes you."

A fluttering explodes in my chest at the thought of a custom wedding dress.

"I'm going right now to buy her a drink and keep them flowing until she's buzzed enough to say yes."

"It's an open bar."

"Even better. Let's go."

I get halfway across the room when a strong arm curls around my waist, folding me into a hard body. "Where're you running to?"

"To plow Ember with drinks until she's loose enough to agree to help with a custom-made wedding dress."

Achilles' lips trail over the shell of my ear. "Heard about a notary who will marry us online so we can do it naked in our bed."

The horror!

I twist, ready to tell him this, and find him smirking in that wicked way.

"Not on your life, buddy! That boat has sailed. I may have agreed to that over a decade ago when you ruled my world. But not now."

His smirk widens. "A decade ago, you were jailbait."

"That's why we'd have gotten married by a notary online, naked, and hid it from my dad. He'd have undoubtedly killed you."

"True. Guess I missed my chance."

"Sure did. Now we are planning a real wedding with a dress. Custom-made if I play my cards right."

He links his hand in mine, tugging me to the dance floor, and situates me in his arms, swaying to the light music.

"What are you doing?"

"Dancing."

"But we're the only ones out here."

"Don't care."

An old memory strikes in my mind. "We haven't danced since your prom."

"I haven't danced since that night at all."

My body melts into his, my fingers tugging loosely at the hair on his neck. He controls our speed, moving us around the dance floor as if we do this often.

"Give me a date, Harley." His smooth voice sends a tingle over my skin.

"A date?"

"The date you're marrying me."

"Well, I've been looking at fall when the leaves change and the weather is cooler."

"Memorial Day weekend."

"Memorial Day? There's no way I can get it all together."

"You have a dozen influential resources. It's possible. Especially if we do it at the Club."

Thousands of twinkling lights with white linen tables seated with people fill my head. Waiters and waitresses float through the area with cocktails and hors d'oeuvres. A hardwood dance floor set up on the side of the property with enough room for a live band.

I'd always pictured something like tonight. A ballroom in a fancy hotel, or a similar venue. Now, all I want is the intimate setting of the Club. And Achilles is right. I have a dozen resources to make things happen. With my new position, I'm an influential resource as well.

"I love that idea."

He brushes his lips across mine. "I left you to become the man I needed to be on Memorial Day weekend all those years ago. It's only right I get my reward the same weekend."

Suddenly, nothing else matters. Not the elegance or extravaganza I've been dreaming of all my life. We can go to the Justice of the Peace, and I'll die happy.

"Memorial Day weekend it is."

He lifts me off my feet, swinging me around as his mouth captures mine. Catcalls and cheering resonate around the room, and I giggle into his mouth, not caring that we are the center of attention.

EPILOGUE

ACE

I POUND UP HARDER, feeling her muscles clamping like a vise. "You there, baby?"

"Oh my God, don't stop," she pleads, her nails digging into my shoulder blades.

My hips swivel twice, my dick scraping her smooth, slick flesh. "You are so fucking tight."

"Love… your… ring…" Her stammers turn into cries as she flies apart. I watch until my stamina snaps and I erupt. My mouth goes to her neck, sucking hard and groaning through the power throbbing in my veins. Pulse after pulse, I release into her tight heat.

Never in this lifetime will that sound and sight get old. Watching, feeling, hearing her come alive while impaled on my cock. The way she reacts from the second I slide inside her until she's writhing and moaning has become my addiction.

I glide in and out, letting her catch her breath and enjoying these last few moments alone for the day.

"Don't let me go. My limbs aren't working."

I smile into her skin, shutting off the water and walking her to the vanity. She helps me dry us off, and I wrap the towel around her.

"I could be a very rich woman if I sold pictures of this right here. People would pay big bucks." Her fingers trail down my shoulders, arms, abdomen, and back up to my chest. She traces the numbers on the newest numerical addition to the dates already there.

Doesn't matter I was just inside her; my dick reacts to the appreciative glint in her gaze as she ogles my chest. She licks her bottom lip before pulling it through her teeth. "So damn sexy."

The rasp in her voice is all it takes. I'm fully hard again.

"I'm so lucky." Her knuckle grazes lower, circling my crown.

"Playing with fire, baby."

"You got to have all the fun this morning."

"It was out of my control. My dick has a mind of its own. It's addicted to your pussy."

"It wasn't your cock that woke me up."

"My mouth has an addiction to your taste."

"I have my own addiction, too." She eases off the vanity, sliding down my body with her purpose clear.

"We can't." The words score my throat.

Her tongue darts out, licking the length and teasing my ring. "Fuckin A'."

"I'll be quick."

"Your—"

"Shhhh." Cool breath blows on the tip, and my argument dies.

"Your stamina is impressive this morning." She takes me perfectly into her mouth and my chin drops, watching her take me as far as she can. Her tongue rolls around my flesh, and by impulse, my hips flex. When she swallows, she sucks me all the way, hitting the back of her throat.

"Fuck," I hiss, my fingers threading through her hair.

She hums her approval, working me faster.

Her fingers tickle my balls, rolling them lightly, increasing her suction.

A knot coils low in my gut, my muscles straining not to pump mercilessly and fuck her face.

My phone blares with an alert, and my blood runs cold. "Goddammit." I want to fucking lose my mind.

She slowly and expertly pulls her mouth away, kissing the slit. "Looks like we have company."

A growl rumbles from my throat.

She rolls on her toes, bringing her mouth to mine. "I'm addicted to your taste, too. As soon as these people leave, it's my turn to have the fun."

"What the fuck am I supposed to do about my raging dick?"

She bites her lip, regret flickering in her features. "Think about Grandma Lucy invading your house in a few minutes."

That does it. The image of her grandmother flashes in my head, and the tightness in my balls shrivels fast.

"Jesus, babe. That wasn't cool. "

"It was the only thing that came to mind."

"Your grandma is a cockblocker."

"Dare you to tell her that." She brushes past me with an amused shimmer in her eyes.

I follow her, dressing in my running clothes quickly. "I'll go let them in. You finish getting ready."

She shoots me a grateful grin and yanks a dress over her head.

All the women are coming up the steps when I open the door. Jewls, Rowan, and Ginger followed by Mom, Amanda, Grandma Lucy, and Aunt Tina.

Every woman's arms are loaded with bags.

"Holy shit, what's happening here?"

"We're planning a wedding, dear." Mom swooshes past.

I take the bags from Grandma Lucy, allowing them to pass, and trail behind them to the living room.

"I'll set up the food samples in the kitchen," Mom declares.

The monitor on the table dings with another arrival. This time Robbie's Suburban drives up the road.

"That's Ember and Presley. They may need help," Jewls instructs. "They are bringing a platform."

"Platform?"

"For Harley's dress fitting."

I go to see what they may need, catching Finn and Robbie with them.

"Thought you could use some help today," Robbie calls over his shoulder, lifting the hatch.

"Help with what?"

"You moving Harley's things to storage?"

"Yeah, but it isn't much. Already moved the furniture."

"Thought Finn and I could lend a hand since the other guys are on shift."

"That really what you want to do on your Saturday?"

"Considering you're covering the bar tab afterward, yeah," Finns speaks up. "Unless you're rushing to get home and discuss centerpieces and flowers."

"Fuck that shit." I jog down the stairs to help Robbie with what I assume is the platform.

Finn pulls out a case of champagne and beer.

"What the hell is that for?"

"Achilles, we're planning a wedding in one day. We need our creative juices flowing," Presley chastises with exasperation.

"You ladies getting loaded or planning a wedding?"

"You're the Roadrunner who set the wedding date. We're the organizing crew."

Ember surprises me by wrapping her arms around my middle in a gentle hug. "Hey, Ace," she says in a soft voice.

"Hey, sweetie, what's with the hug?" I look at Robbie for guidance, and he's eyeing us. There's more amusement than jealousy on his face.

Same with Finn, but Presley is grinning sneakily.

"Because I'm ecstatic with the design Harley chose, and once you see her and how stunning she is, you may cry. Then you may never hug me again."

Jesus, this woman is fucking awesome. "Babe, my girl is always stunning, but the only way you'd make me cry is if you shattered her dreams of this dress. Even then, it may be more of a rampage."

She giggles softly into my chest. "You Marines are ridiculous."

"Us Marines are smart fuckers. Look at the women in our lives."

She stares up at me, her eyes lit with admiration and smile genuine.

"My husband and Finn are heroes like you. And heroes deserve everything, especially to tear up on their wedding day."

"Make you a deal. You get a tear out of me, Harley and I'll babysit for date night."

"I'll take you up on that!" Robbie yells. "My money is on my wife."

She shares a thoughtful look with him and moves to pick up a plastic container. "Fair warning, my cousin and his partner are coming over later. They fell in love with Harley when she came to the shop to look at designs."

"Babe, with Cruz and Alex in the mix, should we plan on everyone being sloshed?" Robbie eyes his wife.

"Yes," she chirps. "They're closing the shop early and bringing the evening cocktails."

"How did a wedding planning party turn into a rave?" I question.

"Because you're Usain Bolt!" Presley and Ember parrot back.

Apparently, Jewls shared her feelings.

"Ember, where you want this?" he asks his wife.

"Living room."

"You need any help?" I offer.

"Nah, I'm used to it." He heads up the steps.

"I'll take these then." I remove the bins from Ember's hands and notion with my head for her to lead.

The prattling goes wild when Ember and Presley join the women. Harley stands in the middle of the room, her wet hair tied back with two ribbons that hang to the middle of her back. She informed me the colors were azure and champagne.

To me, they look blue and cream, but I now know what azure fucking is.

She also informed me that after her day in Ember's formal shop, Clyde's, she wants these as the wedding colors.

Once again, I don't give a shit which colors she chose as long as it ties her to me.

But I kept that to myself.

"Trust me on this, unless you want to answer questions you don't give a shit about, we need to exit fast," Finn utters under his breath.

He read my mind.

"Let me get my stuff. Meet you around front."

I head toward my room when I hear Grandma Lucy declare, "We need more pictures of that handsome fella."

By fella, I assume she means me, so I glance at Harley.

"Your mom brought pictures of you growing up. I have tons of us together, but do you have any from the Marines? It's for a slideshow."

"I may have some in an old box in my closet."

"Let's look." She eases out of the huddle of women and takes my hand.

"You sure you don't want to taste any of the food?"

"You know what we like. I'm taking care of the bar."

"Any additional addresses I should add to the invitation list?"

"Baby, I gave you over a dozen."

"Invites get addressed today and go out on Monday. Don't want to miss anyone."

"Didn't you order extra?"

She nods.

"In the off chance someone's forgotten, we'll send it later."

"I hope your Marine friends come."

It's cute to hear her refer to these men as my friends. The ties that bind us are so much deeper. Any man who will take a bullet for you is a brother for life.

"I'm sure most of them will."

"Really?" she asks hopefully.

"Yeah, if they can swing it. Most of those fuckers won't give up the chance to meet you. Especially since Talon spread that twinkle shit wide."

I let go of her hand, going to the closet and finding a box that would hold any pictures from my years in the service. "Anything I have will be in here."

She scans through the contents and brings out a shot of me with the guys in training after boot camp. "It's like opening a time vault."

I grab my keys, wallet, and cell, bending for a quick kiss. "I'm headed out the back way. Call me if you need anything."

"Sneaking away? All these women scare you?"

"Nope, but seeing as I have a dick, that's not my scene."

"Such a romantic way with words," she teases.

"Tonight, I'll show you romance."

"Love you, Achilles."

"I'll remember that when your mouth is wrapped around my cock finishing what you started."

A heated flush splotches her chest, making its way up her neck and face. The blue of her eyes lightens right before they drop to my waist.

My dick stirs and I adjust myself, trying to stop a full hard on. "Swear to God, Harley, I'll tackle you on that bed if you don't stop staring at me like that."

"You better go before I let you tackle me."

"Go plan our wedding while I transfer your shit to storage and make this move official."

"Okay, Achilles. Suck you… oops," she giggles, "I mean see you later."

This fucking woman is going to be the end of me.

Achilles,

~~Thank you for being my friend.~~

Thank you for being the best, most wonderful, most loyal friend in my life.

Thank you for letting me know the incredible person you are hiding from the rest of the world.

Thank you for not embarrassing me that first day when I declared we were friends, and you weren't getting rid of me.

There are a thousand little things to thank you for, but last, I'll say thank you for being such a good man.

All my love,

Harley

The words are on replay in my brain, making it impossible to beat back the memories of those first few weeks of boot camp.

When Harley handed the letter to me earlier, claiming she was incorporating these words into her vows, my chest seized. I'd kept the letter for a reason, and by the state of it, you could tell I read it frequently my first year.

Then I tucked it away, almost forgetting about it until today, when she found it in the box of mementos.

The door behind me opens, and I twist to find Harley wrapped in one of her ridiculous fuzzy blankets. She cuddles to my side, folding her arms and the blanket around my waist. "Thought for sure you'd be worn out and sleeping off a few bottles of champagne."

She jabs my gut. "I didn't drink that much. And I felt you get out of bed."

"Sorry about that."

"You okay?"

"Great."

"Why are you standing in the freezing cold at one a.m., staring into the darkness?"

"Reflecting."

She jerks at my answer, her expression growing thoughtful. "Reflecting? You sure you're okay?"

"I'm fucking perfect."

"Then why so serious?"

"Not serious. That letter you found today brought up a lot of old memories."

"Good memories?"

"Most of them. It is a reminder of why I was pushing so hard, crushing expectations, and delivering results. That letter and the words inside are the reason I am standing here with you. On the same day you planned our wedding. All of it started when that sixteen-year-old firecracker walked up to me and gave me a shot at beauty for the first time in my life."

She sighs wistfully, squeezing tighter. "It's ironic I found it today. I'd like to think it's fate."

I kiss her forehead and shift her to my front. The scent of her lotion fills the air and I inhale deep, enjoying the tranquility. She holds tight, giving me what I need.

After a few minutes, she breaks the silence. "Are you allowed to marry in your uniform?"

"You don't want me in a tux?"

"Your time in the Marines has been a huge part of our story.

Considering Talon, Ford, and Major are standing up with you, and if they can wear their uniforms, too, it will mean a lot."

"Then that's what we'll wear."

"I didn't even ask you earlier. Did you have a nice day with the guys?"

"Yeah, obviously not as much fun as you."

"Those women are crazy. But a totally cool and awesome kind of crazy."

As suspected, when Robbie, Finn, and I returned to the house late afternoon, there was a party in full swing. Harley explained once all the major decisions were made and her fitting was done, it was time to celebrate.

Talon, Major, and Ford came home shortly after and joined the festivities. Rowan, Ginger, and Jewls crashed in one of the guest rooms. It was late when I finally got Harley to myself.

I learned that a tipsy and happy Harley loves to play dirty.

She tilts to face me. "I know it's pitch dark, but can you picture our wedding out here?"

"I can." Honestly, I didn't know what these women would do with the back of the property. But after seeing the sketches they came up with, it all makes sense. "There's one large flaw in your planning."

Her eyebrows shoot up, and she purses her lips worriedly. "What is it?"

"With three open bars, there is no question some of our friends will end up ass over feet in the pool."

She grins widely. "Actually, we covered that. I personally don't care, but we're putting a decorative barrier around the perimeter. If anyone bypasses, then it's their risk."

I brush my lips across hers. "Smart thinking."

"It's possible for me to come up with a smart idea once in a while."

"Well, then I better get you to the courthouse tomorrow before you wise up and decide to ditch me."

"Not a chance, I think I chose well for my first husband."

I slide my hand into her waistband and slap her ass gently. "Just try to get away from me, see what happens."

She giggles, cupping my chin. The beauty on her face is my undoing. The urge to feel her body against mine takes over.

"Go back to bed, baby. Get ready for me. I'll be right there."

Her eyes spark with desire. "Okay."

When she's back inside, I give the darkened landscape one more glance. Another memory crashes into my brain, this one taking me back to the beginning.

"Um, hi. Achilles, right?" A nervous voice sounded from behind, and I slammed my locker closed, expecting to see one of the snooty bitches vying for my attention. All the girls wanted to take a walk on the wild side, trying to land the bad boy of the school.

Instead, I faced the sweet, quiet, and extraordinarily pretty Harley Jacobs. She thought she was invisible, but I'd had my eye on her since the year before. One thing that kept me from making a move was the fact that her dad was a cop who now had a permanent place on my speed dial. My lips curled and I nodded, trying not to get hard at the blush on her cheeks.

"Yeah, people call me Ace."

She scrunched her nose adorably. "I'm—"

"Harley Jacobs, know who you are."

She stood straighter. "That makes this a lot easier. Ready for science?"

"You're in a senior science class?"

"Yep!" The pop of her 'p' hit me straight in the dick. "Hand me your phone."

On autopilot, I did as she asked and watched her type furiously. Her phone rang as she handed mine back.

"I'm in your favorites and will get your contact set up when we get to class."

"Did I miss something?"

"Not yet, but if we don't hurry, the class will start. It would suck to get the evil eye on the first day."

I decided to play along, because this girl was adorable and made me want to reach out and tug her to my body. "Lead the way."

She let out a little breath and slid her arm around my elbow. "There's a concert this weekend downtown. Indie rock band that my dad and his partner are providing security. Want to tag along?"

At the mention of her dad, my body tensed. If she noticed, she didn't let on, continuing to babble.

"I mean, we obviously can't drink or anything, but it's a cool little dive and Dad won't mind."

"Never been a huge fan of live music, but yeah, we can go." Suddenly, nothing sounded better than taking a chance of listening to a shitty band if it meant spending time with her.

She beamed up at me and my chest constricted, feeling that brightness soak into my veins. A flash of something caught my eye, and I noticed her pink chucks.

"Cool shoes."

The compliment shot that beam of brightness straight to brilliance.

"Thanks! I have an unhealthy obsession with chucks. My mom gripes when we have to replace them every few months. She always offers to buy me…"

The memory fades as I picture those two kids—who are now adults—side by side.

You're a lucky motherfucker, my subconscious reminds me.

I head back inside to the woman in my bed that kick-started my life path all those years ago.

Lucky motherfucker.

ACKNOWLEDGMENTS

There are a lot of people behind the scenes that keep me going, and when the time comes, help me prepare the roll out. Thank you to my editor, graphic designer, and the group of women that throw in your advice and wealth of knowledge to encourage me.

I always feel an enormous sense of gratitude to my family for supporting me in this crazy endeavor. It never gets easier and they stick by me with each release.

A special *THANK YOU* to you- the reader-for purchasing, downloading, and reading this book. Without your support this would not be possible. I love creating these characters and worlds that hopefully bring you enjoyment.

Happy Reading!

For an author reviews are an essential part of helping spread the word of our work. As a reader, your reviews help other readers that may have similar interests. If you enjoyed this book, please consider leaving a short review (or long if you wish). I would appreciate it!

XOXO!

ABOUT THE AUTHOR

Ahren spent her formative years living in an active volcano. There her family made collectible lava art. She studied rock collecting at the Sorbonne in France. There she met the love of her life-her pet pig, Sybil. She returned to the states and started writing. She is happily married to a guy who used to live under a bridge, who she met while pole-dancing.

Now, meet the real me. I grew up in the south and consider myself a true Southerner. Most of the special locations mentioned in my books are reflections of my favorite places. Living on the Florida coast, my family spends a lot of time at the beach, which is where I usually can be found with a book in my hand.

For more information on my books, please visit www.ahrensanders.com

OTHER BOOKS BY AHREN SANDERS

Men of Action Series (Each Can be Read as a Standalone):

Speed King (Achilles & Harley)

Power House (Ford & Jewls)

Mad Jack (Ford & Rowan)

Southern Charmers Series (Each Can be Read as a Standalone):

Pierced Hearts (Pierce & Darby)

Miller's Time (Miller & Ashlyn)

Evin's Fight (Evin & Poppy)

Surrender Series:

Surrendering (Raven & Declan)

Surviving (Raven & Declan Conclusion)

Salvation (Robbie & Ember)

Finding Our Way Series:

Finding Our Way (Bryce & Devon Novella)

Staying On Course (Bryce & Devon)

Finding Our Course - Collision Course Duet

Bennett Brothers Series (Each Can be Read as a Standalone):

Hotshot (Shaw & Bizzy)

Sexy Six (Nick & Grace)

Heartthrob (Mathis & Claire)

Standalones:

Reed's Reckoning

Smokescreen

Finn

Trixsters Anonymous

Fat Cat Liar

www.ingramcontent.com/pod-product-compliance
Lightning Source LLC
LaVergne TN
LVHW050528160826
845677LV00011B/1975

* 9 7 9 8 8 6 9 1 6 2 6 7 0 *